"Not so fast, Mistress Lytton."

A Spanish accent. I looked at the man more closely, seeing a cruel dark face under the cowl of his robes. It was one of the Catholic priests who surrounded King Philip at court, whispering poison in his ear against the English. I disliked being cornered by such a man, particularly in this lonely place, surrounded by long and menacing shadows that seemed to creep in closer as we faced each other.

My tone was cold. "Do I know you, sir?"

He looked down at me through the flickering torchlight, studying me as a man might study an insect before he crushes it beneath his heel. "Not yet," he said lightly. "Nor should you ever wish to. My name is Miguel de Pero of the Inquisition."

I shuddered. So he was one of them, the terrifying Spanish priests whose sole purpose was to torture and destroy any who did not follow the Catholic faith—but most especially those who professed any heretical beliefs or who were suspected of witchcraft.

"I see you know our reputation," he murmured, the shadows thickening around us as he spoke. "Though a girl who consorts so frequently with a novice of the Order of Santiago de Compostela need not fear the Inquisition, surely?"

My heart ran cold at these words. What did he know?

Señor de Pero nodded, seeing my expression. "Yes, your growing intimacy with Alejandro de Castillo has not gone unnoticed at court. He may seem a humble novice to you. But Alejandro is the son of a great nobleman, with a wealthy family awaiting his return in Spain. If Alejandro marries at all, he will be expected to marry a woman of noble Spanish blood." His voice grew stern. "Not the serving girl of a suspected traitor."

Books by Victoria Lamb
available from Harlequin TEEN

The Tudor Witch trilogy

WITCHSTRUCK
WITCHFALL

THE TUDOR WITCH TRILOGY

WITCHFALL

VICTORIA LAMB

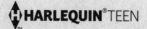

Recycling programs
for this product may
not exist in your area.

ISBN-13: 978-0-373-21100-5

WITCHFALL

A Harlequin TEEN novel/April 2014

First published in Great Britain by Corgi Books, an imprint of Random House
Children's Books

A Random House Group Company

Printed in U.S.A.

For my father, Richard Holland.

Howl, howl, howl, howl! O, you are men of stones.
Had I your tongues and eyes, I'd use them so
That heaven's vault should crack. She's gone for ever
I know when one is dead, and when one lives.
She's dead as earth.

WILLIAM SHAKESPEARE:
KING LEAR, ACT V, SCENE III

PART I

HAMPTON COURT

SPRING 1555

SCRYING

I had been here before in a dream. I was standing in a high place, buffeted by winds and wrapped in a reddish mist that stretched into cloud a few yards ahead. My loose hair whipped about my face, longer than it was now. The wide skirt of my gown billowed around my ankles, flapping like a ship's sail. Power prickled at my fingertips, tingling with familiar heat. Yet I was not permitted to use magick. Not in this place. My senses strained for clues as to my whereabouts, catching strange sounds, a rushing noise like wings.

Sensing movement above my head, I glanced up. A hawk came soaring out of the sunset. It screamed impatiently, tilting its barred body as though hunting for a place to land.

When I looked down again, Marcus Dent was standing in front of me, clothed all in black.

"You always knew it would come to this, Meg Lytton." His words echoed in my mind. "Didn't you?"

I stared at him, too horrified to speak.

I had to get away from him, yet seemed unable to move. My arms hung stiffly by my sides, my feet rooted as though tied to a stake.

"You bested me with your girl's magick last time we met. But now you will find I have the advantage."

The witchfinder showed me what was in his hands: a broad-headed axe, shiny and cruel, its thick shaft wrapped thrice about with holly.

"No," I managed hoarsely.

Marcus Dent watched as I struggled to break free from whatever supernatural hold he had asserted over me. His blue eyes gleamed with malicious amusement.

"Why waste your last moments on this tiresome show of resistance? Accept your fate and kneel for the axe. You have tried before to escape me—and might have succeeded with a little more talent. But you are a mere girl. It is your destiny to die at my hands. You have neither the strength nor the knowledge to fight me. I will always be stronger than you, and your blood spilt in this place today will prove it." With the axe, he pointed to the stone between us. "Now, down on your knees!"

Sweat broke out on my forehead as I battled to break free of Marcus Dent's hold over me. How had the witchfinder managed this feat, binding me so tight to this time and place that I could not escape?

"I will not kneel to you, Dent. I refuse!"

"Meg," he said deeply, leaning closer. The axe blade flashed in my eyes, dazzling me. His voice grew urgent. "Meg! Meg!"

Then a hand came down on my shoulder and I turned, looking up into Alejandro de Castillo's concerned face.

The young Spanish novice was balancing a tallow stump on his palm, its flickering flame reflected in his eyes. As though

I had never seen him before, I drank in the sight of my secret betrothed: strong cheekbones, dark hair swept back from his forehead, a burning intensity about him—and yet a steadiness too, like a rock set in the midst of a wild torrent.

"Meg, it is time to go."

I closed my eyes, dazed and confused as reality flooded back. I was no longer standing in that high place, about to have my head chopped off by the witchfinder Marcus Dent. Instead, I was kneeling on the dirt floor in a tiny disused storage room adjacent to the kitchens of Hampton Court Palace.

My heart was juddering, my palms clammy. It was hard not to let my frustration show as I stumbled over my words. "I must keep scrying...just another few minutes."

"The kitchen servants are assembling to carry the dishes into the Great Hall. Your absence will be noted if you are not at the princess's side when the banquet begins."

"But I must finish the vision! I must see how it ends."

Alejandro pointed to the ground. The copper scrying bowl had been tipped over, the wine almost drained away into the dirt. "Forgive me, I had no choice. It was the only way to wake you."

"You had no right to interfere, Alejandro. What I see in these visions is important."

Alejandro helped me to my feet, brushing the dirt from my skirts. *"Mi querida,"* he murmured, his Spanish accent pronounced, "your fury is quite charming. As is the flash in your eyes when you say 'Alejandro' in your very English voice. Have I ever told you that?"

"The Lady Elizabeth has ordered me to keep scrying and consulting my books of magick, looking for any threat that may lie ahead for her," I countered, ignoring his question as deliberately provocative. He put his arms about me, and it was hard to push him away. "Be serious, please, just for a moment."

"I am always serious with you. I know you serve *la princesa* well, but might I suggest you find somewhere less dangerous to practise your scrying?" His slow, warm smile made my heart flip over. "Now that I have found the woman of my dreams, I would hate to lose her to the Inquisition."

The woman of his dreams? I was hardly that. Not only was I that most forbidden of creatures, a witch, but I was also in the pay of the Lady Elizabeth, whose dislike for the Catholic faith was widely whispered at court. Yet there was no denying the heat between myself and Alejandro. That passion was what had led him to offer me marriage, for Alejandro belonged to a holy order which permitted its priests not only to fight in God's name but also to marry.

Although I felt the same about him, however, and had secretly agreed to be his betrothed for a year and a day, I had not yet been able to give him a final answer. Life would not be easy for such an ill-matched pair, after all.

Besides, our betrothal did not mean he could demand the sacrifice of my craft.

I turned away, tucking the copper scrying bowl away out of sight under a dusty shelf, and stoppering the wine bottle I had used to fill it before carefully hiding that too. They would be needed next time I came here to scry in silence and solitude.

"I am safe enough from the Inquisition," I insisted, though the black-robed priests who prowled the court looking for heretics made me very nervous indeed. I halted before him and smiled up into his eyes. "They do not even know of my existence. Give me your patience a little while longer."

Frustration flickered in his face, though he did not refuse. Instead, he put out a hand and tucked a loose strand of hair back under my courtly hood. "You are beautiful, Meg, but vulnerable too. Do you have any idea of the horrors in store for you if these activities should be discovered?"

How could he ask that? Alejandro had been present at the horrible execution of my aunt, burned at the stake as a witch and a heretic. He must know that my last glimpse of Aunt Jane, screaming in agony as she was consumed by smoke and flame, had been scorched into my mind's eye for ever.

"I shall be more careful in future," I promised him.

"But you will not stop." It was a statement, not a question.

"I cannot," I whispered.

"Not even for my sake?" He held up the candle to see my face better. "Not even though I am your betrothed and ask it of you?"

Beyond the closed door, I could hear clattering and shouts from the vast roaring kitchens as hundreds of servants bustled about, preparing a feast fit for the royal court.

I placed a hand on his chest, feeling the thud of his heart beneath my fingers. "I was born into this path. I cannot be other than a witch, any more than you could turn away from your training in the priesthood. If your Order of Santiago did not allow priests to wed, would you give up your calling to marry me?" I sighed. "Please do not ask me to change who I am, Alejandro."

He looked deep into my eyes, then nodded slowly. "So be it."

For a long moment we gazed at each other without speaking. It was the first time in weeks we had managed to be alone together, and heat bloomed in my face at the sheer intensity of his look. Was this how love always felt, this exquisite tenderness, as though my emotions had been scraped raw and could not bear to be touched? I wanted so badly to speak, to admit that my love for him was as strong as ever, despite the obstacles that fate had thrown between us. Yet I did not wish to break this love spell with the clumsiness of speech. And what if he did not feel the same way?

Alejandro bent his head and touched his lips to mine.

My arms clasped about his neck, and I kissed him back, temporarily pushing all my fears to one side as I let my heart rule my head.

We swayed together, tangled up in each other like strands of wild honeysuckle, and then his arm came round my waist, pulling me even closer. Still I did not resist, lost to reason, wanting the moment to last for ever.

He made a strangled noise under his breath, and the heat of his kiss increased. Then suddenly he took an abrupt step backwards, holding the candle in a less than steady hand. "Meg, we cannot…"

My cheeks were on fire. I knew he was right. But that did not make the trembling ache inside me any less of a torment.

"Yes… I mean, no. We should…go," I managed unevenly, but could not resist brushing his cheek with my fingertips.

"That would be wise," Alejandro agreed with a crooked smile, "before I lose my head."

It was only a joke. But I remembered Marcus Dent with his axe, and shuddered.

After the witchfinder had put me through a sickening trial by water—bound and thrown into a pool, to drown if innocent, to be hanged if I survived—my banishing spell had tossed him into the void. I had thought him gone for ever. Yet now Marcus Dent was appearing in my visions, seemingly unharmed by his ordeal. What could it mean?

Alejandro opened the door and bowed, allowing me to go through before him.

"Meg, the Lady Elizabeth awaits you," he reminded me softly when I hesitated.

I nodded and squeezed past him in the dark narrow space. These were dangerous times at court, and I needed to focus on survival, not on the prickling heat I felt whenever I looked at Alejandro.

I had heard nothing of Marcus Dent since the Lady Elizabeth had been summoned back to court earlier that spring. Now summer was approaching fast, and every day I feared Dent's arrival. I did not know where he had vanished to after Woodstock, nor how long my spell to silence him might last.

It was not a comfortable thought that my vision could be a premonition of my death. If Marcus Dent had indeed returned from some otherworldly void, and was perhaps free to accuse me of witchcraft once more, I would have no chance against him. The word of a witchfinder must outweigh the word of a suspected witch every time.

I rejoined the Lady Elizabeth in the Great Hall, sidling in behind her chair on the high dais and hoping that no one had noticed my absence. I had only slipped away for half an hour during the dancing, after all, and with the Queen still keeping stubbornly to her apartments, these royal banquets never dragged on much beyond nightfall anyway.

Blanche Parry shot me an accusing look but said nothing, pursing her lips and folding both arms across her ample chest as I begged a passing servant for a cup of ale. The princess's lady-in-waiting knew better than to draw attention to my absence when the King might overhear and punish our mistress for it instead.

"Forgive me," I whispered to Blanche. "I forgot the time."

Mistress Parry's gaze flicked across the Great Hall to where Alejandro had joined the black-robed priests at the back wall, his cowl drawn forward to hide his face.

"Indeed," she said drily. "At your prayers again, were you? They'll make you a nun soon, you are so keen on your devotions."

I ignored her jibe, turning to watch the princess. Since Queen Mary had summoned her to court from imprisonment at Woodstock Palace, the Lady Elizabeth had become a favourite with the courtiers. Some said too much of a favourite, and that the Queen would send her sister away again once the royal baby had been born.

Deep in conversation with His Majesty, the Lady Elizabeth was seated on the left hand of the King, simply dressed in a plain black gown with a net of tiny pearls in her hair. Elizabeth laughed at all King Philip's jests and smiled in a flattering way, her face flushed and animated.

I spoke little Spanish, so could not follow what the princess and King Philip were saying to each other. But courtiers throughout the Great Hall were openly staring at the couple, their heads so close together—the Queen's dark-haired Spanish husband and her slim-waisted sister. Indeed, it could not be denied that the princess's youth and shining reddish-gold hair were in contrast to Queen Mary's dour looks.

Not that the court had seen much of Queen Mary in recent months. She still kept to her state apartments, insisting that her baby was late. But King Philip showed so little interest that few still believed their Queen to be with child. Instead, the whispers spoke of a sickly Queen and a young princess who might well be married to the grieving Philip before the year was out.

The dishes were brought out in a long procession that passed in front of the high dais for the King's approval. He applauded them politely, then the cloth-covered board was crowded with platters and wine cups, with honey-glazed pork flesh and a vast roast swan cut open at table that released half a dozen tiny wrens flapping their wings in panic as they flew upwards, seeking the rafters. The whole court exclaimed in delight and clapped vigorously when the spit-cook was brought forward, red-faced and still in his leather apron, to receive the King's compliments.

At one point between courses, the Lady Elizabeth turned to me with greasy fingers. "Meg?"

Hurriedly, I passed her ladyship a bowl of lemon-scented water and a clean white napkin, freshly starched and folded.

Still listening to His Majesty, Elizabeth dipped her long white fingers in the lemon-scented water without even glancing at me. She dried each finger meticulously, draped the napkin over her shoulder to protect her costly gown, then turned back to the King with an apologetic smile.

A sudden shout at the back of the hall stilled the revellers. A courtier, his face pale with terror, was being dragged from the hall by two of the black-robed priests of the Inquisition. His voice could be heard even after he had been removed, raised in high-pitched protest of his innocence. The Spanish priests paid no heed, however, their cowls hiding their faces as they took him away. Those priests who had remained walked among the courtiers with watchful eyes, as though hoping to catch another "heretic" by his guilty expression.

Blanche shivered and crossed herself. "Poor soul," she muttered, but was careful not to speak too loudly, in case she was next.

I saw Alejandro frown at me from across the room, and lowered my gaze with difficulty. He was right. Even to stare could be deemed a sign of guilt or complicity. I wondered how long the Spanish Inquisition would stay at court, their black-robed presence more sinister and alarming with every day that passed. Such arrests had become a common occurrence in recent weeks, as the King and Queen ordered a purge of anti-Catholic feeling at court. Yet none of us dared ask why some courtiers were taken for questioning and not others, nor why a few never came back from the terrifying cells of the Inquisitors.

After the banquet had finished, we were allowed to grab a few mouthfuls of manchet bread and roast meat from the sideboard while the top tables were being pushed back for more dancing. Torches were trimmed and brought forward, for the evening was already darkening to dusk in the high windows. The musicians struck up to the swift beat of the tabor, the hautboys carrying the lively tune, and soon my foot was tapping. The Lady Elizabeth began the dancing with a swift-moving galliard, supported in her leaps by the handsome Spanish King, whose hold on her waist seemed rather too intimate for a married man.

"Do you see that?" Blanche nudged me as she watched the royal couple dancing and leaping together. She whispered in my ear, "They're saying King Philip married the wrong sister."

With so many courtiers crowded about us this was dangerous talk, even if it was no more than the truth. I silenced Blanche Parry with a warning frown. "He married our Queen," I replied warily, "and will soon be father to a Tudor heir, God willing."

"Aye, God willing," she agreed, seeming to recall her surroundings. But she continued to watch our mistress and the courtly Spaniard with an eager, narrowed gaze.

As the music and dancing began to draw to a close, I hurried back from the Great Hall to prepare the Lady Elizabeth's bedchamber for her return. The sheets and bedcovers would need to be shaken out and freshened with herbs, her pot wiped clean and any soiled rushes swept away. Down one of the darker corridors, with only one guttering wall torch to light the way, I found my path blocked by a tall hooded man in dark robes.

"Forgive me," I murmured, and tried to slip past the stranger, but he caught me by the arm.

"Not so fast, Mistress Lytton."

A Spanish accent. I looked at the man more closely, seeing a cruel dark face under the cowl of his robes. It was one of the Catholic priests who surrounded King Philip at court, whispering poison in his ear against the English. I disliked being cornered by such a man, particularly in this lonely place, surrounded by long and menacing shadows that seemed to creep in closer as we faced each other.

My tone was cold. "Do I know you, sir?"

He looked down at me through the flickering torchlight, studying me as a man might study an insect before he crushes it beneath his heel. "Not yet," he said lightly. "Nor should you ever wish to. My name is Miguel de Pero of the Inquisition."

I shuddered. So he was one of *them*, the terrifying Spanish priests whose sole purpose was to torture and destroy any who did not follow the Catholic faith—but most especially those who professed any heretic beliefs or who were suspected of witchcraft. Against my will, I recalled Alejandro's grim description of the Inquisition's methods. Red-hot irons taken straight from the fire and applied to the flesh, spiked cages and barrels to break the limbs, heavy stones and chains that loosened the tongue, and the fearsome rack that could stretch a man's spine until it snapped: these were but a few of the horrors in store for those under suspicion, innocent or not, who did not immediately confess their guilt.

"I see you know our reputation," he murmured, the shadows thickening around us as he spoke. "Though a girl who consorts so frequently with a novice of the Order of Santiago de Compostela need not fear the Inquisition, surely?"

My heart ran cold at these words. What did he know?

Señor de Pero nodded, seeing my expression. "Yes, your

growing intimacy with Alejandro de Castillo has not gone unnoticed at court. He may seem a humble novice to you. But Alejandro is the son of a great nobleman, with a wealthy family awaiting his return in Spain. If Alejandro marries at all, he will be expected to marry a woman of noble Spanish blood." His voice grew stern. "Not the serving girl of a suspected traitor."

"What do you want from me?" I whispered, guessing the answer already but needing to hear it from his lips.

But the priest did not reply. He had stiffened, staring over my shoulder with a hint of anger in his frowning eyes.

I turned. Alejandro was striding along the dark corridor towards us, his cowl thrown back to reveal a tense expression. At the sight of him I wanted to shout his name with relief, yet somehow managed to bite my tongue. I did not want him to get into trouble with his superiors. Finishing his training meant so much to Alejandro, I could not have borne it if my words or actions meant he were refused a place among the other priests of his Order.

"Meg?" Alejandro demanded, reaching me swiftly. He caught my hands in his, his intent gaze searching my face. "Why are you so pale? What was Señor de Pero saying to you?"

"Señor de Pero? Oh, he was just…"

I hesitated, not wishing to be the cause of an argument between Alejandro and his masters. But when I turned back, the corridor was empty except for its host of listening shadows.

The black-robed priest had vanished.

"He was just asking me to convey his compliments to the Lady Elizabeth on her dancing," I finished lamely.

Alejandro did not believe a word of my explanation, I could tell by his frown. He must have already been warned away from me by his masters and knew their disapproval of our relationship. But the danger had been averted for the moment, and at least the Inquisition did not seem aware that I had once been accused of being a witch. They merely saw me as a threat to one of their young Spanish novices, an upstart nobody who must be removed before she ruined a promising career in the priesthood.

"I see," he said drily.

He raised my hand to his lips and touched his lips to my skin. I remembered how passionately he had kissed me before the banquet, and felt my cheeks flare with heat again.

His voice was deep and exasperated. "Don't wander off on your own like that again, do you hear me? I was frantic. I didn't know where you'd gone. With the Inquisition on every corner, looking for ways to trick *la princesa* into some confession of Protestant guilt, you can't be too careful."

"Yes, Alejandro," I said meekly, pretending to agree, but I knew he was not deceived.

"The Queen only allowed her sister to return to court so she could humiliate her with the birth of this new heir to the throne. Do not be deceived into thinking the Lady Elizabeth is a free woman. The slightest indiscretion could see her back in prison—and you with her, Meg." His gaze burnt into mine. "Your lack of caution terrifies me. I know these men. They will *hurt* you, and enjoy their work."

Slowly, Alejandro kissed my hand again, his mouth lingering on my skin, then released it. My hand tingled with the invisible imprint of his kiss, and I found it hard to breathe. Suddenly I could not look him in the eye, fearing the intensity of the emotions his touch stirred in me.

Alejandro insisted on escorting me back through the torchlit maze of courtyards and passageways to the Lady Elizabeth's apartments, and for this I was secretly grateful. In my heightened state of anxiety, it seemed to me that one of the darker shadows had detached itself from the palace wall and slithered behind us most of the way. But I chose not to look at it too closely.

2

THE INQUISITION

"*On days like* this, I almost wish I could be back at Woodstock Palace. At least there I was permitted to roam the grounds with a single guard. Here I am free in name only. I must ask permission even to descend to the courtyard gardens. And then it seems I must make my intention known to the Captain of the Guards and wait for proper accompaniment, whatever that entails!"

The Lady Elizabeth turned from the elegant leaded-windows to look across at me with small hooded eyes that seethed with frustration, like a hawk kept too long on the wrist. Beyond the castle walls, it seemed summer was almost at hand. May sunlight lay in golden strips across the rushes between us. I could see the river gleaming brightly at the princess's back while young lambs played in the lush green fields on the far bank.

"And I miss my old governess, Kat Ashley. More than a governess, for in truth we are so close, she has been like a second mother to me. I had such a nightmare last night—" she shuddered "—and when I tried to wake Blanche, she just snored. Kat would have known how to comfort me. But my sister's advisors consider Kat too Protestant a companion for me. So they keep her away from me."

"A nightmare, my lady?"

Her face was a little flushed that morning, as though she had indeed slept badly, but she had tamed her hair into shining tresses and looked remarkably calm considering the danger of her position.

Since her sister, the Queen, had relaxed the terms of her imprisonment, Elizabeth had blossomed into a regal lady of the court. She still wore the most sombre gowns among those offered to her by the Queen's wardrobe mistress, declining to outshine her sister in cloth of gold or russet satin, and wearing her hair demurely loose as befitted an unmarried lady of the court. Yet there was something about the way she held herself which told the world she was a princess born, and the legitimate daughter of King Henry, whatever the law might say on that contentious matter.

No doubt King Philip's special attentions had helped the Lady Elizabeth feel more confident at court, I considered, then chastised myself for such uncharitable thoughts. The princess was not interested in her sister's husband, and could hardly help it if he was attracted to her. But she was clever enough not to spurn the King too openly, for one day she might need his protection against her sister's ill will.

"Oh, just some hideous creature watching me from the shadows. It was nothing, a foolish dream." The Lady Elizabeth forced a smile. "What else could it have been?"

The door opened and Blanche Parry came staggering in,

red-faced and breathless under the weight of a great heap of silver and black cloth.

"Look what I managed to glean from the royal wardrobe," Elizabeth's lady-in-waiting exclaimed, laughing at our bemused expressions. "Come, Meg, help me with this and there could be a new gown or wrap in it for you. Why, you silly goose, don't frown. You are permitted to look your best. You are at court now, remember?"

"Why can we not go down into the palace gardens again, as we did when we first arrived, and play a game of croquet or quoits?" Elizabeth demanded, watching us rummage through the pile of fine clothing. "I need the sun on my face. I cannot breathe in this stuffy room."

Sitting down heavily beside me on the settle, Blanche Parry shook her head and comfortably began unstitching one of the sleeves.

"Now, my lady, be patient and do not fuss so loud. You know well that the Queen's Grace cannot bear to hear any sound outside her window, so the gardens have been forbidden to us until her child is born."

"That wretched child!" Elizabeth exclaimed, forgetting to lower her voice. "We have been waiting weeks for him to make his appearance. I never heard of such a lengthy pregnancy. My sister must be an elephant, carrying her child a full year. I swear the Queen has been with child since late last summer. Will this much-awaited son and heir never be born?"

Blanche set aside the sleeve she had been working on, its silver stitchwork hanging loose. "Hush, my lady!" she hissed, glancing at the door in case we were overheard. "The dear little prince will be born when he is born, God bless his soul. It may be divine will that his birth is delayed. The stars may not yet be auspicious."

"Then perhaps they should have consulted the Queen's

astrologer on the matter, rather than calling him a magician and dragging him to the Fleet Prison in disgrace." The Lady Elizabeth nodded when I looked up in surprise. "Yes, Meg, I heard of his plight yesterday. Master Dee's house has been searched, his books and papers removed by the Inquisition."

Blanche was even more horrified than before, rolling her eyes towards the door. "My lady!"

"Yes, yes, I know. I must mind my speech and keep my own counsel on this matter. I have not forgotten my precarious position at court." Yet far from taking her own advice, Elizabeth strode restlessly back to the window and stared down at the rolling Thames. Her severe black gown did nothing to disguise the burnished red-gold of her hair, shining in the sunlight. "Poor Master Dee. I only hope they do not find anything dangerous amongst his papers."

She glanced at me, and suddenly I remembered how we had visited the astrologer one night at Woodstock, meeting him secretly at the village inn and discussing Queen Mary's horoscope. But I said nothing, catching a warning look in her face. Blanche Parry was aware that her mistress had gone to see John Dee that night, but knew nothing of what had been discussed. Which was just as well, for it could cost all of us our lives if it ever emerged that the Queen's horoscope had been on the table between us.

"Perhaps once the heir to the throne is born, my sister will allow me to leave court and live quietly in the country." Elizabeth leaned her chin on her hand, looking broodingly across at the shepherds in their fields opposite the palace. "I wish that I was back at Hatfield. Now that would make a pretty prison. Do you know Hatfield, Meg?"

"No, my lady."

"It is not so large and handsome a palace as Hampton Court, but it is homely and quite beautiful in the spring. Soon

the musk-roses will be budding and there will be young cuck-
oos calling in the groves. I miss…ah, so many things, Meg, I
cannot begin to tell you what a wonderful place Hatfield is.
Perhaps one day I shall be allowed to return there, and Kat
Ashley will once again be my companion. Then we shall—"

The door to her apartments opened without any knock
and the Lady Elizabeth turned, her body stiff at the sudden-
ness of the intrusion.

"How dare you, sirs—!" she began, then bit her lip and fell
silent, seeing at once who it was.

Three black-robed members of the Spanish Inquisition
stood in the grand doorway to her apartments. As the princess curtseyed, the men grimly inclined their heads, displaying
only the slightest deference to her status as the Queen's sister.

I recognized one of the priests and scrambled to my feet in
sudden fear, setting aside the book I had been leafing through.
It was Señor Miguel de Pero, the priest who had warned me
to keep away from Alejandro.

Father Vasco, the irascible old priest who had made our
lives so miserable at Woodstock, came hobbling in behind
them, his face greyer than ever, leaning on the shoulder of a
young novice.

Alejandro!

My face flushed at the sight of Alejandro, and I had to look
carefully at the ground, willing my cheeks to cool down. But
it was hard not to remember his kisses in the disused storeroom, the warmth of his arm about my waist as he drew me
closer. What if he had not stopped there?

Furtively, I tidied my cap and gown, then despised myself
for such a show of vanity. Was there no end to my foolish-
ness? I had only seen Alejandro yesterday, yet I was behaving
as though we had been apart for months.

"I am always delighted to welcome those who serve Her

Majesty, my sister," Elizabeth was saying, cleverly reminding her visitors of her own royal lineage.

In a pointed manner she spoke English rather than Spanish, despite her proficiency in that language. Perhaps she hoped that would give her some advantage.

"But I fear the abruptness of your entrance has left my nerves jangling. Do you always barge into the rooms of royalty without knocking or asking permission to enter, sirs?"

"You must forgive us the ignorance of foreigners, my lady," replied Señor de Pero in his heavily accented English. He was taller than the other two men; a great wooden crucifix hung from his belt, and his neatly trimmed beard gleamed with oils where he had recently groomed it. He threw back his hood and smiled, his thin-lipped mouth cruel. "We are not used to your quaint English customs. In our own blessed country of Spain, the Inquisition comes and goes as it pleases, even in the great palaces, even amongst princes and nobles."

Elizabeth shivered at these words. But her chin was raised. She was not ready to show fear before these foreigners. "What is your name, sir?"

"My name is Señor Miguel de Pero and I have come to ask you a few questions on a matter pertaining to Her Majesty's safety," he told her shortly. "These other gentlemen are here to keep a written record of whatever is said by yourself or your servants, so there can be no denials later. I trust this will not be an inconvenience to you, my lady."

"How could it be?" the princess countered sharply. "My royal sister's safety is always my greatest concern."

"Just so." The Inquisitor turned with a bow to indicate Father Vasco. "We have brought a priest with us whom I believe you already know from your time at Woodstock. I fear Father Vasco has not been well since accompanying your household to court, which has sadly delayed his return to Spain. But he is one of our most respected elders, my lady, and it was felt his presence might render our visit less of an intrusion."

Elizabeth curtseyed low to the old priest. "I am sorry indeed to hear of your continuing ill health, Father Vasco. Would you care to sit?" she asked him politely, and nodded to me.

Hurriedly, Blanche and I cleared a place for him on the high-backed wooden settle where the remnants of silver fabric had been laid, then stood back as Alejandro supported his elderly master to the seat and made him comfortable there.

Straightening from his task, Alejandro met my gaze briefly. *Be careful,* his look seemed to say. Then he turned and bowed to Elizabeth with his usual deference.

"My lady," he murmured.

We waited in silence for the interview to begin, the Inquisitors seating themselves at the table where they whispered together, then took out quills, ink and a roll of paper.

Why were the Inquisition here? Could they have some new evidence against the Lady Elizabeth? I remembered my brother William's warnings about Queen Mary's marriage to a Catholic prince, and how England would soon be overrun with the priests of the Spanish Inquisition, hunting down heretics and burning them at the stake. I had thought William too gloomy about England's future. But it seemed he was right. The Inquisition had followed King Philip here from Spain, and now they had come to the princess herself, looking for an excuse to accuse her of heresy—and inflict the death penalty.

I schooled myself to seem as calm as Elizabeth herself, for to show fear in front of these men would be to compound their suspicion that Elizabeth was guilty of some crime. I even tried not to look at Alejandro, though I was sharply aware of his presence in the room, my skin prickling at every slight movement he made. Whatever passed here in the next hour must surely decide my mistress's fate, I thought.

Pale and determined, Elizabeth settled herself on her cushioned seat by the window and spoke briskly to the lead Inquisitor. "Come, Señor de Pero, I am ready whenever you are. Pray ask your questions on whatever pressing matter brings you here. I am my sister's faithful and true subject, and have nothing to hide."

"Muy bien." Miguel de Pero drew up a chair opposite her. His tone was smooth, as though they were discussing the weather. "You will know that the Queen has asked for our aid in purging the court of the evils of Protestant heretics. Unfortunately, some of our enquiries have led us to your household, my lady. Do you know Master John Dee, my lady?"

"Is he not the Queen's astrologer, sir?"

"Master Dee has been sometimes in that position, yes. But this past year he has overstepped his mark and done much to displease Her Majesty."

Elizabeth said nothing but waited, her face cool.

"So you do or do not know Master John Dee," Señor de Pero repeated, writing something on the paper in front of him. When Elizabeth still said nothing, he frowned and looked up at her. "I require an answer to my question, my lady."

"Forgive me, *señor,* I did not know that it was a question." Elizabeth lowered her gaze to the floor and pretended to muse. "Master John Dee…yes, I may have seen him once or twice about the court. Just as I have seen many others in my sister's service about the court."

"But you have never met with him privately?" he persisted.

Elizabeth raised her eyebrows. "Must I repeat myself, sir? Has it been claimed that I have met this man privately?"

Miguel de Pero's eyes narrowed on her face. He looked thoughtful. "What makes you ask that?"

"Only that I know Master Dee to be under some kind of suspicion and now you are here, asking if I have met with him privately. For a maid to be alone with any man would be a sin, but for the Queen's unmarried sister to meet privately with a man now accused of some conspiracy would be not only sinful but also treasonous." Her voice became icy. "I am no fool, sir. I can see a trap when it is set so clearly before me."

Miguel de Pero's mouth tightened with fury. He stared at her for a long while without speaking, his nostrils flared and his eyes as fierce as if another word would see the Lady Elizabeth dragged away to the stake. I guessed he had not often met with such defiance, especially from a young woman in fear for her life.

Eventually he stood and walked about the room for a few moments, his head bowed in thought, hands clasped behind his back. When he returned, he managed a strained smile as he sat down before the princess again.

"Forgive me, my lady, I did not mean to imply that you are in the habit of meeting men privately. It is just that some papers have come to light with your name on them, in connection with this astrologer, and your sister is keen to learn what you know of this matter. Dee is indeed accused of treason, by way of calculating the Queen's horoscope, a charge he does not deny but claims to have done in order to benefit the Queen."

I recalled our secret meeting with John Dee at the Bull Inn in Woodstock. I myself had seen and read the Queen's horoscope that night. My cheeks grew suddenly hot and I felt my palms dampen. Could they see the guilt in my face?

Elizabeth sounded perplexed. "I do not understand. Is it now a crime to cast a horoscope?"

"When it could be used to discover secret information about Her Majesty's health or to time an assault against her throne, yes." The Spaniard gave her a dry smile. "But you stray from the point. How did your name come to be on certain private papers belonging to the Queen's astrologer?"

"I do not know, *señor,* nor am I able to hazard a guess. Perhaps Master Dee intended to draw up my horoscope and read my secrets too, but I can assure you that I gave him no such instruction, nor asked any other person to do so on my behalf. Sir, let me make myself plain. These questions insult me and I do not wish to answer them any further." Elizabeth drew herself up in her seat, cold and straight-backed as though on a throne herself. With that instinctive and princely air of command, I could see why her sister continued to regard her as a threat. "Until you have some proof that I am more than just a name on a piece of paper to Master Dee, I bid you leave me and my ladies in peace."

The Inquisitor stood up and glanced back at his men. Some message seemed to pass between them, and then he bowed and began to pull on his gloves. It seemed indeed that he was leaving, but from de Pero's sneer I knew his questions were far from over.

"I fear it is not possible to take your word alone on this matter, my lady. We will return in a few days with more questions, and perhaps you could set your mind to thinking when you may have had any private contact with Master Dee or sent him any letter. Meanwhile, we shall take your ladies-in-waiting away with us and question them in a room set apart for the purpose."

My heart juddered as I realized that he was looking directly at me, his cruel gaze on my face, enjoying his moment of power. *A room set apart for the purpose.* By that, he must mean a torture chamber where answers could be extracted without fear of interruption.

Seated just behind her mistress in the window alcove, Blanche Parry was looking horrified too.

"I'm not going anywhere with those odd-looking Spaniards," she began loudly, but Elizabeth silenced her with a click of her fingers and Blanche lapsed into a kind of indignant muttering.

Elizabeth's face was white with fear, but I could tell that she was angry too. More angry than I had ever seen her before. Threats against herself I had known her receive with impossible calm, but threats against her own servants seemed to have loosened her grip on that famous self-control.

"Sir, this is unacceptable," she told him. "You have no authority to take my women away from me. If it is my name on Dee's papers, what have my servants to do with this business?"

Miguel de Pero spread his hands wide. "Perhaps nothing, my lady. We have arrested John Dee and intend to ask him the same question as soon as the Queen's councillors have finished their interrogation. But if you are innocent, you can have no qualms about allowing us to question your servants." His smile was terrifying. "In my experience, a servant will often talk where the accused refuses to do so. So I like to begin with the servants and…erm…work my way upwards."

"And how am I supposed to live without my women?" Elizabeth demanded furiously, and I could see how desperately she was searching for reasons why he should not take us. "I am a princess at a royal court. Am I now expected to fetch my own meals and dress myself as best I can without my ladies-in-waiting?"

"Perhaps one of the Queen's ladies would consent to wait on you until your own servants have been restored to you?"

The princess interrupted him, her eyes flashing. "Sir, I refuse to countenance such an outrage. My royal sister awaits the birth of her child and cannot spare her gentlewomen to wait on me. If you will not see sense, *señor,* then I pray you send for the King. I shall speak to His Majesty myself on this matter, since my sister is indisposed."

Having stood silently by all this time, betraying nothing of his feelings, Alejandro suddenly stepped forward. He bowed, then spoke aside in Spanish with the Inquisitors, his voice low and seemingly unemotional.

Miguel de Pero nodded, though once again he looked at me with hostile eyes. "*Gracias,* Alejandro." He turned to the princess. "On this young man's advice, I shall leave your maidservant to see to your needs, and take Mistress Parry for questioning first. She will be returned to you once we are satisfied with her answers."

Blanche struggled as the two men in black robes took hold of her arms and began to drag her from the room. "No, I shall not go with you! I must take care of the Lady Elizabeth."

Ashen-faced, Elizabeth stared first at me, and then at Alejandro. "Will you do nothing to help my servant, sir?"

"Forgive me, my lady, but this is for the best," Alejandro said tersely, stepping between the Lady Elizabeth and the Inquisition as though to protect her. "They will not leave empty-handed, and at least this way you can have Meg to serve you until Mistress Parry's return."

I had no skill for reading thoughts, but I could see that he was afraid for *me*—not for himself, nor the princess, nor even the unfortunate Blanche. It was my neck that was most at risk here, or so Alejandro seemed to believe. That was why he had protected me and thrown Mistress Parry to the wolves instead. Because he already knew that Miguel de Pero considered me an enemy.

His face averted from me, Alejandro strode towards the

door as if he intended to follow the priests and Mistress Parry, but Señor de Pero stopped him in the doorway.

"We shall not require your services any further today, Alejandro." The Inquisitor's voice was cool. "You have been most helpful and I thank you for it. But we can question this woman ourselves. You had best tend your old master before he falls off his seat; Father Vasco appears to have fallen asleep."

With that, the dark-robed priest bowed to the princess and strolled in an unhurried fashion after his men.

We listened in horrified silence as Blanche's shrieks and sobs echoed along the palace stairs and corridors, then abruptly stopped as a door slammed.

I closed my eyes briefly, trying to understand what had just happened. I had watched them drag her away to be questioned—perhaps even hurt and badly frightened—and had done nothing, had used no magick art to confuse their minds or play one man against another. Although Blanche and I had never been friends, she served Elizabeth as I did and for that she deserved my loyalty. Yet like a coward, I had said nothing and thought only of my own safety. Even now I could feel myself trembling like a mouse in a cornfield, hardly daring to breathe in case the Inquisition changed their minds and came back for me too.

I wondered if we would ever again see Blanche alive.

THE CONJUROR'S CELL

Elizabeth shuddered and covered her face in her hands. "Poor foolish Blanche! What will they do to her?"

With a cautious glance at Father Vasco, still asleep on the settle behind us, Alejandro shook his head. "Whatever powers the Inquisition may have been given here, my lady, you are still the Queen's sister. They would not dare harm one of your women."

I looked at Alejandro. His reassurance was well meant, but I knew his words to be empty. The Inquisition were cruel and barbaric in their methods; they were capable of any evil in pursuit of their prey, even torturing innocent women and children to make the men they were shielding come forward. Besides, if they would not harm Elizabeth or her servants, why had he looked at me with such fear?

Rising to her feet, Elizabeth clutched at her full skirts and

stumbled towards her bedchamber. "I am unwell. I must...
lie down."

Alejandro hurried to her side, muttering something in
Spanish. Elizabeth managed an unsteady laugh and replied
in the same language, then gripped his shoulder to stay on
her feet.

He supported her into her chamber while I readied her
bed, plumping the bolsters for her head and tidying the covers
where she had thrown them aside that morning on waking.

Discreetly, Alejandro bowed and left the chamber, though
the look he shot me was grim.

I undressed the princess as quickly as I could. My fingers
fumbled with the difficult fastenings of her gown. Elizabeth
looked sicker every minute, her face becoming deathly white,
her body trembling as she waited for me to finish. It was almost as though she had fallen under a spell, the fit had come
upon her so rapidly. It had to be her old illness, the one she
had suffered so often at Woodstock and which had kept her
confined to her bed for weeks on end. Blanche had claimed
there was no cure for it but bed rest, though the discomfort
could be lessened with herbal remedies and the application of
cool scented cloths to the forehead, wrists and ankles.

No doubt the shock of seeing Blanche dragged away by
the Inquisition had been enough to bring on another bout
of her illness...

I tried to remove Elizabeth's rings, but her fingers had
swollen so much it was impossible. I draped a robe about her
shoulders, then guided her into bed.

"My lady, let me call for one of the Queen's doctors," I
murmured, and drew the covers up to her chin.

Elizabeth lay there shivering, her eyes closed. She shook
her head. "My sister needs their assistance more than I," she

whispered. "What if her baby comes and they are not on hand to help her?"

"It will not take long. The birthing room is only a few minutes away. You are not well and should be examined by a doctor."

She turned her head aside, choking, and I was just in time with a bowl to catch her vomit. I found a cloth and wiped her face clean afterwards, smoothing back her red hair on the pillows.

Elizabeth became more peaceful after that, no longer clutching at the covers with her long swollen fingers, though her body still trembled as though with an ague. I could find no fever in her, but I was not skilled in the treatment of the sick and did not know what signs I should be looking for.

"Try to sleep, my lady," I whispered, though I sensed she was already too far gone to hear me. "I will find a woman to sit with you while I fetch a physician to examine you."

Alejandro had waited for me to finish attending the princess. He was leaning by the window, one fist clenched against the stone, staring down at the broad rolling River Thames below. I could see from the way he held himself that something was eating away at him inside, and when he turned to me, his face spoke of the same frustration.

"It is my fault," he muttered. "I should have done more to prevent this calamity. I knew they were coming to question the princess this morning, yet I did nothing. I thought that by agreeing to accompany Father Vasco, I could somehow protect you. But in the end…"

"You did protect me. They took Blanche instead of me."

"*Si.*" He closed his eyes briefly, as though on a wave of pain. "And God knows what Mistress Parry will suffer at their hands."

"You did your best, Alejandro."

"No!" Alejandro slammed his fist down onto his sword hilt. His fierce eyes flashed open, glaring at me. "I did my duty to my master King Philip and to Spain, yes, but what of my duty to you? You are my betrothed. What of my oath to protect the Lady Elizabeth? I failed both of you, and because of this failure, Mistress Parry has been taken by the Inquisition, and the Lady Elizabeth has fallen sick."

"Her ladyship needs rest, that is all."

"You know this for sure? You have seen this in your…your scrying bowl?"

I heard the anger and self-recrimination in his voice and tried not to get angry myself. "No," I said curtly. "But her illness is a nervous disposition, and comes and goes with her moods. It is not likely to be mortal."

There was an odd snorting noise behind us, then a muffled crash. I turned. Father Vasco was lying on the floor beside the settle, his priestly cap tumbled off and his robes awry.

Alejandro drew a deep breath, then went to help the old priest to his feet. He spoke to him in Spanish, his voice soothing and conciliatory. But the irascible old man brushed him aside.

"Donde esta la princesa?" he demanded hoarsely, peering about the empty apartment, and then his watery eyes lighted on me and narrowed. An old memory seemed to click into place as the priest stared at me. His voice was slurred, yet still coherent enough to condemn me thrice over. "Wait," he continued in stilted English, "I remember you. You are the little witch from Woodstock."

"No, Father," Alejandro said hurriedly, "your illness has made you forget. The accusation of witchcraft was false, do you remember? This girl is innocent."

Alejandro tried to lead him back to the door, but it was too late. The priest had my guilt locked into his head now.

"No, I remember truly. This one is a witch." Father Vasco pointed a bony finger in my direction, his large emerald ring gleaming in the sunlight. "We burn witches in Spain."

"We burn priests in England," I countered, thinking of all the Protestants condemned to a hellish death since the arrival of the Spanish Inquisition.

But I was afraid. For the first time since a kitchen maid had accused me at Woodstock Palace, I knew how it felt to be exposed as a witch—only this time my accuser was no young girl, but an elderly priest revered by the Order of Santiago.

I lifted my own finger and pointed back at the old Catholic priest.

"Forget," I commanded him, wiping the slate of the old priest's mind. My voice shook, for I knew how vital it was to get this spell right. His word alone could see me brought before the Inquisition as a suspected witch. "Let no memory bind, let the past be blind, drive thought from your mind… and leave us!"

The priest had a weak mind, easily brought under enchantment. Caught up in my improvised spell, Father Vasco's face emptied of all his cruelty and hatred. His hand dropped to his side. The old man turned and weaved unsteadily towards the door, leaving the princess's apartments without another word or a backward glance.

"You'd better go with him," I told Alejandro, "in case Father Vasco tumbles down the stairs without your guiding hand."

But Alejandro did not move. He was looking at me. "Why did you do that?"

"What did you expect me to do? Your master would have gone straight to the Inquisition. A witch in the princess's service? What more reason would they need to confine the Lady Elizabeth to the Tower again, and drag me out to the gallows? I did what needed to be done, that is all."

"You had no 'need' to use magick against Father Vasco. He is an old man, his memory is not what it was. You were never in any danger. I would only have had to explain to the Inquisition that the whole thing was a misunderstanding, and that would have been an end to the matter."

I raised my eyebrows at the simplicity of his thinking. "And the Spanish would have believed you without question?"

"You forget that I am Spanish too. Just because we are foreigners does not make us stupid."

Too late, I saw how angry he was. He was still training to be a priest, after all, and to see me using magick on his own master must have hurt him deeply.

"Forgive me," I stammered, catching at his arm as he turned to follow Father Vasco. "I didn't mean to upset you. I was only trying to protect the princess."

"You were trying to protect yourself, Meg," he corrected me, pulling away from my hand. He bowed as he left, but did not meet my eyes. "As you said, I must make sure Father Vasco reaches his room without accident, just as you had better tend your mistress in her sickness."

I stared after him, my heart burning with grief.

Could Alejandro not see the danger we might have faced without my spell of forgetting? If his master had chosen to repeat that accusation to any of the other Spanish priests and King's men in the palace, however rambling and unlikely, they would still have listened with eager interest. Father Vasco might be old and sick, but he was still respected. Otherwise he would never have been brought here today to attend the princess's questioning.

I jerked with guilt, his parting words having recalled the

Lady Elizabeth to me. With Blanche Parry gone, and her other ladies still forbidden to her, Elizabeth's care fell to me alone.

Time was short. I hurried away to find a maid who would sit with the princess. I persuaded one of the Queen's physicians to examine the Lady Elizabeth, but he refused to return with me at once, saying he would visit when his other duties allowed it. Meanwhile I knew what must be done to save us all. I would disguise myself and visit John Dee in prison. It could be done easily with a bribe—you could achieve almost anything in London with a hefty bribe—and then at least we would know if the astrologer planned to name the Lady Elizabeth as a co-conspirator in this matter of the royal horoscope. Or whether he had already done so under torture.

It would be too dangerous to visit John Dee alone, of course. The city was crawling with foreigners intent on troubling the English. It was no longer safe for a girl to travel about London on her own.

But after our argument, could I persuade Alejandro to go with me?

A more hellish prison than the Fleet I could not have imagined. It was a place straight out of the terrifying engravings of demons and spirits my aunt had owned. Inside its high walls the air stank so terribly, it seemed to burn my throat, and the smoking tallow of the guard's lantern stung my eyes until I could hardly see.

Alejandro had agreed to accompany me from Hampton Court to the Fleet Prison, but I had refused his help beyond the gate. I knew how reluctant he had been to agree to this plan, and his lack of trust irked me. "Wait here for me until I return," I had whispered, wrapping myself in my cloak. "A young English maid alone, visiting her unfortunate brother in prison, will rouse no suspicion. But in the company of a Spanish priest?"

"I would not speak a word—" Alejandro had begun, but I had cut him off with a quick shake of my head.

"It's too dangerous for you to come any further," I told him. "Please trust me and wait near the river gate."

He would still be there now, waiting in the darkness beyond the high stone walls. Impatiently too, if I knew my betrothed.

I had faced greater terrors than this place, I told myself firmly. Still, it took all my courage not to turn and run as the guard came to a halt before one of the cells and fumbled with his key chain, swearing when none of the keys would turn in the lock. But I had a duty to the Lady Elizabeth. I could not fail her.

I stood ankle-deep in mire, my nostrils assaulted with the stench of the Fleet Prison, while rats brushed my skirts. At last the rusty iron yielded, and the man threw open the door to the cell.

"A visitor for you, master!"

There was silence. Then a man stirred in the dank shadows. "What's that? A visitor?"

"Your sister, or so she claims, and a sweet young piece she is indeed." The guard turned to me with a grin and spat on his hand, holding it out for the turnkey's bribe. "Three shillings, mistress, was what you offered me at the prison gate to let you see your 'brother' one last time. Though I do not believe for a second he's your brother. What, with his hair as dark as the Devil's and yours yellow as the sun? Nay, never fear, I'll not say a word to the prison warden. Every man deserves a little comfort before the end."

His obscene wink made his meaning plain.

I shuddered, dropping three shillings into his palm. The

guard bit each coin, then pressed the bribe carefully into his belt pouch.

"Thirty minutes is all I can spare you before the guard changes at midnight. But thirty minutes is more than enough for any man to achieve his business, and you must make merry while you can. The Inquisition will be coming for your master tomorrow, and after that…" The guard mimed a neck being stretched by a rope, his face contorted, tongue lolling horribly, then shoved me inside the foul-smelling cell and swung the door shut after me. "God have mercy on his soul!"

I closed my eyes, standing motionless behind the closed door, then muttered a word under my breath. A second later I heard the splash as the guard tripped in the filthy water flooding the passageway, falling heavily to his knees, then his muffled curses as he attempted to get up and slipped again. My lips twitched. It felt wonderful to work magick again. Being at court might be more comfortable than the dilapidated lodge at Woodstock, but with so many unfriendly eyes on the Lady Elizabeth's household, I had hardly felt able to work even the simplest of spells in recent weeks. For I knew that discovery would mean my death, and perhaps the princess's too.

Once the guard's angry oaths had finally died away, I pushed back my hood and looked around. My eyes struggled to see anything in the dim light—the guard had given me just one candle to keep darkness and the rats at bay.

The cell was so chilly, I drew my cloak about myself instinctively, unable to believe anyone could survive even a single night in such a place. The walls glittered with water, a constant trickle adding to the slurry of the mud floor. An iron grate in the wall revealed a black rushing current but a few feet below us, and I realized with a shock that the sound I had taken to be a northerly wind howling about the walls was in truth the Fleet River, flowing down into the Thames.

"Master Dee?" I whispered.

The astrologer stepped forward into the candlelight, a shadowy figure whose gaunt face and piercing eyes I would have recognized anywhere.

"Meg Lytton?"

"I am here on behalf of a mutual friend." I saw from the slight widening of his eyes that he had understood me. "Is it safe to talk?"

"As safe as any place can be for a man charged with treason," Dee replied, but glanced warily at the door. "Come closer, let me look at you."

I approached the astrologer, placing the candle on a small table. He removed my gloves with trembling hands and examined my palms, just as he had done once before in a small upper room at the Bull Inn.

The Lady Elizabeth had been the prisoner then, I realized, and John Dee had come secretly to help her. Strange how rapidly the wheel of fortune had turned to reverse their positions, with the Lady Elizabeth back at court and John Dee in prison himself.

"Let us stand against the river wall," he muttered, dropping my hands as though satisfied. "The water is loudest there."

Following him across filthy rushes to the dampest part of the cell, I watched the black swell of the river rolling below us and thought of the man I had left waiting at the prison gate.

"Who is this friend on whose behalf you visit me?" John Dee asked, his gaze searching my face. "Is it the lady in whose company we first met?"

I nodded, and began the speech I had rehearsed all the way along the river from Hampton Court. "My lady fears you may name her when they ask why you drew up the Queen's horoscope. I trust you will remember that she neither asked nor paid to see the chart, but was offered it freely."

"Her name will never pass my lips, I swear it."

"Not even under torture?"

"Not even then."

"You might not mean to betray her," I pointed out gently, "but even the strongest of men have failed to stay silent under the torments of the Spanish Inquisition."

"I am not afraid of the Inquisition," John Dee insisted, and indeed I saw no fear in his face. "I have read the stars and my life does not end in this foul place. My only true fear is that I may lose the last of my family estate over this matter. My confiscated papers will prove beyond doubt that I did cast the Queen's horoscope, which is considered treason."

"How do you think to escape a traitor's death when the Inquisition hold such proof against you?"

He shrugged, strangely calm as we discussed his possible death. Perhaps he truly had astrological proof that he would survive this accusation. "I shall argue that my only thought in casting these horoscopes was for the Queen's welfare and that of her unborn heir. My defence will be that I was consulting the stars on her behalf, as any court astrologer should do during a royal pregnancy."

"They will never believe you. These Spaniards are fanatics. They see the casting of a horoscope as akin to working magick, and as such your life will be forfeit."

"We shall see," was all John Dee said, and his smile made me suspect he had some deeper game to play.

God defend him if he has not, I thought, for all the world knew how dangerous a pregnant woman could become when threatened—and Mary was no ordinary woman, but the Queen of England herself.

"But can you know for sure that you will not betray my lady under torture?"

"I have asked the spirits and been given a sign of good

omen," he told me quietly, and the hairs rose on the back of my neck at his words. "I know that you understand such things. When voices call us from the celestial spheres, we must respond."

The celestial spheres?

He meant the stars, I realized. One of his horoscopes covered with tiny black scrawl, the symbols I did not fully understand.

"Voices?"

"We live in light and darkness beneath the Sun and the Moon. But there are spirits dwelling above us. Not only the spirits of the dead, but also of the celestial realm itself. Some call these spirits daemons, others elementals. I think of them as the spirits beyond the stars. Certain men are destined to be born with the power to conjure and converse with those spirits." He hesitated, running his finger over my palm again. "And certain women too."

I recalled what John Dee had asked me at our first meeting. *Can you speak with the spirits?*

This was too near my own dreams and imaginings to be comfortable. I shook my head, pulling my hand out of his grasp. "Only my aunt possessed such power and she is dead."

"So I heard. Burnt at the stake by Marcus Dent, a man at whose name every English witch must tremble." His eyes narrowed on my face. "Yet somehow you escaped him."

"I was lucky," I lied.

"Some might call it destiny, not luck. The celestial spirits wished you to live. But for what purpose?"

I did not like his searching gaze. "I should go."

He called after me. "Before you leave, Meg Lytton, do you wish to see your aunt again? To speak with her as I am speaking with you? For I can bring her spirit to face you in this godforsaken cell—even poor as I am, stripped of my books and instruments. This is my power, and I wield it whenever and wherever I choose."

He held out both hands towards me in a dramatic gesture, his long thin fingers pale in the candlelight.

"To summon spirits is a power you too could possess, if only you would drop your girlish fears and learn from a master."

I stared at the man, deeply shocked by his offer. "My aunt is dead. It is not possible."

"Anything is possible."

"I would not see her peace disturbed."

"The dead have no thought of life or death, of peace or disruption. Your aunt would be here with us, but not of this world."

Dee took my hand and began to stroke my palm, watching me. I did not resist, for to own the truth I was curious to see the extent of his power. I did not believe he could summon my aunt from the grave, nor did I wish him to try. But his power fascinated me, made it hard to deny him.

His gaze fixed on my face. "What was your aunt's name?"

I hesitated, then whispered, "Jane Canley."

He closed his eyes and spoke in Latin, muttering under his breath, and I heard him weave my aunt's name into the spell. His fingers continued to squeeze and stroke my hand as he spoke. Suddenly his eyes snapped open and his narrowed gaze lifted to stare over my shoulder. His lips twitched as he glanced down at me.

"Look behind you, Meg," he whispered hoarsely. "Slowly, slowly! Show neither fear nor surprise."

My skin prickled. Following his instructions, I turned my head with exquisite slowness and looked over my left shoulder. There in the darkness stood Aunt Jane. Not as I remembered her in those last terrible moments as she slumped against the village stake—a smoking husk of blackened skin and bones—but as she had looked in her younger years, when I was but a child. My dearest Aunt Jane, her skin smooth again, her fair hair rich and glossy under her white cap, dressed in a simple gown and apron.

Terrified as I was, I found myself smiling at her instinctively. My lips opened to speak her name. "Aunt Jane!"

But my aunt did not reply, nor did she smile back at me. She stood—or possibly floated, for I could not see if her feet were touching the dank floor—in perfect stillness, staring at a point beyond us in the dark cell as though not even aware of our presence. Her mouth remained level and closed, her blue eyes tranquil and empty of all emotion.

Staring, I was suddenly aware that I could see through my aunt's body to the filthy wall beyond. There was her gown of coarse linen, yes, but through it I could see the wall's rough-cast stones glistening with water. It was as though Aunt Jane had performed the spell of invisibility on herself, and it had only partially worked.

I could not stand it. My heart rebelled, knowing this was not my aunt as she had been in life, but a shadow of her soul, a phantom that could never replace the woman I had known and loved.

"Begone, spirit!" I cried, wrenching my hands from John Dee's grasp and pointing at the wavering vision.

And we were alone again in the prison cell.

John Dee looked at me oddly. "Impressive," he said, commenting on my ability as a witch. "Though your aunt would have spoken, if you had waited to question her."

"That was not my aunt."

"No," he agreed mildly. "But it was as close an embodiment of her spirit as you will get now, this long after her death."

Dee poured some ale from a flagon into his wooden bowl and sipped at it, then offered the bowl to me. I shook my head, still a little angry with the astrologer, and he smiled. "If you wish, I can teach you to work the spell yourself. It is a powerful magick for a woman, but I can see you are not without talent. You never know when it may come in useful to call a spirit to your side."

"I came here to serve my mistress, not to learn how to summon the dead."

"Wait," he insisted as I turned to the door. Dee set the bowl of ale on the table and beckoned me forward. "Look into the bowl and tell me what you see."

Did he intend me to scry for him? Curiosity brought me to the table's edge, but I did not wish John Dee to know the extent of my skill. I pretended not to understand.

"What do you mean?"

"If you are a woman of power like your aunt, not a country witch, then a simple act of divination should come easy to you."

The astrologer was taunting me, and I knew it. A child's trick, goading me to play his dangerous game.

Still listening for the guard's return, I lowered my gaze to the bowl. I waited a while, trying to empty my mind of thought. Still nothing stirred in the cloudy liquid but the flicker of candlelight.

My reflection looked back at me helplessly: a pale, wide-eyed girl, her face tense and unsmiling under a plain white cap. The silence dragged on. My eyes began to sting and my belly hurt in anticipation of his contempt. From somewhere in the depths of that vile prison I caught what sounded like a scream, muffled by thick walls. Some unfortunate captive being tortured in pursuit of a confession, guilty or not.

At my side, Master Dee stirred at last, perhaps growing uneasy as he contemplated his fate, and I drew breath to admit my failure.

"I cannot read the future, I do not have the skill." Suddenly I frowned, my attention snagged by some movement in the cloudy liquid. "Wait, what was that? I thought I saw something."

"Yes?"

My gaze fixed on the bowl as the dark vision inside it swirled and shifted. With a chill sensation, I recognized what I was looking at. "I see a girl. A girl kneeling in a high lonely place. I cannot see her face, her head is bent. It is sunset and there are dark clouds on the horizon. At her back, I see—"

I gave a horrified cry and broke off.

"Speak on," he urged me, close at my ear. "Do not be afraid of what has been shown to you. These visions have no power to hurt you and may bring much secret information."

I shook my head and was relieved to hear the heavy tread of boots and jangle of keys outside in the corridor. It was the guard at last, returning to release me from this hellish place.

"My time here is done," I muttered, averting my eyes from the bowl and hurrying to the cell door. I dragged on my gloves with shaking hands, banishing the vision from my mind. "I wish you good fortune when they come to question you tomorrow. And I pray you most fervently, Master Dee, to remember my mistress and the terrible hurt that might be done to her by uttering the wrong word—even under torture."

This time John Dee did not attempt to stop me, and I was soon outside again in the night, gulping at the river air, desperate to rid my lungs of the foul stench of his prison cell.

Alejandro was waiting for me near the river gate as he had sworn. He looked more Spanish than ever in the moonlight, his eyes keen and fierce as a hawk's beneath his feathered cap, his cloak hiding a jewelled sword and the richness of his court suit. I remembered standing by another riverbank in the daylight, listening to his proposal of marriage and promising to give him my answer in a year and a day's time.

His sharp gaze searched my face. "What is it? You look pale. Did the meeting go badly?" He frowned when I did not reply. "Does the astrologer plan to betray the Lady Elizabeth?"

I shrugged helplessly. "He said not, but I do not know for sure. We must return to court as quickly as possible. The princess will wish to hear what I have learned. If you want to help me, call a linkboy to light us back to the barge."

Alejandro did as I asked, then turned back, still frowning. "You are cold." He removed his cloak and swung it about me. His hands lingered on my shoulders. "I wish you would trust me, Meg, and tell me what has upset you so much."

"It's just the stink of this place," I muttered, and hugged myself into his fine cloak, still warm from his body. "I can't stomach it."

"Hampton Court does not smell much better," he pointed out.

"But the court is there and the Lady Elizabeth, and it is my duty to serve her." I tried to distract him with my chatter. "At least summer is nearly upon us. Perhaps the Queen will finally allow us to depart for the country before the stench of the palace infects us all with some plague."

I felt safer once we were on board the barge and heading back along the dark Thames towards Hampton Court. The ancient timbers creaked and protested beneath us, oars struggling against the current, the return journey far slower as we hugged the central streams of the river, avoiding jetties that we knew to be watched by the Queen's spies.

Wishing to avoid the winks of the bargemen, bribed to

keep silent about our secret journey, I stood apart from Alejandro and gazed out over the blackness that was London asleep. Once or twice a small boat approached us, with men and torches on board who looked to be portsmen, and I feared we would be discovered. But each time I raised my hand and softly spoke, "Depart!" in Latin, then watched as my power steered the boat away from our barge and sent it dancing violently across the current, leaving them no chance to turn in pursuit.

As we left the city behind, I gripped the barge rail and stared down at the water, sick at heart. There was little profit in telling Alejandro that the astrologer had conjured a semblance of my poor dead aunt, nor had I any desire to discuss what I had seen in John Dee's scrying bowl. For from what I had been shown in that last terrifying vision, it seemed I had neither future nor husband ahead of me—and no head either.

DEAD QUEEN

Another day and an evening went by before one of the Queen's physicians finally came to visit the Lady Elizabeth, by which time I had managed to beg more logs for the fire and warmed the room as I remember Blanche used to do at Woodstock when the princess was sick. A tall Spaniard with a domed forehead and bulging eyes, his skin the colour of beaten copper, examined the drowsy Elizabeth with only mild interest. It was clear he thought little of her Protestant leanings.

"A disease of the spirit," he proclaimed, straightening from his cursory examination. "Very common in young women of an hysterical disposition, and hardly worth calling me away from the care of Her Majesty for such a trifling matter. Your mistress will recover with bed rest and good care. Meanwhile, let her take a cup of wine every three hours, and perhaps some mutton broth if she can keep it down."

"And the swelling?"

The Spanish doctor shrugged. "It is a simple imbalance of the humours. The Lady Elizabeth is melancholic and suffers from an excess of black bile. An hourly application of cold cloths steeped in hyssop should help to alleviate the swelling in her lower limbs."

I stared as he packed away his instruments and turned to leave the room. "*Señor,* is there nothing else you can do for her ladyship? She suffers badly."

"You could pray for her soul," he suggested helpfully after a moment's pause. "In my opinion, this affliction is a punishment from God for the wicked heretical views she has embraced in the past. Let the Lady Elizabeth do penance to our Lord Christ with constant prayer and daily communion. Then she may see an early recovery."

"Thank you, Doctor," I said drily, and showed him to the door.

I returned to the bed to find Elizabeth awake, a faint smile on her lips. Her forehead drenched in perspiration, she sat up slightly to let me rearrange her covers. "So this is all God's fault."

I smiled, though in truth I was desperately concerned for the princess. Her skin was almost grey now, and her eyes lacked their usual spark of light and humour. If only Blanche Parry were there to advise me, I thought, busying myself with her pillows. But we had seen nothing of her since she had been dragged away by the Inquisition.

"Would you like me to fetch you a cup of wine, my lady?"

"Not yet."

I wiped her forehead, trying to sound cheerful. "At least your sickness should mean a respite from their questions, my lady."

"Do not be so sure," she murmured.

"It's late, but I must find cloths and an infusion of hyssop to reduce the swelling as the doctor suggested. And your sheets will need to be changed. But you will not be alone while I am gone. I have found a girl to sit with you until I return, my lady."

"Not that half-witted maid you left with me earlier? She kept staring and crossing herself whenever I looked at her."

"Forgive me, my lady, she was the best I could find in a hurry." I laughed at her expression. "This time I asked amongst the Queen's maids of honour and finally found one who was not required in the birthing rooms and could be more easily spared from her duties. This one should be rather less inclined to cross herself, though I cannot promise anything about her staring. Her name is Alice Upton, and I believe she's the granddaughter of one of King Edward's old stewards."

I paused meaningfully, in case anyone was listening at the door, and Elizabeth nodded, lowering her eyelids to hide the expression in her eyes. "Then let her come forward and sit with me, Meg, while you play hunt the hyssop. This may be the sickness talking, but I am inclined to like the name Alice Upton; it has a good ring to it."

I knew then that she had understood me. Her brother Edward had been a fierce Protestant, and had tended to keep men about him whose allegiances and beliefs lay in the same reforming direction. It was unlikely that anyone of that blood would feel any loyalty to Queen Mary and her burning Catholic zeal.

"First though, while we are still private, tell me of your visit to John Dee. All I recall is you whispering in my ear that you had visited him in prison. Then I must have slept again, for I remember nothing else. Was that a true memory or my delirium?"

"We had better speak softly then, for fear we may be over-heard," I whispered, and pretended to fuss with her covers, stretching across the bed to smooth them down. "I have indeed visited Master Dee in the Fleet Prison. He said he would not betray you, even under torture. That he was more powerful than the Inquisition. And then Master Dee…" I stumbled painfully over my words. "He…conjured the likeness of my aunt to demonstrate his power."

The Lady Elizabeth stared up at me. "Master Dee conjured your aunt's spirit? I have heard tales of necromancers who summon the dead to speak with them, but never believed it could be true. Was it indeed your aunt and not some magician's trick?"

"It was a good likeness," I admitted. "But whether it was her spirit or not, I could not tell."

"Did you not speak with her?"

I shook my head, wishing now that I had not admitted what John Dee had shown me. The princess seemed excited by the news that Dee could conjure spirits. For myself, I hoped he would never play such a trick again. I was still haunted by my aunt's blank stare. If I had not refused to marry the witchfinder Marcus Dent, he would never have become my enemy, and my aunt might still be alive—for it was through his cruel determination to make me suffer that she had gone to the stake.

"But you believe that I am safe?" Elizabeth prompted me.

"I trust Master Dee's word."

"Then I am as safe as anyone may be in a country such as ours. And it seems I owe you my thanks again, Meg, for undertaking this dangerous task on my behalf." She sat up, her face flushed, and took a silver link bracelet from the wooden jewellery chest beside her bed. "Here, accept this as your reward."

"I need no reward for serving you," I protested.

"But I wish you to take it. The Spanish ambassador gave me this silver bracelet as a gift, though I suspect it comes from his master, King Philip." Her mouth tightened in fury and contempt. "What a husband! With my sister laid in a birthing room night and day, struggling to give life to his babe, His Majesty sends me secret gifts and compliments as though he would get me with child next. And I must smile and dance with this man, and say nothing, for he holds the key to the prison my life has become."

Faced with her fury, I did not argue any further but accepted the bracelet with a curtsey. The tiny silver chain glittered on my palm as I looked down at it, its links so fragile I was afraid it would be broken in my daily work. I would have to hide it away under my floorboards with my secret books, and only wear it on special occasions. The tale of how she received the bracelet interested me though, and I glanced at her curiously, slipping the beautiful thing into my belt pocket.

It was unlike the princess to be so forthright about King Philip, for while the Queen lay abed he and his Spanish Inquisitors ruled the court. But perhaps Elizabeth too was uneasy about our long wait here at Hampton Court, days stretching into weeks with no news from the Queen's darkened birthing room. It seemed strange indeed. Yet if the Queen was not pregnant, why would none of her doctors admit this?

Not that we were alone in this suspicion. Every day courtiers kicked their heels in the richly tapestried corridors, listening for women's cries or the slam of doors, anything which might indicate the birth of a royal child was imminent. Visitors came to our rooms each morning to pay their respects to the Lady Elizabeth, yet rarely spoke of the Queen's condition above a whisper. Nor had the cloud of accusation above her head lifted, though it had lessened, with her ladyship allowed to move freely about the palace—though she could not leave court without permission.

So despite the royal banquets she could now attend at the King's side, Elizabeth's position had not much improved. The princess was still essentially a prisoner, tied to these dark corridors and dreaming of the day when she could return to her beloved Hatfield.

Leaving the princess's bedchamber, I went in search of Alice. She had been waiting patiently for my summons, a tall, clumsy-looking girl with curly chestnut hair and a snub nose. That she had a sweet nature I had been able to see without using any art, for she had jumped up on hearing of the princess's sickness and begged to be allowed to serve her. But whether Alice was discreet and stout-hearted enough to join the princess's raggle-taggle household I was less sure. Only time would tell whether her apparent love for Elizabeth was true or feigned, for she could have been put forward by one of the Queen's spies with instructions to watch the princess and her servants while they were at court.

Now, however, Alice was gushing. "Oh, you can trust me, never fear. I shall watch her ladyship like a very hawk, mistress, and not stir a step from her ladyship's side without permission."

"Please call me Meg," I begged her. Being called "mistress" by a girl my own age was rather like wearing a gown that did not belong to me, too richly trimmed for my status at court. "And I shall call you Alice. We do not stand on ceremony in the Lady Elizabeth's household."

Entering the princess's bedchamber, Alice peered tentatively round the heavy bed curtains, and bobbed a curtsey when she found her royal mistress awake and waiting for her. "My lady, my lady," she muttered several times, and curtseyed again, clearly flustered, very deferential in her manner. "An honour to serve the Queen's sister, my lady."

Elizabeth managed a weak laugh. "Good Alice, pray find a seat and sit on your hands there. Otherwise you will wear yourself out with all this courtesy."

"Yes, my lady."

I looked at the Lady Elizabeth. "Alice will fetch you wine and a bowl of broth when you feel able to take some. I shall return as soon as I can, my lady."

Elizabeth was looking exhausted, but nodded me away on my errands. I guessed her swollen body must be aching badly; no doubt she could think of nothing but the cold herbal compresses which might reduce her discomfort.

"Godspeed, Meg."

Hurrying away with a list of essential supplies in my hand, I soon found that the Queen's doctors were not the only people at court to despise the Lady Elizabeth. Although I had no trouble begging old rags and hyssop water from one of the kitchen servants, and bearing it back to Alice so she could begin the lengthy task of steeping and preparing the cold cloths, I had little luck with my search for fresh linen.

First I found our door guarded by two of the King's men, swarthy Spaniards who stared at me whenever I entered or left the princess's apartments. Some might have said they were protecting the princess, but it seemed to me the guards were there to prevent her from leaving. Then, asking for linen, I was sent to the wrong part of the palace, returning footsore and empty-handed. Sending for the head housekeeper, I was told she was already abed and could not speak with me until the morning.

By the time I discovered the whereabouts of the linen store, the hour was almost midnight. The woman in charge of the linen chests was resentful and heavy-eyed at having been roused from her bed at such a late hour. She looked me up and down with barely disguised contempt when I explained my errand, then handed me an armful of linen so stained and poorly patched it was not fit for a servant's bed.

"I cannot take these to my mistress," I said, frowning over the stains and thin, fraying edges. "Perhaps I did not explain myself clearly enough. I need good clean linen for the Lady Elizabeth's chamber. She is sick and taken to her bed."

"I heard you," the woman said sharply. She was plump and dark-haired with slanted eyes. "This is all we can spare."

"This?"

"All the best linen is reserved for the Queen and her ladies." Ending the discussion there, the woman shut the chamber door in my face. "Goodnight."

The back courtyard was dark and empty as I trudged across in my clogs, linen in hand, my eyes half closing with drowsiness. Few logs for the fire, poor linen for her bed, and now two grim-faced Spanish guards on her door. So this was all the courtesy my mistress was to receive, summoned back to court as though all charges against her had been false, yet still suspected and under guard. No doubt they would be whispering against her until the Queen gave birth, for until then Elizabeth must still seem a threat. Meanwhile my lady suffered badly, and had none but me and Alice to care for her.

Torches flamed above me on the ramparts, and I could hear the men in the guardroom playing some game, dice probably. The rest of the palace wing seemed to be in darkness, the windows shuttered and locked, for beyond them lay the Queen's apartments in its strange, deathly hush.

I thought of the dark-eyed, sharp-chinned Queen and tried to imagine her lying in pain and fear amongst her rich bed hangings as she waited for her child to finally emerge. I wondered again if my prediction had been right, that Queen Mary had no child in her belly and dared not tell her husband. I could see now why it could be considered a treasonous act to draw up and consult a horoscope on such a delicate matter. For any man to be in a position to tell if and when a royal birth—or a death—might occur was a dangerous thing, for that was the kind of information which could shape a country's fate.

Then I forgot all about the Queen and her unborn child. I stopped dead on the path, my skin creeping with fear.

A rat had come scuttling out of the bushes just ahead of me. At least, I thought it was a rat, though as the creature moved closer it seemed to grow and shift shape, until it was almost shuffling on its hind paws like a man. Its body was unnaturally large-boned, its head long and gleaming black as though it had just slipped out of the river.

Its whiskered face turned towards me with a malicious air. For a horrifying second I thought it would speak.

"Evil spirit," I began hurriedly, tripping over my spell, "in the name of great Hecate, in the name of the four directions, begone and take thy foulness far from here!"

Still the rat came on, staring at me with its shiny black eyes, and I realized that my spell was having no effect. How was it possible that a creature so small could resist my magick? Sweat broke out on my forehead as I backed away, my gaze locked with the rat's. Had I chosen my words poorly, or was I losing my skill as a witch?

Suddenly the door to the guardroom was flung open with a crash, throwing light from its well-lit interior across the yard.

Two men wearing the King's livery and with dark complexions hurried down the steps and past me with little more than a brief glance, arguing heatedly with each other in Spanish.

I turned back, my gaze searching the shadows under the tower, but the rat had gone.

Wary now, glancing from left to right as I climbed the tower stairs, I hurried back along the corridors towards the princess's apartments. It was not the first time I had seen such a creature, I realized, casting my mind back to the day on the river bank when Alejandro had asked me to marry him. Could that have been the same rat who slipped from the river that day? I had thought instinctively of Marcus Dent at the sight of its mad eyes, part of me wondering if the witchfinder had returned from the void in rat form, not as a human.

Shaking away such wild imaginings, I elbowed my way through the half-open door into the Lady Elizabeth's bed-chamber. My spell had failed because I was weary and needed sleep, that was all it was.

The heavy bed curtains had been drawn back as though to encourage the heat of the fire, and a flushed Alice had fallen asleep beside her royal charge, her curly head resting wearily on the counterpane.

As I entered the room, the Lady Elizabeth woke with a start and cried out, "God defend us!"

Alice woke with a snort, gave a strangled shriek and fell backwards off her stool. She struggled to her feet and stood wild-eyed, staring at us as though she could not remember where she was.

Dropping the pile of linen, I hurried to the princess's bedside. "What is it, my lady? Are you in pain? Has your sickness worsened?"

"No," Elizabeth said hoarsely, shaking her head as I reached for a cool cloth to lay on her forehead. "I had a dream. The most terrible dream. I saw my mother standing before me in this very room. It was Queen Anne, I swear it! I have a portrait of her in my locket, and as soon as she came towards me, I recognized her face. She held out her hands and they were…they were covered in blood."

"Oh, my lady!" Alice crossed herself, her hands shaking. "You saw a ghost? Saints preserve us!"

I took a deep breath and helped the Lady Elizabeth to sit up against her pillows. "Rest yourself, my lady, and be easy in your mind. It was no ghost, but a nightmare brought on by your sickness." Turning to Alice, I managed a flustered smile. "Alice, would you run to the kitchens and heat a cup of sweet posset for the Lady Elizabeth while I change her bed linen?"

Alice nodded and hurried away, though I could see her glancing dubiously about the chamber as though expecting to see a ghost lurking in one of the corners.

"Listen to me," Elizabeth insisted, grabbing at my arm as I shook out the linen. "In the dream, my mother was trying to tell me something, but I woke before she could speak."

"You are exhausted, my lady," I said soothingly.

Her face flared with sudden anger. "Fool, why will you not listen? I know what I saw and it was my mother, not some nightmare conjured by a fevered brain." The princess stared at me commandingly, her eyes hard and dark as jet. "Summon my mother's spirit, just as Dee summoned the spirit of your aunt, and let me speak with her."

I was horrified.

"I cannot conjure the dead, my lady. I do not have the power."

"Don't lie to me, girl. I know in what high esteem Master Dee holds you." Elizabeth fumbled for the cross at her neck. "What is the matter? Are you afraid, Meg? I do not fear the dead, only the living. I pray you, use your powers and summon the spirit of Queen Anne for me. If I am in danger, my mother will warn me of it."

SUMMONS

I stooped to pick up the linen I had let fall, my voice shaking. "I promise you, my lady, I am no necromancer like Master Dee. I do not know the right words and to get the spell wrong could be disastrous."

"My mother would never harm me," she said stubbornly.

"Queen Jane died at Hampton Court, perhaps in these very apartments, soon after your brother, King Edward, was born. Do you think it could have been Queen Jane you saw, and not your mother?"

"It was not my stepmother," Elizabeth said hoarsely. She turned her head away, staring at the hearth as though she hoped to see her mother's spirit emerge from the ashes of the dying fire. "It was the ghost of my mother, coming to bring me comfort in this place of torment. It was Anne Boleyn, I tell you!"

I struggled not to shout at the princess to be silent and drop this madness. It was hard to remember that she was my mistress and the Queen's sister when she was forcing me into dark magicks I had no wish to perform. To witness my poor aunt's spirit called forth by an adept like Master Dee had been terrifying enough. But for a country witch to try to call forth the tortured spirit of Anne Boleyn, an executed Queen of England, felt like an affront against nature.

Everyone knew the story, of course. The Queen's mother had been married to King Henry for years, with Mary their beloved daughter, until the day that Henry fell in love with one of the court ladies, Anne Boleyn. Then he had split from the Holy Roman Catholic Church because they would not dissolve his first marriage, divorced his Spanish Queen himself, allowed poor little Mary to be neglected and forgotten, and married the beautiful Anne instead.

Before long, the Lady Elizabeth was born—though she was called Princess Elizabeth in those days. But King Henry grew weary of Anne, and soon fell in love with another woman, Jane Seymour. He caused charges of adultery and witchcraft to be brought against Elizabeth's mother, and had the unfortunate Queen executed at Tower Hill.

"Hush, my lady," I whispered, glancing over my shoulder. The door was shut, but instinct warned me not to speak too loudly. "Why not try to get some sleep first? There are guards on the outer doors. King's men, Spaniards. It is not safe to speak of this here. When you are back on your feet and can walk unaccompanied in the gardens, we will talk then."

"No, it must be tonight." It was clear that Elizabeth was determined. She folded her arms across her chest. "Fetch whatever you need. Work your spell and bring her back to me. If you do not obey me, Meg Lytton, you will leave my service tomorrow morning and return to Oxfordshire." Her mouth tightened. "You understand?"

If I was sent home in disgrace, I would never see Alejandro again. But to call forth an unquiet spirit of this magnitude might endanger all our souls. I clutched the linen, trying to stare her ladyship down, then finally capitulated. The anger of a Tudor is not an easy thing to bear, I thought grimly.

I had no wish to call forth the spirit of an executed Queen. Yet I could see that the Lady Elizabeth would fret herself to death if I did not at least try to call her mother's spirit to that place. I did not have the power to succeed in such a spell, so it could cause little harm. I held out no hope of making so much as the shadows quiver.

"Very well, my lady," I said quietly. "Since you command me to do it, I will try my best. But if the spell goes wrong, remember that I warned you of the danger."

"I have been warned," she agreed, then lay back against her pillows with a faint smile of triumph on her lips. "Quick, the hour is already late. If you are to perform the spell before dawn, you had best go to work."

Returning to the little room I shared with Blanche and now also with Alice, I lit a tallow candle and slipped my hand down between two loose floorboards, searching about in the narrow space until my fingers hit leather.

The book was thin and the ink barely legible, it had faded so badly, but I knew my old book of shadows contained what I would need tonight: a spell to make manifest that which is lost or absent. It was not quite a spell for raising the dead, but it would have to do. My aunt had often said that no spell was perfect for every occasion, but must be made to fit the witch's need. And this was the closest spell I had to the one Master Dee had used to conjure my aunt in his cell.

My conscience pricked me as I flicked through the pages of spells copied out in a childish hand when I was still young and under the discreet tutelage of my aunt. Was this too dangerous even to contemplate? If we were discovered in the act of summoning the dead, my own death would be nothing compared to the public humiliation and execution of the Lady Elizabeth for witchcraft. By summoning her mother, Elizabeth might end up suffering the same terrible death as Queen Anne.

Yet the princess's mind was made up, and I could not entirely blame her curiosity. Before I was forced to burn them to avoid discovery, I had often looked at such spells in my aunt's books and wondered how it would be to call up my own dead mother from the world of shadows. But something had always held me back. A fear of what I might meet in her eyes, perhaps. Or a more secret fear that my power would not be strong enough to contain the spirit once conjured.

I needed very little by way of magickal instruments. The spell called simply for a candle, a black cloth for a blindfold, and a few sprigs of rosemary, which I sent an unsuspecting Alice to collect from the herb gardens. These I took back to the princess's bedchamber, the only room where we could be reasonably sure of not being disturbed during the ritual, and began to cast the circle.

I had to admit to some light-headedness, excited to be working magick at last. I had known it would be difficult to practise my craft at court, but I had not realized how painful it would be for me to stifle my talents in this way, for fear of being caught. Lighting a candle and arranging the rosemary sprigs now seemed acts of such significance they elevated this spell to some great feat of magick. Which, I thought with some trepidation, it would be if I was indeed able to conjure the spirit of a long-dead Queen.

Alice came to me as I prepared the ritual in the closeted darkness of the Lady Elizabeth's chamber, her face pale. It seemed the girl had been thinking while I was gone, and had come to a natural-enough conclusion.

"Meg, are you…are you a witch?"

I looked at her sharply. "What answer will get me hanged?"

"No, no." Hurriedly, Alice shook her head, her eyes very wide. "I will say nothing. My grandmother knew a little of the old ways, though she was not a witch. But I saw her work a few spells when I was a child…just to heal my grandfather when he was sick, and once so my older sister would bear a son instead of a daughter. I would never tell anyone such secrets. You can trust me."

"I am glad to hear it."

"You must forgive me though, for I do not wish to stay to see whatever it is you and the Lady Elizabeth are doing," Alice muttered uneasily. She looked at the array of strange implements I had gathered, the open book with its crabbed lettering. "We could hang for this. It looks like black magick."

"Then go," I told her. "It makes no odds whether you stay or go. You are not needed here."

I glanced at the Lady Elizabeth for confirmation that Alice could leave. But her ladyship was too absorbed to have noticed our whispered discussion, bent over a locket which I guessed must contain a miniature portrait of her mother. I smiled at Alice and gestured her towards the door. I bore her no ill will for wishing to be absent during this ritual; I did not wish to be here myself, though a certain curiosity drove me to see how much power I truly possessed.

"But at least watch the door for us, would you?" I asked as Alice left. "If we are interrupted, stamp your foot three times as a warning to clear the circle."

Alice nodded, curtseyed to her ladyship and hurriedly

withdrew. She had a stout heart, I had to give her that. It was clear she disapproved of this summoning. Yet now she was in the Lady Elizabeth's service, her loyalty lay with the princess, and I had no fear she would betray us.

I turned to the princess. "You will need to come into the circle too," I told her, lighting the candle that stood in the centre. "There is no other way."

Elizabeth nodded and slipped out of bed, throwing a shawl about her shoulders against the night air.

"Bring the locket," I said, noticing its silver chain still lying on the covers. "It bears a portrait of your mother, doesn't it?"

Nodding, Elizabeth fetched the locket.

I pointed to the cushion I had positioned safely within the circle. "Sit there, my lady, and place the opened locket in front of you. That's it."

She put down the locket and settled herself cross-legged, staring up at me, wide-eyed. Her face had lost its colour now, as though she had finally grasped the dangerousness of the spell I was about to perform. Yet she made no move to stop me.

I tilted the lit candle until the tallow began to drip, then walked around the edge of my circle, dripping hot tallow among the rushes and whispering in Latin beneath my breath, *"Claudite, claudite contra malum,"* meaning "close the door to evil."

I knew the charm against evil would not hold, not without better preparation. But I hoped an additional barrier of tallow would ward off any malevolent influences until the ritual was over.

I turned to the princess, the black cloth dangling from my hand. "My lady," I said haltingly, "this spell calls for the summoner to be blindfolded. This will make it easier for you to reach out to those who have died and are in darkness."

But she did not explode with temper as I had expected. Instead, Elizabeth stared at the black cloth and shuddered. "A blindfold? That is what my mother would have worn to her execution."

"Forgive me," I muttered, and tied it about her head, giving the black cloth one last tug to make sure the knot was secure and her eyes were completely covered.

I knelt opposite the princess and held out a small green sprig of rosemary to the candle, watching as it caught light and began to burn, its sweet fragrance swirling in the smoke above us.

"If you have any memories of Queen Anne, call them to mind now and let them fill you," I murmured, lowering my gaze to the candle flame. It beat steadily against the darkness, casting its soft yellowish glow about the circle. "When you are ready, stretch out your hands towards the locket and call your mother to you. Whatever happens after that, my lady, you must on no account leave the circle. You understand?"

"Yes," she said huskily, and bent her head as though in remembrance of her dead mother.

It seemed to take for ever. The sprig of rosemary burnt out while I waited and turned to smouldering ashes in my hand. I dropped it to the floor, my fingers tingling, and wondered if Elizabeth had changed her mind. But at last the princess stirred and stretched out her pale long-fingered hands to where the locket lay.

"Mother," she whispered first, like a child in pain, and I heard her voice begin to tremble. "Queen Anne, Anne Boleyn, mother to Elizabeth, wife to King Henry, I summon thee to my side!"

"Again," I instructed her.

She repeated her summons, more forcefully this time, and

I looked at the candle as its flame suddenly dipped almost to nothing, then flickered back into life.

Someone—or something—had heard Elizabeth's call and had answered. But who?

I encouraged the princess to continue. "Again," I said faintly, lifting the larger sprig of rosemary to the flame. It soon caught alight, and the fragrant smoke filled my senses until I could hardly breathe.

"Anne Boleyn! Anne Boleyn! Anne Boleyn!" she repeated breathlessly. "I, thy child Elizabeth, do call on thee in death. Appear before the living, Anne Boleyn, and speak thy mind!"

In the deathly stillness that followed, I found myself unable to move. My eyes were caught and held by the candle, its flame standing tall and bright now, unnaturally bright in the shadowy chamber. Above our heads, I heard the roof timbers shift and creak, like the timbers of a ship in sail, yet dared not look up. I knew that if I moved, the spell would be broken. Then the full weight of Hampton Court, all its tapestried halls and bedchambers and the great pomp of its red brick battlements and towers, seemed to come down on my back and shoulders like a burden I would be forced to bear until the ritual was over.

I knelt before the princess and struggled with the terrifying weight of it, sweat running down my forehead and into my eyes, seaming the court gown under my arms and breasts. It felt as though I was supporting the palace roof itself with nothing but sheer nerve and the light of a candle.

The Lady Elizabeth gasped and shuddered. "I am so cold, so very cold," she whispered. "And someone is looking at me. I just know it!"

Before I could stop her, she had tugged down the blindfold. There was both fear and joy in her face as she pointed towards the fireplace. "Look," she breathed, and crossed herself in wonder. "My mother!"

Barely daring to turn my head in case I broke the spell, I managed to strain my eyes round to look in the direction of her pointing finger.

The silver woman hovering beside the hearth turned and stared back at us, perhaps responding to the sound of Elizabeth's voice. This was no figure like my aunt, her body strong, her face blank. No doubt I lacked the power of Master Dee to make his summoned spirits look human again. The Anne Boleyn we had conjured between us was more spirit than apparition. I could see the bricks of the fireplace through her floating robes, and her feet did not seem to touch the floor.

Even in death she was beautiful, a slender but elegant lady in a rich, courtly gown such as a Queen might wear. Yet her face was wrenched with terror and hopelessness, and her eyes were the saddest I had ever seen.

She looked at me. Instantly the room lightened and the candle flame seemed to swell, burning steadily and strong. I felt sorry for her and my heart clenched in sorrow, certain that a great wrong had been done to this woman. Then I remembered what my aunt had told me about the spirits of the dead, how they could secretly manipulate the minds of the living and were not to be trusted.

As though sensing my sudden distrust, her silver-eyed gaze passed from me to the princess. At once I felt the weight of the spell on my back again, a terrible force crushing me to the floor so that I could neither move nor speak, and I knew that we were in danger.

"Elizabeth," the spirit of Anne Boleyn said mournfully, and held out her hand to the princess. Her voice was like the rustle of dead leaves in the winter. "Come to me, my daughter. You must come to me."

Staring back at her mother's ghost in a kind of trance, the Lady Elizabeth stirred, gathering her skirts as though to rise.

Frantically, I sought her gaze, struggling to say the word "No!," but all I could manage was a muffled groan from behind enchantment-sealed lips. I knew Elizabeth must not leave the circle I had marked out with hot tallow or she would no longer be protected. Yet she seemed oblivious to my warning.

Elizabeth stood up, swaying, and walked to the edge of the circle. As though in a trance, she took one step towards the conjured spirit, then another, and stood at last outside the circle.

The candle blew out as though a window had been thrown open in a wind, plunging the chamber into darkness. The fire was little more than glowing embers by which I could still see the floating silver ghost of Anne Boleyn, hands outstretched, waiting for her daughter.

Elizabeth gasped and missed her footing, stumbling in the dark. As she righted herself, the shadowy room began to break apart in waves, the white-washed plaster disintegrating and flying away. The four walls of her chamber peeled away to reveal a high, desolate place and a storm howling about our ears. A violent wind tore at Elizabeth's hair as she stood outside the circle, her face hidden from me, her thin body buffeted by forces I could not control.

"My Lady Elizabeth!" I cried, the weight on my back immense now, my head bowed almost to the floor by its burden. "Hurry, step back inside the circle!"

But my words were whipped away by the wind, nothing but a cry in the darkness. Desperate to save my mistress, I staggered to the edge of the circle and reached out an arm, groping for the hem of her gown in the whirling maelstrom.

"Come…back…my lady!"

For a second, my fingers brushed some silken fabric, and I

gripped hard, knowing I had her. But before I could drag the princess back inside the safe territory of the circle, the calamity I had dreaded finally happened. The seething darkness above us, the weight I had been carrying on my back ever since we began the ritual, suddenly came crashing down and split the darkness asunder. For a few moments there was chaos. Light on the one side battled dark on the other, jagged lightning bolts and storm clouds raging above our heads. At last there was a terrifying crack, and the place of desolation juddered beneath our feet, as though the earth itself had broken in two.

Then up out of the centre of the circle, the very spot where I had set the candle and told Elizabeth to call forth the spirit, came a roaring black wind like a tornado. This wind swept up and round with immense power, scattering everything in its path and spinning me backwards like a top. I fell into what remained of the tallow-marked circle, still holding onto the hem of the princess's gown and dragging her on top of me.

As soon as Elizabeth's body crashed back into the circle, there was an incoherent cry of rage from the darkness. The black wind funnelled itself into a body and soared upwards—up, up, up, until it was almost out of sight. Then the air steadied and I realized that I was lying on my back on a hard wooden floor, staring up at the hearth in Elizabeth's bedchamber, where a dark cloud had just vanished up the chimney.

What on earth had just happened?

The silver ghost of Anne Boleyn put her face in her hands and wept, her outline growing thinner and less distinct until she too was gone, her spirit fading into nothingness like the last shreds of a mist.

Elizabeth, kneeling beside me in the darkness, also wept and called on Anne Boleyn in vain. Nobody answered.

I thought the terrible noise of the summoning must surely

bring down the whole palace on our heads in moments. My hands shook as I hunted for the tinderbox, eventually managing to relight the candle. I held up its fragile light to reassure myself that the four walls were still there and the roof intact. The fire, it seemed, had long since gone out.

I knelt by the chimney and held out a hand experimentally to the stones. The hearth was cold as though no fire had been lit there in months, though I plainly remembered the embers glowing red before we began the ritual. The chamber itself was painfully icy; the skin on my arms had come up in goose pimples and I could feel my teeth chattering.

Of the black wind there was no sign.

"Forgive me, Mother," Elizabeth whispered into the shadows, then looked across at me with an expression of complete loathing. "Why did you do that, Meg? Why did you pull me back? You've ruined everything. I nearly touched my mother's spirit—and now she's gone."

"She didn't come alone," I muttered, but the princess was not listening. I pulled myself to my feet and cleared away the remnants of the circle, my body aching now the ritual was over. I felt as though I had been kicked all over by a mule.

"You must get back into bed," I told her, fearful that we would be interrupted at any moment. "If the priests of the Inquisition come to the door, you must pretend to have been woken by the noise…just like everyone else will have been, I expect."

Shivering, I threw back the covers on the princess's bed and helped her slip miserably between the sheets, her face ravaged with tears. I stood a moment by the hearth, listening to the stones. What we had done here tonight had been more powerful than any magick I had ever performed before. Yet whatever that black wind had signified, the room was silent now and it seemed to have gone.

"Send Alice to me," Elizabeth said coldly when I bent to tuck her into bed. "I do not wish you to attend me."

I made my way outside to find Alice waiting by the door, her face drawn with weariness but her eyes alight with curiosity and fixed on my face.

"Her ladyship is asking for you and she's not in the best of moods," I managed, adding drily, "You were right not to stay."

"Wait," Alice insisted as I stumbled past her, almost too exhausted now to stand. "You can't leave it like that. What was the spell you cast? Did it work? What happened?"

I stopped and turned, staring at her. "You didn't hear?"

"I heard nothing, except the mice scratching in the walls. The night has been still and silent since I left you."

There was nothing but confusion and innocence in her face. I could scarcely believe it. Alice had been only a heartbeat away from the chamber door throughout the ritual, yet she had apparently heard none of it. Not the noise of our cries, nor the roar of the black tempest whirling about our heads. What had happened in that room had stayed in that room, as even the most violent and terrifying dream stays locked within a sleeper's head. No wonder the guards had not come running when the storm was at its most furious and vindictive. It had been a magickal storm, a tempest of the mind, confined only to that room and its occupants.

"It doesn't matter," I said, after a moment's hesitation. "Goodnight, Alice. You'd better hurry. She's waiting."

It was just after dawn when the priests of the Inquisition returned, this time with a tearful Blanche Parry in tow. For the second time they entered the princess's apartments without knocking, and demanded that I should rouse the Lady Elizabeth at once. Not bothering to argue, I sent a sleepy

Alice in to wake the princess and see to her needs. Elizabeth had said she did not wish me to attend her again, and I suspected that one night's sleep would have done nothing to change her mind.

I turned and looked at Blanche Parry.

Blanche did not meet my gaze, but stood shivering behind the men in their long, black robes, her cap askew, a nasty bruise on her cheek and her skirts soiled with filth along the hem.

"Mistress Parry," I murmured, indicating the settle, "will you not sit down? You look unwell."

Saying nothing for once, Blanche sat down and began to weep, hiding her face in her hands. A coldness pierced my heart as I regarded her bent head, then looked at Señor de Pero, noting the smugness of his expression. What had Blanche told them under torture? I did not believe they would have racked her or inflicted any other kind of outrage on her body, despite the bruise on her cheek. But there were certain kinds of torture that did not need to be physically inflicted, tortures of the mind and soul, and I guessed that Blanche might have been unable to stay silent in the face of a priest's cunning words, whispered in her ear.

I could hardly blame her, even if she *had* betrayed us. The Inquisition were experienced in making people talk, and Blanche was not used to holding her tongue.

"The Lady Elizabeth is not well," I explained to the priests. "She may not feel able to rise and speak with you."

Señor Miguel de Pero gave me a sneering smile, just as he had done on his previous visit. But there was something in his face this time that made me feel deeply uncomfortable. What did he know?

"Nonetheless," de Pero said smoothly, "she will speak with us, either here or in her chamber if she is too sick to leave her bed. Her lady-in-waiting has been most helpful, and now we must discuss our findings with the Lady Elizabeth. I am sure your mistress will be anxious to know without delay what we have discovered, don't you agree?"

I did not reply, but saw with some relief that Alejandro was standing silently behind them in the doorway. So I was not to be entirely alone in this trial.

But then, as Alejandro stepped clear of the shadows, I saw his face and was suddenly more frightened than I had been even when Marcus Dent took me prisoner and tried to drown me as a witch. For there was no hope in Alejandro's face, only a cold fear that told me we were in danger of losing our lives. But for what reason? What had Blanche told these men to make Alejandro look like that?

The bedchamber door opened and Elizabeth stood there, hands clasped loosely before her, regal even in her simple white gown and wrap. She came forward with Alice behind her, the girl holding up her train as though Elizabeth was already Queen in her sister's stead. Her cheeks were still flushed—with fever or anger, I wondered?—but otherwise she looked calm and collected, not like a girl who had spent half the night trying to summon the spirit of her dead mother.

"Sir," she said coldly, inclining her head to Señor de Pero. "It is very early for you and your men to be calling on me. What is so important that I must be roused from my sickbed to speak with you?"

"You must forgive our intrusion, my lady, but there are several matters we would discuss with you immediately." He paused, looking at her closely. "I regret that you have not been well, but it seems you are not in danger. Perhaps if you were to sit for my questions?"

"Thank you, I shall stand." Elizabeth glanced across at Blanche, still sobbing into her hands, then returned her gaze to the Spaniard. "Ask your questions without delay, sir, so that I may return to my bed before my sickness grows."

"Very well." Señor de Pero's voice became as cold as hers, no doubt sensing that no amount of politeness on his part could thaw this princess. "You have denied knowing the astrologer Dee. But from what your lady-in-waiting has told us, it seems you have no need of such men about you. For Mistress Parry tells us that one of your own servants is skilled in the dark arts. Indeed, that her aunt was so well-known as a witch, she was burnt in the marketplace for her sins."

My throat constricted, and I could hardly breathe. Standing numb with fear, my palms clammy, I felt my heartbeat grow sickeningly fast. It was over. We were betrayed. There could be no escape from this revelation. Only death and disgrace could follow: death for me—and for the princess, disgrace, yes, but if I were to deny that I had ever worked magick in her service, she might yet survive this blow.

If they were to search under my floorboards…

I stared painfully at Señor de Pero, the two men in black robes who had accompanied him, the guards standing curiously at the door, and wondered how it would be possible to subdue them all to my will, and whoever else might be privy to this secret knowledge.

But no spell came to my mind. I stood helpless as a rabbit in a trap, waiting for the blow that would kill it. I did not even have my white stone about my throat, the stone my aunt had charmed to protect me in moments such as these, for it was under my floorboards with my secret books.

Then Elizabeth spoke, her voice cool, musing. "I know nothing of this aunt, but it is true one of my young maids was once accused of some dark knowledge. It was investigated, and found to be false. The girl who had accused her was simple-minded and envied Meg's position as my maid, wanting it for herself."

Miguel de Pero's eyes narrowed and he turned to look at me. "Nonetheless, we will need to question your servant for ourselves."

"She was very thoroughly questioned at the time, as I recall, by the local witchfinder. No proof was ever found."

The Spaniard's eyes flickered back to Elizabeth. "Yes, Mistress Parry let slip that she was examined by one Marcus Dent."

Alejandro made some involuntary movement towards his sword hilt as though he would draw steel and strike the man down. His jaw was clenched, his eyes smouldering with anger.

I glanced at him swiftly, for no more than a second, begging him, warning him with my eyes to be calm and do nothing. *Calm!*

I could hardly be calm myself, with my heart pounding, and my cheeks so icy with fear it felt as though all the blood had drained from my face. But we had to keep our heads. Or Elizabeth might lose hers.

"Was that the man's name? I can hardly recall, he was there less than an hour. But if Blanche is sure…" My admiration for the princess grew as I saw how steadily and with what resolve she met his killing thrusts and sent them straight back again. "I was sick in bed at the time, and Blanche always oversaw the other servants at Woodstock, so she would know what happened that day better than I."

Blanche gave another great sob at this and cried, "Forgive me, my lady. I could not help it. They hurt me and twisted my words so."

Señor de Pero ignored her tearful outburst, still watching Elizabeth as though hoping she would suddenly crumble and admit to some terrible guilt. "And this aunt of hers, this proven witch—"

Elizabeth dismissed his words with a gesture. "I have no idea who this woman could be and have never heard of her before this day. I am not privy to the lives of my servants and their families. Are you, sir?"

He conceded that point with a dry shake of his head.

Glancing at Alice, still standing wide-eyed at her back, Elizabeth nodded towards the sobbing Blanche.

"Alice, take Mistress Parry into my chamber and see if you can calm her nerves with a cup of stout wine. I shall call for you when I am ready to retire myself." She looked at Miguel de Pero with glacial dislike while Alice supported the shuffling Blanche into the bedchamber and quietly closed the door behind her. "You have hurt and frightened my old servant, sir. I trust you had good reason."

"You may dislike our methods, my lady, but they work. Mistress Parry proved stubborn and loyal to her mistress. She would never have spoken so freely without a little push towards honesty."

"You mean that you tortured her."

He smiled unpleasantly. "Oh, hardly. We persuaded her, rather. Though I am afraid we must now take your maid Meg Lytton away with us. We would like to know more about this aunt of hers. Indeed, I am surprised you are not more curious yourself, Lady Elizabeth, given the charge of witchcraft once faced by your maid. But perhaps you are content to be served by one in whose blood flows the stench of eternal damnation."

"That is arrant nonsense, sir, and well you know it," Elizabeth retorted, and held up a hand as his men moved to seize me. "No, you shall not take another of my faithful servants to your torture chamber. If this witchfinder Marcus Dent had found anything of note when he examined Meg Lytton, would he not have sent word to the Queen, my sister?"

"Perhaps he was prevented from doing so," Señor de Pero remarked simply.

"Or perhaps there was nothing to report."

"All the same, we will take Meg Lytton to be examined."

The Inquisitor nodded to his men to continue. Elizabeth looked on in cold fury, helpless to prevent them from dragging me to the door. My mistress had done more for me than I had expected, however, given that I had refused to help her, though it was hard not to imagine that Elizabeth had tried to prevent my arrest by the Inquisition for fear of what I might reveal, like poor Blanche before me, under torture—and not because she cared for me or valued my service.

I passed Alejandro in the doorway and saw his furious expression, his hand still hovering above his sword hilt.

Deliberately I averted my face and stared coldly at the ground, hoping Alejandro would understand that he must not interfere with my arrest. *Say nothing! Do nothing!* Alejandro wanted to fight, because he was not only a man of God but a trained soldier. As a woman I knew that fighting was futile. We were outnumbered and on their territory. This was a time to be patient, not rush in without thinking of the consequences.

"It is both God's will and the Queen's wish that we root out evil and unholy practices in her court. If your maid servant knows nothing of the dark arts, you will have nothing to fear." Miguel de Pero bowed to the princess with a mocking flourish, then waved his men to take me away. "*Adios,* my lady."

6

INSTRUMENTS OF TORTURE

Evil and unholy!

That was a better description of the cell into which the priests had thrown me than of myself, I thought. The place was cramped, wretched-smelling and thick with tiny black flies that stirred from the straw like a breeze every time I shifted position. I might not be pious and devout, yet I believed in God and had always tried my utmost to do what was right. It was surely God who had given me the power to work magick and a keen ambition to better myself in the craft. Had He done so in order that I should reject that gift as "unholy" and spend my life on my knees instead, praying to be deaf and blind to the power I possessed?

The black-robed men of the Inquisition had chained both my wrists and my ankles to the wall, then locked the cell door when they left me there alone—as though they expected me to escape without these precautions. I could not imagine how

I could have achieved such a feat. The cell was high up in one of the eastern towers, a part of the palace I had never visited before. Through the narrow sunlit grating that passed for my window I could hear birdsong from the stately gardens below, and the occasional clatter of wheels in some unseen courtyard.

What had Blanche told them of my talents? That I could scale sheer walls and gnaw iron bars with my teeth? I felt a sudden anger towards my betrayer, and clung on to it as a source of strength. My head could not blame Blanche for speaking under torture, but my heart did, and my aching body too. I had thought we had become friends in the past few months. But in her pain Blanche had seized on my name, and given it to the Inquisition to save herself.

The iron cuffs chafed at my skin with every movement, so I stayed as still as I could. With nothing better to do, I watched the slotted sunlight crawl across the walls as morning turned to afternoon. Then the sun swung away, and the tiny room became dark and chilly.

For hours nobody came to the cell door. I tried not to dwell on my growing need to relieve myself. This must be part of my test, I thought drily. Another was the foul, unrelenting stench of the straw at my feet, which smelled as though many others had been left here for hours without a pot.

Some of the flies entertained themselves by exploring my nose, then my eyes and cheek, while I jerked my head impotently to drive them away. This was how a horse must feel in harness, I thought, unable to shake off the flies which plagued and stung its hide.

No doubt I could have dreamed up some spell to make my imprisonment less of a torment, perhaps even made myself invisible—for all the good that would have done me, chained as I was to their filthy wall. But one of Señor de Pero's men had stuffed a cloth into my mouth before leaving, and the closest I could get to speech was an angry stifled moan.

Eventually I heard footsteps stop outside my cell, then the door being unlocked. This was it. They had come back to question me.

My heart juddered and I felt sick, watching the door swing inexorably open.

How long could I withstand their torture before I broke as Blanche had done? Perhaps I was not as brave as I hoped. Certainly I did not feel very brave just at the moment, about to face the Inquisition.

Except it was not Miguel and his men come back to skewer me alive, but a dark-hooded priest standing in the doorway to the cell, a silver cross about his neck.

"I bring spiritual solace," he murmured, and I saw that he held a small, leather-bound book of prayers. "Will you repent your sins, or risk an unshriven death?"

Alejandro!

For a second I was overjoyed, my heart singing with love at the sound of his voice. Even the dark little cell seemed to lighten with his presence. Then I remembered the terrible danger he had put himself in by coming to me, and I shook my head violently, groaning, "No!" behind my gag.

Alejandro stepped inside, his head still bowed. Beyond him I could see one of the guards looking at me with a sort of leering stare, then the man pulled the cell door shut and we were alone.

"Forgive me, my love." Alejandro removed the cloth from my mouth, his gaze searching my face intently. "I wanted to come earlier but they were questioning me too. Have they hurt you?"

I shook my head. My mouth and throat were dry as sawdust. "Thirsty," I managed.

He looked about but there was nothing for me to drink. "Damn them," he said angrily.

I closed my eyes in despair, then opened them as a new thought struck me. "The Lady Elizabeth?"

"They're searching her rooms now for forbidden writings, anything that might link her to Dee and his accursed horoscopes. I bribed the guard, told him I could not bear to see such a young girl face the Inquisition without bringing her prayer and spiritual comfort." He smiled grimly, throwing back the deep cowl of his hood so that I could see his face clearly. "I look the part, at least."

"If they catch you here—"

"I know," he agreed calmly. "We have maybe a few minutes, then I'll go. Hush, don't look like that. I'll be careful."

"How should I look?"

Alejandro leaned forward, his gaze fixed on mine, and covered my mouth with his own. A kind of warm, glorious darkness enveloped us both as we kissed, and for that moment I forgot the horror of our situation. I was waiting to be questioned and tortured, while he had put himself in terrible danger just by coming to see me.

Yet as soon as his lips touched mine, all of that became meaningless. All I knew was that I loved him, and my soul soared as our lips and then our bodies touched.

After a moment, he pulled back and gazed down into my face. "That's how you should look," he said softly.

"If I wasn't chained to this wall, I'd put my arms about your neck and kiss you back," I whispered.

Alejandro smiled, but I saw his restless fury grow as he looked about the room. His dark gaze paused on the brazier, not yet lit, but with thin irons poking out that would sear flesh once red-hot. Then he glanced down at the metal cuffs at my wrists and ankles, no doubt seeing how cruelly they dug into my skin. "What savages they are, to treat a woman worse than a dog. Let them hurt you, I'll fetch my sword and hack their hearts out, one by one," he breathed angrily. "They do not deserve to be called men."

"Fire-eater! You know, this is the second time you have bribed a guard to visit me in prison," I said lightly, hoping to distract him from his fury.

I remembered how Alejandro had visited me secretly in my little room at Woodstock, the night before Marcus Dent came to interrogate me on a charge of practising witchcraft. How frightened I had been then! We had only left Woodstock a month ago, yet already the time I had spent there seemed a thousand years ago. Now I was at court and still suspected of being a witch, facing torture at the hands of the Inquisition.

It was like facing death.

I managed a faint smile when he did not reply. "You seem to be making a habit of bringing me 'spiritual comfort,' Alejandro."

"Only because you have a habit of getting yourself into trouble."

"Well, you may not have noticed this, but I'm not very good at being *good*." I took a deep breath, knowing what I must do. "Which is why you must go, Alejandro. You cannot help me, but you can help the Lady Elizabeth."

He touched my cheek, his expression intense. "I have a plan. Let me marry you. Tell them we are betrothed. I can protect you once we are man and wife."

"No," I whispered, though it nearly killed me to refuse such an offer.

It was sweetly tempting to agree and let him protect me, in the hope that being betrothed to a Catholic novice in the King's service would restore my reputation and save my neck. But in truth it was more likely to do neither of those things, but stretch Alejandro's neck instead. And I would not drag him into this dangerous hotchpotch of guilt and suspicion.

"It would do no good. Señor de Pero has already warned me to stay away from you," I told him, "and I think he warned you too. He'd be more likely to want me dead if I said we were betrothed."

His eyes flickered, but he did not press the point. So I was right and Miguel de Pero had spoken to him about me, perhaps instructed Alejandro to steer clear of English country girls like me, so clearly beneath his status as a Spanish nobleman and a novice. But whatever had been said, he was still here beside me. I had to give him that. And he knew me well enough not to waste his time trying to change my mind once it was made up.

"Then my advice is to confess straight away that you dabbled in the dark arts, but only at your aunt's insistence. That she led you astray with her cunning witchery, and now you repent. Tell them you renounce the Devil and wish to be a good Catholic." He frowned when I shook my head. "No, hear me out. They'll be more excited by a confession of witchcraft than this other business with John Dee, which seems to be leading nowhere. You will not be tortured if you confess straight away, and if you can demonstrate true repentance they may even release you without trial as an example to other transgressors. Then once you are free I will take you away from here, somewhere they can never find you."

"And what will happen to the Lady Elizabeth?"

He hesitated, then lied. I needed no magick art to tell me that he was lying. "She will come to no harm. Your mistress need not be implicated in your confession."

"A witch in her household, and you say she will not be implicated?"

His voice became strained. "I love you, Meg Lytton. I will

not leave you here to be tortured and abused. I know it sounds bad, but a confession will save you the worst pain."

"Alejandro, you know I cannot do that. A confession would destroy the Lady Elizabeth."

I loved him back fiercely but I could not make myself say the words. Not now, not here in this cell. To use those words would glue him to my side as surely as if I had used a spell of cleaving.

"Now leave me, Alejandro. For my sake, you must say nothing of our betrothal to anyone. You will never become a priest if you openly associate with me, especially now that I have been arrested by the Inquisition. And if you are found here, what can your masters think but that you are somehow involved in my wickedness?"

He stared at me despairingly. "At least protect yourself, then. I know that you are capable of it."

I almost laughed, but did not quite dare, seeing his grim expression. "Are you giving me permission to use magick?"

"I do not believe a just and loving God would wish to see you suffer under the instruments of the Inquisition," he muttered, and glanced about the walls of my cell where vicious metal tools and contraptions hung, waiting to be used on unfortunate prisoners like myself. "Nor remain locked up in this cruel place, though you had cast a thousand witch's circles."

We both heard the sound of footsteps coming up the tower's circular staircase. Alejandro turned to look at me, his eyes very dark.

"Please go," I managed huskily. "And put the cloth back in my mouth. Hurry!"

By the time Miguel de Pero stepped into my ugly cell, ducking his head to avoid the low doorway, my betrothed had disappeared—probably slipping higher up the stairs to avoid meeting the Inquisition as they climbed to my tower room.

The black-robed Spaniard loomed above me, holding a torch aloft to banish the growing shadows. I blinked up at him and his men in the torchlight, unable to hide my fear of what would come next. Now that I no longer had to appear strong in front of Alejandro, my inner defences began to crumble and I could not seem to hold a single spell in my head.

How could I withstand this man's methods when I already felt so weak, so alone and vulnerable? My arms ached from hanging in chains, and my body was deeply uncomfortable, my belly cramping like a woman's in labour. His eyes were cold as he looked me up and down, examining my captive body; they froze the blood in my veins.

Would it not be less painful to follow Alejandro's suggestion, confess to having "dabbled" once or twice as a witch, then plead a contrite and heartfelt repentance?

But that would leave the princess open to accusations of harbouring a witch in her household, I reminded myself.

De Pero handed the torch to one of his men, then unfastened his cloak, watching me.

"I trust the long wait has not been too tiring for you. I'm afraid it could not be helped. I had more questions to ask and rooms to search. But now, Meg Lytton," Señor de Pero said pleasantly, picking up a hooked metal tool from a side table, "I aim to discover what steel you are made of."

I woke to darkness for the fourth or fifth time, my head hanging. There was something sticky on my chin: spittle perhaps, or it might have been blood. My mouth had been gagged again, no doubt to prevent me from casting a spell against my tormentors. Under my gown, my thighs were damp and sore, and I suddenly remembered the humiliation of wetting myself after a futile and nauseating battle to control myself.

That embarrassment seemed the least of my troubles though. I knew there was more to come, and worse. Far worse.

I stirred painfully against my bonds. The sky outside the window grating seemed to be lightening. How long until dawn?

I had no idea what the hour was, nor even how long I had been asleep. The night seemed to have been one long round of torment, broken only by the marvellous absences and horrifying returns of the Inquisition.

There was something lying on the filthy straw at my feet. An unidentifiable blur of white. As my eyes struggled to make out what it was, the door opened and someone came in, a flaming torch in his hand.

I did not need to look up to know who it was.

"Well, *señorita?*" Señor de Pero demanded, dragging the soiled gag from my mouth. "It will be daybreak in another hour. Are you ready to speak to me yet?"

"Go to Hell," I muttered.

He came closer, thrusting the smoking torch into the wall bracket so he could look into my face. "What was that you said?"

But I said nothing more, my bravado abruptly deserting me. Previous remarks like that had been rewarded with pain, and I was tired of hurting. So desperately tired I knew it could not be long before I weakened and began to give him, word by stumbling word, the confession he craved. It did not seem to matter what I confessed to having done, so long as it would incriminate the Lady Elizabeth and allow them to arrest her. That had been clear from his questions, which always seemed to return to my mistress in the end.

He had come at me gently enough the evening before, one of his men merely pricking the soles of my feet with a hot needle at each "wrong" answer. "Are you a witch, Meg

Lytton? You can tell me the truth, I shall see that your death is not a painful one."

"I am no witch, sir."

"What does the Queen's sister know of your powers?"

"I am no witch," I found myself repeating, wincing as the hot needle was pushed deeper into my bare sole.

"Is the Lady Elizabeth a witch too? Have you heard her call upon dark spirits? What spells does she perform against the Queen?"

"None, no spells." I cried out as the needle bit into me again. "The Lady Elizabeth is a devout, God-fearing Catholic. She is no witch."

A resounding slap round the face sent my head lolling. Miguel came close, spitting in my face with venom as he spoke. "Don't lie to me, Witch. Everyone knows what the Lady Elizabeth is. She will burn in Hell for her sins." He changed his tack, stepping back. "Tell me, have you met the conjuror and astrologer known as John Dee? Have you ever seen him in company with the Queen's sister?"

"No!"

"Letters, then. Have you brought your mistress secret communications from him or seen her reading any privately? Charts, perhaps, folded into a book to hide them? The Queen's own horoscope?"

I would shake my head at all these questions, then groan as the chains that held my arms were inexorably shortened, drawing me higher and higher up the wall until I was perched on the far tips of my toes. My terrified mind grasped at spells I could work to prevent him hurting me again, but it was useless. I knew there would be no hiding from a charge of witchcraft after that, for no one would believe me innocent if I showed my power so openly. And then the princess would suffer for my weakness.

"Tell me everything you know, Meg Lytton, and I will spare you pain. Keep lying, and I will tear your fingernails off and leave you bleeding in the dark." He had turned away to the lit brazier while I hung shaking. A hot needle pricked under one of my nails, making me hiss with excruciating pain. I had struggled to drag my hand away, but was held grimly in position by one of his men. "Speak the truth now, girl, have you ever taught the Lady Elizabeth how to work magick?"

"No, sir! I swear it!"

"I know that you are lying just as I know dusk from dawn. You will weep blood before this night is out, Meg Lytton."

I had screamed then as he prised one of my fingernails off, then plunged my hand into a bowl of steaming hot water so that my whole body shook violently in shock.

Then darkness had come but no rest from the interrogation. There had been visits by torchlight, repeated demands that I should tell the truth, and then more pain when I refused.

Now Miguel de Pero had come to examine me again in the pale early dawn, his fingers tilting my chin up to look into my face. "Did you sleep? No, I imagine not in that position. Few can."

Carefully, he removed the gag which had held me silent and unable to work magick—an important precaution when examining a witch, as I knew from my mock trial in Oxfordshire. I had survived that ordeal. But would I survive this?

My lips had begun to bleed where the rough cloth had rubbed against the corners of my mouth. I licked at them painfully.

"It would go better with you if you were to speak to me, Meg Lytton. Do you fear to betray your mistress, is that it?" When I said nothing but looked him in the eye, he smiled wearily. "Such loyalty is commendable. I am not an ogre, I would not wish to see the Queen's sister in this cell. But it is my duty to uncover the hidden sources of evil in this court and destroy them. And it has come to my ears that your mistress not only knows Master Dee, but met him secretly when she was at Woodstock."

My eyes widened but still I said nothing. Had someone betrayed us?

"However," Miguel continued smoothly, "I have no evidence of this, no proof whatsoever. All I have is the word of a man who has some old score to settle, I would guess."

He held up a letter. I stared, but in the flickering torchlight I could not make out the handwriting, let alone read what the letter contained.

Miguel noted my interest. "Yes, even the young and beautiful Lady Elizabeth has enemies. And not just at court. This letter comes from Oxfordshire."

My heart was thumping now. Oxfordshire?

"It is probably all true, what this fellow writes to me. Or enough of it to put your mistress in the Tower for treason. Except that another player has entered the game. The King heard testimony last night from one of the men who was with the Lady Elizabeth in Oxfordshire. He swears on his life that your mistress never left the palace of Woodstock and was never seen in the company of Master Dee, that this letter contains nothing but hearsay and lies." He smiled unpleasantly. "One man's word against another. The simplest contest, and yet often the hardest."

I waited to see what else he might reveal, though my tired mind could not fully comprehend what he was saying to me. Some enemy from Oxfordshire had written to the Inquisition about us. But who?

It was far easier to work out who had spoken to the King on her behalf. It had to be Alejandro de Castillo. Who else in this palace of hatred and suspicion would have risked his reputation and his own neck to stand up to such an accusation?

I felt unaccountably angry at the thought. What could have possessed Alejandro to risk his chance to become a priest by defending the princess? He must know such a connection would mark him out for ever as a traitor to his own countrymen, for this was a court where all Spaniards followed the Catholic King and Queen, not the little half-sister whom many still believed to be secretly Protestant.

Miguel came closer, looking down into my face. "You have nothing to say?"

I shook my head, and watched in a kind of exhausted stupor as he nodded to the Spanish guard on the door to unfasten the manacles about my wrists and ankles.

"In the absence of further evidence, His Majesty the King has sent orders for you to be returned to the Lady Elizabeth's service." His voice crackled with frustration. "But I still have my suspicions about you, Meg Lytton. Do not think this means we will not be watching you and your mistress."

Released at last, I fell forwards onto the filthy straw with a cry, for my legs were too weak to support me, my arms prickling with pins and needles from having been raised so long above my head. The white blur that I had seen was my cap, trampled into the straw and spattered with blood. I lay beside it like a corpse, incapable of movement despite the appalling stench, and hardly daring to believe that I was being set free just at the point when I had thought the end had come.

Was this a trick? I wondered feebly. Was it still part of my ordeal, to be allowed a tantalizing moment of freedom before being jerked back to my iron bonds?

Miguel de Pero said something in Spanish and the guard came forward to help me to my feet, his hands rough and unfriendly, his face dark with contempt.

I picked up my soiled cap, wiped my freshly bleeding mouth on my sleeve, and staggered to the door before my captor could change his mind. My first thought was that I had to get back to the princess, to satisfy myself that she had not been harmed. I was still concerned over how exactly my freedom had been achieved, but at least this question of her involvement with Master Dee might now be dropped.

It occurred to me that my hands were free again now, and my mouth no longer gagged. I could use my magick to hurt them as they had hurt me, or to make them run mad and dash themselves down the brutal stone steps of the tower.

But no, it would still be too clear to everyone who could have worked such a spell upon them, and I would soon find myself back in this cell with another zealous torturer—only this time there would be no reprieve.

Glancing back at Señor de Pero, I saw the same contempt in his eyes. Like master, like servant. It was clear they both believed me to be a witch, bound for the everlasting bonfires of Hell, and they were right to do so. Yet neither of them could do a thing about it.

7

RELEASE

Nursing my swollen and bleeding hand against my chest, I limped back to the Lady Elizabeth's apartments in the thin dawn light, accompanied by two disapproving Spanish guards. Passing through hallways and richly decorated, high-ceilinged chambers, I found a new excitement in the air of Hampton Court. The palace was alive with servants already awake and bustling about their duties, courtiers staggering bleary-eyed from their beds, doors slamming and shouts in the distance. I watched as several serving women bent over a dark wooden chest, arguing about what to put in; they seemed to be packing the chest with jewel-encrusted clothes and shoes.

Along one of the long corridors in the east wing, I caught the faint din of hammering, its echoes muffled by the lavishly embroidered tapestries hanging on the wall. Curious, I hobbled to the window. Looking down into the stable yard below, I saw groomsmen at their work, leading out horses to be reshod by the leather-aproned farrier. Beyond the farrier's glowing brazier lay a covered wagon on its side with two men crouched over it, replacing one of its thick-spoked wheels.

I glanced at my two Spanish guards as we turned down towards the princess's apartments, but their faces revealed nothing. It seemed the court would soon be on the move again, leaving Hampton Court to be swept and purified. A good thing too, for the palace rooms and grounds were now unpleasantly pungent, the enclosed privies buzzing with flies and everyone choking on the stench of the gong farm where many months' sewage lay waiting to be shovelled out.

But how could the court be allowed to leave the royal residence while the Queen was still locked away in her birthing room? Unless Queen Mary had given birth while I was hanging by my wrists in that dark little cell? Perhaps I had been kept there longer than I realized.

"Meg!"

For once Blanche Parry seemed genuinely delighted to see me. She had been sewing with Alice as I came into the room, but jumped up from her seat when she saw me, abandoning her stitchwork to clasp my hands.

Blanche did not seem to notice my wince as she squeezed my abused hand. "The Lady Elizabeth will be so pleased that you are back," she exclaimed. "She has been awake since dawn, awaiting your return. Come, her ladyship will want to see you at once."

Blanche dismissed the guards with a sharp-eyed look and ordered a relieved Alice to finish the stitchwork on her own. Then she led me into the princess's sunlit bedchamber, whispering conspiratorially in my ear, "You look pale. And you are limping. Did those vile men hurt you? Forgive me for having given them your name. I could not help it, truly I could not. They tortured me until I no longer knew what I was saying."

"I forgive you," I managed hoarsely, though it was said with an effort.

The Lady Elizabeth was sitting up in bed with her head bent, studying some leather-bound tome with great intensity. She laid her book aside as soon as she saw me, staring rigidly at my face as though she hoped to read all my secrets there.

"Blanche, shut the door," she said shortly, then gestured me closer. "Well? What did you tell them?"

"Nothing, my lady," I reassured her.

She did not believe me, that was clear. Her eyebrows were raised as she gazed coldly across at me, no doubt examining my dirty face for the telltale signs of torture. I could hardly blame the princess for distrusting me. Few survived a day and a night in a cell with the Inquisition and came forth with their consciences clear. And the Lady Elizabeth's secrets were enough to condemn her thrice over.

"Nothing?" she echoed. "And they let you go?"

"I was told that someone had interceded on my behalf with King Philip, and His Majesty had ordered my release," I said, and a note of bitterness crept into my voice. "I am grateful for my freedom, of course, but Alejandro de Castillo should never have interfered. This will cost him his hope of becoming a priest."

Elizabeth looked astonished. "Alejandro?"

"Who else?"

"No, no," she said, shaking her head. She seemed relieved now that she had heard me out. "It was not the young novice who went to the King. It was Sir Henry Bedingfield."

It was my turn to stare. Sir Henry Bedingfield had been the princess's gaoler at Woodstock. "I don't understand, my lady."

"I owe him a debt of gratitude for this," Elizabeth said,

and smiled at my frowning bewilderment. "I could not allow them to torture you, Meg. Not only are you my servant, but you know things…things I would never wish the Inquisition to discover. It was imperative to achieve your release as soon as possible. So I wrote a note to Sir Henry yesterday and begged him, for my sake, to speak to the King about this matter and explain that the accusations against you at Woodstock had been false. I had only a short reply from him last night, to say that he would do his best. And now you are here, albeit filthy and bruised, so it seems my former gaoler was true to his word."

"Sir Henry Bedingfield agreed to speak to the King on my behalf?" I stood amazed, remembering how much the man had mistrusted me at Woodstock. I could not imagine why he should have agreed to clear my name. "But why?"

Elizabeth's mouth twisted in a wry smile. "Because," she murmured, throwing aside her covers and swinging her legs out of bed, "Sir Henry is no fool. He knows I may not always be a disgraced princess, and that if I should ever come to power, he would rather be remembered for having helped to free my servant from the Inquisition than for having been my gaoler at Woodstock for the better part of a year."

So it was not Alejandro who had spoken up for me. I felt a foolish moment of disappointment, then joy that he would not suffer because of me. I helped the Lady Elizabeth out of bed, though in truth I was in no fit state to be serving anyone, let alone a princess of the House of Tudor. My shoes stank, my legs were shaking badly, and I knew my face and gown must be filthy, encrusted with dried blood and sweat.

"Señor Miguel de Pero told me a letter had arrived from Oxfordshire, accusing you of meeting John Dee secretly. He did not say who wrote it."

Elizabeth moved to don the ivory-coloured robe that

Blanche was holding out for her. She froze at my words, looking round at me in horror. "I was not told of this. Who could have written such a letter?"

It was time to share my suspicions with her. "I have been wondering that myself, my lady, and I can think of only one man. Marcus Dent."

Her eyes widened with fear. "The witchfinder? But I thought you said he was as good as dead, that you had dealt with him?"

"I thought him beyond recovery," I admitted, then lowered my voice. "But I may have been wrong. The letter did not accuse me of being a witch though. So if it is from Marcus Dent, my charm to prevent him speaking of my witchcraft is still working."

"Well," she muttered, "that is good news, at least." Elizabeth wrinkled up her nose as she passed me on her way to her dressing table. "Merciful heavens, what is that appalling stench?"

"Forgive me, my lady," I said awkwardly. "That stench is me. I badly need to take a bath and change my gown. I should have cleaned myself before I came to your chamber. But Blanche thought you would want to see me first."

"I did, yes," she agreed sharply. "I have been worrying myself to death half the night. But now you should certainly take yourself away and bathe. And perhaps burn that gown. You smell like a pony that's fallen in the mire."

I almost smiled. "I feel like one too."

Elizabeth looked away, and I suddenly remembered how desperately she had begged me to summon her mother's spirit. I had failed her there. The spell had gone wrong, though I was not yet sure how. But it seemed she had forgiven me for my failure.

"My lady," I said quietly, "before I leave you, I must tell

you something else. On my way back from the east wing, I saw servants packing chests and horses being reshod as though for the road. I could be mistaken, but it seems to me that the court is getting ready to move." I hesitated, seeing the princess glance sideways at Blanche. "Has the Queen given birth?"

Blanche let out a little cry of fear, then hurried to make sure the door was shut.

"Hush, keep your voice down. These walls have ears." Still in her plain nightgown, Elizabeth came nearer, and her face was alive with barely suppressed excitement. "There was a rumour about the court after they took you away yesterday, a rumour that the Queen was no longer with child. We waited all day, expecting news of a stillbirth, or some indication that an heir had been born and died. No news came. Then late yesterday evening Blanche heard a story from one of the tirewomen, who had heard it from one of the Queen's ladies, that there had *never* been a baby. That the Queen had not been with child at all."

"Not with child?"

"It seems she and her doctors were mistaken about the pregnancy," Elizabeth whispered. "So the court will be moving to Oatlands by the end of the month, and although I am to accompany them there, I must not live too near. I think Her Majesty has no wish to see my face about the court, reminding her that she has no other heir but me. Instead, she is making provision for me to stay near the court at Oatlands, in a little house of my own."

I did not know what to say, but bent my head as Elizabeth paced restlessly back and forth. There was much to think about in what she had said. "I am pleased for you, my lady."

"I begged again to be allowed to return to my childhood home at Hatfield. But the Queen sent a note this morning forbidding it absolutely."

I stared, still reeling from the news that the Queen had not been pregnant after all.

"Meg, it was just as you said that evening at the Bull Inn," she reminded me in a whisper. "You knew, even before we were sure that she was carrying a child, that my sister's pregnancy was not a true one. You told us, but I did not believe you."

"The chart..." I breathed, suddenly recalling how John Dee had shown me the Queen's horoscope and asked me to interpret it, and I had declared that there would be no child.

Elizabeth put a finger to her lips, urging caution. "You have a great power within you, Meg Lytton. Greater even than I realized. But we must be careful not to let them know it or they will try to destroy you."

I nodded my agreement, and again nursed my swollen hand as it began to throb and ache.

Elizabeth caught sight of my tortured hand, the red scalded flesh and the fingernail that had been ripped out, and hissed angrily. "Is that what the Inquisition did to you? But that is monstrous."

She clapped her hands. "Blanche, where is your salve for scalded flesh? Hurry away and fetch it!"

I allowed the princess to take my injured hand and press it gently, though the pain made me sick. "It will mend in time, my lady," I managed hoarsely, not wishing to have a fuss made over it.

The door opened and I looked over my shoulder, gritting my teeth in agony, expecting to see Blanche there with the healing salve. But it was not Blanche. It was Alejandro de Castillo standing quietly in the doorway, the priest's robes gone, a white silk shirt and fine red doublet in its place, his cloak thrown back to reveal his sword.

I drew a sharp breath, his presence like a burning light in a dark room, and felt myself slip uselessly to the floor.

I woke to find myself in Alejandro's arms, being carried like a child to the bedchamber I shared with Blanche and Alice.

"What are you doing?" I demanded, furious with myself for having shown such weakness before him. But I knew it had not been my fault. The pain in my wounded hand had become suddenly unbearable, and no doubt my mind had closed like a door against its terrible fire. "Put me down! I must smell awful!"

"You do," he agreed calmly.

Mortified by that reply, I said nothing else, but wished the earth would swallow me up.

Reaching my bedchamber, Alejandro obliged by setting me down on the narrow cot in which I slept when I was not tending the princess at night. He shut the door and fumbled to light a candle, for the place had no window and was dark as pitch.

His face was grim as he approached the bed, candle in hand. "Show me," he ordered me, and I laid my hand in his, not bothering to hide the extent of my hurts. He examined me briefly, then took a pot of salve from his pouch and began to unstopper it. "I seem to be forever mending your hurts."

I said nothing, but set my jaw as he began to apply the salve. My skin stung horribly. My lips twitched, but I kept my hand steady in his, determined not to cry out or faint like a fool again.

His fingers moved most swiftly where the skin was red-raw. I drew breath, struggling against faintness, and Alejandro glanced up at my face.

"I did not think to see you alive again," he muttered savagely. "Do you enjoy putting yourself in danger? Is death a game to you?"

"Where is Blanche?" I countered, ignoring his anger with a little fury of my own. "Or Alice? I should not be alone with you, Señor de Castillo. Or do you want the world to know we are secretly betrothed? Because I do not think your masters will be too happy about the arrangement, a young Catholic novice promising himself to a suspected Protestant witch."

"Shut up," he said thickly, and took me by the shoulders. He stared down at my lips, still sore from the coarse gag they had used on me, then kissed both my cheeks instead, my eyelids, my chin. "Why did you not use your power against them? Look what they have done to you."

"If I had used my power against them, as you put it, then everyone would have known what I am, and the princess would have been arrested and tried for harbouring a witch." I managed a lopsided smile. "So I did the only thing I could do, which was hold out."

Alejandro looked down at my battered hand, at the shiny red scalds, at the bloodied finger where my nail had been ripped out, then he raised his gaze to my face. "You are the bravest woman I know, Meg Lytton."

"Then you do not know very many," I replied sharply. "If he had used a hot brand on me, I would have told him everything. I would have betrayed everyone I have ever known, even you, even my brother, even the Lady Elizabeth herself. I would have sworn the Queen's sister could fly like a bat and turn herself into a snake if de Pero had tortured me long and pitilessly enough."

I held up my hand. "This is nothing compared to what he wished to do to me, given the chance. I saw it in his face whenever I cried out in pain. Señor de Pero is like Marcus

Dent, I fear. He is a cruel man who believes utterly in the ways of the Inquisition, and he enjoys inflicting pain."

"I shall kill him!"

"No, for then you would be condemned for his murder and there would be another torturer in his place within a day. It's better to wait and see what will happen at court. The Lady Elizabeth tells me the Queen has all but admitted she is not with child and the court is moving on to another royal house. So there will be no heir to supplant Elizabeth. The Queen is too old to have a child, and everyone knows it. Perhaps the feud will be over between them now."

Alejandro managed a wry smile. "My love, they are sisters of the same father by different mothers. There will always be a feud between them."

I winced at the pain in my hand, and he bent again to kiss me, this time on the mouth, but exquisitely gently so he would not hurt my stinging lips. His lips were the best medicine on earth. The aches and pain of my tortured body were soon forgotten as I floated away on a sweet dream of pleasure and comfort.

"You should sleep," he commented, and stroked my hair. "Sleep first, then rise and bathe. I will send the girl Alice to help you."

"I do not need a servant!"

"Let her be a friend, then. But you cannot bathe alone. You are hurt, and your hand will not be strong enough to pour the water."

Reluctantly, I accepted the wisdom of this and let him lay me down to rest. The luxury of a warm scented bath such as the princess sometimes had before the fire; that would be welcome. Yet already my head was drowsy and I longed to close my eyes for a space.

Had I imagined all this? My release from the torturer's cell, his kisses, this soft bed? Perhaps I was still being tortured by Miguel de Pero and had fainted with pain and terror. Perhaps Alejandro was only here in a dream I was having, not flesh and blood at all. Indeed, now that I was lying back on the soft covers, I found it hard to see his face clearly, my vision was so weak and blurred.

"Alejandro?" I murmured, half-asleep.

"Sleep, my love," he told me firmly, and rose from my bedside. "I will guard the door and let no one come near you until you wake."

8

INTO THE WOODS

It had been no dream, I discovered, waking later that evening to find myself deliciously refreshed. I rose from my bed, with Alice's help, and managed to bathe myself until my aching body was clean. Alice gasped and shook her head at the vicious marks of torture on my body, and even wept a little in sympathy over the missing fingernail. But since I had no more tears to cry on my own behalf, Alice soon grew cheerful again and found me a clean gown to wear about the court. My old one I reluctantly sent to be washed, though in truth I would have preferred to see it burnt. But we could not afford to waste a well-made court gown just because I had once worn it to be tortured and humiliated by that devil, de Pero.

Someone came to the door as I was dressing, and Alice went to see who it was. Through the half-open door, I could see Alejandro there, still guarding me, and another girl delivering a message.

Alice closed the door and came back, grinning, a folded bundle in her hands. "You are summoned to attend the Lady Elizabeth at supper. She is to dine with the King and court. You had better hurry for her ladyship is waiting. Blanche Parry has been taken ill with a bellyache and the Lady Elizabeth does not wish to be attended by any of the Queen's ladies."

I let the girl brush my hair until it hung smooth and neat, then stood still while she fixed a smart black velvet hood on my head in the French style. "That's not mine," I said hurriedly, and felt uneasy when Alice explained that the hood belonged to the princess.

"Your best cap is ruined, and you cannot go down to the Great Hall wearing any old gown. Her ladyship will be laughed at for not being able to dress her servants in a manner befitting the Queen's sister."

"Then the Queen should make her a larger allowance," I muttered, but did not argue when a pair of old but comfortable, well-cut shoes were produced and slipped on my feet.

The princess and I were about the same size and her cast-off clothes fitted me well. I fussed and fidgeted while Alice dressed me, for I did not wish to keep the Lady Elizabeth waiting. To my relief, the court gown I was already wearing passed Alice's rigorous inspection, though she did insist on adding a thin silver belt chain at my waist, which she assured me was all the fashion.

Before we left, I slipped the bracelet onto my arm which the princess had given me. Its fragile silver links looked beautiful against my pale skin.

Finally, Alice declared me properly dressed for the court and ready to attend her Queen's sister. I hurried out, and found that Alejandro had vanished. I tried not to be disappointed—he had other duties to perform, I was sure—but my heart ached a little at his absence. Perhaps I had grown too accustomed lately to having him always within reach.

That was a dangerous habit! I warned myself.

Alejandro was not bound to me; at my own insistence, we had never made our betrothal public. He might at any moment return to his family in Spain, or leave with the court and never see me again, and no one would ever know we had once been promised to each other. *If a love is kept secret and locked inside a heart for ever,* I wondered hopelessly, *does it truly exist?*

"Walk behind her ladyship and make sure you lift her train out of the dirt and the rushes," Alice whispered in my ear, following me to the Lady Elizabeth's apartments. "Remember to hand her a clean napkin and water bowl between courses. The King does not like dirty fingers at table. And look no one in the eye. You must be invisible."

"I have served before in the Great Hall, you know."

"Have you?" She looked surprised. "I've never seen you there."

"I've only done it a few times, and I was hidden away behind the Lady Elizabeth's chair. Blanche Parry is jealous and prefers to wait on the princess herself. But her ladyship said I should come along too once or twice, for she wished me to learn how to serve at table." I looked at Alice, interested in her history. "How do you know so much about waiting on high table?"

Alice grinned. "I was trained from my cradle to serve royalty, but have rarely been allowed to serve the Queen myself. There are too many other ladies above me in rank who take that honour. It is a great privilege you have been given tonight, Meg."

So don't make a mess of it, I finished for her silently. Sweat began to run down my back as I thought of the trial ahead of me. With no Blanche Parry at my side to remind me when to move forward and when to stay still, I was going to be desperately nervous about making a mistake. As a girl I had been trained to cast the sacred circle and work magic, but never to serve a royal mistress as my mother had done when she was at court during Queen Anne's brief and ill-fated reign.

God forbid I should trip over carrying the Lady Elizabeth's train or drop her finger bowl in the King's lap. I would almost rather be back in chains in the Inquisitor's cell than embarrass my mistress with my woeful lack of training.

I had never seen anything to equal the dazzling splendour of the banqueting hall that summer evening. Now that the Queen was no longer confined to her apartments, it seemed as though the whole court was assembled in that one place, though Alice insisted that many of the lesser nobles had already slipped away ahead of the royal party to find lodgings at Oatlands. Yet the Great Hall with its tapestried walls and arched wooden roof beams still seemed impossibly hot and crowded, unused as I was to such a great company of nobles, their silks and fine velvets glittering with jewels.

Yet for all its splendour, the court felt close and stifling, as though at the height of summer. The Spanish courtiers and priests whispered amongst themselves, or stood in shadowy groups away from the torches, their hostility towards the Lady Elizabeth obvious.

As we entered the Great Hall, the King stepped down from the dais to greet his sister-in-law. To my surprise, the Queen was nowhere to be seen.

"Stay behind me," Elizabeth murmured, seeing my hesitation. The King beckoned her forward and she sank into a deep curtsey before him, then seemed to blush as the King smiled and gestured to her to rise.

"I was sorry to hear you had not been well, my lady. I

would have come to you myself if it had not been for various pressing matters of state. I only hope these visits from the Inquisition, and their questioning of your servants, have not added to your woes. My countrymen can be overzealous where God is concerned. But every accusation must be tested in order to prove your innocence, as I am sure you understand." He took her long pale hand, lifting it to his lips in a courtly kiss. His dark eyes flirted with hers quite openly. "How are you, sister?"

"Much improved, Your Majesty," Elizabeth replied softly, and it was clear from her purring tone that she enjoyed being reminded of her royal status as the Queen's sister. "The news that I was to dine with you tonight seems to have restored me. My rooms overlook the Thames, and I fear river air is not good for my health at this time of year, with the spring tides swelling the river and bringing its debris so high up the banks." She paused, and looked at him daringly. "But I hear the court is soon to move from Hampton Court, Your Majesty. Is that so?"

It was a bold question, perhaps even a dangerous one, given that no official announcement had been made concerning the dismal end of the Queen's lying-in.

King Philip hesitated, and then his smile broadened. "Indeed, it is true. We are bound for Oatlands. I am told it is not far, a mere day's ride across easy country. Will you accompany us, sister?"

"Thank you, Your Majesty." Elizabeth bent her head, but could not quite conceal her satisfaction at his reply. "I shall come if my royal sister, the Queen, is disposed to welcome me there."

The King nodded, stroking his dark beard as he looked her up and down, no doubt admiring her tiny waist in the black gown she had chosen that evening, its sober colour broken only by a silver belt like my own, but more ornate and ending in a dangling cross. No crucifix such as the more devout Catholics wore, her cross was plain and defiantly Protestant in flavour. But the King's pale blue eyes skipped across it without comment, preferring—it seemed to me—to linger over the low neckline of her gown.

King Philip held out his arm to the princess. "I had hoped the Queen would join us this evening. But alas, she is still abed with an affliction that keeps her from leaving her apartments at present."

"I am saddened to hear it, brother."

"I am sure she will welcome you at Oatlands though, for my sake at least. Never did a King have such a fine sister-in-law." He kissed her hand. "Come and sit next to me at table, since my wife cannot join us. We shall eat well tonight and toast a merry farewell to Hampton Court. Soon our best cooks will be leaving us to set up their ovens at Oatlands. Do you know the place?"

"Indeed, my lord," Elizabeth murmured.

Listening to my mistress laugh heartily with the King all evening and accept food from his hand, it was not hard to see how her mind went. Queen Mary might secretly loathe her younger half-sister and instruct her spies to make Elizabeth's life a misery, but King Philip found her charming and attractive. And Elizabeth was not a woman to throw aside a weapon, however trickily it came to her hand.

After they had eaten, the King asked the Lady Elizabeth to walk with him in the moonlit gardens. Half the court descended with them to admire the newly planted walkways, their lines and circles designed to impress the senses with an idea of order and beauty. The courtiers kept their distance from the royal pair, muttering behind their hands or standing in silence as they waited for them to return to the Great Hall.

Torches flamed along the paths at intervals, lighting the low
hedges of lavender and privet, their flickering lights reflected
in the central pool into which a fountain played incessantly.

As they walked ahead of me, King Philip pointed out the
young plants he had ordered to be brought over from Spain
for these gardens.

"If the climate will support them is not yet known, but we
shall try. In my own country these grow freely, but here…"
He made an impatient face, gesturing to the evening sky
above us, already prickling with stars like tiny diamonds on
black velvet. "Here in England it rains too heavily and too
often in the summer for plants which need the sun. And the
winters are too cold and wet, the seed will rot in the ground
before it is spring again."

Elizabeth laughed. "Then you must learn to appreciate the
beauty of our woodland plants, Your Majesty, which do not
need the sun and have their own deep colours and rich scents
to recommend them."

We were passing a small wooded area of the grounds. The
trees grew thickly there, overarching the path. I glanced about
us, suddenly uneasy. It seemed to me there were shadows
in the woodland, shadows with unfriendly eyes that moved
when we moved and held still when we stopped. The Queen's
spies? Or unnatural creatures that had no place in our world?

My skin crept and I spoke a spell under my breath, hoping to throw a barrier around my mistress that would protect
her from any harmful influence. But the further she moved
away from me, the more I felt that protective barrier weaken
and grow thin.

The King paused, then drew the Lady Elizabeth aside into
a narrow copse thick with the scent of bluebells. "Will you
show me this tender English beauty, sister? I am a Spaniard

and know only the coarse flowers brought out by the dry heat of our summers."

Elizabeth bit her lip, clearly uncomfortable with the suggestion. "It is too dark under the trees."

"The stars will light our way. Come, let us leave your servant behind and enjoy the place alone. I am curious to see these charming woodland plants."

"Very well, Your Majesty."

I waited in shadow as they disappeared under the trees, unsure whether it was quite acceptable for the young princess to walk alone in the dark wood with her sister's husband. But with the Queen absent, still keeping to her bed as though she were sick, which of us would dare to comment?

The shadows seemed to thicken and lengthen once I was alone. I remembered the giant rat I had seen twice now at Hampton Court and turned, staring hard into the shadowy woods. My senses searched for an attack, but could find none. Then a rustling in the bushes stiffened the hair on the back of my neck.

"Meg," a voice whispered huskily behind me. My heart leaped, exalted. I knew who it was even before I turned.

"The King and the Lady Elizabeth are in there alone, without even a guard or chaperone," I told Alejandro, forcing myself to sound calm. "What would the Queen say if she knew?"

"Nothing very complimentary," he said drily, and raised my sore hand to his lips, kissing it just as the King had kissed the Lady Elizabeth's hand, though I saw how careful he was not to hurt me. Bent over my hand, Alejandro looked up at me as a cat looks at a mouse it has caught, something mischievous in his expression. "But on this occasion I shall not complain, for it gives us a chance to be alone as well."

These Spaniards certainly knew how to make a woman feel loved and desired, I thought, my skin tingling at his touch.

Sometimes I felt safe in his company, safer than with any other man on earth, and my heart would sing with joy. But then sometimes his eyes looked at me so fiercely and with such heat, it was as though he wished to eat me up and leave nothing but the bones behind. It was not always a comfortable thing, being alone with Alejandro de Castillo.

"This is a fine gown. And a smart new French hood too." Alejandro smiled, releasing my hand. "I saw you at dinner tonight, Meg, carrying the princess's train as though you had been born to serve royalty. You looked so noble and lofty, like a princess yourself. I hardly recognized you."

"It felt very strange," I admitted. "A far cry from our ramshackle life at Woodstock."

"Ramshackle." He ran the difficult word around his tongue, then laughed. "The English have such unusual words. Yes, our life at Woodstock was certainly *ramshackle*. And how does court life suit you, Meg Lytton?"

I looked into his eyes and knew I could not lie. "Being at the royal court is the most dizzying thing. I can hardly believe where I am when I wake up each morning. I enjoy the honour of being able to wear fine gowns like this and walk behind the Lady Elizabeth when she talks with the King himself. I have never been anywhere but quiet Oxfordshire all my life, and now to be here at court… It is exciting, it is miraculous." I hesitated, then finished in a low voice so that only he could hear me, "But it is not the life I want. I miss the open fields and the rain on my face, Alejandro. I miss casting the circle and calling down the spirits. I miss the power of magick in my fingertips. As a witch, I am the servant of the goddess. Here I am only the servant of a princess."

He said nothing for a moment, but watched me closely. It occurred to me that I did not know much about Alejandro, except the few things he had told me about his Spanish family—very wealthy and noble—and his childhood, how he had been the unwitting cause of a witch's death. He kept his past to himself, his eyes darkly secretive even when telling me how much he loved me. It made me wonder what else I might discover about Alejandro in the future—and whether any of those discoveries could make me love him less.

"So you could never be content to throw away your skill on this life of courtly indulgence," he suggested quietly, "with spies at every corner and the block waiting for the unwary?"

"I'm not sure," I replied in a whisper, looking over my shoulder in case anyone might be listening. But the shadows no longer seemed dangerous, not now that Alejandro was with me, and the moon had slipped behind a cloud, hiding us from the view of any covert watchers.

"It may be possible to be a witch at court, if the thing is done secretly. My mother practised the craft when she served at the court of Queen Anne, the Lady Elizabeth's mother. But Aunt Jane told me that when she returned home to Oxfordshire, my mother abandoned the craft in favour of marriage and motherhood, as so many women choose to do when they fall in love."

Alejandro did not smile. "Did she regret it?"

"I believe she did, yes. But I never knew my mother so I cannot know for sure. She died young."

He nodded sombrely. "There is no greater risk for a woman than to be with child. You know the curse that has been laid upon me, and what it could mean for my future wife. I would not have you die young, Meg. Even if it means we must never marry."

He meant the curse a dying witch had laid on him as a boy, that his wife would die in childbirth. "I have no intention of dying. Trust me."

He smiled at this and drew me so close I could hardly breathe. His hands clasped my waist, his gaze searching mine.

"Always," he agreed.

"Shall I call down a nightingale to sing for us?" I whispered, afraid what might follow if we allowed our hearts and hands to do what they wished.

Alejandro said nothing but waited, still watching me.

I whispered a few words in Latin, and sketched a brief pass in the darkness, willing the branches to part and bring us a nightingale. I did not know if such a summoning spell would work without any preparation on my part, but I was hopeful that the night would favour us.

Suddenly there it was, a small brown bird with unassuming plumage, gazing down at us from a nearby beech tree. The nightingale tipped back its throat and a glorious peal of notes filled the air.

Alejandro stared at the bird in disbelief, then gave a hoarse laugh. He gathered me in his arms and kissed me, pressing kisses on my forehead, my cheek, even my lips. "Sweet astonishing Meg!"

We listened to the nightingale's song as we kissed, drowning in its music. My heart swelled with joy.

We stood in the shadows a long while, pressed together like two leaves of a book, until the King's deep voice woke us from our dream and we shot apart, our faces flushed. I looked up into the leafy branches of the beech tree but the nightingale had fled. The spell was broken.

Much to my relief, the royal pair had not seen our intimacy.

"Meg," the Lady Elizabeth said, turning to me with a large single pearl on her palm. Her smile was strange and unnerving as the beautiful pearl glinted in the moonlight. "A gift from His Majesty. Look after it for me, would you?"

"Yes, my lady," I murmured, and slid the priceless pearl into the small leather pocket hanging from my belt.

There was another rustle from the bushes behind us. I looked round, but there was nobody there—not even my betrothed. Alejandro too had vanished, along with the nightingale's beautiful song.

There was no time to regret his absence. Elizabeth snapped her fingers and I busied myself with her gown, lifting the trailing silk and lace off the damp ground as the King and the Lady Elizabeth walked back towards the rest of the courtiers, still talking together merrily, sometimes in Spanish, sometimes in English.

Back in the dimly lit safety of her rooms later that night, Elizabeth tore at her gown with angry fingers. "Get me out of this!" she insisted, and stared furiously out of the window as Alice and I struggled to release her intricate and expensive clothing.

"What is it, my lady?" Alice asked, rather daringly I thought, given Elizabeth's notorious temper. "Are you unwell again?"

Elizabeth shook her away impatiently, turning her sharp eyes to me instead. "Meg, did you not see her in the bushes?" she hissed.

I was bewildered. "Who, my lady?"

"One of the Queen's ladies. That stiff-necked old Spaniard who served her mother, Queen Katherine of Aragon. She was there amongst the trees tonight, I tell you. I saw her clear as day when the moon came out from behind a cloud." Elizabeth gasped and leaned against the wall, holding her side as though it hurt. "She was *watching us!*"

"Watching us?" I repeated stupidly, thinking of how Alejandro had kissed me, of what we had been whispering about.

Could we have been seen or overheard in the shadows? And what of my spell, drawing down the nightingale to sing for us? I had been foolish and reckless to work magick in the open like that, where anyone could have seen me.

To my relief, I realized Elizabeth meant the lady-in-waiting had been watching her and King Philip. "No doubt she will be taking great pleasure right now in telling the Queen how I went apart with the King, alone and unaccompanied. How we came out laughing like lovers, and how her husband gave me that enormous pearl as a gift." Elizabeth's face drained of colour as she stared at nothing, seeming to remember what had passed between herself and the King when they were alone together. "God knows what else she might have seen!"

"Forgive me, my lady. I was watching but saw no one. I heard a gentle rustling in the bushes that I thought was the wind."

Elizabeth drew a hand across damp eyes, then nodded and gestured us to continue undressing her. "No matter," she muttered. "My sister has been sending her spies to watch me ever since I arrived, looking for an excuse to banish me from court again. Now I will be able to leave court and live quietly elsewhere for a while."

Alice's eyes bulged. "Elsewhere?"

"Hatfield House," Elizabeth said determinedly as we unlaced the kirtle from her hips and left her in nothing but her thin shift and woollen stockings. "After this, my sister cannot continue to refuse me permission to return to my old house at Hatfield. Mary may wish to have me at court where I can be kept under close watch, but she will not want her husband constantly fluttering about me like a moth at a candle flame."

Leaving court. That would mean leaving Alejandro.

My chest hurt dreadfully but I said nothing, bending to put away her finery in the wooden chest.

I looked up to see an odd smile on the Lady Elizabeth's face. She was standing perfectly still while Alice brushed her long reddish-gold hair, staring at nothing and smiling.

I felt a flutter of rage and amazement as I understood. "You did it deliberately. You knew your sister's spies were watching and you wanted them to tell her."

Elizabeth looked at me sharply. "And what if I did? I am sick of life at court. It is little better than a prison, and Mary would never have released me otherwise."

I said nothing but looked hurriedly away, sensing something boiling under the surface of her calm. There was a terrible stillness about her slender frame that made me wary.

As I held out her nightgown a moment later, the Lady Elizabeth suddenly stamped her foot and hissed, "Leave us, Alice!"

Startled by this outburst, Alice dropped the hairbrush with a clatter and almost ran from the bedchamber.

I had frozen at her order, nightgown in hand, but as Elizabeth turned to me I took a step backwards, only too aware of her appalling temper. But I was wrong; the princess was neither laughing nor angry, but distressed. Her eyes were full of tears, her lip trembling.

"I had no choice tonight," Elizabeth whispered, staring at me. "I had to force the Queen's hand. If I stay at court any longer, he will ruin me. You understand?"

I nodded, then instinctively held out my arms and embraced her. Her thin body shook against mine as she sobbed.

I was taken aback by her torrent of emotion, and said the only thing I could think of that might comfort her. "Don't cry, my lady. We will go to Hatfield if Her Majesty permits it and never come back to court."

"It is so hard, Meg." Her voice was muffled against my shoulder. "I was born to be Queen and can never forget who I am. You are lucky to be a servant. I am not like you, free to love or be loved. Whatever happens, whatever choices I make, I must always remember that I may one day be Queen of England."

I am not free to love or be loved either, I thought, but did not contradict her.

After a few moments the tears stopped and Elizabeth straightened, wiping her eyes. I picked up the nightgown and gently helped her into it. Then I took up the fallen hair-brush and finished Alice's task for her, counting in my head as I brushed the Lady Elizabeth's hair one hundred times.

"We will never speak of this again," she said into the silence.

9

A VILE THING

To our amazement though, the Queen did not allow her sister to leave court for the quiet retirement of Hatfield House. Three days after the incident in the garden, Queen Mary descended from her apartments in a stiffly swaying gown of black silk and lace, clustered about by her Spanish ladies-in-waiting in their severe gowns and black lace headdresses. The royal party swept through the high-ceilinged corridors of Hampton Court like a storm, with courtiers falling to their knees as the Queen passed, heads bowed, their smiles gone as they saw her grim expression and still-bloated stomach.

It was whispered that Her Majesty's chief steward had dismissed the doctors assembled for the royal birth, and warned them not to speak of the Queen's condition under pain of death. But that had not stopped the gossip. The abrupt and unexplained loss of the Queen's pregnancy was the only talk on everyone's lips.

The King accompanied the Queen into the gardens after lunch, his face averted from his wife. It was hard not to wonder if the royal couple had argued. But about what?

There was a muted feast that first evening, with music and dancing to follow. King Philip, much to my surprise, asked the Lady Elizabeth to dance the too-intimate galliard more than once, as though deliberately flaunting his interest in front of his wife.

Hunched on her chair like a sick black crow, Queen Mary glared at the two of them with reddened eyes. Elizabeth smiled carefully for the King, not quite daring to refuse his invitations to dance, but her discomfort was apparent to everyone.

The next morning, the King and Queen held a joint audience in the Great Hall, hearing petitions and speaking at length with their courtiers. The rest of us stood against the walls and listened as the petitions dragged on for hours, only able to converse in whispers in case we disturbed the royal couple's deliberations.

Finally summoned forward to the dais, the Lady Elizabeth dropped lightly onto both knees and kissed the ruby ring on her sister's swollen finger. "Your Majesty," she murmured in a reverent tone, her head still bent. "I am glad to see you so much improved today. It has been too long since Your Majesty graced the court with your royal presence."

Watching them, my skin began to creep. My heartbeat became sluggish, and the room was suddenly darker than before. It felt as though a storm was coming.

I looked at Blanche Parry beside me, and saw her eyes widen, intent on what was happening on the dais. The princess's lady-in-waiting had not noticed anything amiss. Nor had anyone else, by the calm look of the courtiers around us.

Yet something was wrong. What?

Glancing up, my attention caught and snagged on the wooden roof beams of the Great Hall. My blood chilled at what I saw there.

There was a *thing* on the ceiling. A vile *thing*. I did not know how else to describe it, except perhaps as a bloated black shadow, clinging like a vast upside-down bat to the curved beams that supported the roof.

There was no doubt in my mind that this black creature came from another realm, not our world of daylight. Yet it was no conjuration. It possessed form and substance, and had come with some deadly intent into that place. Whatever demon or spirit had produced it, it was a creature of utter malevolence, I knew that much, whose mission was to make mischief of the most deadly kind.

Two or three old spells came faltering to my mind, spells of dispersal and scattering, though I knew they would be too weak to hold sway against such an emanation of pure evil.

I tried to speak, to drive the creature out with a spell, but found I could not make a sound. My mouth was dry, my tongue stuck to the roof of my mouth.

No one else seemed to have noticed the malignant black shape creeping across the ceiling towards the Queen's throne. If I was the only one able to see it, perhaps it was a mere fancy of my mind and not real. Was I going mad? I wondered in horror.

I had heard talk of witches whose minds had snapped under the pressure of power, who had writhed in fits upon the floor and called out for the witchfinder to take them to Hell.

"Here, Your Majesty."

Miguel de Pero and the other black-robed priests of the Inquisition passed me, approaching the dais. I lowered my head, my skin prickling at their presence. It was hard not to imagine myself back in de Pero's cell, tortured as I lied to save my skin.

At their back came Alejandro in a fashionable red doublet, but with his silver crucifix dangling from his neck as though to proclaim his faith. My breath caught in my throat at the sight of my betrothed, though I was careful not to give myself away; with the Inquisition watching everything so closely, we dared not acknowledge each other in public. At his side limped white-haired Father Vasco, stooped over a stick, his gaze moving across my face without recognition. I felt a stab of guilt that I had laid a memory spell on such an elderly man, then reminded myself that his great age would have been no barrier to Father Vasco naming me to the Inquisition as a witch.

My aunt Jane had often said, "Lay no spell or curse against the weak and innocent, yet do what you must to protect yourself from discovery."

As the priests came level with me, I sank into a curtsey and did not look up, not sure I could trust myself to conceal my feelings for Alejandro.

Once he had passed, and it was safe to raise my head without catching his eye, I glanced up at the roof again. The intricate arch of beams above our heads was empty.

I did not know what to make of it. Had I really seen a vile black mass creeping from beam to beam above the dais? Or was it some sick fancy, the product of a feverish brain after my long hours of torture at the hands of the Inquisition?

"Señor de Pero," the Queen greeted the Spanish priest eagerly, "you and your men must accompany the court to Oatlands too. I could not be without your reports." She signalled the Inquisitor to rise from his low bow. "How goes the true faith in England? I pray each night for my subjects to come with one accord to the Lord's feast, though in my heart I know many of them are stubborn and wanting in faith."

"Their stubbornness will be burnt out of them, Your Majesty, as you have so wisely decreed. There is no greater trial for a heretic than fire. No fewer than five and twenty have gone to their deaths unrepentant this month, and I expect that number to rise as the summer passes into autumn."

Queen Mary nodded, her narrow dark face solemn. "Those wretched unhappy people. I hate to think of their suffering, both in death and in Hell. But I know it is the Lord's work we do in this heathenish country. You are right, Señor de Pero. After so many years under false priests and teachers, there is often no remedy but to burn these unbelievers as an example to the rest. Only remind your Inquisitors we are not barbarians. Do not fail to offer any Englishman mercy if he will agree to embrace Catholicism with all his heart."

Miguel de Pero bowed his head at her command. "You are a merciful Queen indeed. The question is asked of each man and woman as they are sentenced, Your Majesty, and yet again as they are whipped to the stake. A few accept the wickedness of their error, and so gain their lives. But I fear the English must be thick-headed as bulls," he told the Queen, and I could hear contempt in the priest's voice, "for many still consent to be led to their deaths in the marketplace like holy martyrs, their hearts all swollen with pride for having refused Your Majesty's edict. Poor fools! These heretics will dance in Hell for ever after our bonfires have put them on the path to the Devil."

The Queen looked over his shoulder at Alejandro. "I recognize that young man."

De Pero gestured Alejandro forward. His tone was reserved. "Your Majesty, may I present Alejandro de Castillo, the eldest son of one of Spain's most respected noblemen? De

Castillo serves as a novice in the Order of Santiago, one of our most prestigious orders, only open to the highest families in the land."

King Philip leaned forward to gaze at Alejandro with interest. "An eldest son in the church? That is most unusual."

"An accident of fate, Your Majesty," de Pero explained, turning to his sovereign. "Alejandro entered his priestly training as a younger son. But now his elder brother has died, he stands to inherit his father's title and estate. Indeed, his family have requested that he should return to them at once. Nonetheless, I am told by his masters that de Castillo has a great career ahead of him in the Order of Santiago if he wishes to pursue the priesthood."

This was news to me. Alejandro's brother had died and he was now the heir to his father's title? I tried not to appear too interested, for fear of betraying my feelings.

Queen Mary looked down at Alejandro as he swept off his cap and knelt respectfully before her throne. Her eyes narrowed assessingly on his figure. "You were in attendance on my sister at Woodstock with the venerable Father Vasco."

"I was, Your Majesty," Alejandro agreed, his dark head bent.

"I remember your reports. They were always very welcome to me, even when not wholly positive." The Queen's mouth tightened and she glanced briefly at the Lady Elizabeth. It struck me for the first time that her care for the princess was not wholly driven by malice and resentment, but also from a very real fear for her sister's soul. She gestured her sister to stand, for the Lady Elizabeth had been kneeling all this while. "You did well to ensure my younger sister continued to attend daily Mass during that time. However, I fear her lax nature has reasserted itself since then. Some who are close to the Lady Elizabeth tell me she has slipped from such strict observance since returning to court."

Elizabeth's eyes widened at this, a flash of anger in her face, but she said nothing, moving silently to the left of the dais.

"This lapse may be partly my fault," her sister continued, a slight flush rising to her cheeks. "I have been too long in my own apartments and have taken Mass there privately instead of before the court. It is the duty of a prince to teach by example, after all. But once we are at Oatlands, I would have you attach yourself to my sister's train and serve as her spiritual advisor. She is a young woman, and it may be that she will heed your teaching more keenly than that of an older priest."

Miguel de Pero stirred uneasily at this startling suggestion. I remembered how he had warned me to stay away from Alejandro, and knew it would not sit easily with him to know that Alejandro was being given such an elevated status within a royal household.

"Your Majesty, I am not sure if such an honour would be entirely appropriate," de Pero said smoothly. "There are other priests better placed to undertake this duty, if you would permit me to suggest one or two names. Father Vasco must soon return to Spain and I had hoped young Alejandro would accompany him. While his reports from Woodstock may have been glowing, I am far from convinced this was because your sister—"

King Philip held up his hand, interrupting the priest. "We have heard your objections. The Queen has made her decision. Your novice will attend the Queen's sister as her spiritual advisor and make weekly reports to Her Majesty as before."

The Chief Inquisitor hesitated—and I swear his nostrils flared—then swept them both an exaggerated bow and backed away from the dais, his head low. "Forgive me, Your Majesties."

The Queen looked at her husband with a shy smile, no doubt to thank him for his intervention. But King Philip did not smile in return, glancing away as though he could not bear to look on her, his English-born wife who had not produced their longed-for heir—no, nor ever would now, for many believed Mary too old to bear a child.

The Queen's countenance fell and she stammered, "My lord King," then fell quiet, twisting a handkerchief between her fingers.

As I watched, Queen Mary summoned the Lady Elizabeth to her side. For a few moments, with the whole court holding their breath, she spoke to her sister in a low tormented voice. Elizabeth nodded and curtsied to her sister, then left the Great Hall with only Blanche Parry in tow, her reddish head bent over a rosary, her skirts rustling gently in the silence.

I did not know where her ladyship was going. I had no choice though but to remain where I was, not having been summoned by my mistress to accompany her. Perhaps she would be returning soon, I thought, and glanced down at the small lined basket of sweetmeats the princess had given me to carry. Should I wait here, or should I return to the Lady Elizabeth's apartments so her sweetmeats did not spoil in the stuffy heat of the Great Hall?

"I have heard there is still good hunting to be enjoyed, despite this changeable weather," the King remarked, clicking his fingers for another cup of wine. "Once the court has settled at Oatlands, I shall go up to Leicestershire for the month of August and hunt deer."

Queen Mary's face was rigid. "Go hunting for the whole of August? But my lord, I have been so unwell. I shall be in great need of your company at Oatlands."

King Philip stroked his neat beard, frowning with displeasure. "But your ladies and your priests will be on hand to amuse you. I have done little these past few months but play chess and chequers. Your English court is nothing like my own in Spain. I tell you, I am half dead with boredom. And what better sport than hunting to blow away the cobwebs?"

Someone tugged on my gown from behind.

I turned, a quick reproof on my lips, and found myself looking into my brother's face.

"William!" I cried in joy, then embraced him.

My brother smiled and stepped back. It was a warm smile, but his face was strained. "Dearest Meg, how well you look. That court gown is so fine, I almost did not dare kiss you for fear of creasing it."

Alice was standing behind him, a smug look on her face. "This one swore blind he was your brother. He does have a strong look of you, Meg, so I brought him to find you. I told the guards he had permission to be at court. I didn't do wrong, did I?"

"Only if we are found out in a lie," I told her, but could not blame Alice for doing exactly as I would have done. "Never mind, it's done now. And I am certainly glad to see my brother again!"

Some of the courtiers were glaring in our direction, their faces hostile. The King and Queen were still arguing, His Majesty's voice raised in anger now. I realized it would not do to draw attention to ourselves at such a dangerous moment. Hurriedly I led Will into the passageway outside, which had the virtue at least of being less crowded than the Great Hall, and Alice followed us, her face alight with curiosity.

"I thought you had found employment as a clerk in London, Will," I said, examining my brother's face for signs of trouble. "What are you doing here at Hampton Court? Is anything amiss?"

William had looked close to despair when I had last seen

him that spring, following the princess's entourage back to court bedraggled and downhearted. But some grief was only to be expected. He had betrayed my aunt by helping our father steal the letter that should have saved her, hoping the mere sight of Elizabeth's signature would sway English exiles to attack Mary's throne. But with no last-minute stay of execution, Aunt Jane had perished at the stake. "For the good of England," my father had claimed, showing no remorse except what lay at the bottom of a tankard of ale. But I knew my brother, William, had loved our aunt, and had perhaps not fully understood that she would be executed without the Lady Elizabeth's plea for mercy. Though of course we had no way to be sure the letter would have made any difference to her fate.

He glanced at Alice, then back at me. "Perhaps we could talk more privately?"

"You can speak in front of Alice," I said, and squeezed the girl's hand, for I was beginning to think of her as a friend.

Will still looked wary however, so I gathered my skirts and hurried down the passageway, taking a turn which led out into the courtyard. It was hot and close outside, a dark bank of cloud blocking out the sunlight that earlier had streamed in through the high windows of the palace. It had been a strange unsettled summer, with periods of fierce heat and cold rotting damp following closely on each other's heels, floods and droughts by turn across the country, and nobody ever sure from one day to the next if the sun would shine or rain would fall.

I waited for William and Alice to catch up with me, watching the farrier as he rapidly shaped a hot shoe to one of the Queen's own horses. A young boy of perhaps nine or ten years old leaned against the wall of the smithy, holding a bucket of water for the farrier, his chest bare for the heat but so filthy he might as well have been clothed. As I watched, the farrier straightened and turned, dipping the hot shoe in the bucket of water. There was a violent hiss and steam filled the air like fine mist. The chestnut gelding shifted slightly in the farrier's grasp, rolling its eyes, but did not seem otherwise alarmed.

"We will not be overheard here," I told my brother impatiently as he and Alice emerged from the gloom of the passageway. "Say what is troubling you—and quickly, please, before I burst!"

"You are right, Meg. I did find work in London," William told me, and I was surprised to hear his old childhood stammer return as he told his story. "I was private secretary to a merchant near Aldgate. His name was Lumsden and he was quite a wealthy man. I lived well for the first month. Nor was the work too difficult, little more than keeping his accounts each day and overseeing shipments at the docks. I thought to have stayed with Lumsden a good few years, perhaps even settled there in the east of the city. But then one day we had an unexpected visitor." My brother shuddered, real fear in his eyes. "A Catholic priest, one of those they call the Inquisition."

I began to understand. I gripped his arm as he faltered. "Go on, you are among friends now."

"My master was one of those who had sought reform before Her Majesty came to the throne. Everyone knew that in Aldgate and no one held it against him. Once the Queen's rule was heard, that we should all be Catholics again, Lumsden returned to the old religion like everyone else. That is what he told us and I believed him." William hesitated. "Only… only he did not burn all his papers and books, as he ought to have done."

"So they arrested him?"

William nodded, swallowing hard. "And charged him with

heresy before the week was out. Once they searched his house and discovered his chest of forbidden writings, my master was put to the rack and confessed it all. It seems he and two other men had been meeting secretly each Sunday night to worship as Protestants. One of their servants got wind of it, told the local priest, and that was when the Inquisition came to his door."

Alice was staring, her blue eyes wide with horror. "The poor man. What happened to him?"

"Master Lumsden was burnt before the city wall at Aldgate, him and his two friends." William crossed himself and closed his eyes. After a moment, he seemed to shake the memory away, then carried on in a low voice. "It was only by the grace of God that his wife did not burn with her husband, for they arrested her too. But the priests could find no evidence against her. Though her life was ruined anyway. After my master's death, his goods were forfeit and his land confiscated by the crown. His widow and three young children were turned out of their home and forced to leave London." William's face was hard. "I wanted to help the family, but Mistress Lumsden would have none of it. She said I was as much a Protestant as her husband and should have burnt too."

"Oh, William!" I embraced him tightly. "She must have been in great distress to have said such a thing."

He nodded grimly. "I know it, and hold her no grudge."

"So you came straight to court?" Alice asked.

"Not quite," my brother admitted. He looked at me warily. "I wanted to see our father first, so I went home to Lytton Park."

I was shocked at first, then found myself ridiculously eager to hear news of home. I had always felt out of place at Lytton Park, a misfit who did not deserve such a delightful ancestral home, even if the house itself had become a dilapidated heap under my father's care, its roof forever needing to be repaired, its lawns and formal gardens overgrown. But now, even more of a misfit as a witch at the court of Queen Mary, I had to admit to a little homesickness. It would cheer my heart to see the twisted red chimneys of my childhood home rising above the leafy trees in the park. Yet I was far from home at Hampton Court and could not indulge such childish fancies for fear they might weaken me.

Besides, my father would be at Lytton Park, unless he was on one of his lengthy trips abroad. The last time I had seen my father had been in a smoky upper room at the tavern in Woodstock, where he had drunkenly confessed to being part of a secret rebellion against Queen Mary and having left my aunt to the witchfinder rather than betray his cause.

"Was our father at home?" I asked awkwardly. "How is he?"

"Father is well enough, though he drinks more than he should. His conscience troubles him sorely, I think."

"So it should," I said sharply, thinking how he might have spared my aunt that hideous death.

"But there is worse."

I frowned. "What is it?"

"Dearest Meg, I hardly know how to tell you this…" William laid a hand on my shoulder, his voice dropping to a hoarse whisper. "It's Marcus Dent. He's back."

I stared, feeling the blood drain from my face. Marcus Dent, the witchfinder, was back from whatever violent hell-hole I had flung him into when last we tangled. I had known this day would come, for powerful though my banishing spell had been, it had not dealt the man a killing blow. Anger alone had seemed to fuel that moment of power, channelling everything I knew into one purpose. But my anger had not been great enough to kill a man. Instead, I had hurled

Marcus Dent into some other dimension, some hellish void I could not begin to imagine, and ever since I had thought myself safe from his malignant influence.

Now Marcus was back from the void, and that meant only one thing. He would soon be looking for me—and vengeance.

My skin crawled with horror as I tried to imagine where Marcus might have been all this time. I had spoken the words of the spell which banished him from this world, yet I had no inkling of where he had gone, nor how he had managed to return. It must have been hard for him to explain his long absence when he finally returned. No doubt when he caught up with me, I would discover the truth. Because I knew for sure Marcus Dent would find me one day, no matter what spells I used to conceal and protect myself from him.

Suddenly, Alejandro was there at William's shoulder. His urgent glance barely acknowledged my brother's presence before searching my face. "Meg, there you are! What are you doing out here? You are needed at once in the Great Hall. The Lady Elizabeth has returned from her prayers."

"She will not miss me," I muttered defensively.

Alejandro looked at me grimly. "She needs you, Meg. You had better hurry too. The King and Queen have argued in the Great Hall. His Majesty has overturned a table and sworn that he will leave England."

Alice's eyes bulged. *"What?"*

"The whole court is in uproar." Alejandro took my hand in a firm grasp and refused to let go. "Come, all of you. The Lady Elizabeth will need friends about her after this."

Hurrying back into the Great Hall with the others, the atmosphere hit me like a dark wave of evil and I recoiled from it instinctively. It felt like a poison slowly creeping through my veins.

I stopped dead in the ornate doorway and stared up through

the excited, whispering crowd at the dais. The Lady Elizabeth was motionless against the far wall, her face very pale but with red burning in her cheeks as though she had been struck. Queen Mary sat stiff and upright on her throne in her black gown finely threaded with silver, skirts spread wide to conceal a still-swollen belly. Her husband stood in the midst of his Spanish courtiers, arms crossed and with his back turned to his wife as though he had been raging against her. No one dared look either monarch in the face but all there gazed at the floor or studied the brightly embroidered tapestries on the walls. I dared to look at them though, staring from King to Queen in a horrified daze, and wondering why I felt so sick.

"My lord King, my good Philip," the Queen was entreating him, her voice shaking with anger and fear, "you cannot leave England. I...I am with child again. I feel it."

The King shot her a contemptuous look that sent half the courtiers bowing swiftly from the room, sensing a battle ahead which might end in disaster for anyone too close to the throne. "You are not with child, nor is it likely you will ever be now."

The Queen blanched, clearly distraught at such a cruel statement delivered in front of the court. "Your Majesty!"

"I had already made arrangements to leave by the end of this year. Our quarrel merely brings my plans forward a few months. Don't pretend you thought I would remain here for ever. I cannot stomach this English climate, nor the blandness of your food and the rank acidity of your wines." The King made a disgusted face, turning as though to leave immediately. A few strides took him to where we stood shocked in the doorway, but a wild cry from the Queen made him turn. He sounded furious. "What was that you said?"

"I only brought my sister back to court for your sake, because you said that...that you *desired* her...her presence. Now you would leave me with her?"

The Queen seemed to choke over her words, her cheeks flushed and her eyes swollen with tears.

I shook off Alejandro's hand. For I had finally seen what I had somehow missed before, this horror hanging over the court, all of them as blind as I had been...

Behind the Queen's head was the vile misshapen creature I had seen clinging to the roof of the Great Hall. Now it was perched on the canopy above the throne like some kind of monstrous insect, glossy-backed and swollen, its ringed body convulsing and contracting. As I watched, it turned as though satisfied with its work, and leaped for the wall. The noise it made as it scaled the panelling was disgusting, like something squelching through mud. Yet no one else seemed able either to see or hear it.

I stared up at the creature, half out of my mind with terror. I could not think of a single word of power that might destroy it. Part of me feared that I had summoned this monster myself. When I had first reentered the hall, I had seen the creature as a mere shadow above the throne, shadow and light naturally rising and falling as the sun shifted behind a cloud and the Great Hall darkened. But now I saw it for what it truly was, evil incarnate in a hideous nightmarish body, shining like a vast black maggot. And I recognized its wickedness and greed, its darkness...

I recalled the summoning of the Lady Elizabeth's mother, her ethereal silver spirit—and the furious black cloud that had accompanied her back to life, not retreating into oblivion as the dead Queen had done afterwards, but roaring up the chimney and out into the world.

Was this creature my doing?

King Philip looked at his wife with pity in his handsome face. "It did not seem right that your sister Elizabeth should be kept away from court once her innocence was no longer in doubt. However, you are Queen here. You must do as you see fit."

Turning to leave the Great Hall, King Philip stopped and hung on his heel as he passed us. The King looked briefly at me, then reached out and gripped Alejandro's shoulder. He made no attempt to lower his voice, as though the Queen was already far from his thoughts. "Take care of *la princesa,* de Castillo. I leave her in your charge as a fellow Spaniard and a nobleman, and would have no harm befall her. The welfare of the Lady Elizabeth is of great concern to me—and to Spain."

For a moment after the King had left, there was a terrible silence in the hall. The shiny black maggot on the ceiling writhed and gloated over its prizes in the stifling heat, a broken marriage and a divided court. I looked at Alejandro, sensing his stillness, and saw the strain on his face as the King's command sank in. The princess's safety lay in his hands now, and her enemies were many.

Realizing she had failed, that nothing would stop her husband from leaving, the Queen looked wildly about the Great Hall in search of supporters. But most of her English courtiers had slunk away during the shouting, and the Spanish had departed with their King, their faces haughty and disdainful. Even her closest advisers seemed to have left the chamber, perhaps fearing the consequences of this latest blow to England's stability.

Humiliated and alone on the dais, Queen Mary's voice broke as she pointed an accusing finger at the Lady Elizabeth.

"As soon as the Spanish fleet sets sail, you can take yourself and your entourage back to your precious house at Hatfield. Yes, go… I will not hold you any longer against your will. Though if you value your immortal soul, Bess, you will listen to young de Castillo's teachings and embrace the true faith before it is too late."

I saw Alejandro glance at me inadvertently, his eyes very dark. Since both the King and Queen had made it clear he was now part of the princess's household, that must mean Alejandro would be accompanying us to Hatfield as Elizabeth's spiritual advisor. My heart leaped with joy at the thought, even while I shuddered at the horrors I had seen here today; we would not be separated after all.

Hiding her triumphant expression, Elizabeth curtseyed and began to back out of the Great Hall. The Queen called after her bitterly, "And when it is your turn to marry, may your husband make your life as wretched as mine is now!"

PART II

HATFIELD HOUSE

10

RAIN, LUTES AND PIGS

It began to rain the day we left Hampton Court, early in the autumn, and did not show any signs of stopping even after we had arrived at the modest country house the Lady Elizabeth had called home as a child. For the first few miles, riddled with guilt, I tried to shake off the image of the hideous black creature I had seen on the ceiling at Hampton Court. Was I going mad, or had my summoning of Anne Boleyn somehow brought the monster into being?

Looking back, it seemed too incredible to be true. Yet my instincts told me I had not imagined the creature—nor its evil purpose. It seemed to hate the Queen and wished her ill, even to the point of destroying her. Perhaps it was because Mary had not been intended to inherit the throne; both she and Elizabeth had been termed "illegitimate" by their father, King Henry, and disinherited in favour of a male heir. Now that their younger brother—Edward, a mere nine years old when he had succeeded to the throne for his short reign—had died, however, it seemed likely that a female Tudor would reign for years to come.

Was it the thought of a woman on the throne that the hideous creature could not stomach?

But the trials of our journey soon distracted me, for in such terrible weather the roads were not easy, and even our covered wagon was damp and uncomfortable. The horses struggled the last few miles to Hatfield, sometimes halting exhausted on the road, sometimes lurching with their carts into marshland and standing there, trembling and knee-high in muddy water, waiting to be rescued. Several times Alejandro jumped down from the saddle to help the driver guide her ladyship's wagon back onto the road, the two horses pulling her covered litter being nervous of heavy rain and shying at every unfamiliar object along the road. Yet the only time I heard the princess complain about these constant stops and starts was when a crack of lightning split the grey sky and the horses reared frantically, whinnying and almost throwing the old wagon onto its side.

At last we arrived and found the place in darkness, not a single candle in the windows. It was nearly dusk, the rain still pouring down relentlessly, a strong wind flapping the litter curtains. The Lady Elizabeth waited impatiently in her covered wagon while Blanche and I ran through the rain and mud ruts to hammer at the great studded door.

An ancient old man peered out at us suspiciously, holding up a lantern that swung and shook in his hand. "Who is it?"

"Do you not recognize me, John? It's Mistress Parry." Blanche leaned into the doorway so he could see her face by the light of his lantern. "Bless us, we are hardly strangers, will you not let us in? I'm getting soaked to the skin standing here.

The Lady Elizabeth has come back home at last and needs a clean dry bed, a good fire and a hot posset."

"The Lady Elizabeth? Well, why did you not say so at once?" John, the elderly retainer, opened the door wide enough to let us stagger in one by one, Alejandro trying to shield the princess with his cloak from the worst of the weather. He bowed low to the Lady Elizabeth, but looked flustered when Blanche asked again about her ladyship's bed-chamber. "Alas, we are not ready to receive you, my lady. I had no word of your arrival. There are no sheets on her ladyship's bed and the fire's not been lit in her chamber these three months."

At our arrival, a thin-ribbed, mangy-looking hound had uncoiled itself from the great hearth and now came loping towards us, barking as though under the impression that we were intruders.

Elizabeth gave a cry and bent to embrace the grey-haired old hound, who stopped barking at the sight of her and began to wag its tail enthusiastically.

"Rufus, my dear old friend!" She grinned up at Alice, who had shrieked at the sight of the barking hound. "Don't be afraid, Rufus doesn't bite. Well, not since he was a puppy. I helped to rear him myself when his mother died. Dear sweet Rufus, I can hardly believe you are still alive. But what a loving welcome! We shall take him out across the meadow once the weather is better, see if we can find him some rabbits to chase. Rufus always loved a good walk."

Blanche turned to the old man with an impatient expression, stripping off her wet cloak and gloves. "Where's your wife, Margaret?" she demanded loudly, as though the man was hard of hearing.

"Dead," John replied sourly. "They said it was the plague. We lost five in the village last spring."

"I'm very sorry to hear that," Elizabeth told him gently, and even managed a smile as Blanche helped her struggle out of her sodden cloak. Meg thought Elizabeth had never looked less like a princess. Her cap was lopsided and her damp hair hung bedraggled down her back. But the Lady Elizabeth seemed at home here, her eyes warmer and her smile more natural, as though the cold persona she adopted at court was already falling away. "I liked Margaret. But what of your daughters?"

"Our Bessie married a sailor, but he was drowned away in the Indies, so she's a widow now and looks after me. She's in the pantry with young Lucy, a-hanging a hare for next week's pie. But I'll send Lucy up with kindling and logs for the fire, and some clean sheets for your ladyship's bed." The old man shook his head as he limped away down a narrow passageway, presumably heading for the kitchen. "There's no hot food to be had tonight, mind. We've a pig in the sty but it would take too long to kill and skin it. Nor is there a drop of wine in the house."

"Then I will drink ale tonight, if you have any, and take bread instead of meat until that hare has hung long enough." The Lady Elizabeth seemed cheerful considering the sorry plight in which we had arrived at Hatfield. She gazed around at the hall, a wistful look on her face. "How I have missed this place, and often feared never to see it again. Yet here I am, back in Hatfield with my head still on my shoulders, and here I plan to stay until…" She hesitated, glancing warily at Blanche Parry. "Until it is time for me to leave again."

Until my sister is dead and I am Queen, I finished for her in my head, and guessed from the awkward silence that every-one else was thinking the same thing.

Blanche snapped her fingers at me. "Well, look sharp, girl! We must ready her ladyship for bed before the poor mite

catches her death of cold, standing about in these wet clothes!"
Impatiently, she gestured me to lift the Lady Elizabeth's sodden train, then turned to Alice who had been trying uselessly to wipe the worst of the mud from her thin court shoes.
"Alice, help the maid carry up the logs, and mind they're dry
enough to burn. Her ladyship's bedchamber will smell as foul
as a badger's rear end in this damp weather, I have no doubt,
so let's not make it smoky too. Then you can fetch her ladyship a hot posset against the cold. And be sure to sweeten it
with honey, or she'll have none of it."

"Yes, Mistress Parry," Alice replied meekly, and scurried
away to find the kitchen.

The rest of the house felt chilly, away from the hall with
its huge stone hearth and high-backed wooden settles on either side of the fire. It did not improve my impression when
I found the stairs to be dark and winding, nothing like the
grand, torch-lit staircases at Hampton Court. Struggling to
negotiate each step without tripping over my own cumber-
some skirts, I dropped the princess's train and earned a reprimand from the eagle-eyed Blanche.

At the top of the stairs, I began to feel distinctly uneasy. I
was a born witch. I had never been afraid of the dark, not like
other children, and had not shied away from wandering the
deserted rooms of Woodstock Palace at night, though many
had claimed the ruins were haunted. Yet somehow this thick,
dusty darkness and the closed doors to empty bedchambers
made my skin creep. Blanche had brought the lantern, but its
flame was too poor to provide more than a puddle of light before her feet. I found myself peering down at the fine sodden
material of Elizabeth's train rather than looking from right
to left, remembering with horror the vile black thing in the
Great Hall at Hampton Court. It had seemed half shadow,
half monster from another world, and it was hard not to imag-

ine it clinging to these walls too, hiding in deep shadow as it awaited its next chance to cause havoc.

Nonsense, I told myself firmly. Whatever that hideous creature had been, it had wanted the Queen. Not anyone here.

Indeed, Hatfield House seemed an excellent place to hide from our enemies. It certainly felt as though the house had been left to fall into disrepair since the princess had spent her childhood there. The air was damp and chill, just as Blanche had predicted, and cobwebs brushed my cheek more than once. The floorboards were misshapen and seemed to creak in protest under every footstep; one or two along the narrow landing were even missing, showing a drop into darkness below.

"Here we are," Blanche said, a little too heartily, hiding her fear from the princess as she pushed open the door. "Your old room, my lady. And just as you left it."

She had been right too about the smell, I thought, and wrinkled my nose. I hurried to close the shutters across the window, shivering with cold. A tendril of ivy was slapping against the cracked glass, the rain still lashing down outside. It was hardly a welcoming night to have arrived. But once the shutters were closed, the bedchamber did seem a little cosier. Though not much, I considered. The panelled walls were hung with old sun-faded tapestries to keep out the draughts, but the room itself was sparsely furnished with a covered bed, a rickety three-legged stool and a low table. It seemed strange to me that the Queen's sister should prefer to lay her head in such a grim place when she could have stayed at court and lived in the kind of comfort that befitted a Tudor. But perhaps Hatfield House had some hidden virtues which would become plainer in daylight—and when it was not blowing a gale outside.

Blanche set the lantern on the table and began to remove

the princess's black foreskirt, then the beautiful Spanish bodice which had been a parting gift from King Philip, sent privately with a note which Elizabeth had read and then torn into pieces, her face stiff and cold. Nonetheless, I noticed that Elizabeth had worn the gorgeous bodice twice on the journey now, perhaps because it was warm and well-made, perfect for travelling.

I helped, carefully unlacing the silk-embroidered sleeves from each shoulder, and then the princess's mud-soiled shoes, laying them aside to be scraped once dry. Alice struggled in with a basket of logs and a blushing young girl of about sixteen who seemed overawed by the Lady Elizabeth, despite the princess's kind reassurance that she remembered Lucy well. The two girls knelt to set the fire together, arguing in fierce whispers over the best way to make the twists until Blanche knocked their heads together. William and Alejandro came to the door soon after, having carried up the princess's clothes chests, and soon the Lady Elizabeth was sitting on the stool in a dry nightshift and woollen wrap, enjoying the heat of a fire while Blanche dried her hair with a clean rag. A plate of bread and cheese was produced by young Lucy, along with a pint pot of ale, and the princess consumed these in a daze, clearly exhausted by our long journey from court.

The bed was sagging and in serious disarray, so I set about thumping the feather mattress, straightening the bolsters, and shaking reluctant spiders out of the hangings. Clean sheets had been provided by Bessie, only a little musty-smelling from storage, and with Alice's help these were soon tied across the mattress. A hot brick wrapped in a fleece was positioned just below where her ladyship's feet would go, and left to heat the bed for a space. Several old furs and lacy woollen coverlets were found to keep the Lady Elizabeth snug and warm, and just as well, for the princess sneezed several times as she climbed into bed.

"Lord preserve us, I said you would catch your death in that wet gown and here you are sneezing!" Blanche exclaimed, hurriedly tucking the heavy furs in around Elizabeth's chest. "Did I not say so, my lady? This terrible rain will kill us all. There, there, take my handkerchief in case you should sneeze again, for I have not yet unpacked your own. Don't fret, Lucy is bringing you a hot sweet posset and then you shall sleep for as long as you like."

"Thank you, Blanche," Elizabeth murmured sleepily, her eyes already closing.

Blanche handed me a lit candle and shooed us out the door. "Hush, go now, and let her ladyship rest. Best find yourselves somewhere to sleep too, and don't come knocking with her breakfast until at least nine o'clock, for my Lady Elizabeth never gets up early at Hatfield."

Lucy showed me and Alice to the room we would be sharing, then left us alone to tidy ourselves while she hurried downstairs to prepare a "cold plate and ale" for us too. Our chest of clothes had not yet been brought upstairs, so we contented ourselves with brushing the mud from our skirts and straightening our damp caps. The fire in our room was unlit and the room was chilly, but the old retainer arrived after a few minutes with a large bag of straw and two mattress covers, which we sat on the floor to stuff.

A deep growling thunder rolled overhead several times.

Alice looked up, quivering with nerves. "Dear Lord, the thunder is so loud! What if the next bolt of lightning should strike the house?"

"Don't be such a goose, the storm's almost over," I told her, tying my mattress cover with a firm knot, then shaking it out so the straw was well-distributed. "Besides, why should it? We are all good Catholics here."

Alice stared, then saw that I was joking and covered her giggle with a nervous hand. "Meg, you should not say such things," she whispered. "It's…it's almost blasphemous."

"I'm sure God has better things to do than strike me down for making a jest," I told her tartly, and went to the window to close the shutters.

Lightning flashed at that moment, a brilliant white sheet of light that illuminated the grounds as though it were noon. I stared, my hand frozen on the shutter.

There was a hooded man standing on a flat stretch of grass between trees, gazing up at the house from the shadow of his hood. It seemed to me in that terrifying instant that he was looking right at my window, right into my soul, that he knew my name and everything about me. That he had come here to find me, in fact.

Then it was pitch-blackness again outside the window, only black rain lashing the glass and wind howling in the chimneys.

"Meg? What is it?" Alice asked, coming alongside me. Her eyes were wide as she too peered into the darkness.

"I thought I saw—" I began breathlessly, and then another lightning bolt lit up the grounds in a repeat of that brilliant flash, silencing me.

The grass between the trees now stood empty. The man had vanished into black rain and howling nothingness.

Were my fears still playing tricks on my mind? Ever since William had told me Marcus Dent was still alive, I had found it hard to sleep, imagining in the creaking darkness that Dent was standing at the end of my bed. But this fleeting vision was something new. It made no sense though. Not even a man as determined for revenge as Marcus could have found me so quickly, not when we had only just arrived at Hatfield

House—and when so few people had known we would be coming at all. Only a witch skilled in the ancient art of divination could have managed such a feat, and that was hardly likely for a witchfinder.

"Meg?" Alice was impatient, tugging on my gown.

I shook my head, forcing a laugh. "It was nothing," I told her firmly, and closed the window shutter. "Let's go down to the hall and find what there is to eat. If we don't hurry, I fear my brother will soon have eaten it all."

We met Lucy again below, running past us and up the stairs with a steaming hot posset for the Lady Elizabeth. "I'll be back to serve you by and by," she gasped in passing, her face flushed with the exertion and excitement of suddenly having a princess to wait upon—not to mention her entourage of ravenous servants.

I imagined it must be odd for the poor child to have this quiet secluded house suddenly full of people again. And what strange people! By the light of our candle, we looked like two giants entering the hall, great spidery shadows that stretched to the roof.

Alice grinned, finding my brother on the settle by the fire, poring over a shallow dish of the princess's sweetmeats. "You'll be in trouble now! Those are my lady's sweetmeats."

"Rain must have seeped into their wrappings during the journey and spoiled them; they are no longer good for the Lady Elizabeth to eat," he said defensively, and showed her the dish of sticky sweetmeats. "It seemed a waste to throw them out."

"Well, don't eat too many," she told William, "for more than a handful can cause an imbalance of the humours. One of the Queen's own doctors told me that. Well, one of his apprentices. He said it was not wholesome to eat too many sweetmeats."

William looked sceptical. "What did this 'apprentice' say we should be eating instead, then?"

"Goose fat," she said promptly.

I laughed at this nonsense and sat down comfortably next to my brother. It felt as though the past wrongs between us had been laid to rest over the journey here from Hampton Court. The fire down here had been well built-up at least, and the heat warmed my damp bones. I stared into the flaming heart of the logs, piled haphazardly in the vast stone hearth, and tried to shake off my sense of unease.

The older daughter, the widow Bessie, came bustling into the hall with a great bowl of ale. She placed this on the settle beside William and wiped her hands on her apron. "There's enough there for everyone to share. That's the last of the ale, but we'll have more brought up from the village tomorrow, with poultry and spices for the pot. I've made a hot pottage now and some bread to go with it too, if you've a mind to eat. It's only a poor meal, but should warm you."

"Sit and drink with us," William suggested as she turned to go.

Bessie looked horrified. "Oh, I couldn't do that, sir. It wouldn't be right. Besides, we had our ale at supper."

"Meg saw something outside," Alice said blithely, ignoring my warning stare, "from our chamber window."

Now Bessie turned to stare at me. She was a big girl, and puffed when she walked, yet suddenly she was still. "What did you see, mistress?"

I hesitated, unwilling to share my fears in this company. Now my brother was frowning at me too. Even the shadows seemed to bend in from the darkest corners of the hall, listening to our conversation. I felt under scrutiny, like a tiny insect in the palm of a child's hand.

Why did Alice have to meddle?

"Just for a moment, I thought I might have seen…a man." I tried to dismiss the whole incident as unimportant. And indeed perhaps it was. "A man standing out there in the rain. That's all. Then he disappeared."

"What was this man doing?" William asked intently.

Lucy had come back and was listening too, her eyes fixed on my face. I saw no point in lying. I shrugged. "Looking up at the house."

My brother's voice was insistent. "Did you see who it was? Did you see his face?"

I knew what he was thinking. The hairs crept up on the back of my neck. But I shook my head. "No, it could have been anyone. One minute he was there, and the next he was gone." I managed a laugh. "I…I'm so tired after that journey, I might even have imagined him."

Bessie sent Lucy back into the kitchen for the bread and a bowl of hot pottage. "Well, it could have been a poacher," she mused, "come here a-rabbiting or maybe after one of the deer. Some deer do come out of the woods on bad nights. Or it might have been Master Pollox, the groundsman. He likes to check all's secure around the place when the wind gets up."

Balancing pottage and bread along her arm, Lucy came back into the hall. "Or it might have been old Jack," she offered.

I frowned. "Old Jack?"

Bessie laughed and shook her head, stirring the vast pot, then setting it before us. "She means old Jack of the Woods," she explained, then made a hidden gesture to indicate that Lucy was simple. "Folk hereabouts used to call him the Green Man or Jack-a-the-Greenwood, and leave offerings to him at harvest. But don't pay my sister no mind. She's a good girl, but she still thinks the faeries brought her, you know?"

Lucy looked annoyed. "I do not!"

"Hush, child, they don't want to hear those old heathen stories. They're more used to songs and dancing at court. Go and make sure our father does not need any help in the kitchen. There'll be the pots to scour, and the oven to heat for tomorrow's bread."

Alice had been stuffing her mouth with bread and pottage—I could not blame her for this lack of manners, for it was many hours since we had eaten on the road to Hatfield—but on hearing this, she sat up eagerly. "We've been so gloomy at court this past year, I cannot remember when I last had a dance." She looked from one sister to the other. "Do you keep a lute here? Or any instrument?"

Bessie's face lit up with inspiration. "There's my lady's lute, that she used when she was a girl. It's still in the storeroom. Wait, I'll not be long." She hurried out of the hall. "You finish up your supper while I see if I can't find it."

I was not very hungry, but took a little dry bread and dipped it in the last of the pottage. It tasted surprisingly good, so I dipped the bread in again. I felt a little guilty that the princess had taken nothing but bread and cheese, but at least there should be a proper meal for her in the morning. There was the sound of feet on the stairs, descending softly, then Alejandro stood in the entrance to the hall.

I looked up at him longingly. It seemed an eternity since that sunlit day when Alejandro had ridden into the grounds at Woodstock, stern in his armour and white surcoat with its red cross. Sometimes it felt as though there had never been a time when I had not known him. Yet our very first meeting had been not much more than a year ago.

Impossible thought!

Alejandro smiled, stepping out of the shadows and into the firelight. He wore a black cap with a feather and carried a book under his arm. His damp cloak and muddied riding boots had been cast aside for a superb black doublet, double-slashed to reveal white silk beneath, and a pair of elegant black court shoes. I noticed that he was not wearing his sword, but carried a curved dagger on his belt instead, its handle ornate with gold and tiny rubies.

He looked every inch a Spanish nobleman, born to lead and command armies—and now that he was to inherit his father's title and estate, perhaps he might. Certainly, I thought wryly, no one seeing him would ever guess that he was still hoping to be admitted into the fighting priesthood, into the coveted Order of Santiago de Compostela.

My breath caught at the sight of him, heart clenching like a fist under my ribcage. Could this be love?

Sometimes my body ached and I thought, *Yes, this must be love.* In my darker moments though, I wondered if it was fear. For no one but Alejandro could ever have the power to destroy me with a single word, to shrivel me up inside like a dead leaf. No, not even Marcus Dent, nor the priests of the Inquisition with their terrible instruments of torture.

Except for a few golden hours, we had been kept apart from each other at Hampton Court. Kept apart by thick stone walls and endless corridors, by constant observation, by the stupid rules and conventions of courtly life. Yet here at Hatfield House there was little to separate us. Part of me dreaded being alone with him here, for I knew how vulnerable this secret courtship made me. But another part of me yearned for a chance to know Alejandro better, to return to the halcyon days of last summer when we had spent so many hours in each other's company.

"There you are at last, Señor de Castillo. Could you not

find the way down to us?" Alice had turned from the bowl
of pottage to admire him. "How very Spanish you look. Do
you play the lute?"

Sombrely, Alejandro inclined his head. His eyes met mine
as he answered her, and I wondered what he was thinking.
"I do indeed, *señorita*. To play the lute is a required skill for
all young men at the Spanish court."

"Such an accomplished priest!" she teased him, more talkative than I had ever seen her. It seemed the country air was
loosening her tongue. "I have seen you dance at court, but
can you sing too?"

"Again," he murmured, "it has been known to happen."

"But that's marvellous. You sing, you dance, you play the
lute...and you are an excellent swordsman too, they say." Alice
looked from him to me, a mischievous light in her eyes. "I'm
beginning to think you must be the perfect man."

His smile did not quite reach his eyes. "Oh, not perfect, *señorita*. No man is that. As I'm sure your friend would agree."

I felt uncomfortable, for that last comment was aimed directly at me. Alejandro was impatient that I had not yet formally agreed to marry him, even though he had given me a
year to make my final decision. But how could I marry him?
That would mean sailing to Spain with him, meeting his
family and perhaps settling in that strange hot country so far
away. And my first duty was to the Lady Elizabeth, who was
paying for my keep as part of her new household, and she was
far from safe, even here in Hatfield.

The danger was not over yet, I could feel it with every
step I took in this house. And until whatever threatened her
was dealt with, I could not be free to love Alejandro. There
was a gathering darkness above this place, a malignancy that
had followed us from court on the wings of the storm. I did
not yet know what it meant, but guessed it was connected to

the vile black shadow I had seen in the Great Hall at Hampton Court. Was it some kind of spirit-demon, feeding off the hatred and fear that surrounded the court? Whatever it was, this was not a good time to ignore my obligations to the Lady Elizabeth and accept a proposal of marriage.

Besides, I was a little nervous about the prospect of meeting his noble family in Spain.

After all, ours was not exactly an ideal match.

Briefly, I pictured their horrified faces at the family reunion: 'Mother, Father, I have the honour to introduce to you the witch I intend to make my bride." Then I had to bite back my wild laughter, for Alejandro was watching me again, a frown in his eyes.

Blowing out her cheeks, Bessie came hurrying back with the Lady Elizabeth's old lute. She dusted the instrument off with the edge of her apron, then presented it to Alice, who curtseyed and handed it to Alejandro with a smile and a wink.

"This old lute belongs to the Lady Elizabeth. I am sure as a nobleman of the Spanish court your skills must be at least equal to hers. Will you play us something, *señor?*"

The hall was suddenly lit up with a bright white sheet of lightning that flashed through the long windows, illuminating our astonished faces. Its dazzling light was followed almost immediately by a deafening crack of thunder so loud it sounded as if the storm was right above the house.

Alice gave a startled cry and hid her face in her hands. Bessie muttered something about "the Devil slamming a door in Hell!" My spine stiffened in instinctive warning and I glanced up, half expecting to see some malevolent black creature clinging to the painted ceiling of the hall. But there was nothing to see above us except shadows.

In the tense silence that followed the thunder, Alejandro

strummed a few experimental notes. "This lute needs to be tuned," he remarked. "Though it's not bad for its age."

At that moment, the door to the servants' quarters burst open and a grunting black-and-white pig ran in, closely pursued by Lucy.

The young girl was beating the pig with her apron, shouting, "Get out! Get out of here, you wicked, filthy creature!" while the rain-drenched animal ran round and round the echoing hall, squealing and knocking over a table in its terror. Everywhere it ran, it left muddy trotter-prints behind, like boundary marks on a map, so that Bessie exclaimed in dismay at the mess as much as the confusion. William jumped up with a gleeful shout and joined in the chase, grinning like a schoolboy. Lucy made a dive for the pig as it ran between his legs, but could not seem to get a grip on its slippery body. The pig easily wriggled free and doubled back, its large black ears flopping over its white face, no doubt hoping to escape the way it had come.

"Begging your pardon, but she must have pushed her way in from the back yard. She's terrible afeared of the thunder and lightning, you see!" Bessie explained to us, rather unnecessarily, then ran after the escaped pig in the direction of the kitchen, berating Lucy loudly as she went, until both sisters had vanished along with the unfortunate swine.

My brother grabbed Alice by the waist and spun her round, pretending to dance grotesquely with her while she shrieked with laughter.

"Time for a country dance after all that argy-bargy!" he cried. "Play us a pig pavane, de Castillo!"

I looked at Alejandro in disbelief, but he merely smiled at my brother and struck a jangling chord on the lute.

"Welcome to Hatfield House, welcome all," he sang gently, "where the rain never stops and pigs run about the hall."

★ ★ ★

That night, I dreamed again of the high tower, the wind in my hair, and Marcus Dent with his axe. When I awoke, it was with a fast-beating heart and a sweat-riven forehead, gasping in panic.

I saw now that by leaving court and accompanying my mistress to this quiet country house at Hatfield, I had left myself more open to attack. Marcus Dent, as my brother had warned me, was back and would be hungry for revenge. I did not know in what guise he had reappeared, nor how close he might be to hunting me down. But it was about time I found out.

1-1

THE CONJUROR'S APPRENTICE

I have never been particularly brave, and have often felt that if bad news will do me no good, I would rather not hear it. So it was with mixed feelings that I sat down privately with my brother a few days after our arrival at Hatfield to ask him about the witchfinder Marcus Dent.

Although I had hoped never to hear that vile name again, it had kept cropping up at court, and thanks to my recurring dream of the tower, would not be banished from my mind. After all, if Marcus Dent ever managed to shake off the tongue-tying spell I had laid on him at Woodstock Palace and regained the power to accuse me of witchcraft, it was better I should know with what strength he had returned. I was also keen to learn, if I could, what Dent had done since writing that discredited letter to the Inquisition, accusing the princess of some forbidden association with the Queen's astrologer.

It was no idle fear. I knew now that the witchfinder was

on my trail again, worrying at me like a dog with a bone. At any moment Marcus Dent might come hammering on the door to demand my arrest. Yes, and the Lady Elizabeth's too, for harbouring a witch in her household.

"I want you to tell me everything you know about Master Dent," I told William. "Leave nothing out."

We were sitting on a grassy bank under an ancient oak tree, the knotted roots of the tree stretching away in every direction. Behind us lay miles of woodlands and meadows bathed in sunlight where sheep grazed peacefully, calling out to each other from time to time as they ambled about the rough grasslands. Ahead of us stood the pretty side view of Hatfield House, a long building of red brick softened by tangles of ivy and climbing roses, and adorned with high twisting red chimneys which smoked thinly to keep out the autumnal chill. On top of the nearest chimney, the only one from which smoke was not issuing, a ragged crow sat and cawed hoarsely in the sunshine, surveying us with gleaming black eyes.

"I know almost nothing worth the telling," my brother began, then caught my look and sighed. "Very well. I do not pretend to understand this power you have, Meg. Nor do I entirely approve of it, for everyone knows that witchcraft is the work of the Devil." He picked a long stem of grass and twisted it between his fingers, his expression distracted. "But I know your power has served you well in the past, and I have never once seen you work evil with it."

I waited calmly, guessing from his hesitation that there was something more he needed to say.

"Except perhaps when you…" William shifted uncomfortably, not looking at me. "When you cast that terrible spell on Marcus Dent, the day in Woodstock village when he tried to drown you. I shall never forget it. One minute Dent was standing there, screaming insults at you, and the next he was gone. Sucked into that black wind you conjured out of nowhere. I don't know what spell you cast, but it smacked to me of dark magick, of the work of Satan."

"Dent would have murdered me, surely you understand that?" I thought for a moment, trying to decide how best to answer his fears. "Look, I don't know what I did that day either. It just happened. But I can assure you, I am no Devilworshipper. I am a witch, yes. But I always strive to use my skills for good ends and to follow the same path that Aunt Jane followed, the path of the hearth fire."

William nodded jerkily. "I know, I know. And I do want to believe you. But you're my little sister, Meg. I used to carry you on my back when you were a child. I can remember you being terrified of spiders and screaming for me in the night because you'd found one on your bed. I love you more than anyone else in the world, and I'm truly sorry for all the trouble and pain I've caused you this past year. But I never again want to watch my sister calling up a black wind that...that *swallows* people whole. It's just not natural."

I counted silently to ten, not wanting to lose my temper with him. I had already lost my aunt, and I was not sure I would ever forgive my father for his treachery, so William was all the family I had left.

"So, about Marcus Dent, what do you know?"

He shrugged. "The first I knew was when he came to Lytton Park to see our father, a few days after I'd got back from London."

"He spoke to Father? What about?"

"I don't know. It was early one morning and I was asleep. I heard them arguing and came downstairs, but Dent was already leaving. He had two men with him—apparently he never goes anywhere these days without a personal bodyguard—and I only caught a quick glimpse of his face, but he looked…well, he looked *wrong*."

"Wrong?"

"His face was badly scarred." Reluctantly, William traced two lines across his cheek to the corner of his mouth. "As though he'd been scratched by a wild animal. His skin was a coarse dark red, as though he'd been travelling under a hot sun all summer. And…"

"Go on," I prompted him when he hesitated.

"He wore his cap pulled low, so I did not see this myself. But when I spoke to Father afterwards, he told me Dent had lost an eye."

This description filled me with foreboding. What precisely had my spell of banishment done? I might have cast a spell on Dent so that he could not accuse me either by word or in writing, but that did not mean he could not take his revenge in some other way—perhaps by hurting me physically, or accusing those nearest me.

I wondered why Dent had visited Lytton Park. Had he been looking for me? That did not seem likely. I had made no secret of my allegiance to the Lady Elizabeth, nor that I was following her to court. Anyone in Woodstock and the surrounding villages could have told him where I was.

"You said he argued with our father. You do not think Dent means to do him some harm?"

"I may not have your powers of sorcery, Meg, but I am not a fool. I would never have left Oxfordshire if I had thought Father was not safe on his own there."

"I hope you are right," I said. "It sounds to me as though Dent is in a dangerous mood and looking for revenge."

William looked at me broodingly. "If he is, it was your spell that made him so."

I would have liked to point out that Marcus Dent had always been a dangerous man, and indeed that he would have drowned me as a witch if I had not used that spell on him. But I could see Blanche Parry heading towards us from the house, carrying what looked like two large cushions. Behind her came the retainer's two daughters, Bessie and Lucy, with covered baskets in their arms. Then I saw the Lady Elizabeth herself leaving the house, followed by Alejandro—who looked rather like a court minstrel with a lute strung across his back—and Alice, clutching the hem of the princess's gown and trying not to let it brush the still-dewy grass.

"It seems we are eating lunch outside today," I murmured, and allowed William to help me to my feet.

The Lady Elizabeth pointed to a spot near the oak tree, and Blanche threw down the cushions, rearranging them to her satisfaction. The two maids bobbed a curtsey and hurried back to the house for their own lunch. I watched them go, noticing that the last chimney was smoking now and the ragged crow had flown away, no doubt fearing to be cooked alive on its perch.

My brother seemed uncomfortable at the sight of the Lady Elizabeth. He was not attached to the princess's household and had been sleeping in the stables since accompanying us here from Hampton Court. Now he looked guilty for having been seen in her grounds by the princess, like a boy caught scrumping apples from his neighbour's orchard.

"I am not supposed to be here," William muttered in my ear. "I should leave Hatfield. I only wished to be sure you were safe, Meg, and that you knew of Marcus Dent's return. But now that is done, I will return to London and seek new employment."

"Wait," I whispered, hanging on to his sleeve. "Stay with me here a while longer. The princess will not turn you away." I saw his uncertainty, and begged, not wishing to lose touch with my brother so soon after fate had pushed us together again. "Please?"

William smiled. "Very well, Meg. If her ladyship is kind enough to permit it, I will stay until I am no longer of any help to you."

The Lady Elizabeth turned to us. "Señor de Castillo is going to play some Spanish songs for us while we take a small luncheon under this tree. Come and sit by me, Meg. I had a strange dream last night and wish you to interpret it for me." Her dark gaze flickered over William with sudden interest. "This is your brother, is it not? I have seen him about the house, but do not believe we have been introduced."

I introduced them with a curtsey, watching hopefully from under my lashes as he bowed over her pale hand and made a few flattering remarks about her beauty. Elizabeth liked young men, especially those with a neat figure and a handsome face like my brother. And if William was lucky, the princess would not remember his part in the theft of her letter.

We sat on the grass together, protected from the damp by cushions and blankets that had been strewn about there. The baskets were uncovered to reveal delicious cold meats and pies, with a tankard of local ale to be shared between us, the Lady Elizabeth joining in thirstily as the cup went round and wiping her mouth on the back of her hand afterwards, like any other girl.

Later, while we picked drowsily at dishes of sweetmeats, Alejandro stood in the spreading shade of the oak and played the lute for us.

He began with a well-known tune from court, a lively dance that soon had Alice's feet tapping.

"Now sing to us in Spanish, *por favor*, Señor de Castillo," was the Lady Elizabeth's request, applauding him with pleasure. "But make it a love song this time. And a sad one. I am too full of eel pie for dancing."

"A Spanish love song," he repeated musingly.

"But a sad one," she reminded him, smiling. "A song of parted lovers and aching hearts."

"*Muy bien, mi princesa.*"

His dark head bent over the lute strings, his fingers strumming gently as he considered what to play. Then Alejandro began to sing softly in Spanish. I did not know what the words meant, but his voice was so sad and tender my eyes soon filled with tears and I lay back on my cushion, my fingers knotting themselves helplessly in the grass as I listened.

Alejandro lifted his head and looked straight at me as the song came to a close, his voice dropping to a husky murmur, the Spanish barely audible. Yet the sense of his words was communicated by his eyes and fingers, and by the achingly mellow notes of the lute.

I love you, he was saying with his whole body, *but I know we can never be together.* His fingers slowed on the lute strings, each note drawn out, poignant. *I love you, though our love must end.*

Alejandro's gaze darkened, his eyes staring into mine. His voice rose and fell for the last time. *I love you, but death will soon part us.*

In the long silence after his song had finished, I slowly became aware of the rhythmic thud of hoof beats in the distance. One horseman, approaching at a breakneck pace from the road to London. Nor was I the only one who had heard him.

My brother was already on his feet, shielding his eyes against the sunlight as he tried to make out the horseman's identity.

"Who is it?" the Lady Elizabeth whispered, suddenly very still, a hand to her throat. No doubt she thought this might be another accusation of treason on its way. Or else that miraculous news she never quite dared hope for, that her sister was dead and she was Queen at last.

"I cannot see, my lady. A single rider. But he will soon be upon us. Do you wish to return to the house for safety?"

Alejandro had laid down his lute. Now he trod swiftly forward as though to guard us from attack, his hand falling to his sword hilt. His gaze met mine briefly, and then he swung to face the approaching danger.

"Yes," Elizabeth muttered, letting Alice help her to rise, then stood there indecisive, measuring the distance from the lawn to the house with an uncertain eye. Her voice grew stronger. "No, no. I shall not flee from a lone messenger. Let the dice fall where they may. I am the Queen's sister and I have done nothing wrong."

The horseman came into clearer view, kicking up sods of turf as he galloped hard along the grassy track. He looked like a young man, his body bent low over the horse's neck, cloak billowing out behind him like a black cloud, the reins held short as he wrenched the horse off the track and towards where we were standing.

"Whatever message he bears is urgent," Alejandro commented, "or he would not risk killing his horse to deliver it."

Dragging hard on the reins, the young man pulled his sweating horse to a stop and slid from the animal's back. He took one swift assessing look at us all, his gaze touching on me a moment longer than the others, then dropped to one knee before the Lady Elizabeth.

"My lady," he said hoarsely, "I come with a letter from Master John Dee. It has been written in code, but my master says you will understand what it means."

Her face very pale, Elizabeth took the letter he was holding out in his gloved hand. She handed it to me, then carefully removed a small scrap of paper from the leather pocket hanging from her belt. This she unfolded, then took back the letter from Dee. Glancing from one to the other as she checked the code key against Dee's writing, her body stiffened as she read. When she had finished, she looked down at the kneeling messenger. "You are Richard, apprentice to Master Dee?"

"I am, my lady."

"If I have understood this letter aright, your master says he has been released from prison and means to visit me here. Where is he at this moment, and how long does he intend to stay?"

The young man glanced at the rest of us, not replying.

Surprised, she glanced round at us too, her gaze lingering a moment on my brother, William, then gestured him to continue. "These are members of my household. You may speak freely before them."

"Yes, my lady," he muttered, but did not bother to hide his reluctance. "Master Dee intends to leave London tomorrow. He has been released only on the agreement that he will take up work on behalf of the crown, though I do not know what that work might be. So he will not stay long, perhaps a few days. My master told me he would travel mainly by night, taking the back roads and making several diversions to shake off any of the Queen's spies who might be following him. By my reckoning, he should arrive by Thursday."

"Three days?" Elizabeth sounded surprised. But she nodded, folding Dee's letter very small and concealing it within her belt purse. "You may stand, Richard. Do you know the contents of this letter?"

Dee's apprentice stood up, dusting down his knee with his gloved hand. He was not as tall as he had seemed on his horse. He was perhaps a head shorter than Alejandro, and far leaner too, his build wiry but muscular, like a hunting hound. Dressed all in black, his clothes were mud-spattered from the road and serviceable rather than well-cut, an indication of his status as an apprentice. I guessed him to be around eighteen or nineteen years of age, a slight stubble on his chin revealing that he had not shaved that day. He had not removed his cap in the princess's presence, which I felt was an act of insolence, but could see that his hair was dark and unkempt, curling at the back into his shoulders like a beggar's.

Richard was not unattractive, I thought, yet there was something about him that made me uneasy. And it was not just his rough appearance. His mouth was straight and un-smiling as he looked back at the princess.

"I do, my lady."

She smiled, not angry as I had expected, but seeming to want to cajole him. "Come, Richard. Is it such a hardship to join my household until your master arrives?"

So Master Dee had asked the Lady Elizabeth to accept this young man into her service. I was taken aback, and looked him over more carefully. Certainly he would not be hired for his charm. Richard said nothing in reply but held her gaze flatly, amazing me with his churlishness. But perhaps as apprentice to a man like Dee, who lurched from being in great company to being an outcast and a prisoner, he was unused to courtly manners.

At this point, Alejandro stepped forward to intervene. I could not remember ever seeing him look so cold with dislike.

"Here, boy, allow me to show you the way to the stables," he said pointedly, taking up the horse's slack reins. "Your mount is tired, and in need of fresh water and hay. William has been sleeping above the stables. Perhaps we can find you a bed there too."

Dee's apprentice stared at him, then held out his hand for the reins. "I can lead my own horse to the stables. Yes, and make my own bed too."

Shrugging, his face full of disdain, Alejandro handed him the reins. "As you prefer."

Not moving, Richard met his gaze with a hard look of his own. "You must be the Spanish priest."

If Alejandro was surprised by this, he did not show it. But his back was stiff, and I could tell that he was angered by the boy's lack of respect. "My name is Alejandro de Castillo, and I am a novice in the Holy Order of Santiago de Compostela."

"Yes, like I said." He glanced over his shoulder at me, then turned back to Alejandro. I had the suspicion he was mocking us. "My master told me of you. Before I left London, he gave me a message for you."

"A message? What possible message could John Dee have for me?"

"Only that your life is in danger," Richard replied shortly, then bowed to the princess and turned to lead his horse to the stables.

"Is that all?" Alejandro threw after him with a sceptical laugh. "I thank you for the warning, and shall be sure to sleep with a dagger under my pillow from now on."

As Richard walked away, I saw for the first time that he was limping. Badly too, as though one leg was considerably shorter than the other. Alice had noticed his limp too and was crossing herself to ward off evil, for like many folk she feared that an imperfect body must be a sign of the Devil's favour. For my own part, I did not think it a sign of anything but some misfortune in the past.

On the other hand, Richard was certainly rude and surly enough to be a servant of the Devil. But was his message from John Dee true? Could Alejandro's life be in danger?

12

DARK OF THE MOON

Master John Dee himself arrived, as promised by his apprentice, on Thursday evening at dusk. He came disguised as a travelling tinker, his pony's sides clanking with pots and pans, his cloak patched and stinking of horse droppings, and with what appeared to be a dead badger strapped to his head. Calling at the back door with samples of his wares, he was taken in that way by a fascinated Bessie, and news of his arrival carried up to the princess by Alice while he rested by the kitchen fire.

William was sent down to smuggle John Dee and his apprentice across the darkening lawns to a place where the astrologer could stay unseen at Hatfield—a rough low hut about a quarter of a mile from the house, hidden amongst trees in an abrupt dip said to be the site of an old midden, or rubbish heap. Bessie had recommended it as a hiding place, not knowing the identity of this silent tinker, but eager to help her royal mistress to conceal him. I believe the hut had been built to house goatherds, when there were still goats kept around there, but the place had been long since abandoned and left to rot.

"I cannot allow Dee to be recognized while he is staying here," the princess muttered, pacing her chamber while she waited to be given the signal that all was quiet below. "No one would believe any meeting between us to be innocent."

Since their meeting was far from innocent, I found this amusing. I bent my head to hide my smile though. The Lady Elizabeth had no sense of humour where her sister was concerned.

"It is imperative that I consult with Master Dee while he is here, but we must be careful," she insisted, perhaps guessing my thoughts. "I am not sure how far we can trust the servants, though I believe old John's two daughters are loyal to me and not the Queen. But my sister's spies watch us even here at Hatfield. I feel their eyes on me every time I set foot outside the house."

Once night had fallen, the Lady Elizabeth carefully wrapped herself in a hooded cloak, and went to see the astrologer.

Alice and I accompanied her through the shadowy grounds, with Alejandro as our guard and lookout. In case the house was being watched, we left by the back door and walked in darkness to the edge of the trees. Then Alejandro produced a tinderbox from under his cloak, lit the lantern for us, and we continued on into the woods.

It was the dark of the moon, when the nights are at their blackest, and the thin light of our lantern showed little but a circle of scrubground beneath our feet. My senses prickled as we came closer to Dee's hiding place. The ground suddenly sloped away there, steep and pitted with rocks, and the prin-

cess clutched at my arm for balance. The swaying light of the
lantern touched on a hawthorn growing aslant on the slope,
the faeries' tree under which no man should fall asleep for
fear of being taken. I took care not to touch it, but Elizabeth's
fingers brushed its leaves quite deliberately, the tree rustling
beneath her touch, and I suddenly recalled that the hawthorn
was associated with the house of Tudor.

There was a flicker in the darkness, then a door creaked
open and I saw the goatherds' hut right before us, a ramshackle building with ancient leaning timbers and mud walls.
Dee's apprentice stood in the doorway. Behind him a small
fire smoked in the centre of the hut.

"My lady," Richard muttered, and stepped aside for her to
enter. He met my gaze as I followed the princess inside, and
I wondered what I had done to offend him, his eyes were
so hard.

Dee was waiting for us behind a roughly made table, his
head bent as he pored over an open book. He had removed
his disguise and washed the dirt from his face and hands, but
although the false beard and hair had gone, there was still a
goatish stench about him. Or it could have been the hut's previous occupants we could smell. I said nothing but wrinkled
my nose, and saw Alice doing the same.

The astrologer closed his book and came forward to greet
the Lady Elizabeth, bowing deeply.

"I thank you for agreeing to see me, my lady," he murmured. "I did not wish to endanger you, given my recent
incarceration at the Fleet, but I believe my visit here may be
vital to your safety and to the future of England."

"Indeed?" Elizabeth asked coldly, and I knew she was angry
at having been put at such risk by his visit. Nonetheless, her
powerful desire to know if and when she would ascend the
throne was still stronger than her fear of discovery.

Dee gestured her to a low stool. "I am afraid this is the only seat in the place. The others must stand or wait outside, for there is little room to sit on the ground." His curious gaze dismissed Alice as unimportant, but hesitated on my face before moving to Alejandro. "Ah, the young Spaniard."

"Sir," Alejandro said stiffly.

"My boy Richard tells me you did not much care for my message."

"I did not believe it, sir."

Dee raised his brows in mild surprise. "Really? I was told of your death by a most reliable spirit, and that it would come soon. Or rather, that you would surely die if certain conditions were not met."

My skin was cold. I saw Alejandro about to remonstrate with him and interrupted, "What were these conditions, Master Dee?"

Dee smiled, turning to me at once. "Nothing you could alter by knowing them, and indeed to know them might prove dangerous. It is good to see you again, Meg Lytton, though I could have wished for a more congenial setting. So much power, so much potential…" As he had done before, he took my hands, turning them over again to trace the lines on my palm. His gaze lingered on my finger, where the nail had been ripped away by Miguel de Pero. The torn skin had healed but was still discoloured, the fingertip a dull purplish red. "What happened here?"

"The Inquisition," I murmured.

"I see." Alejandro moved instinctively to my side, as though furious that the astrologer had dared to touch me, and Master Dee dropped my hands. "This young man is your protector?"

I could not at first reply. How to answer Dee truthfully without revealing our betrothal to everyone there?

Something in me balked at the thought of the Lady Elizabeth and her whole household knowing our private business, not least because I knew it would displease the princess to discover that her priest had fallen in love with one of her ladies. She might tease me at times about Alejandro's attentiveness, but I guessed she found him quite attractive herself. Besides which, the princess made no secret of the fact that she preferred her female attendants to remain chaste like her—and uninterested in marriage.

I said at last, "It's not like that," and caught a gleam of mockery in the eyes of his watchful apprentice. Damn him! But the anger had cleared my head, and I answered more confidently, "Señor de Castillo is a soldier, as well as a novice. He protects us all."

"*Señor,* would you watch the door for us outside? We must not be disturbed," Elizabeth asked.

Alejandro bowed and left the hut without speaking, closing the door behind him quietly. But I had seen his hand clenched on the hilt of his sword and knew how angry he was. Not being one to believe in this talk of spirits and stars, he probably thought John Dee was simply trying to scare us and make himself look more formidable as an astrologer. And perhaps it was safer for now if Alejandro held on to that belief, for his faith was like a great light shining in this darkness.

Elizabeth turned back to Dee, a deep concern in her face. "This is most worrying. I need Señor de Castillo by my side. He is a necessary barrier between me and my sister, and I would not lose his strength for all the world. What can be done to prevent this death, Master Dee?"

Apologetically, Dee spread his pale hands wide. "I cannot say for sure, my lady. The spirit was not at all clear in his message. But he did suggest that a sacrifice would be required if the Spaniard is to live."

"What kind of sacrifice?" I demanded, and felt myself shiver before he even replied.

"Human," Dee murmured.

Alice cried out and put a hand to her mouth. Beside her on the stool, the Lady Elizabeth drew a sharp breath, then crossed herself.

"May it never come to that, God willing," she responded, and I could see that she was shocked and perhaps even a little disbelieving.

To me, it seemed inevitable. Of course it would take nothing less than a human sacrifice to save Alejandro from death. My fingertips buzzed painfully with the need to work magick, my scalp prickling as I tried to keep myself calm. My powers were running high that night, responding perhaps to the proximity of the great conjuror John Dee. I had not forgotten what Dee had shown me in his cell at the Fleet Prison, nor the vision that had haunted me for months now, of the desolate place where I would kneel for my death, Marcus Dent behind me with an axe in his hands.

I wanted to scry in the dark mirror again tonight; beg Dee to show me what the stars held in store for Alejandro. But I must not forget why we were there—to allow the Lady Elizabeth to consult John Dee in safety and secrecy. Nothing else mattered.

In the uneasy silence, Dee unrolled a chart and weighted it down on the table with two large rocks. "Shall we look at your stars and their transits, my lady? You see here? This symbol represents the planet Mars, that has proved most troublesome to you this year. It provokes anger and conflict in a man's chart and suggests marriage for a young woman. But in the chart of a princess, it may indicate war."

"War?" Elizabeth looked startled.

"A war between countries," Dee suggested, frowning over the chart, "or a war between sisters."

"And who will win this war?"

He studied the chart for a moment in silence, then conceded, "That is not shown. I can consult the angels on this question, however, for often when a chart is unclear they can provide enlightenment."

Her brows rose. "What else?" she asked icily.

"Saturn may be a growing problem for you," he indicated a symbol on the chart, "both natally and in transit. As the planet swings around the zodiac, it will make a troubling aspect to your Moon in Taurus."

I craned my neck to see what he was pointing at, but it was unclear. The crabbed black symbols were too tiny and intricate for me to make out. I had not been invited to view the princess's horoscope so did not dare lean in to study it. But even from a distance of several feet I could see the powerful lines criss-crossing her diamond-shaped chart.

"A dark spirit comes to haunt you," Dee concluded thoughtfully, tapping the house containing her Moon in the sign of Taurus as though it held all the answers.

"A dark spirit?" I repeated, staring at him in horror, and saw Elizabeth's head swivel like an owl's.

Angrily, the princess flicked her fingers at me to take a step back, and I had no choice but to obey. But my heart was beating fast. *A dark spirit. A dark spirit comes to haunt you.* What could he mean but the vile shadow-thing I had seen at Hampton Court?

There was sweat on my forehead and I wiped it away with my sleeve. The fire was so hot in this little space. My gown felt too tight and it was getting hard to breathe.

I had felt for several days now that the vile creature had followed us here from court, maybe some vicious Hell-spirit intent on destroying Elizabeth. But without proof I could hardly speak of my fears to the princess, or indeed to Alejandro. They would think I was mad. I had often wondered myself if I was mad, for what I had seen in the Great Hall at Hampton Court made no sense—except perhaps to an inflamed brain.

"This is a subtle transit," Dee continued, "but a powerful one that may change you for ever. I urge caution though. Saturn is a malevolent planet and often the harbinger of death."

Something was happening to me. I began to clench my fists as Dee was speaking. Then my mouth stiffened into a grimace, I could not control it. Everything in my body was reacting to his reading of the chart, the tiny hairs standing up on my arms and on the back of my neck, my stomach aching, my head throbbing with the pain of a megrim that had come on sudden and violent as a thunderclap.

I must have made some sound, because Elizabeth suddenly glanced round at me, exasperated. "Stand away from us, Meg! I do not need a village witch to interpret my horoscope. Astrology is not a woman's skill but a man's."

I willed myself to obey. Yet I could not seem to move. I could hardly speak either, I felt possessed. My eyeballs were burning in their sockets, my tongue heavy and leaden in my mouth.

A voice inside me was whispering, *Look at the horoscope. Look at the stars. Speak to the lines they draw across the chart. Look to the transits.*

The small hut began to burn in my vision. My gown had caught fire, I was going up in flames. I would be consumed for all eternity, damned as a witch. The shadows danced crazily about the walls, heaving up and down like a tidal river in flood.

I stared, fixed and intent on the princess's horoscope, and

heard the voice inside shouting, Look to them! *Look to the lesser and the greater lights!*

Elizabeth stood. Her face was contorted, as though she too was possessed. "I commanded you to stand away, Meg! Why do you not obey? Don't make me dismiss you from my service."

Dee met my eyes for a moment in silent warning.

I stepped back, gasping and trembling, my blood thundering at my temples.

I had not shouted. I had not even spoken. My gown was not on fire. The room was smoky and warm, but pleasantly so. Whatever powerful creature had possessed me for those few moments of madness had left me empty. I slumped against the wall, limp and used-up, a weak-minded fool who had allowed herself to be violated.

"Elsewhere in the chart," Dee continued more quietly, his voice so low that I could hardly hear him, "I fear that the transit of Venus to your natal Jupiter may bring you too much into prominence at court this winter, when it might be better to lie quiet in the country."

They spoke together in murmurs for some time while I pressed my back against the wall of the hut, feeling sure I must be mad. The voice in my head had gone, but for those few seconds it had utterly consumed me, left me wrung out like a cloth, my body so cold away from the fire that I began to shiver.

Alice stood fretting and white-faced by the door, not looking at me any more. I was not surprised. My odd behaviour must have frightened her, left speechless, staring like a madwoman at Dee's horoscope. I tried to catch her eye but Alice bent her head to examine her own foot, looking as though she wished she was anywhere but here, stuck in this dangerous place with a crazy witch and a man who had already been arrested once as a suspected traitor. In the end, I gave up trying to bring her round and focused on the astrologer instead, catching the occasional remark whenever Dee raised his voice.

Richard came in from outside, stamping mud off his boots. It had been a damp start to the autumn and some of the grounds were still flooded from the last heavy rainfall.

"Your priest is not very talkative."

I glared at him, but was glad of the excuse to give up my vain attempt at listening to Dee. "Alejandro is not mine," I whispered, not wanting to disturb the horoscope reading again, "and he's not a priest either. He's a novice."

He shrugged. "Still not very talkative though, is he?"

"Perhaps you said nothing to interest him."

"Or perhaps he's an arrogant fool who will one day need my help and won't get it." Dee's apprentice came very close to me in the cramped, smoky hut. I longed to shrink away, finding his presence disturbing, but did not want to give this boy the satisfaction. His skin was swarthy, like a Celt's, and his eyes were almost black. He narrowed them now, watching me. "You have courage, don't you? I admire that in a woman."

I did not reply, looking back at him coldly.

Richard seemed to mistake my stillness for encouragement. He seized my chin and wrenched my head towards the firelight, studying my face. "I doubt your priest would ever be interested in what I have to say. But I know something that might interest a witch."

"Take your hands off me!"

"Easy, girl, I was only looking. I don't bite." His hands dropped away, yet he did not move, still standing so close we were almost touching. "Not unless you beg me to."

He was laughing at me.

My temper flared and I stepped away. I spread my fingers

wide and pointed at him, opening my mouth for a curse that would teach this rude, black-eyed, upstart apprentice a lesson.

Suddenly I was flat on my back, my ears buzzing as though filled with bees, unsure exactly how I had got there. My body hurt though. My back was aching, and I felt dizzy and badly winded as though someone had punched me in the stomach.

I tried to sit up and the beamed ceiling of the hut swam violently above me. Laying my head back down on the rough ground, I closed my eyes and tried to regain control. That vile black creature on the ceiling at Hampton Court. Was it here again now? Was that *thing* the unknown force that had suddenly knocked me off my feet?

Dimly I heard Elizabeth exclaim in horror, then opened my eyes to find that John Dee had come to stand over me.

The astrologer helped me to my feet. "What happened?"

I shook my head, staggering slightly. "I...I don't rightly know, sir. It felt as though something threw me across the room."

Dee turned to look at his apprentice accusingly. "Richard, did you do this?"

It seemed like the stupidest question to be asking at such a moment, and I stared blankly at the astrologer. Of course his apprentice had not thrown me to the ground. Was the man a fool? Could he not tell this had been some kind of supernatural attack?

To my amazement, Richard did not deny his master's accusation. He shrugged, watching me through the smoke. "The witch was about to curse me. What was I supposed to do?"

"Duck," John Dee suggested drily. "Now, why don't you three young people wait outside until we are finished? And don't forget to apologize to Meg, Richard. Or I may be tempted to send you back to the gutter where I found you."

★ ★ ★

It was considerably cooler outside the hut. Banished while Dee finished his consultation with the princess alone, I stood a little way from Alejandro and tried not to register his brooding stare. Yes, he was angry with me, as well as angry with Richard, and it was something we would need to deal with before long. But for tonight, the only thought in my head was, *How on earth had Richard done that?*

"What happened in there?" I demanded, staring at Dee's apprentice. I saw Alejandro's head turn. "Are you a witch?"

Richard was fiddling with the pin on his cloak, which had become entangled in its folds. He looked up at my question, raising his eyebrows. "I beg your pardon? Do I look like a witch?"

"I don't know, what does a witch look like?"

"Nothing like me, that's for sure." His face turned hard as granite, giving nothing away. "I can see you at the end of a hangman's rope though, Meg Lytton. Best be careful what you say."

I considered trying to force him to answer me with magick. A spell to reveal the truth. Then I remembered his trick of knocking me flat on my back, and changed my mind. My aunt had often said there were many paths to the truth. Rather than continue to argue and make him angry, it might be better to try another route.

I smiled, leaning close to him. "Don't worry, I understand."

"You do?"

"I was afraid to admit it myself at first. There's no shame in that. Not when our kind are hunted down like wild animals, then hanged from a gibbet for all to see." My voice grew warmer, drawing him in, making him drop his guard. For a moment the soft light from the lantern glowed brighter, a shining circle of protection against the darkness. Our eyes met. "But you are amongst friends. You may speak freely here. We will not betray you."

"You think I'm afraid?"

"We are all different, Richard." My voice was honeyed, seeking to ensnare him in the spell. Eyes, voice, words, breath. My hands moved slowly, tracing an ancient sign in the air. "Those of us who are given the power must choose our own road. I do not judge you for yours."

But Dee's apprentice was wholly unaffected by the spell, observing my efforts with what I knew to be scorn. My heart sank as he bowed with a mock flourish. "I am glad to hear it, mistress. Did you bring anything to drink, or can you perhaps conjure me up a large cup of ale? I'm parched."

Alejandro had been listening to this exchange with a puzzled expression, his brows knitted together. Now he came forward. There was a threat in his voice. "This boy is a witch?"

"Less of the *boy,* if you please, Señor Priest." Richard smiled coldly, showing his teeth. "And no, as I have just been at pains to demonstrate, I am not a witch. Though I do possess certain powers. Powers a mere woman could never hope to understand."

"Oh, I see," I muttered, trying to rein in my temper. "And what are these powers? Where did you learn them?"

Richard looked at me with undisguised contempt. "I did not need to 'learn' them, as you might learn a mathematical table or a foreign language. They were mine by right of birth. Some have been worked upon by practice and study, it's true. Master Dee helps me with that. But most of my powers are natural and come to me from God."

At this, Alejandro gave a snort of disbelief.

Shooting him a look of acute dislike, Richard continued, "Master Dee tells me he has never met anyone else with such powerful God-given gifts, that I am a true adept."

"But what can you do?" I demanded.

Richard's glance was dry. "You mean, besides flattening you like a buzzing fly before you could work your woman's magick on me?"

"You did *what?*" Alejandro came fiercely between us, his hand on the hilt of his sword, his dark stare fixed on the apprentice's face.

The difference in their heights was more noticeable now, the Spaniard easily taller and more broad-shouldered than Richard. Alejandro was also the more angry of the two, his temper rarely roused but far more intense than my own. He meant every word when he was angry, and that determination was what made him dangerous.

"I swear to you, sirrah," Alejandro growled, "you hurt this lady, I will make you hurt in your turn a thousand-fold."

Richard glared back at him. "Try it, Priest."

His sword was halfway out of the scabbard before I could intervene. My hand gripped Alejandro's right arm. "Stop, Alejandro! Put up your weapon. We must not fight amongst ourselves, we are all here to serve the Lady Elizabeth and keep her safe from harm. Or had you forgotten your promise of allegiance?"

The two young men stood staring at each other by the pale light of the lantern, face to face, like two rams poised to lock horns in battle.

To my relief, Alejandro's good sense seemed to return. He took a deliberate step backwards and sheathed his sword again. I could see from his eyes that he was still burningly angry, but in control of himself.

"Don't touch her again," he muttered, but directed this remark to the air rather than the apprentice, so it wouldn't need to be answered.

Alice had covered her face with shaking hands during their

abrupt confrontation, but peeked again now. "Oh, good, you're not killing each other. Please don't start fighting." She sat down heavily on a fallen tree trunk. "I can't bear men who shout. They remind me of my father."

"Forgive me," Alejandro said unevenly. He looked at me, then away. "I lost my temper."

"Well, I'm not sorry," Richard remarked, seeing my expectant glance, "so don't expect me to apologize. The priest started it."

"He has a name," I reminded him.

"Yes, and I'll stop calling him 'priest' when he stops calling me 'boy,'" Richard promised, and crossed himself with utter solemnity. "I swear on my life."

Alejandro's jaw clenched. He turned to face him again, the anger back in his face. "Are you blaspheming now?"

This time I put a hand on Alejandro's chest and pushed him away. Forcefully. "Look, why don't you go and stand over there by Alice?" I suggested, and shook my head in disbelief. I couldn't understand why he had become so tense and aggressive since Richard's arrival. The last thing we needed was to fight amongst ourselves and risk drawing dangerous attention to John Dee's presence here. "Go look for spies. Guard the doorway. *Please,* Alejandro."

Reluctantly, he obeyed me and at last I was able to speak to Richard without interruption. I led Dee's apprentice a few feet away from the hut, out of the narrow circle of light cast by the lantern we had brought, so we could talk without being overheard. All the same, I was careful not to arouse Alejandro's temper by standing too close to Richard.

"So, these powers. You can push people away with your mind, like you did with me before? You don't need to use words?"

Richard frowned, not understanding. "Words?"

"Spoken spells."

"I told you, I'm not a witch."

I digested that, confused. I had once or twice managed a familiar spell without using words, but in general my spells tended to work better when accompanied by exhortations and commands in Latin. That ancient tongue just seemed more in tune with the natural universe.

"What else can you do?"

He folded his arms across his chest, staring at me broodingly. "Why should I tell you? You give me nothing in return."

I hesitated, wary now. "What do you want in return?"

"That depends what you want to give me."

I was annoyed by his mocking replies. "This isn't a game, Richard."

He raised his eyebrows. "Isn't it? That's a pity, I was just about to break the rules."

"What are your other powers?"

He contemplated me in silence for a moment, then shrugged. "I can speak with spirits."

I shuddered, remembering my terrifying interview with Dee in his cell. The astrologer had conjured my aunt's spirit against my wishes; I had looked into her dead eyes and felt real fear. Such spells were neither right nor natural, though they were a great show of strength by the conjuror.

"You mean the dead?"

"No, I mean spirits. Don't you know the difference?"

"Enlighten me."

Richard smiled. "Maybe one day. Not tonight." He saw me shivering and took off his cloak, offering it to me. "Cold or frightened?"

"Cold." I took the cloak gratefully, swinging it about my

shoulders, and only hoped Alejandro would not interpret that acceptance as a sign of some special favour. "Thank you."

He hesitated, as if considering whether or not he should speak further. Then clearly reached a decision. "I heard you'd had trouble with Marcus Dent, the witchfinder from Oxfordshire?"

I stiffened at the sound of that hateful name. "You could say that, yes. Marcus Dent burnt my aunt as a heretic, and would have hanged me as a witch if he could."

Richard was watching me closely. "Did you know that Marcus Dent and my master were friends at university?"

"What?"

"I guessed you did not know." Richard looked satisfied. "Yes, as young men they studied together for several years at Oxford. Afterwards, Dent went to Germany to complete his studies. My master chose the Low Countries instead, enrolling in the university at Louvain. Clearing out an old chest once, I found a letter that Dent had written on his return to England, and asked who this Marcus was. He told me they'd been friends, and had shared an interest in astronomy and alchemy, but that Dent had grown obsessed with witchcraft and the Devil. So obsessed, by the time he returned from Germany, that he could talk of nothing else."

I felt sick. "Why did Master Dee never tell me this?"

"My master was not aware that you knew Dent until it was too late to warn you what kind of man he was."

"And what is your part in all this?"

"When I speak to the spirits, Meg, they tell me things to relay to my master. Secrets presented in coded images, or clues on how to interpret the deeper meaning of the Scriptures. Once or twice a month, the spirits will speak of this sublunar world, and give warnings or information they think might be helpful to my master."

"Sublunar?"

"This planet," he murmured, gesturing around us. "All that lies beneath the moon."

I glanced across at Alejandro, feeling his gaze steady on my back. I did not want to make him any more jealous, but I had to hear what Richard knew. "And these spirits told you about Marcus Dent?"

Richard nodded, watching my face. "When Dent was in Germany, he supervised the burning of a whole coven of witches. The youngest was only fourteen but she was the most powerful. The spirit said this girl prophesied his death as she burnt."

I felt my tongue dry in my mouth. "What...what did she say?"

"That he would die at the hands of a witch. But not any witch. An English witch with the power to raise a dead King. That's why Marcus Dent is so obsessed with hunting down every witch he can find. He's killing them before they can kill him."

I felt a warning in my spine and spun round, so nervous I nearly cried out in shock when I found Alejandro standing right behind me, listening to the apprentice's story. He was very still.

His eyes met mine, a remembered pain in them. Suddenly I understood. He too had once unwittingly caused the death of a witch and been cursed for it. But not like this. This was no error.

I struggled to understand what Richard had told me. "A witch who could raise a dead King? Are you sure that's what the spirit told you? Not...not a dead Queen?"

Richard raised his brows. "Why, do you have a preference?"

The door to the hut opened at that moment and our conversation had to end. The Lady Elizabeth emerged, thanking John Dee for his reading. She looked tired, but seemed to be arranging to meet him again the following night, for there were other secrets he wished to share with her before he returned to London.

"I'll come back at nightfall tomorrow," Elizabeth promised him, and let him kiss her hand. "I shall not forget your loyalty, Master Dee."

"I pray you will not, my lady," Dee murmured, then hesitated. "I have been sent word by Bishop Bonner that I must join his household next month, for he has need of certain skills of mine. I am not sure what that means, but I cannot refuse such a man. He could have me back in prison with the slightest word. I trust you will not hold this against me in the future, my lady."

Elizabeth looked aghast. "Bishop Bonner? He who has condemned so many true Protestant souls to the stake?"

"Forgive me, my lady. I have no choice. To refuse him would arouse too many suspicions and lead to an accusation of heresy against myself."

She nodded, thinking rapidly. "No, no, you must go. These are dark times, and what purpose would your death serve but to deprive me of another faithful servant? Accept Bonner's invitation and keep yourself safe. But do what you can for the poor souls under his charge."

John Dee bowed. "With all my heart, my lady."

That night, I was woken by the sound of terrified screams. Alice and I staggered out of the bedchamber in our nightshifts, bleary-eyed, to find the household in darkness and confusion. Young Lucy came running from the servants' quarters with a lit candle to see what was wrong, old Rufus lolloping up the stairs after her, barking hysterically. Blanche Parry was shouting for help, and from the Lady Elizabeth's room we could hear her struggling to restrain our mistress.

"My lady?"

Blanche looked up as we rushed in, white and shaking as she pressed a writhing and bucking Lady Elizabeth down into the tangled bedclothes. "Quick! Help me to hold her ladyship still. I fear she will do herself a mischief in this fit."

"But what is it? What has alarmed her?"

The Lady Elizabeth clutched at my arm as I helped to restrain her. I had never seen her so wild, even in the grip of one of her violent tantrums. She was flushed and panting like a lunatic at the full moon, her face upturned to mine.

"Oh, Meg, Meg, please, you are the only one who can help me. I woke and saw him in the darkness. He was a terrible black shadow above the bed, with such long teeth! Yet I would know those cruel eyes anywhere. It was him, I tell you, in this very chamber!" There was sweat glistening on her forehead and cheeks, and her hooked fingers dug like claws into my bare arm. She began to weep. "Do not leave me alone, I beg you. The shadow will creep back down the chimney as soon as the candle is out. He means to murder me, I know it!"

I could not understand her ravings. "Who, my lady?"

"My father!" she gasped, almost incoherent with fear. "My father that was King Henry when he was alive. He took my mother's life, and now he has come back for me."

13

CAPUT DRACONIS

The next day it began to rain heavily again. The rain poured down relentlessly all day, the sort of rain that soaks through a cloak to your skin in a few moments. It pooled and puddled under every ill-hung door and window frame in Hatfield House, leaving everyone miserable and the air damp as a grave. The Lady Elizabeth stayed in her room, stricken and with dark bruises under her eyes from want of sleep. I had sat in a chair at her bedside until dawn, for she would not let me leave for fear of the shadow creature's return. Then I had stumbled down to the kitchen to beg some ale, for I did not wish to go back to bed myself even though it was now daylight. My body ached with exhaustion, yet my mind was sharp and keen, watchful for every shadow that moved in the house. I had left Elizabeth reading fervently from the Bible, and Blanche snoring on a hastily made-up trestle bed beside her, her hair in disarray, still wrapped in the cloak she had worn half the night to tend her mistress.

Bessie had gone out at first light in the cart with one of the grooms, to fetch flour from the mill to make bread. She came back sodden and in tears, the sack of flour ruined by the rain.

"Father Toms is to be executed!" Bessie exclaimed when her father asked what was wrong. Her eyes red-rimmed with weeping, she stared around at us in wild despair. "As soon as the rain has dried, the miller says he will be burnt as a heretic, right there in the market square in front of his own church. Old Father Toms, the gentlest man in the world, who never harmed a soul in his life. To burn him for not saying the Mass right... Oh, it's wicked! Wicked!"

Her father, John, was horrified, but said nothing, shaking his grey head. No doubt he did not wish to say anything that might sound treasonous. He looked at me, standing silent by the kitchen table, then pushed the ale across to me.

I thanked him and poured a fresh cup for Bessie. "Here, drink this," I said, putting my arm about her. "It will calm you."

She drank, then sniffed, wiping her wet mouth on her sleeve. "Father Toms buried our mother. He married me and Ned, then buried Ned. I remember the holy Father at Lucy's baptism, making the sign of the cross on her forehead." She shook her head, her mouth agape. "I don't understand it. He's a good man, Mistress Lytton. You've been at court, have you not, with the Lady Elizabeth? Tell us, why does the Queen do this? Burn an old man, almost in his dotage, and for what? Because of some old book?"

"Hush now, Bessie, that's enough," her father warned her. He glanced nervously at me, clearly unsure if I was a servant of Elizabeth's choosing or planted in her household by the Queen. "Please forgive my daughter, Mistress Lytton. She's upset, that's all. Father Toms has been our priest all her life. It goes hard to see him brought to such a cruel end. But we take Catholic Mass like everyone else and won't hold with any other way of worship. I'm sure Queen Mary only does what's right, God bless and preserve her. It's not for us to question her ways, is it?"

I nodded, and left the kitchen. There was nothing I could say to help with their grief which would not sound like treason, or heresy, or both—and we all knew it. I made my way back to the Great Hall, fumbling along the unlit walls. It was hard not to be overwhelmed by the sense of creeping horror that I had been holding at bay ever since Elizabeth's description of her nightmarish visitor. Her shadow monster had sounded remarkably like the vile creature I had seen on the ceiling at Hampton Court. But had her ladyship's visitor been dream or reality?

King Henry. A dead King, indeed. What had Richard said of the witch who would eventually destroy Marcus Dent?

An English witch with the power to raise a dead King.

Well, I had not raised a dead King. The spirit I had called for the Lady Elizabeth had been her long-dead mother, Anne Boleyn, and she had slipped back into the spirit world afterwards as easily as she had slipped from life. So the prophecy could not refer to me, could it?

It was dark and chill in the stone-flagged passageway that led to the Great Hall. The wall tapestries flapped uneasily in the draught and I could hear the constant depressing lash of rain outside, echoing about the walls. I felt something brush the back of my neck, light as breath, and turned, instantly on my guard against whatever evil might be baiting me.

But there was nothing there. Only shadows.

Alejandro was standing alone in the hall. My heart lightened at the sight of him, and I smiled, barely able to restrain myself from kissing him. "Looking for me?"

He nodded sombrely, but did not speak.

"Very well." I glanced about; the hall was dark, the fire still unlit, and there was no one within earshot. "What is it? Are you still angry with me for talking to Dee's apprentice? He knows many useful things that may help us."

Alejandro looked at me, tight-lipped, and I knew I was right. He was jealous of my long conversation with Richard last night. "Such as?"

"That Marcus Dent and John Dee were at university together." I saw his eyes widen and nodded. "And that Dent was once told he would die at the hands of a witch. Hence his deep hatred of witches."

He frowned, searching my face. "And this is the only reason why you were so close with that boy last night?"

Daringly, I put my hand to his cheek. His skin was warm and rough, as though he needed to shave. Alejandro did not flinch away this time as he so often did when we might be seen, but let me touch him, his eyes intent on my mouth. Suddenly I was glad the fire was unlit and rain was darkening the high windows along the length of the hall, the shadows deep and intimate enough to hide us.

"Can you doubt it?"

"You smiled at him, Meg. I saw you."

"I smile at lots of people."

"I wanted to run him through with my blade." His dark eyes brooded on my face. "Then drag you away to Spain and force you to be my wife."

I raised my eyebrows. "Is that all?"

"Don't laugh at me, Meg. I'm serious." His eyes closed briefly. "Do you know why I didn't do that?"

"Because you knew I would have turned you into a toad long before we reached Spain?"

Alejandro smiled and shook his head, his eyes opening. He put out a long finger and slowly traced the line of my mouth. "Because I am in love with you, Meg Lytton."

My heart lurched to a halt, then juddered back into erratic life. I said nothing, largely because I did not know what to say. Though I knew what I wanted to do.

"I want you to be in love with me too," he continued softly, taking a step closer so our bodies were almost touching. "I want you to choose to be my wife with all your heart and soul, not feel you have been forced to marry me. In my country, it is common for marriages to be arranged between noble families before a girl is even a woman, and for a man to meet his bride for the first time on their wedding day. For myself, I do not believe this is how it should be done. So I will wait until the day you are sure and come to me willingly."

"Thank you," I managed huskily.

We were standing face to face, his finger stroking my cheek, my hand resting lightly on his shoulder. I wanted so badly for him to kiss me but did not dare suggest it, for I knew his desire was held on a tight leash when we were together, and it was unfair to tease him.

His voice was ragged. "It's killing me, but I'll wait."

Our eyes met.

"Meg…" Alejandro gave a groan under his breath, then bent and brushed his lips across mine. On impulse, my hand curled about the back of his neck and held him there, my prisoner. He did not seem to object. Instead, the kiss deepened. His mouth explored mine. I could feel the full length of his body pressed against me.

His arm slipped about my waist and pulled me closer. My eyes closed and my cheeks began to flush with heat. I felt as though I was drowning again. Only this time I welcomed it, my whole body longing to be his.

A loud giggle from behind us broke the spell. "Well, I didn't think priests were allowed to do that kind of thing!"

Alejandro released me abruptly and took a few steps back, a hard colour in his face.

"Forgive me," he managed huskily, the words meant only for me, and then he bowed and left the hall.

I struggled to catch my breath, straightening my gown as I turned to glare at Alice, her face alight with mischievous laughter.

"What are you doing, creeping up on people like that?" I demanded. "That wasn't funny, Alice!"

"I didn't know you and Señor de Castillo were…" She tried to hide her smile. "I take it he isn't going to be a priest any more?"

"For your information, he belongs to a Catholic order that is permitted to marry. And fight in battle too, so you can wipe that smirk off your face!" But it was impossible to stay angry with her. I could still feel the imprint of Alejandro's lips on mine, a warm glow spreading throughout my body. Was this how it would feel to be married to him, to have him kiss me like that every day of our lives? "Anyway, what did you want? I take it you had a good reason to interrupt us?"

"Oh, yes. Her ladyship is sleeping now, but she gave me this message for you," she said blithely, and handed over a folded note. "What does it say?"

"It says, mind your own business," I muttered, opening the note and ignoring Alice childishly putting out her tongue at me. Though in truth it was impossible to remain angry with her for long. We had become friends over the past few months and I knew that I could trust her…except when it came to sneaking up on me when I wished to be private!

Go to Δ and ask to be shown how to banish that which we know has been loosed. E.

I puzzled a moment over the odd symbol of the triangle, then realized it must stand for Master Dee, since Δ was the Greek capital letter *D*.

The rest of the message then became clear. After last night's bad dream, Elizabeth was determined that the spirit of her father had been summoned by the conjuration of her mother's ghost, and that he meant her harm.

I remained unconvinced by the Lady Elizabeth's explanation, however. Since seeing that shadow monster for the first time, I had grown to associate it with Marcus Dent. To me, it seemed a more logical explanation that Dent had somehow learned a few tricks of his own, perhaps in the dark world of the void into which my spell had banished him. Dent must be an intelligent man, after all, for he had studied astronomy with John Dee himself at Oxford, then gone on to develop his dubious skills of witch-hunting in rural Germany—where those unfortunate enough to be accused of witchcraft were burnt to death or boiled in oil, or sometimes both.

Alice was watching me impatiently. "Meg! Well?"

"I am to visit our friend from last night," I said carefully, in case anyone else might be listening. Then I tore the princess's note into pieces, took the tinderbox from the hearth and struck a few sparks, setting light to them.

Her face had filled with comical dismay. "Rather you than me," Alice said. "Whatever for?"

"Best you do not know," I told her, then smiled when she stared at me. "Where is my brother?"

She brightened. "Still a-bed in the stables, I should think. Should I fetch him?"

I nodded. "I don't think the Lady Elizabeth should be left

unattended today. I know Blanche is with her, but in case Blanche leaves the room or falls asleep, William should keep watch outside her ladyship's door at all times. Tell him to keep a candle lit, and not let it go out."

"And what should I do?" Alice was pouting.

The torn pieces of the note were almost burnt to ash now. I straightened and took my friend's hand, squeezing it encouragingly. "Well, you could...you could keep William company. He will be hungry sometimes, and thirsty too, I should imagine. You could fetch him ale and sweetmeats, I am sure he would not turn you away."

We both laughed, then I looked up to see Alejandro in the entrance to the Great Hall. I fell silent, watching him. Part of me was glad that Alice had disturbed us, for while he was kissing me, I had felt the strongest urge to accept his offer of marriage and leave this life behind. Now that we had been separated though, even if it was only by a few feet of light and shadow, my desire to learn whatever could be learned from John Dee had returned. I loved Alejandro, but I was not yet ready to become a wife.

Yet how to make him understand such a subtle thing without losing his heart?

"I must risk the rain to speak with our guest," I told him, fetching my cloak from the settle. "Will you walk with me?"

"Gladly," Alejandro replied, and held out his hand.

The fire was burning in the centre of the goatherds' hut again, no doubt keeping out the worst of the damp weather, though I could see that the roof leaked in several places. John Dee was at his table, pacing rather than sitting, and reading often from a great book that lay open there. His apprentice invited me in and closed the door on Alejandro, whom he told to "return at dusk."

So it was to be a long day, I thought, and unfastened my sodden cloak. I stopped to gaze without understanding but with much fascination at a chart that had been scratched upon the wall: strange figures drawn in concentric circles, some that I recognized from the zodiac, others unfamiliar to me, uneven triangles and circles dissected by lines or ending in moons or arrow shapes.

The astrologer looked up and saw me. "Ah, Meg Lytton! You are come in a fortunate hour."

He took my hands, removing my wet gloves and handing them to Richard to be dried before the fire.

"The Moon conjuncts Jupiter, and the planet Mercury is almost upon the Ascendant. Quick, quick. We must make a start." Briefly, he held up a scrap of paper, creased and torn, then crumpled it back into his belt pocket. "A note from your mistress, sent to me at first light. In it she tells of her dream last night, and your great act of conjuration in her chamber at Hampton Court. Why did you not speak of it before?"

He meant my summoning of Anne Boleyn, of course. My heart sank for I had hoped John Dee would never find out about it. He seemed excited but agitated at what I had done, and a little disapproving too.

"It must have been an astonishing act," he commented, not waiting for my reply, "To have brought forth not one royal spirit, but *two*—how did you summon Queen Anne, by the way? No, not yet. Tell me the incantation later. For when the dead Queen answered your summons, it seems her husband came through from the spirit world with her. And now he will not return to his proper place in the halls of the dead."

"But we cannot be sure it is her ladyship's father, King Henry."

"Who else?"

"Marcus Dent," I suggested, and saw the astrologer's face

darken. "The Oxfordshire witchfinder. I cast a spell on him this spring, and he…vanished. He has been seen in the county since, but much changed, his face scarred and otherworldly. I cannot help wondering if what they have seen is no man, but an unquiet spirit, walking this earth in search of revenge."

"Unlikely," Dee said dismissively. "If you found no body, then there was no death. Except perhaps a magickal one. And a magickal death can often be reversed—if one possesses a talisman or dedicated token against death, and the knowledge of how it should be applied."

I frowned, remembering how I had watched Marcus Dent being sucked into the whirling black void that my spell had opened up in the village square at Woodstock.

"You knew Master Dent, I believe."

"A long time ago, yes." John Dee made a complex sign in the air, as though to clear away evil influences, then sat down on his stool. He clasped his hands together, then raised them to his chin, thinking aloud. "We met at Oxford while I was still unsure what direction I wished my studies to take. Dent was several years older than me, with a powerful grasp of mathematics and philosophy. He was greatly admired in the school of divinity too and could have become a doctor—or even a priest. But he knew little of astronomy until I shared my learning with him." Dee mused for a moment. "Marcus became obsessed with the stars. Not just their mathematical patterns, but the implications of their uses here on Earth."

"I don't understand."

"To properly comprehend the zodiac, the movements of the planets and stars, and their influence upon us, is to learn how to control and transmute the matter of life itself." He stared blindly ahead, his voice husky. "To change that which cannot be changed by any other means."

Richard was standing behind him. He looked at me over the astrologer's head and mouthed the word, "Alchemy."

"Are you saying Master Dent became interested in how to change base metals into gold?"

"That is indeed what I mean. Marcus went off to Germany in search of the philosopher's stone, the secret elixir which turns lead into gold. I did not follow him. We had argued and my interests lay elsewhere at that time, though since those days…" He smiled drily, and looked up at me as though he had suddenly remembered why I was there. "Well, some of us come to it early and some late. But for Dent, as for so many others, the search for the philosopher's stone was fruitless. Through the study of alchemy, he came to research magickal properties, and thence to witchcraft. In Germany, he fell in with some fellows whose chief joy in life was the burning of witches and Devil-worshippers. One of these women foretold his death at the hands of one of her kind here in England, and so Marcus came home with no elixir, but with hatred in his heart for all witchkind."

"So he is not a witch himself?"

John Dee raised his eyebrows. "Define *witch*."

"One who works magick."

"We all work magick to a greater or lesser extent every day of our lives," Dee commented. "Magick is but the achievement of marvels, whether they be true marvels or merely seem so to those who are ignorant of the workings of God's universe. Does that make us all witches?"

"I think it may be Master Dent that the Lady Elizabeth saw in her chamber last night," I blurted out. "I have seen him too, a vile shadow creature crawling across the ceiling of the Great Hall at Hampton Court, though only I was able to see him there." They were both staring at me now and I tailed off, feeling more than a little foolish. "Marcus Dent may also have appeared to me in the guise of a giant rat."

It was Richard's turn to raise his eyebrows at me now. His lips twitched with amusement. "A giant rat?"

But John Dee was not smiling. He turned to his book and leafed urgently through it. "You saw a 'shadow creature' on the ceiling of the Great Hall, you say?"

"Yes," I said stubbornly.

"What day was this?" He glanced at me when I did not speak. "Speak, girl. What was the date? The time?"

"I'm not sure. Late morning. Maybe mid-July?"

The astrologer slammed his book shut with a violent bang. "*Maybe?* How can I draw a conclusion from this supernatural event if you cannot give me the exact date and time that it occurred?"

I looked at Richard and he smiled, making a soothing gesture. "Master, the summoning…"

John Dee put down the book with a heavy sigh. "Yes, of course. Let us move on and establish what can be established. Tell me instead about the act of summoning. You called forth the spirit of Queen Anne, she who was sent to the block by her own husband, King Henry, for committing the sin of adultery?"

I nodded, relieved that neither of them had called me mad for suggesting the shadow creature was Marcus Dent. "Yes."

"And what made you attempt such a dangerous and fool-hardy act on your own, untrained and ignorant of true magickal procedure as you are?"

I felt my face grow hot as I looked from Dee's cool disapproval to Richard's mocking smile. "I am not untrained," I objected, my temper rising as I realized the low opinion they held of my skills as a conjuror. "Nor am I ignorant of true magickal…whatever you called it. My aunt was a witch and taught me most of what she knew before she died. The rest I have learned from magickal books."

"Women's magick," Dee said dismissively.

My teeth ground together. "I still managed to summon Queen Anne though, didn't I?"

"And brought a terrible darkness into the land with her."

"No, that is Marcus Dent's doing, I swear it. It is not King Henry. It cannot be. I did not summon him by name or thought or deed. I called on his Queen, Anne Boleyn, and she came. She came to us and spoke with her daughter."

Dee leaned forward on his stool. He was staring now, suddenly rapt and attentive. "You saw the Queen's spirit?"

"Yes."

"She took on a *physical form?*"

"Yes."

"And she spoke to the Lady Elizabeth? You heard her voice too? It did not sound in your mind, but aloud on the air, as I am speaking to you now?"

"Yes."

He glanced round swiftly at Richard, who was also intent on my description. "A true manifestation."

His apprentice nodded. "So it would appear."

"Are you a sensitive? What the Chaldeans used to call a 'prophet'?" Dee demanded, leaping up and knocking the stool over.

"I don't know."

He seized my hands and examined them again, then stared into my eyes. "To be able to conjure a spirit in physical form and with an audible voice is almost unheard of, except in ancient texts. We have long since lost the art… Would you sit with me at an appointed hour and call on the spirits for me? It can be tiring work—Richard will tell you—but your mind would be utterly opened to the true universe, far beyond this dull earth that we see every day."

I hesitated, seeing a flash of anger in Richard's face. "I am in the Lady Elizabeth's service, Master Dee, and can only work with you further if her ladyship commands it. She requires me to learn what I can from you about this shadow from her dream, and nothing else."

Dee sat back down, drawing me with him. "Yes," the astrologer agreed reluctantly, still holding my hands. "I shall ask her ladyship. But first, this shadow creature. You think it is Marcus Dent, but why?"

Briefly, I explained my previous encounters with Dent and the spell I had worked that had finally sent him into the void. The astrologer listened without expression but Richard folded his arms, his cold eyes never leaving my face. I wondered if he suspected I was there to take his place as Dee's apprentice. "It is just a feeling, of course, that the shadow is Marcus Dent. But it is my best explanation for why this is happening. Master Dent wants revenge, both on me and on the princess."

Richard did not believe me. "And Queen Mary? What does he want with her?"

I thought for a moment, painfully aware that Dee's apprentice had pinpointed the only part of my explanation which made little sense even to me. "I'm not sure. Perhaps he just wanted to fill me with horror. To show me what he could do."

"No one else saw this event?"

"He seems able to make himself invisible at will. Or visible only to a certain person. Like me—or the Lady Elizabeth last night."

Dee released my hands and turned back to his book. Dragging it onto his knee, he ran his finger erratically down the columns of numbers, pausing now and then to whisper some calculation under his breath. I realized then that it was an ephemeris, a book listing the positions of the planets and fixed stars on any day at any given moment.

"Yes, yes," he muttered. "Mercury rising. And here, *Caput Draconis.*" He stood and looked up at me, his light-coloured eyes narrowed to bright slits. "The Head of the Dragon, auspiciously placed for divination. No infortunes applying, and although it is the dark of the Moon, yet this may work in our favour for such dark and secret matters. Tell me, girl, when did you last eat?"

"Pardon?"

"Did you break your fast this morning? Answer truthfully, for it is important. To avoid evil influence, the stomach must be empty and the body cleaned for conjuration."

I had to think. "I took a little ale, but no food. I was not hungry after last night's excitement."

He nodded to Richard. "Prepare her," he muttered, and turned to a saddlebag on the floor behind the table, bending to retrieve various wrapped objects which he began to place on the table.

"What's going on?" I whispered to Richard.

Dee's apprentice did not smile. I had been right. He was angry that I was taking his place as seer.

"My master wishes to test your visions," he said coolly, and poured water from a flask into a bowl. Into this he stirred what smelled like a mixture of ground herbs and spices—I caught a hint of pine, nutmeg, sage, and something exotic I could not place—then carried the bowl to me. When I merely raised my eyebrows, he gestured to the stool. "Sit, I need to wash you."

I repressed a giggle, and he grew even more stern. "Forgive me," I managed. Trying to look serious, I held out my hands and watched in fascination as Richard dipped each finger in the odd-smelling concoction one by one, then dried them afterwards on a red cloth. As each finger was dipped into the water, he muttered in Latin, *"Sanus,"* and then *"Gratius ago,"* as he dried it.

When Richard came to the finger with the missing nail, its skin still red and puckered, he glanced at me but said nothing, drying it more carefully than the others.

Master Dee stooped to burn a handful of incense on a platter. The small hut filled with a strange, sweet-smelling smoke that left me a little light-headed. The astrologer then lit four candles and placed one ceremoniously at each corner of the table, in a way that was very reminiscent of my own casting of the circle.

"Thou shalt honour the North, the South, the East, and the West," I muttered. This I could understand.

Richard's hard gaze lifted to my face. "Head back," he said softly, then dipped his finger in the bowl and drew a wet line down from my forehead to my chin, then across from one cheek to the other. He's making the sign of the cross, I realized, and was surprised by it.

Master Dee was now chanting in Latin. The chanting went on for some time. He swung a black hooded cloak about his shoulders and pinned it with a gold-and-red brooch which glinted in the firelight. The centre of the table he draped with a black silk cloth, on which he placed a greying ram's skull with curved horns, a quill and an inkpot containing red ink.

At least, I hoped it was red ink.

Raising his hands to the ceiling like some priest about to say Mass, John Dee cried out, "Hear us, O Mars, great lord of battle and feverish visions, in whose name all blood is spilt. Grant that our seer Meg Lytton may call on you for strength through this talisman of your power, the Ram."

As I watched, he dipped the quill in the red ink and drew on the ram's skull the spidery shape of a conjoined circle and cross on the skull, then topped this symbol with a crescent curving upwards.

"O Mercury, swift and cunning ruler of petitions and messengers, may your bright wings guide us in this endeavour, you, whom the Romans called the god Mercurius and the Persians the lord Tyr." He touched his forehead to the table three times, then pointed at me. "I conjure you, O Mercury, to bring this girl to a place where she may speak with that spirit which troubles us, and learn its will."

"You know," I whispered to Richard, "I managed to summon Anne Boleyn without any of this nonsense."

Richard's mouth twitched, but he did not reply. He merely took away the bowl of scented water he had used to wash my hands and face, and returned with a comb. Carefully, he unpinned my white cap and set it aside, then began to comb out my hair.

He paused, frowning down at me. "Why is your hair so short?"

"I fell asleep in a field and a goat ate it," I replied.

"You are a very strange girl, Meg," he commented, then went back to combing my hair with short, careful strokes.

He was not to know that my hair had been chopped off by Marcus Dent at our last encounter, and had not yet fully regrown. But the brutal memory stung and I stiffened under his touch. I found it disturbing that John Dee and Marcus Dent had known each other at university, and shared an interest in astronomy and mathematics.

What else had Marcus shared? Dee's fascination with magick, perhaps, and not merely as a witch-hunter?

There was a threatening rumble of thunder overhead. Rain began to fall more violently, drumming on the weak roof and smashing against the shuttered window. Water leaked through the cracks and ran down the walls. The broken door banged in its frame as the wind started to rise, as though at any moment it might suddenly fly open. I hoped that Alejandro had sensibly taken Richard at his word and gone back to the house until dusk fell. But I knew he would not have left me here alone and might be sheltering nearby, probably in a thorn bush. If so, he'd be drenched by now.

Master Dee lifted one of the candles and sketched the sign of the cross in flame. Long shadows bobbed uneasily with the flame, then settled again into wavering darkness.

"Let us pray to the Lord," Dee announced, much to my amazement. He bent his head and began to mutter, "Our Father, who art in Heaven, hallowed be Thy name…"

Richard knelt at my side and joined in with the Lord's Prayer, his voice cool and calm. I had not been told to kneel so stayed where I was on the stool, but bent my head and repeated the Lord's Prayer along with them, long-familiar words I had learned as a child from my hornbook.

I had to stop myself gaping like a fool. But it was the oddest magickal act I had ever witnessed. If my demure white cap had not been removed, and I had not been sitting eyeball to eye socket with a horned skull covered with symbols drawn in blood, I might almost have been at a Church Mass.

The howl of the wind grew so loud, it began to drown out our words. The rain was lashing down, hammering at the roof, bubbling under the door, trying to get in. That was how it felt, anyway.

"Amen," Dee finished triumphantly, bowing to the horned ram's skull as though the table was an altar.

"Amen," we echoed.

Richard stood and also bowed to the skull. He looked sideways at me as he straightened, half mocking, half in deadly earnest.

I'm not bowing to a skull, I thought defiantly, and stayed upright on the stool.

Dee pitched another handful of incense on the platter and set fire to it, beginning another invocation in Latin, this time to the Moon. My eyes stung with the acrid smoke and I could feel my hunger now like a dizziness that threatened to overwhelm me. As Dee moved and swayed with the ritual, his tall hooded figure seemed to merge with the shadows behind him, until he was part of the darkness, himself one of the shadows.

I began to feel a little sick.

Uncomfortable, I shifted on my stool, an icy trickle running down my spine as though the roof above me was leaking. How much longer would this ludicrous ritual take?

John Dee crossed himself, muttering, "Let it be done in the name of the Father, and of the Son, and of the Holy Spirit. Amen."

He dropped a thin, coiled cord in front of us on the table, and a neatly folded length of black silk. His voice was hard as flint.

"Bind the witch's hands behind her back, Richard, then blindfold her. It is time."

14

DEAD KING

I knew the place. I had seen it before in my dreams and in the scrying bowl, and once, in a prison cell with John Dee. John Dee. The name seemed to mean something to me. I struggled to retrieve the information but already it had gone, flitting away like a bat into the darkness.

It was nearly dusk in my vision and I was standing on the edge of a high place. At my back I could hear the wind blowing. Was I on a cliff? A tower?

Below me lay a kind of wilderness, stretching to the horizon. Stunted yellowing trees, straggling bushes, lichened boulders strewn here and there in the rough grasses, hills and valleys under the touch of autumn. On one of the hilltops opposite I could see markings and mounds in the grass where an ancient stone circle must once have stood, long since dismantled, its greatest stones carted away to build new monuments and temples—or left for the grasses to cover up.

A bird screeched overhead and, instinctively, I glanced up at its wheeling shadow. A hawk. Just like every other time.

Of course, he was there when I lowered my gaze. Marcus Dent. In his hand was the ribboned and gleaming axe I had seen before, its thick shaft wound with gleaming holly almost down to the grip.

"You again," I said wearily. "I should have known."

My enemy looked back at me, unsmiling, unspeaking. This time there was something different about the dream.

Then he turned his head slightly, as though to stare out into the wild air, and I realized what had changed. Marcus had an ugly scar running across his face now, and one of his eyes was coloured silver as though it was blind. So reality had caught up with my dreams.

I crooked an eyebrow. "Lost for words, Marcus? This is where you say, 'On your knees, Witch, and die!' Or something like that."

Marcus Dent hefted the great axe in the air, grunting with the weight of it. "On your knees, Witch, and die!"

This was where my visions had always ended in the past. Sweet and safe, with me waking up and wondering what that strange dream of the high place and the axe was all about.

But to my alarm, this time I did not wake up. This time, my legs buckled and I found myself kneeling before him on the hard ground.

"No, no, this isn't what's supposed to happen," I muttered, trying to get up again.

His hand forced me down. "Your neck," he growled hoarsely. His breath sounded like a blade being sharpened. "Bare your neck to my axe, Witch."

"Wake!" I exhorted myself in Latin.

He was fumbling with my hair, drawing it back to expose my neck. I had a sudden memory of Richard gently combing my hair. Richard, the astrologer's apprentice, preparing me to speak to the spirits. The smoky little hut where I had been sitting on a stool when suddenly a spell had been cast upon me. A spell of candles and incantations, then the ringing of a bell, once, twice, three times, and then I was here, kneeling before Marcus Dent, my old enemy, my executioner.

"This is just another vision," I told myself frantically, but kept struggling just in case I was wrong.

Marcus was strong. Far stronger than I was. I could not seem to get up. His voice was in my ear. "What is your name?"

"You know my name!" I spat bitterly.

"Rise up and answer me. What is your name? What planet rules you? Are you of air or water?"

My face was in the dirt. I could not breathe, I was choking on the foul earth of this place. I remembered how Marcus had tried to drown me, my body succumbing to the murky cold depths of the water, and wondered if he had actually succeeded that day in Woodstock village, if everything since then had been a dream after death, an imagined life from beyond the grave, and I was in truth dead. Dead and cold, my heart stopped, my body lost to breath, my love for Alejandro buried with me, and the Spanish novice grieving over my tombstone.

Not for long though. Soon Alejandro will take ship for Spain and meet another woman there, a beautiful dark-skinned Spanish bride, and marry her instead.

I struck out with my whole being and cried, "Banish!"

My face was still in the dirt, but suddenly I could smell flowers. Roses, thyme, fragrant jasmine, the tall spikes of purple-headed lavender, a sweet knot of herbs in a formal garden to my left, camomile springing soft under my cheek.

"Look up," a voice whispered, close to my ear.

I lifted my head. I was standing in a garden, a beautiful

garden, with red brick walls and high towers above me. The sky was blue and the air was warm.

A man was standing beside me. He was tall and muscular, and stood on the grass barefoot. His body was wrapped in a yellow glittering cloth, like starfire, and as I turned to see him properly, I realized he was holding a small child in his arms.

"Who are you?" I asked. "What is your name?"

"My name is Raphael," he replied.

I looked into his face and found that I could not see him properly, for all about his head was a glowing fire, emitting golden beams in all directions like a beaten image of the sun.

"Why am I here, Raphael?"

"You came to seek the name of the spirit who troubles you."

With a shock, I remembered John Dee making the sign of the cross with his candle flame, then my hands being bound, my eyes covered with black silk, and the sound of a bell ringing.

"Yes," I managed. My mouth was dry. "What is that spirit's name?"

Raphael put the small child into my arms, saying, "Seek not that which is not thine to seek, but look to the one star still shining. There is thine own salvation and the salvation of Albion. Repeat these words."

I repeated them, stumbling a little as I spoke. Then I looked down into the face of the small child in my arms. It was a girl with reddish-gold hair and small solemn dark eyes.

When I raised my head, the angel had disappeared.

"What do you see?"

It was John Dee's voice in my head. I stared about myself. There were shouts from the far end of the garden. Men in armour running towards me. The child was wriggling in my arms.

I lifted her up and called, staring up at the open casement above me, "Your daughter! Look on your daughter, my lord King!"

There was a man staring down at us. He was broad-chested and large-bellied, his face reddened with wine. There were jewels on his cap and on his large hands that clutched at the wooden frame of the casement. Then I looked into his eyes, so unexpectedly familiar, narrowed in hatred as he stared at me, and I knew in that instant who he was.

It was King Henry, father to Queen Mary and the Lady Elizabeth; he who had ordered the arrest and execution of Elizabeth's mother, Queen Anne Boleyn.

As I watched, the King seemed to grow in the window, his body blackening, his face blurring, becoming darker and more grotesque until he was nothing but a terrible vast shadow with hooded eyes that looked down into me and knew my true self.

"Take her away!" he roared, and slammed the casement shut.

Someone lifted the child from my arms, wrapped her in a cloak and carried her away. I missed her scent as soon as she was gone, my heart wrenched away with her little body.

"Be gentle with her!" I exclaimed. "Do not be afraid, Bess. I will come back to you."

Then the guards were upon me. They seized me roughly by the arms and dragged me away through the gardens. The gold and red skirts of my gown brushed the heady clumps of lavender, snagging on the rose bushes.

I heard a woman crying fiercely, "I am the Queen! I am the Queen!" until the sky seemed to darken and my eyes closed.

As soon as Richard removed the blindfold, I looked up at him, shaking with anger. "How dare you? Untie my hands!"

"Welcome back," he said drily, and bent to wrestle with

the thin cords with which he had bound my wrists together at my back.

At that moment, the door was flung open. Standing there, rain and wind howling about him, was Alejandro with a drawn sword in his hand.

His face wet with rain, he stared into the smoke-filled hut. His swift gaze took in my bound hands, Richard crouched over me, then John Dee himself, a hooded figure holding a candle aloft behind a table that boasted a horned ram's skull decorated with strange symbols drawn in what was clearly blood.

"Stand away from her!" he said harshly, and took two hasty steps towards Richard.

Before I could warn him of the apprentice's gift, I saw Richard raise his hand and then Alejandro staggered back, like a man in a high wind.

The Spanish novice groped for the silver crucifix which always hung at his neck. Finding it, he muttered, *"In te spero, Domine. Salva me."*

Richard sighed. "How very tiresome he is." He spread his fingers and pointed at Alejandro, who dropped to his knees, his whole body struggling against the enchantment, the veins standing out on his throat.

"Leave him alone," I told Richard furiously. "Untie my hands."

"What, so you can try and throw me against the wall with your witch's magick? No, thank you."

His master intervened, throwing back his hood and snapping his fingers at Richard. "Don't be such a fool. Our work is finished here anyway. Untie the Lytton girl and release the Spaniard from your hold." He drew a sharp breath when his apprentice did not move. "Now, Richard! The Lady Elizabeth is fond of her young priest."

"Oh, very well." With a muttered oath, Richard released Alejandro from whatever spell he had used against him.

Alejandro leaped to his feet at once, his sword levelled at the apprentice. His face was flushed with anger. "What have you done to her, sirrah? What gives you the right to treat a lady in this way?" Reaching me, he slit the cords binding my wrists with one stroke and put his arm about my waist, lifting me as though I weighed nothing.

"Put your arms about my neck," he ordered me, and I obeyed, my head dizzy from the smoke.

His chest was sodden with rain, but I lay my head against it gratefully.

John Dee held out his hands in a conciliatory gesture. "It was part of the ritual. We could not risk her using magick and disturbing the angelic powers. She was not harmed."

"You could just have asked me not to use magick," I muttered.

"You are a woman," Dee said apologetically. "Sometimes the visions can be very intense and frightening. Even Richard has sometimes defended himself without thinking and angered the spirits. We could not trust you to remember, not on your first attempt."

"Her last attempt," Alejandro told them bitterly, and turned as though to carry me back to the house.

"No, no, I want to do it again," I insisted, struggling free of his grip. Alejandro released me, staring in amazement as I stepped away from him. "I have to choose my own path."

"Meg, you were screaming," Alejandro reminded me. "These men had you tied up and blindfolded."

"I know, I know. And I'm truly grateful you came for me. I was scared, at that moment, and I do feel safer, knowing you are there if I need you. But that doesn't mean I never want to try it again. It was astonishing." I struggled to find the right words to describe how it had felt to live and breathe a vision like that. "Miraculous."

Alejandro recoiled at my use of that word, then crossed himself against the taint of blasphemy. His dark eyes sought mine through the smoky air.

"Tell me truthfully, are you under a spell?"

I shook my head, though I was still a little dazed from what I had seen and felt in my vision. "I thank you with all my heart for coming to my aid, Alejandro," I murmured, not wanting to hurt him, "but it would be best if you returned to the house. This is no place for you."

Alejandro looked at me, disbelieving. "You expect me to walk away and leave you here?"

"Yes."

"With this conjuror and his boy?"

Richard had come silently to my side. Now he gave an angry laugh. "One more word, Novice, and I swear—"

A fight was stirring here, their faces taut with aggression. I put up a hand between them, looking from one to the other. "I don't want any more disputes. Alejandro, please do as I ask and leave me. I am not in any danger, as you can plainly see. My mistress asked me to be here, to see this business through to the end, and that is what I intend to do."

Alejandro stood there a moment longer, his face a cold mask, his sword in his hand, still pointing lethally at Richard. When I raised my eyebrows, he reluctantly sheathed his sword and bowed to me with customary politeness. But I could see the fury in his face.

Then he stalked out without another word, dragging the door shut behind him.

I closed my eyes in silent apprehension after his departure. Perhaps I had done the wrong thing. Perhaps I had driven

him away for ever. Yet if Alejandro truly desired us to become man and wife, he must accept this side of my nature.

"Meg?" the astrologer asked gently.

I turned back to Master Dee and nodded, putting my grief
behind me. There was still much to be done this night if we
were to make sense of my outlandish visions.

"So I was in a high place, and then somehow in the body
of Queen Anne. But what does any of it mean?"

When my throat was dry from talking, and every inch of
the astrologer's paper was covered in his fine black scrawl,
Richard rose and threw me my cloak. It stank of wood smoke,
but I wrapped myself in it gratefully, too exhausted to care.
Everything I could remember from my visions had been noted
down meticulously, yet I suspected we were no nearer solv-
ing the problem of what was haunting Elizabeth. Master Dee
seemed more puzzled than enlightened by the words of the
angel, and if he could not understand what I had seen, it struck
me that nobody could.

"Time for you to sleep," Richard said shrewdly, looking
into my face. "It will be dawn in a few hours. There is little
more we can learn tonight."

"But was it enough?" I asked, glancing at Master Dee.

"There is much here to ponder. And one of my books may
yet reveal what we do not understand." Dee stood up from
his seat wearily, stretching. He gestured to Richard to clear
the table. "I must return to London, but I shall leave Richard
and the more arcane books at Hatfield. He can search through
them in my absence, and perhaps discover an answer to these
most perplexing visions."

I shuddered. "I wish you did not have to leave."

"I have no choice." John Dee closed his eyes, pain twitch-
ing the thin brows together above his sensitive face. "Bishop

Bonner demands my presence in his house, and I have no power to say him nay. To refuse would be to draw down the same terrible fate on my head as the heretics he burns daily. But I have seen in the stars, his time is nearly at an end. Another year or two, and I shall be free again." He opened his eyes and gazed at me intently. "Meanwhile, you must serve the princess and help to keep her safe from those who would harm her. Marcus Dent is such a man. If you ever have the chance again to destroy him, take it. And this time do not hesitate."

Annoyance pricked at me. "I already tried to destroy him. I thought he was gone for good."

"Then try harder, Meg Lytton. This is not a game. More than your own life and that of your mistress may be at stake here. If he can, Marcus will take great pleasure in condemning your mistress to the Tower, and you to everlasting torment, and England will not be far behind." John Dee turned away, staring into the dying embers of the fire. "Marcus was always cruel as a young man, taking pleasure in the suffering of others. Now I fear his cruelty has grown to monstrous proportions. He may not even fully be a man any more, but a creature of darkness. In a way, your banishing spell may have made him stronger, perhaps even given him the power he needed to trick death."

My voice was high with incredulity. "You mean he cannot die?"

The astrologer shrugged. "The only way to tell if you can still kill Marcus Dent is to face the man—and defeat him."

There was a long and terrible silence during which I struggled not to weep at this news. Even though I had long suspected he might not be properly alive, I had still hoped Master Dee, with all his knowledge and experience, might have some simple answer that would solve everything. Perhaps a magickal instrument to keep the witchfinder away from me, or a darker

spell than those in even my aunt's most secret books which
would allow me to banish Marcus for good.

Instead, he seemed even more convinced than I was of my
own impending failure.

Richard held out his hand. "Come," he said brusquely, and
there was no sympathy in his face, "I'll see you safely back
to the house."

The path back through the woods showed a glimmer of
light above the trees; dawn on its way, in the far east. We
walked slowly, for I was cold and tired, and Richard's limp
slowed his progress over the uneven ground. Once or twice he
caught me looking at him sideways, though I tried to contain
my curiosity. By the time we reached the back of the house,
Richard was frowning heavily, a sneer on his lips.

"Not as fleet of foot as your tame novice, am I?" Leaning
against the wall beside the back door, Richard looked hard
at me as though expecting an answer.

I was embarrassed. "That wasn't what I—"

"Were you wondering if I was born like this?" His near-
black gaze held mine angrily. "A cripple with one leg shorter
than the other?"

"Forgive me."

"Why? It's not your fault, but my father's. Would you like
to hear the story?"

I did not know what to say, but waited.

"My father liked to beat me when I was a child. Once,
he got drunk and beat me until my leg was broken, for giving him 'black looks.' When he had passed out, my aunt hid
me in the cellar. So he beat her too. I lay in the dark there
three weeks, barely alive, living off what she could smuggle
down to me. By the time my aunt was able to bring help, my
leg bone had knitted wrong." Richard slapped his right hip,

watching me. "So now I walk with a limp, like the Devil's child that I am. That's what my father used to call me. Said my mother played him false with the Devil one night, and I was the child that came of it. My mother died when I was five years old, so I could not ask her if it was true."

"Cruel man," I muttered, my face averted.

"No, for it allowed me to hope he was not my father."

Instinctively, I touched his hand and was surprised when he flinched, jerking it away.

"I was not looking for your pity, Meg Lytton," he said harshly.

"You have it, nonetheless."

His eyes narrowed on my face. "Why did you send your novice away like that tonight? He'll not have you now. They're arrogant, these Spanish priests. They don't like a woman telling them what to do."

"You know why. It was no place for him."

"True, but that won't stop him trying to save you from our evil ways. I could see it in his face."

I know he was speaking the truth. Alejandro would not give up easily. Nor did I want him to, for my heart had thrilled at the sight of him bursting through the door to save me tonight. I was in love with Alejandro—what other sign did I need of my feelings for him, when my heart beat faster at the sight of him, and everything else fell away into dust before my need to be with him, to have him at my side for ever?

Yet my head was confused, for our love could only end in disaster. A marriage between a witch and a priest was unnatural, as I had told Alejandro many times before, and a malevolent star would almost certainly darken our sky if we were to wed.

So why could I not let him go?

"Master Dee said Alejandro was in danger." I reminded

Richard of his message the day he had ridden into Hatfield. "Perhaps he needs my protection."

"Or perhaps he is only in danger because of his nearness to you."

Now he was voicing my own fear. I looked away, unable to hold his gaze any longer, and stiffened in horror.

"What is it?" he demanded, turning to follow my stare.

Just for one fleeting instant, as dawn lightened the skies about Hatfield, I had caught a glimpse of something— *someone*—watching us, half-hidden in the shifting shadows between trees, out there beyond the low wall of the herb garden. Then a soft breeze blew, rustling the dark leaves, and there was nothing between the trees.

"I thought I saw—"

He turned back, apparently having satisfied himself that no one was there. His eyes searched my face, careful and astute. "Your witchfinder?"

"Perhaps."

"My master says this Marcus Dent may be more powerful than he seems. That you should be wary of him."

"I am, thank you."

Richard noted my wry smile, and shrugged. "You said that you'd laid spells of protection about this place. So he cannot come at you here."

"Hopefully not." But I shuddered, remembering the axe Marcus always carried in my dreams. "He means to kill me. That much is certain. I have seen it in my visions."

"A vision is not a prediction of the future, though it may hold elements of truth."

"Now you sound like John Dee."

I caught a flash of irritation in his face. "Then I am proud to do so. Dee is a great man and has saved my life on more than one occasion. Everything that I am, I owe to my master.

He found me starving on the streets and near to death when I was nine years old. He took me home with him, nursed me back to strength, and taught me his craft. He said it was in the stars that we should meet." Richard looked at me stonily. "As it was in the stars that you and Marcus Dent would come to blows."

The wind blew again, suddenly chill, and the trees beyond the walled herb garden swayed, their branches creaking and rustling in the glimmering darkness. I drew my cloak about my shoulders and put a hand to the door. It had been left unlocked for me. Alejandro?

"Thank you for walking back with me," I murmured.

Richard said nothing, but scowled a little, as though in pain, then turned and limped away towards the trees.

Pushing inside, I made my way silently through the unlit passageways and up the stairs to my chamber, expecting at any moment to see Alejandro waiting for me. But there was no sign of him, and when I passed his room, there was no light under the door. I slipped into my room as quietly as I could. Alice, who often slept there too when she was not tending the princess, was snoring gently on the straw mattress.

I drew back the shutters and undressed by the rosy light of dawn, my fingers fumbling wearily with the fastenings of my gown. I knew I should soon be expected to rise and attend the Lady Elizabeth, but I was too tired to sit up until then. An hour or two of sleep was all I needed...

My eye was caught by a movement among the trees surrounding the lawns below. My fingers stilled on my gown, and I stared down, my heart thudding frantically as I tried to make out the cloaked figure slipping between the mossed trunks.

I thought at first it might be Richard, then realized the

figure was too painfully stooped, shuffling like an old man as it moved from tree to tree.

As the man turned to look up, staring almost directly at my window as though he had sensed my gaze, his hood fell back a little and I saw the face beneath.

Except there was no face beneath the hood, only darkness.

As I watched, the cloaked figure dwindled away, shrinking to a black smudge roughly the size of a rat. Then even that horrible thing disappeared into the undergrowth, leaving the lawns empty.

I finished undressing with the wooden shutters closed tight, then lay on my back in the darkness, staring up at the ceiling. I wondered if I ought to say a prayer, but soon gave up, struggling to whisper even the daily prayers I knew as well as my own name. Into the dawn, the walls mocked me with their creaks and groans, wind whistling through the shutters. I had been right to hedge this place with protective spells, for I was more under siege here with every day that passed. But how long would my defences last?

15

BURNING

I spent the next morning, at the Lady Elizabeth's imperious command, sitting cross-legged in Dee's hut, wrinkling my nose at the smell of goat as I leafed through his collection of ancient grimoires and books of conjuring. Some of these he was taking with him to London, discreetly tucked into a saddlebag, but the rest he left behind for Richard to conceal and protect.

"If you fear they may be discovered by the Queen's men," Dee advised Richard later as the astrologer prepared to depart, once more disguised as a swarthy-faced tinker, "have a large hole ready dug outside the hut. Wrap the books in leather or stout cloth, and throw them into the pit, then cover the place with leafy branches. It has taken me many years to assemble this library, and I will not lose more of it to these superstitious fools."

I frowned, following him out to where his horse stood waiting, tethered to a tree.

Master Dee saw my expression and shot me a nervous half smile. "You must think me overcautious, young Meg, with all this talk of burying books. But although some of my most valuable books are still hidden at my home, I cannot be sure the Inquisition will not have burnt those they found by now. For they searched my house when I was in prison, and took away many rare parchments and books. It is soul-destroying to think what may have happened to them."

"I will take good care of these," Richard promised him.

"Good lad." John Dee smiled, then spoke to him privately for a long while before taking his horse and turning it towards the woodland road where few would see him pass. He raised a hand in farewell. "*Vale,* Meg Lytton. Follow my apprentice's instruction, and you will not go far wrong. I have told him how to guide you safely through the ritual again, so you need not fear my absence. Perhaps this time you will be more successful in laying this troublesome spirit to rest."

Once his master had disappeared into the woods, Richard walked back with me towards the house. The weather had turned drier, and the leaves were now a brilliant red and orange on the trees, the autumn sunlight dancing amongst them. I did not believe we would be any more successful without Dee there to guide us, but something had to be done. The Lady Elizabeth had woken feverish and unhappy that morning, complaining of another bad dream in the night. Everything seemed to point to my first conjuring of Queen Anne as having been the point of origin for this spirit, the magick which sparked the troubles now afflicting the princess—and indeed her sister, Queen Mary, and the whole of England— and if so, it must be me who set the fault to rights.

I only hoped it would be possible to find a remedy for the

country's woes. For all I had to help me were John Dee's magickal grimoires, his rather difficult apprentice, and my own power. Which, if I admitted the truth, was fast weakening by the day. I could not remember the last time I had laid a simple spell, such as to light the candles without tinder, or open a locked door with only a word.

It was as though the power had been draining out of me for months. Since I had banished Marcus Dent from this world, perhaps. I had summoned Anne Boleyn, it was true, but Elizabeth herself might have influenced that spell, her desire to see her dead mother so powerful that it lent weight to my incantations.

Had some of my skill as a witch gone with Marcus into the void?

"Is it possible for a witch to lose her power?" I asked Richard as we wandered towards the sunlit lawns. "Or to forget how to work a spell?"

Richard looked at me from under dark brows. "You are losing your power?"

"I didn't say that!" But I hesitated, unable to hide much from that piercing gaze. "Well, it's true that I don't seem to work magick as often as I used to. And when I do make a spell, the words don't come as easily as before. I just wondered if the two were connected—this spirit haunting us, and my loss of power."

"Perhaps," he conceded after a moment's thought, not particularly helpfully.

I could see my brother and Alejandro practising swordplay on the level grass, William struggling to keep up with the Spaniard's speed and agility. The two young men seemed to get on well together. I wondered if Alejandro was remembering times spent with his own older brother, now dead, when he was with William. He had never spoken to me of his brother's death though; perhaps they had not been close.

"How long will you stay here at Hatfield?" I asked.

"As long as my master instructs me to, or until the Lady Elizabeth grows weary of having to feed an extra mouth. There is plenty for me to do though. Not least laying this spirit to rest."

To own the truth, I was a little nervous at the thought of performing magick in front of him, or having to go into a trance while he acted as my guide. It had felt natural enough to allow Dee to be my guide, the astrologer's power and experience well-known to everyone.

But could I trust this surly apprentice enough to put my life in his hands while I stepped out of my earth-bound body and into the dangerous world of my visions? Would Richard be strong enough a guide to protect me against attack by Marcus Dent?

Alejandro stopped fencing with William as we approached, and turned, his quick frown an indication of how much he disliked seeing me with Dee's apprentice. Nonetheless, he bowed his head in a courteous gesture. "Meg," he murmured, and even managed a brusque nod for Richard, who was now inspecting the large sycamore tree that straddled the edge of the upper lawn. "Has Master Dee left?"

"Just," Richard answered.

Alice was sitting on the grass on a cushion, mending a thick winter cloak that was strewn across her lap. Beside her was a basket full of garments waiting to be mended. She looked up and shook her curly head in disapproval. "The Lady Elizabeth was very agitated this morning. She could not even bring herself to take breakfast. I do not think she wished Master Dee to return to London. Not with these terrible dreams she's been having."

Richard shot her a glance, then pulled himself easily up into the lower branches of the sycamore. "The matter is in hand," he said tersely. Sliding along one of the thick branches, he made himself comfortable and stared out across the fields. "What is that smoke?"

"Where?"

My brother had come forward to stand under the tree as though to climb it too, but at this he stopped and shielded his eyes against the autumn sunlight.

Even Alejandro had turned. He sounded puzzled. "It's coming from the village, I'd say."

I stared at the thin coil of black smoke creeping above the trees. Then I shuddered in horror as a sudden realization hit me.

"It must be the old priest," I muttered, then wished I had not spoken when they all turned to stare at me. I stuttered, "Father Toms? Bessie said the priest here had been found guilty of heresy for not reading the Mass according to the Queen's new edict, and was sentenced to death. But then the rain came on, and the floods. They were only waiting for a dry day to…to burn him."

"Oh, the poor old man!" Alice exclaimed, and crossed herself. "Such a terrible death. And a priest too."

Alejandro sheathed his sword and came towards me, pity in his face. "Meg," he said softly.

He knew I was remembering my aunt's death by burning. My eyes pricked with tears. But I could not crumble now, even though the whole country was going up in flames, it seemed.

"No," I whispered, and held Alejandro off with my hand. I bent my head and willed the tears away. I loved him, but his presence weakened me. I knew he would be hurt by this rejection, but more than ever I must be strong now. Strong for the princess, strong for England.

At dinner that night, the Lady Elizabeth came down from her room, supported by Blanche, her face very pale and her small eyes wide as she surveyed our company around the table. "So this is to be our little band," she murmured, and settled herself on the high-backed chair at the top of the table. At her signal, we scraped back the benches on either side of the table and sat down too, Alice on my left side and Blanche on the right, the men sitting opposite. "I had hoped for more servants here at Hatfield, and a greater company. But we shall be merry together this winter, away from the dangers of the court."

Blanche set a trencher before her mistress with a low curtsey. "More will come in the spring, my lady. You still have many followers. They only keep away for fear of the Queen."

"Well, my purse is nearly empty anyway; I have no money to keep a dozen hangers-on or knights at arms," Elizabeth said, and shrugged, pretending to laugh. "And if my household grew too large, my sister would no doubt have words to say about it. Words and deeds. Indeed, it is well we are so small a company. I should not wish to find myself at loggerheads with such a fearful Queen, who burns her subjects for failing to lift a dish of bread."

She meant old Father Toms, I realized.

Blanche looked aghast. "My lady, please…"

"I am amongst friends here, am I not?" Elizabeth hesitated, then sipped at her wine, looking at us all over the rim of her cup. "Or is one of you here a traitor, ready to write these heretical words of mine to my sister—and bring your mistress to the flames as well?"

"Not I," swore William fiercely, adding belatedly, "my lady."

"Nor I," muttered Richard.

"But the servants…" Blanche whispered.

Bessie had just emerged from the kitchen with a vast platter of pork slices glistening in gravy, her face streaked with sweat.

"My lady," she managed breathlessly, setting the heavy platter down before the princess with unsteady hands. Then she curtseyed and slipped away again down the narrow passageway to the servants' quarters.

The Lady Elizabeth nodded, closing her eyes briefly as though in pain. "I shall be careful," she agreed quietly, then opened her eyes with a frown as Blanche began to serve her meat. "Only one slice, Blanche. No, not the pinkest. Yes, that's better. I have no appetite tonight."

Alejandro came round silently to her elbow to replenish her wine cup as though he were one of the hall servants. His voice was pitched very low, so that only those at the table could hear. "More bad dreams, my lady?"

The Lady Elizabeth looked at him sharply, as though about to deny it. Then she gave an abrupt nod. "It is a terrible shadow on the wall, staring down at me as though about to attack. I wake shaking. Sometimes it is gone. Sometimes—"

But she could not finish, her eyes wild.

"Her ladyship cries out in the darkness like a lost soul in torment," Blanche muttered, watching him with hope mingled with despair. Perhaps she thought Alejandro might be able to exorcize this ghost with his priestly power. "She insists there is someone else in the chamber with us. But when I rise and light a candle, I see nothing. Only our own shadows."

He asked, "Do you pray?"

The Lady Elizabeth nodded, taking more wine. "Constantly."

"Perhaps I should stay with you and watch tonight."

Blanche's eyes bulged with horror at Alejandro's murmured suggestion. "In my lady's chamber? At night?"

But Elizabeth was already nodding, her face lit with relief. She ignored her lady-in-waiting's choking refusal. "Thank you," she agreed, and laid her hand on his. "We will pray together and read from the Scriptures until I fall asleep. I will sleep better knowing you are there to protect me, Señor de Castillo."

As I watched them together, and saw her white hand resting on his, a flash of jealousy split my heart in two. I imagined him with Elizabeth in her candlelit bedchamber tonight, her ladyship in nothing but her thin nightshift, and Alejandro sitting intimately by her curtained bed, perhaps even on the bed itself, his silver crucifix dangling about his neck as he bent to kiss his princess goodnight.

Savagely, I stabbed at a dripping slice of pork with my knife and dragged it to my trencher. Then I pinched rather more salt than was necessary and sprinkled it across the meat.

"Careful," Richard murmured, watching me from across the board. His foot brushed mine under the table—perhaps accidentally, perhaps deliberately—but he did not break the contact. "Too much salt can burn the tongue."

"I don't care," I replied shortly, and caught Alejandro's frowning look. Let him stare. Let him spend the night beside Elizabeth in a darkened bedchamber, whispering prayers into the darkness. It was none of my affair.

But guilt seized and shook me. The Lady Elizabeth was my mistress, and had always tried to keep me safe from Marcus Dent and the priests who might have tortured me until I died. If she was suffering each night from these evil visitations, it was my fault alone. It was I who had unleashed this horrific shadow-thing upon the world, after all. And was this how I repaid her kindness and patronage? With anger in my heart because she had asked Alejandro for his prayers?

John, the old retainer, came into the hall with a heavy armful of logs for the fire. As he crashed them down onto the stone hearth, I raised my head and looked broodingly across at Richard.

"It should be tonight," I mouthed at him over the noise.

Now it was Richard's turn to frown. He put down his knife. "Tonight?" he mouthed back silently.

"The summoning."

His eyes widened and he looked cautious. "But the stars... I moth result the books first."

I hesitated, unsure what he meant. "Pardon?" I mouthed back at him.

"I moth result the books," he repeated.

Utterly perplexed, I screwed up my face, throwing my hands wide in a bewildered gesture that meant, "I have no idea what you are saying to me," and only then realized that everyone at the table was staring.

"Something you wish to share with us, Meg?" the Lady Elizabeth demanded icily.

I straightened, my cheeks flushing, and saw Alejandro's fixed stare move from my face to Richard's. I did not know what to say, for it was hardly safe to discuss our planned summoning before this company, not when my brother was not entirely privy to everything, and certainly not with the Hatfield servants waiting on us at table.

"Forgive me, my lady," I stammered. "I was being foolish, that is all."

But Elizabeth was no longer listening to me. She was staring beyond me, at the far end of the table. She dropped her knife with a clatter. Her cheeks, always pale, grew even whiter until I thought she would faint. Then her hand raised, pointing into the shadows past the table. "Who...*what* is...that?"

I turned, and my heart clenched in fear.

The shadow creature was there, standing a few feet from the end of the table. No, not standing, but hovering. It looked more and more like a man every time I saw it. As I stared, horrified, its bloated shadowy form began to move inexorably towards us.

The Lady Elizabeth stood, her chair scraping noisily as the creature seemed to darken, rising into the air above the table.

"No!" she cried, and crossed herself feverishly. "Begone, foul fiend! Back to Hell whence you came!"

Even the old hound seemed to have sensed that something was wrong. Rufus leaped up from his place beside the hearth and stood stiffly, legs apart, barking into the shadows beyond the table.

The bench fell backwards with a crash as Alejandro sprang to his feet, staring about the hall as though expecting some hellish creature to leap on us at any moment. It was clear he could not see the spirit.

William had fallen with the bench but struggled to his feet now, his expression perplexed. He drew his dagger, perhaps thinking we were under attack. "What in God's name...?"

Backing away in a crouch, Richard looked at me. "Is it the spirit?" When I nodded, he asked, "Where is it now?"

I lifted a trembling finger and pointed.

From his vantage point at the hearth, the old retainer was staring at us, then into the shadows, his brow wrinkled. It was clear that he could see nothing either, but thought perhaps that the Lady Elizabeth had lost her mind.

Blanche had seen the old man staring at us too. Urgently, she waved her hand at him, hissing, "What are you staring at? Leave us!"

Not waiting to be told twice, John nodded and hurried away, dragging the dog with him. No doubt he was glad to be free of such a deranged company.

Elizabeth's hand shook as she gestured Alejandro to her side. "Speak your name, creature, if you possess the power of speech."

But the black shadow-thing merely laughed at this command. Its laugh filled the hall, deep and repellent, echoing off the walls and ceiling. The room was suddenly colder, the damp rushes underfoot more noticeable, even the smell of the roast pork unappetising now, as though the shadow's presence tainted everything. The fire itself seemed to darken as the creature rose, undulating across the table towards the princess in a mass of ragged black ribbons, their ends coiling upwards like smoke.

Alejandro took the silver crucifix on its chain from about his neck and held it up like a weapon—or a shield.

"You are not welcome here, demon!" he called in a clear voice, looking about himself as though hoping to find the spirit visible to him. "Quit this place and get back to Hell where you belong."

Again, the shadow laughed. Then it grew huge, spreading further and further, until the hall seemed dense with smoke, and I could no longer see Alejandro's face. But I could hear him calling aloud in Latin, only a few feet from me, commanding the creature to leave.

I felt the heat of the fire at my back, but could not see it, nor my hand before my face, the place was so thick with darkness. Then I heard someone close by begin to whisper in my ear, a terrible hissing that got inside my head and left me dizzy. It was like a fly that would not leave me alone, my scalp tingling, the hairs rising on the back of my neck as I tried to bat it away.

"Meg!"

It was the princess's voice. But where was she? I stared wildly about, seeing nothing but a grey wall of coiling smoke. It was like dust in my throat, grit in my eyes. I staggered back, coughing, half blinded, helpless to find the Lady Elizabeth. I heard her voice again, but it was no use. I could not see her, nor Alejandro, nor any of the others…

Clasping my hands in despair, my fingers met the small leather thong wound about my wrist. My charm-stone!

I unlooped the charm-stone and held it up, still unable to see anything in the dense smoky darkness. I thought of Aunt Jane, her quiet strength, her knowledge of the forests and fields, her understanding of the spirits, and willed her spirit to be with me in this banishing.

"Depart!" I cried, not expecting it to work but hoping.

Miraculously, in an instant, the smoky darkness was gone and we were left standing in the Great Hall like fools, the fire burning bright at my back, illuminating our stunned faces.

William was still crouched, dagger in hand, staring about himself in search of his unseen enemy. Alice stood by his side, white-faced and still. I could see she did not know what to make of any of this but, brave girl, had chosen not to run but to stay with us. Richard was near the windows, his face turned to the wall. He shook himself and stared around, blinking as though his sight had just been restored.

Alejandro was guarding the Lady Elizabeth, crucifix raised before him, his duty always to the princess. Blanche was kneeling near the stairs, her head in her hands; when she saw the smoky darkness in the hall was gone, she gave a low moaning cry and struggled to her feet.

"My lady," she managed croakily, and hurried to her mistress, crossing herself frantically. "Are you hurt? All that terrible smoke… Lord love us, what was it?"

The Lady Elizabeth shook her head, staring past her lady-in-waiting at me. "What did you do, Meg?" she asked in a low voice. Her gaze dropped to the charm-stone. "Was it the white stone? Did you destroy it with that?"

I shook my head, and sank to the bench, my strength almost gone now that the moment of need was over, not caring that I should not sit while the princess was still on her feet.

"It's not destroyed, my lady, though gone for now. When it returns, it will have found a way to master me…and this." I wound the charm-stone about my forearm again and dragged down my sleeve to hide it. "The spirit is cunning. It will discover a counterspell to my aunt's charm-stone, just as it has found a way to sidestep other forms of banishment."

Alejandro nodded, tight-lipped, and hung the crucifix about his neck again. "Yes, the cross had no power over it." His dark eyes sought mine. "You are unharmed?"

"I feel as though I have been disembowelled with a spoon," I muttered, "but otherwise, yes."

The Lady Elizabeth was impatient. "But are we to expect another visitation tonight?"

"We should be safe enough now."

"Good," the Lady Elizabeth said decisively, and sat down again at the head of the table. With a brisk snap of her fingers, she signalled the others to return to their seats. "Come, do not stand about the place amazed. You heard what Meg said. Are we cowards here, or stout-hearted Englishmen and women?" She pointed with her dagger to a dish of devilled kidneys. "Blanche, my appetite has returned. I'll take some of that, and a goodly slice of pork. Señor de Castillo, more wine if you please."

"My lady," Alejandro murmured, and brought the flagon to pour more into her cup. His gaze was frankly admiring as he bowed. "*La princesa con el corazon valiente*. You have a courageous heart, my lady."

I tried not to let my jealousy show, but smiled instead at Richard as he passed me the platter of greasy slices of pork. "Thank you."

His smile was lopsided. "I was not much help to you just then, was I? Forgive me. I was stumbling about like a fool, my head in a daze."

"There is nothing to forgive," I told him, seeing the bitterness and self-loathing in his eyes. He was too quick to condemn himself. "The spirit rules by fear, that is its power. We were all in a daze."

"Not you," Richard pointed out.

I touched my sleeve where the charm-stone was hidden. "But without this, the power my aunt left me, I should have been lost too."

The Lady Elizabeth had been listening to this exchange. She put down her cup of wine and looked at me sharply. "Master Dee's apprentice is right, Meg. You alone of us kept your head. But tonight's visitation proves one thing beyond any doubt. The Church cannot control this evil." Her gaze flashed to Alejandro's face, perhaps sensing his instinctive denial. "No, *señor*, you had your chance with the holy cross, and its power only seemed to increase tenfold at the sight of it. Yet it heeded Meg's command and fled. How much more evidence do we need that she should be the one to exorcize this creature, not a priest?"

"My lady, it is too dangerous—" Alejandro began, but she held up her hand, silencing him with an imperious gesture.

"Dee's apprentice will prepare her. There will be no danger if it is done properly. No, the thing is decided." The Lady Elizabeth looked at me coldly. "Master Dee seems to think you summoned this horror into our lives, Meg Lytton. So to-morrow you will send it back to Hell, if you please—or else live to feel my displeasure."

16

GENIUS LOCI

I felt curiously empty and light-headed as Richard led me by the hand through the darkening woods to a place he had prepared. Looking up through the yellowing leaves, I caught occasional glimpses of the sky, cloudy this evening and already flushed with the coming sunset. The air felt close and troubled, as though a storm was on its way, a fine sweat trickling down my back under my gown.

Dee's apprentice had sat for some hours that morning, consulting his master's ephemeris and magickal books, then finally announced that "one hour after sundown" that day would be the best time for the summoning of hostile spirits. Yet his mood had grown steadily more sombre as the day progressed, for the more he read in those ancient grimoires, the darker the outcome seemed to be.

All day I had fasted, taking nothing but a few sips of boiled water and honey at noon, according to the detailed instructions left by Master Dee. Now my body was like a hollowed-out reed, waiting only to be played upon by the powers that I knew lay all around us.

About ten minutes' walk from the house, we reached a narrow clearing amongst the trees. Here Richard dropped my hand and unswung the leather pack from his shoulder, setting it on the ground. Unfastened, it fell open to reveal an array of magickal objects: black feathers, tapering hazel and ash wands, small crystals, a rusty old nail with red thread wound about it, some small squares of parchment with arcane figures in boxes scrawled across them, and a collection of tiny brownish bones in a cloth bag which he drew out, selecting a few and weighing them thoughtfully in his palm. Some of these objects he placed on a large flat stone he had designated as an altar, arranging them according to a diagram in one of Dee's books, which he kept consulting as he knelt before the altar, his expression distracted. Others he replaced in the pack, and a few—such as the knotted cord they had used to bind my wrists last time, and the blindfold—he laid to one side.

I stood watching, not wishing to distract him during these preparations. Then finally, unable to contain myself any longer, I asked, "Why must the summoning take place outside?"

Richard glanced at me sideways. "Believe it or not, it's safer this way."

"Safer for whom?"

"For everyone," he said drily.

Without bothering to elaborate on that point, Richard set a horn-cup and a fat black candle on the altar, to the right of the scattered bones, then turned to rummage in his pack for the tinderbox.

"Allow me," I said quietly.

I focused on the dead candle and willed it into life, imagining the flicker and spark of a tiny flame, then its steadily glowing light. Suddenly the candle was lit.

"There," I murmured with satisfaction, pleased to know I had not completely forgotten my power.

Richard rocked back on his heels, gazing at me. I caught a flash of pity in his near-black eyes and was afraid. Did he think I was going to die in this confrontation?

"You have real power, Meg," he said grudgingly, then ran a slow finger across the top of the candle flame, as though needing to feel the sting of its heat before believing. "A power that cannot be counterfeited. You will need it tonight."

"You think this spirit is going to defeat me?"

He hesitated, not looking at me any more. This reluctance to share what he had discovered in those ancient books seemed more ominous than anything he could have said. "I think… I think we should stop talking and make ourselves ready. If Master Dee were here, we would spend the next hour in prayer and contemplation."

I smiled. "But since he is not here?"

"I am not my master. Make your peace with God in your own way," Richard muttered, brushing the soil off his clothes as he got to his feet, "then come and kneel before the altar. I have to cast the circle about us. In less than an hour, we shall begin."

As he began brushing away some of the fallen leaves and twigs that cluttered the ceremonial space, I heard a cracking behind me and turned to see Alejandro standing at the edge of the clearing.

My heart skittered nervously at the sight of my betrothed, and I went to him swiftly.

"Alejandro? What are you doing here?" I demanded, rather more sharply than I had intended. But I could not bear the thought that he might try to interfere tonight, and perhaps get himself killed. These powers were stronger and darker than he realized, far beyond what he had known and experienced in his life, and he would only be hurt if he stayed.

Richard's head swivelled, and he regarded Alejandro with a brooding expression. The two stared at each other for a moment, and then Richard turned back to his work.

Alejandro caught at my hand. "Don't be angry, Meg. I'm not here to stop you. I know this must be done."

"Then why—"

"I brought you something." Alejandro gestured for me to hold out my hand; when I did so, he placed something cold in my palm. His silver crucifix! I stared down at it dumbfounded, then at his face, seeing his eyes intent on mine. "I know the magick you work tonight is dark. But I would still like you to wear this. Will you do that for me?"

"Your crucifix had no power against the spirit," I reminded him.

"It had no power to banish," he agreed. "But forgive me, I have been reading about such matters, and if a token is given with the intention that it will protect the wearer from harm, it has more power than it possessed before."

I stared, incredulous and a little dazed at this thought. "You have been…reading about such matters?" I repeated. "In what book?"

"That does not matter now. What matters is that you go into this dark magick with as much protection as possible." He pressed the crucifix deeper into my palm and closed my fingers about it. "I pray you take it, if you love me."

I looked up and met his eyes, hearing bitterness in his voice. "I do love you, Alejandro," I whispered.

He glanced across at Richard, as though about to say something, then seemed to change his mind. But I saw his face tighten.

Did he think I cared for Dee's apprentice?

The thought shocked me. I remembered Alejandro's mock-jealousy the other day because I had "smiled" at Dee's apprentice. I had dismissed it as a jest at the time. Perhaps I should have heeded his fears and been more distant with Richard. I did not wish to risk losing Alejandro over a misunderstanding.

"Alejandro? What is it?"

But he turned away, shaking his head. "I've done what I came here to do. Wear the crucifix, Meg. Don't forget."

I trod swiftly after him, reaching on tiptoe to kiss him gently on the lips.

He hesitated, then his arms came round me, almost convulsively. "Meg!"

We stood together in silence. I laid a hand on his chest and felt the unsteady beat of his heart beneath my fingers. Long might it continue beating! I did not want to turn him away tonight, any more than I truly wished to confront and do battle with the dark spirit I had accidentally conjured. But I had long since accepted that life was not perfect, and that the thing we most wished to avoid was often the thing we would have to face in the end.

Standing like this in his arms felt like a farewell, like a parting of the ways for ever. Yet it was just possible that I would return victorious, that Richard's grim looks were mistaken.

Then again I had not been known for being lucky so far.

Richard came limping towards us, a hazel wand in his hand pointed rather ominously at Alejandro. "I hate to interrupt this touching moment," he told us, "but I cannot cast the circle until you are clear of the woods. Your presence here disturbs the ground."

I shot him an irritated glance over my shoulder. "Richard!"

But Alejandro's arms were already dropping away, and he shook his head. "No, for once I agree with your apprentice friend. I should not be here." He looked at me intently. "I'll be waiting for you at the house."

"This ritual may take several hours," Richard informed him deliberately, the hazel wand still poised in his hand as though he was about to turn Alejandro into some undesirable creature. "It is late now. We may not return to the house until after midnight."

"Then I shall wait until *after midnight*," Alejandro replied with grating emphasis, "and for as long as it takes. Just be sure she wears *that* about her neck," he added.

Richard looked incredulously at the crucifix dangling from my hand. "You believe that will help? I knew you for a fool, Priest. But I did not know you were also a madman."

I expected them to come to blows following that insult. But to my utter amazement, Alejandro did not respond, almost as though he had not heard a word.

"Wear it," he told me softly, backing away. Then he turned and soon vanished, light-footed amongst the trees in the gathering dusk, his dark clothes fading between the trunks.

"Now perhaps we can get on," Richard muttered, and swept the hazel wand in a long circle, beginning the incantation.

In a ringing voice he called on the spirits of the North and South to make our intentions true, then honoured the East and West, sources of the rising and setting sun, of beginnings and endings. Then Richard took a wand of blackthorn in his left hand and walked the circumference of the circle against the direction of the sun, touching the ground at each point of the compass, his face averted from mine. I knew how he felt, for it was always in those first moments of casting the circle and beginning to walk its power that I felt the pull of the earth beneath my feet, and the great wheeling stars and planets above me, looking down with terrible dispassionate faces. It was a lonely time, the walking of the circle.

I sat huddled before the stone altar, watching the candle flame dip and flutter. It was a foolish thing, but I felt bereft now that Alejandro had gone. I was somehow more vulnerable, as though while he was with me, nothing could touch me, no harm befall me. Now the very air was oppressive, the sky weighing down on me as dusk turned inexorably to night.

Richard could feel it too. Raising the blackthorn wand, his slow circuit at an end, he glanced about at the too-silent woods. There was a strange tension humming between the trees, a thickening of the air about the circle he had cast.

"There will be a storm tonight," he commented, but I knew there was more he was not saying, his face shuttered as he knelt beside me and carefully placed the blackthorn wand on the altar.

I looped the chain over my head, allowing the silver crucifix to settle on my chest. I saw Richard looking at it, and pulled a face. "It does no harm. Think what you like. Alejandro is my betrothed and he has asked me to wear this."

"I see nothing but darkness ahead for both of you." I had been right to think him reluctant to speak. The words seemed dragged from him, and he shrugged when I turned on him angrily. "Peace, girl, I shall not speak against your beloved again. Well, not tonight anyway. You do yourself no good by this. Calm yourself and think of the ritual ahead."

I resisted the urge to stick my tongue out at him. He was right, much as I disliked the way he spoke to me as though I was a child. Alejandro's visit had shaken me, brought heat and fire back into my body. I could not call the spirit like this, flushed and confused, lost to my true self. Somehow I needed to return to the hollow state I had reached earlier, my fingertips tingling with power, my mind drifting like an empty boat on a river.

His eyes very dark, Richard looked about the edges of the circle. Night had drawn in while we were talking. He counted seven twigs from a tied bundle he had brought in his pack. These he set before the altar, then looked at me sideways. "Kindle the fire, Meg."

I licked my lips, suddenly afraid. The ritual was beginning. Like a whisper, fire licked tentatively along one of the twigs, then all seven were alight.

He set a small iron crucible atop the flames, waited until it was ticking with heat, then sprinkled a few pinches of dark powder inside it. The powder began to smoke at once, its fumes thick and black, almost overwhelming me as I knelt alongside.

"It is time. Stay within the circle, Meg. Do not break the circle by so much as one step, whatever happens," he whispered urgently, not looking at me but at the smoking crucible. "For the god of the place," he muttered, and poured a thick red liquid from the horn-cup across the altar stone, thick as blood and as acrid-smelling, waiting as it trickled darkly into the earth below. *"Genius loci."*

This done, Richard drew a short, black-handled dagger from his belt and sketched the six-fold sign in the smoky air, then passed the blade through the flames as many times.

"Now!"

I stood and let my head fall back, staring up at the stars just starting to prick the night sky. My arms spread wide, I called aloud on the powers to guide me, on the spirit of my aunt to look down kindly on me, on Hecate herself to strengthen my work that night.

I unwound the white charm-stone from about my wrist

and held it up, using whatever power it possessed to summon the spirit.

"By these tokens, by these offerings, by the blood, by the
fire, by the smoke, by the stone, by the six-fold sign, and by
this charm, I bid thee come to us, unquiet spirit!" I waited,
listening to the silence of the night, the crackling of the fire,
then called again. My belly turned to ice, my veins running
cold, as I saw the darkness thicken about us, drawing towards
our circle. "Shadow creature from the otherworld, heed my
call and appear before us as you were in life. I conjure thee,
appear!"

A mass began to form and grow in the shadows, a few feet
beyond the invisible confines of the circle. The bulky figure
of a man hunched over in sickness, his legs swollen, his vast
body riddled with pain. A bearded face glimmered through
the darkness, skin flushed and mottled, a high forehead shining in the flickering light from the fire.

The spirit's malevolent gaze moved around the circle until
it came to rest on me.

I started in shock, almost dropping the charm-stone. His
were the same dark narrow eyes I knew from the face of the
Lady Elizabeth, seething now with rage and contempt.

"Who dares summon me?"

"It is Meg Lytton who summons you!" I cried, my voice
cracked with the effort of standing unmoved by that glare.
"What is your name, spirit?"

The bearded mouth smiled cruelly. "Henry Tudor is my
name."

My tongue was dry, sticking to the roof of my mouth.
The little white charm-stone seemed to be growing steadily
heavier in my hands; it was all I could do to keep it lifted towards him.

There was a fog in my mind. Had the spirit infected me? I struggled to speak, fumbling over the words I had prepared.

"This is no longer your place, Henry Tudor. Your time has come to depart this earth and return to the world of shadows whence you came." The charm-stone was now as heavy as a rock; my wrists strained and trembled under its weight. "Begone, spirit!"

The thin lips parted again. The spirit-king laughed. The sound was like dead leaves blowing along a desolate track at dusk.

Despair filled me. I had no power over this man. He was Henry Tudor, King of England. His was a great royal dynasty. His name glittered across the world's oceans, his power immense beyond measure. I was nothing before him. A girl in a wood, crumbling under the weight of her own feeble spell. Soon he would lift his hand and strike me down, and I would deserve my death, sinking without a murmur into the nameless oblivion that was my destiny.

Someone else was speaking in the glowing dark. A low voice chanting. I looked down and saw a figure hunched over the smouldering fire, passing the thin knotted cord through the smoke, then looping it between his fingers, muttering, "By this third knot, I close thy eyes! By this fourth knot, I strip thee of thy power! By this fifth knot, I name thee a dead King! By this sixth knot, I open the gates of death!"

In my fear, I had forgotten Richard. I was not alone in the circle; I was not alone in the spell.

He faltered momentarily in his chant though, the spirit of Henry Tudor snarling at him from beyond the circle, "Traitor! Dost thou not know me for thy King? Thou shalt find thy death in this treachery, conjuror!"

Not looking round, Richard continued more strongly, a steely note in his voice, fingering each knot with strong deliberation, "By this seventh knot, I bid thee turn about! By this eighth knot, I call on angels to light the way! By this ninth knot, I conjure thee *depart!*"

A terrible roaring filled the wood, rising in intensity, almost deafening. I longed to cover my ears yet had to keep holding the charm-stone aloft, for it was my only shield against his fury. The dead King seemed to change, blurring and growing, transforming back into the vile shadow creature I had first seen at Hampton Court. His glittering eyes stared down at me through the darkness, the only human thing left about him. Then the hovering cloud of his body began to spin, faster and faster, a vast whirlpool of black smoke. The trees swayed and bent before it like a great wind, their yellow leaves stripped and sucked into the void.

The skies opened above us and rain hammered down like the violent deluge which took the Ark. I was soaked within seconds, my wet gown clinging to my skin, my teeth chattering. The charm-stone was heavy beyond human endurance; I could not hold it aloft any longer. It was like the weight of a mountain on my chest, cracking my spine, crushing me to death.

My knees buckled under the strain of resisting him. I staggered a few steps forward, my arms dropping to my sides, drawn by those eyes, the vicious stare, the black wind sucking at my gown, my hair. Even the silver crucifix and chain about my neck had lifted like a dowsing stick, pointing at the shadow-king, almost dragging me towards him.

"Don't break the circle, Meg!" Richard cried in alarm, dropping the knotted cord and leaping to his feet. His hand clutched for and missed my shoulder.

There was a blinding flash of light, then I fell into darkness.

My eyes focused on chill daylight, rough grey stone under my feet, a curious sensation of height. When my head finally stopped spinning and I was able to raise it, I looked about myself. A mist surrounded me, its thick dew wetting my skin. As I stared, the mist rolled away, showing me damp hillsides in the distance, a barren ravine, gnarled and twisted trees far below.

From the winds blowing my hair, I knew at once where I was. Back in my vision, on top of the tower. I heard the rush of air about my ears, the sound of wingbeats, then a hawk screamed furiously above me.

Which meant…

Glancing over my shoulder, I saw the man with the axe in his hand. Only it was not Marcus Dent this time. It was the shadow-king, half smoke, half man, his bearded, heavy-jowled face glaring down at me from the heart of darkness.

The King raised his axe. "Kneel for thy death, witch!"

I fumbled for a spell that would send me back to the woodland circle, back to Richard, to the world of the living. But my mouth had been sealed by some magickal charm, and I could make no sound, only shake my head. I tried to raise my hand to bind my attacker with a gesture, then found my wrists had been sewn to my sides with invisible thread, a mischievous spell I had used on my nurse as a child, only to be threatened with a whipping by my aunt if I ever showed off my power like that again.

So I stood, effectively gagged and bound, before the gloating fury of the dead King.

"You see how weak you are, witch?" the spirit-voice hissed in my ear as the cloud rolled over me, enveloping me in its terrible clammy darkness. "You are nothing. You dared to summon me? I do not answer to a woman. No, nor to any man either. I am Henry Tudor, King of England."

How could any spirit have such power over the living? I did not understand how it was possible. It seemed to break all the rules my aunt had ever taught me about the boundaries between worlds.

Yet what could I do? My neck was bare, my hair blown to one side by the wind so the fragile nape of my neck was exposed—almost as though I was being prepared to meet the axe.

But I refused to die. Not here, not today.

I conjure you, depart!

I thought my spell at him instead, thinking so furiously it felt as though my head would burst with the effort.

You are a spirit, not true flesh. By the breath in my living body, by the blood in my living veins, I conjure you—depart!

Untouched by my silent spell, the shadow-king snarled at me, "Your magick cannot touch me, witch. I shall have your head this night. Then I shall return to my daughter's court and have hers too, for she is but a woman and weak-minded. I shall consume her heart and rule through her, and this disobedient land shall come to suffer such a burning and a darkness as it has never known before."

The triumphant power of his voice was like a hand, thrusting me to my knees. My hands bound by his spell, my mouth sealed, I found myself kneeling on the cold top of the tower, unable to save myself. Was this real or merely a nightmare? If I was killed here in my vision, would I die back there in the woods? It felt real enough. The air was cold on my face, the stone hard under my knees, and my heart was beating so loudly…

I looked up in sudden terror as his axe swung. The sun glinted evilly off the blade, dazzling me, the whole world a blur of shadow and light, with death waiting for me beyond it.

Too late I realized the face behind the axe had changed. The shadow-king had vanished, and Marcus Dent stood in his place.

"This was always your destiny, Meg," he cried, his voice ringing with triumph. His scarred face turned towards me, one sharp blue eye fixed on my face, the other a dull and empty socket. "Now die!"

The axe came down before I had a chance to move. The whole world shuddered sideways, then turned black.

DEAD WITCH

My body was soaring like a bird's, flying above dark woods. Below, I could see the trees in incredible detail, each reddish leaf glinting in starlight under heavy rain. It looked as though the treetops were bristling with jewels. The rain fell about me, wet pinpoints like hundreds of thousands of thin silver pins hurtling past my body. Yet I was not wet, and the bright narrow rain passed straight through me as though I was not there.

I looked down, catching sudden movement between the trees on the dark ground. I was following someone who was running below. An odd limping figure, crashing noisily through the woods, carrying a burden in his arms: it looked at first like a dead swan, her long graceful neck dangling back over his arm, her body limp and lifeless.

Then the man running came clear of the trees, staggering

across the waterlogged grass under the downpour, and I saw at last what he was carrying. No swan, but a dead girl.

As he approached the entrance to the great house, the studded door was flung open and Alejandro ran out into the rain, fully dressed as I had last seen him, his head bare, but with a sword hanging from his belt.

"Meg!" he cried out, seeing my limp body in Richard's arms. "*Madre di Dios,* what have you done to her?"

"She stepped out of the circle," Richard gasped, shouldering his way past Alejandro into the house.

Suddenly I was inside too, floating just below the rafters, looking down at them in the Great Hall. The fire was dying, a soft glowing light that lit up their faces as Richard carried me to the table and lay me down there as gently as though I had been alive. The old hound jumped up from the hearth and began to bark, no doubt sensing something was badly wrong.

"Is she...? *Dios mio!*" Alejandro took my wrist and felt for a pulse there, then put his fingers to the side of my throat. I had never seen him look so sick and haggard. "No, no, no, no, *no!*"

Richard smoothed back the wet hair that was stuck to my forehead, staring down into my face, then stepped aside for Alejandro.

"It was raining so hard. There was a lightning strike. I think she was hit. I can't be sure, it happened so fast." Richard shook his head, wiping the rain from his forehead. "Meg had summoned him, King Henry. He was strong though, so strong. I didn't think she would be able to exorcize him, and I tried my own spell to help her, but I was too late. He held her in some kind of trance. She took a step out of the circle and the bolt of lightning struck her where she stood."

"Lightning?"

"There was a great flash of light, then I heard the thunderclap. The ground was on fire all around our circle and she was lying there dead, her shoes gone, her bare feet blackened and burnt. The creature was gone. I picked her up in my arms and ran for the house." Richard ran a hand through his wet hair, his face flushed, his dark clothes sodden. His voice was hoarse. "I was there to protect Meg, and I failed her. Forgive me."

"Forgive you?" Alejandro choked. "Forgive you?"

He spun from my body and dragged the sword from his belt. It shone between them, lethal and naked, pointing at Richard's heart. Dee's apprentice stepped back, though there was no fear in his face—only a wariness that told he had half expected this from the Spaniard.

"I shall kill you for this night's work," Alejandro ground out, his eyes hard and glittering. "She was in your care, dog! Now she lies dead, and all you can say is, 'Forgive me'?"

Richard sank into a defensive crouch. There was anger in his voice too. "I told you, it was not my fault. But kill me if you can, novice," he snarled, his dagger suddenly in his hand. "You are not the only one here who knows how to fight. I shall not make it easy for you."

"Put up your weapons! How dare you brawl in my house?"

There was a stirring on the dark stairway. Elizabeth was descending the stairs in her cloak and nightshift, staring down into the Great Hall. Beside her came Blanche, holding aloft a burning torch, and Alice at their backs, rubbing her eyes, sleepy and confused.

The hound continued to bark hysterically. But the two young men turned, falling back from each other. Neither put away his weapon though, still watching each other with furious eyes.

"Hush, Rufus. Lie down, boy." The Lady Elizabeth shooed away the barking dog, then halted beside the table, seeing my body stretched out upon it as though I were sleeping. Her face froze. "What is this? What has happened?"

"My lady—" Richard began, his voice croaking, but Alejandro interrupted him.

"Meg Lytton is dead, my lady. She served you too well and has died for her loyalty." Alejandro sounded half-demented with grief and rage, yet somehow he was controlling himself. His face was taut, his bare sword still in his hand—though he had lowered it now, with an effort. "Dee's apprentice reports that she achieved her end though. The spirit that haunted your house has been banished back to Hell—and taken your servant with him!"

Blanche began to speak angrily, but the Lady Elizabeth held up her hand. "No. Señor de Castillo is a passionate man and must be allowed to speak his mind. There is no fault in the anger of an honest man."

She approached my body on the table. She stared first at my bare feet, blackened by the lightning strike which had killed me, then at my hand, hanging down from the table, palm open.

I saw true regret on her face. "Poor, poor Meg. I would not have had this happen for the world, I swear it. If I had known how dangerous…"

William, who had been sleeping in the stables since our arrival at Hatfield, appeared from the passageway to the kitchens, rubbing his eyes and stretching. "What's all the noise? I heard shouts, and that blasted hound barking…"

My brother frowned at Richard, standing silent and defeated to one side, then saw me lying on the table. His face grew pale and he staggered forward. "Sweet Jesu, is she—?"

"A lightning bolt," Richard muttered. "It came out of nowhere. She had no chance."

"Oh, Meg," William gasped. He seemed stunned, averting

his horrified gaze from the terrible black marks of scorching on my bare feet. "My dear sister."

The Lady Elizabeth laid a hand on his shoulder, comforting him. "She died bravely, William, as she lived," she murmured. "You should be proud." She bent over me as though looking into my face, perhaps searching for signs of life. I watched from above as she seemed to tremble a moment, then turned away, straightening. "Not a magickal death, then. I had hoped…"

Briefly, I saw Alejandro close his eyes, and wondered if he too had hoped my death might prove magickal—and therefore reversible.

Perhaps noting his pain, Elizabeth continued more gently, "The new priest should be called to administer the last rites. And the coroner must be summoned to bear her body away. Let one of the servants ride with a message for them at first light. Meanwhile, poor Meg cannot lie here in the Great Hall. Nor should her body be left unattended. It is not fitting that she should be alone tonight." She glanced at William, who was crossing my arms gently across my chest, then raised her small dark eyes to Alejandro's face. "*Señor,* you are the closest we have to a priest here. Will you light the candles and keep vigil over her body until dawn?"

Alejandro managed a bare nod. "I shall carry Meg to my chamber and light the candles for her there. My Bible and prayer books are there, it is a quiet space."

"I will help you," William muttered, tears in his eyes.

"I need no help," Alejandro said harshly, then checked himself, holding out his hand to my brother. "Forgive me. She was your sister…but I have as much cause as you to mourn her death, William. We had not announced it formally, and I beg your pardon for keeping such a secret from you, but your sister and I were betrothed to be married."

Stiffening at this revelation, the Lady Elizabeth's face grew cold. She looked hard at Alejandro, but said nothing. No doubt she found the very idea of a Catholic novice in love offensive. But to be in love with one of her own servants...

For once paying the princess no heed, Alejandro turned, looking stiffly across at Richard. "You must forgive my temper too. I know Meg's death cannot be laid at your door. We will talk in the morning, when...after—"

Seeing that he could not finish, Richard limped forward, thrusting his dagger back into his belt. He held out his hand, palm upwards, and offered Alejandro what was there: a thin chain from which hung the silver crucifix, still wet with rain.

"Here, this is yours. It must have fallen from her neck when the lightning struck." His face was grim. "I found it on the ground beside her."

Alejandro took the crucifix, staring down at it broodingly. "So she was wearing it. When I didn't see it around her neck, I assumed—"

"She was wearing it," Richard agreed wearily. "And she had her charm-stone too. Though they availed her little in the end."

Alice, who had been sobbing quietly into her hands all this while, her head turned away as though she could not bear to look on my body, came haltingly forward. She embraced both Richard and William, then came to Alejandro, her eyes full of pity.

"I cannot believe she is gone. She was the sweetest friend... my dearest Meg... Oh, I cannot bear to say her name, it is too horrible." Alice dried her eyes with the back of her hand, whispering aside to Alejandro, "Would you like me to keep vigil with you over her body, *señor*? I shall not speak except to pray."

"Forgive me, Alice." He tried to smile, but could not. "I

thank you, but I must be alone with her tonight. There are things that should be said, even though it may be too late for Meg to hear them. They will weigh on my conscience for the rest of my life if I do not…"

Abruptly, Alejandro bent and scooped me up in his arms as lightly as though I weighed nothing, carrying me towards the dark staircase. Blanche fell back, staring at my limp body as he passed, the burning torch shaking in her hand.

Like a hound on a leash, I floated up the stairs after him, beginning to feel more and more distant from the cold shell that had once been my body. It seemed cruel to keep me here so long, watching my beloved in pain and knowing I could not reassure him that I had felt nothing at the end, that my death was no one's fault but my own.

I had arrogantly assumed I could defeat the shadow-king, and that my vision of Marcus Dent with the axe was not something to be feared. I had been wrong on both counts, and although I was not entirely sure how it had happened, my death was the result. It seemed fitting that I should spend my last hours alone with Alejandro before being committed to the grave.

Kicking his door open, Alejandro carried me into his bedchamber. A small fire smouldered in the grate, but otherwise it was in darkness.

With the gentlest of hands, he lowered my dead body to the bed, then stood a while in silence, staring down at me. I could hear him breathing, and thought oddly, *I shall never breathe again.* Already I was forgetting how to breathe, watching incorporeal, part of the darkness, a shadow myself now—just as the shadow-king had been, watching us from the ceiling. At last Alejandro turned away and painfully set out four candles, one at each corner of the bed, like guardians against evil spirits. He lit a spill from the grate and touched its flame to each candle, murmuring, *"In te, Domino, speravi, non confundar in aeternum,"* reciting the psalm in Latin for me, "I have put my trust in You, O Lord, may I never be cast into confusion."

This done, Alejandro made the sign of the cross above my body, and bent his head to pray.

Suddenly, his calm demeanour broke, and he took three swift strides across the narrow chamber. Gasping in agony, he beat his head and fists against the stone mantel above the hearth.

"Meg, Meg, my little love…" His shoulders heaved, and I realized he was weeping. He groaned, "Not you. Not you. Not you. Anyone but you." A flame of anger singed his voice, his pain catching light. "Lord, why did You have to do this? How could You take her so soon?"

Moments passed while I watched his bent head. Then he came back to the bed, his eyes dark with agony.

"Since there is no help for it… May the Good Lord guide your steps in Heaven, my beloved."

He placed the silver crucifix about my neck, rearranging my damp hair on the pillows with a tender hand.

Now it looked as though I were asleep on his bed, my pale eyelids closed, lips slightly parted, the silver crucifix resting on my chest.

"You will be buried with the cross about your neck. That at least I can do for you." Alejandro leaned forward, touching his lips to mine, then whispered, "I was a fool, *mi alma,* and never fully opened my heart to you. But I love you to the edge of madness, to the gates of death itself. If it were possible, I would take your place in the afterlife. I pray to God you are in Heaven soon, whatever your offences may have been on earth. For there can be no place in the torments of Hell for such a soul as yours. You are the truest, the most courageous woman I have ever known."

He knelt beside the bed, clasped one of my hands between his, and began to pray over me in Latin.

I felt an odd tugging deep in my belly. I was suddenly too threadbare a spirit, too scarcely there to remain. Without a sound, my ghost began to scrape through an invisible hole in the air like a thread being pulled from one side of a tapestry to another.

Was this the end of my haunting? Was I now to be taken up to Heaven—or down into Hell?

As soon as the crucifix had been placed about my neck again, I had felt a change stealing over me, as though remembering something I had forgotten. Something in me resisted the call though, reluctant to leave this wonderful effortless floating, my new world of half-light and shadows. I did not wish to leave Alejandro. I wanted to be with him for ever.

But as Alejandro prayed for my soul, his voice ragged in the darkness, I gradually realized that I was no longer watching from above, but was inside my dead body again. My limbs were too heavy and stiff to move, and I could not lift my eyelids to look at him. But I was struggling to breathe, wanting to breathe, though it seemed I had a wet leather sack in my chest. It hurt so badly, it was like trying to breathe grit, sand, broken glass.

My body fought the agonizing sensation, hating it. Yet it could not help but keep trying, made to draw breath and let it out again, to be human. Then my fingers tingled, warmed by the blood in his living hand; the cold skin was coming back to life, beginning to feel again.

I drew breath and spluttered, my chest jerking as I gasped for air, my body suddenly and brutally alive again.

"*Dios!*" His eyes wide with shock, Alejandro shot back from the bed, dropping my hand and crossing himself. He stared at me in disbelief, then tried my name. "Meg?"

I drew another rasping breath, unable to speak.

He addressed me rapidly in Spanish, his voice hoarse and urgent. Then—perhaps remembering that I could not understand a word he was saying—he seized a wooden crucifix from his table and held it out in front of him. "Are you the Devil? Speak, what are you?"

"I'm thirsty," I managed croakily.

He was barely breathing himself. Slowly, he lowered the crucifix. Raw incredulity was in his voice. "Meg, you are truly alive? *De verdad?*" He stumbled over the words. "How has this happened? You...you were dead. I held you in my arms."

I looked helplessly at the cup I could see on his table.

"It's wine," he said blankly, following my gaze, then seemed to shake himself awake. He fetched the cup and tilted it to my lips. I took a sip, wetting my dry throat, then another. He watched me drink, then set the cup down on the floor.

"Not a ghost, then," Alejandro commented, still dazed by the sight of me alive. "As I understand it, spirits neither eat nor drink."

"You can see well I am no spirit," I muttered, then lay back against the pillows, exhausted even by the small effort of drinking. Being dead seemed to have sapped my strength. I only hoped remaining alive would be easier than dying had been. Already my feet were tingling and itching, the blackened skin tortured by its burning.

"Yet you *were* dead." Warily, he touched a finger to the crucifix about my neck. "Was it this that brought you back?"

I hated the look in his eyes, how careful he was not to brush my skin accidentally, to make any physical contact. Did he think me so very dangerous?

I shrugged, too weary and in pain to struggle for an explanation. "Perhaps."

At that moment, I cared little how it was possible for me to have been dead one minute, then alive the next. All that mattered, surely, was that I was alive again. Time enough to examine this strange miracle for flaws later, when I had grown more accustomed to being back in my body. For now, it was not merely my feet that were hurt. My heart too was feeling a little bruised by the coolness of his welcome back.

"You don't seem very happy that I have survived this ordeal," I remarked, watching from under lowered lashes as he rose and paced the room. "Would you rather I was still dead? So you could love me 'to the gates of Hell,' yet never have to pass through them at my side?"

"You heard that?" He stopped pacing and turned as though stunned by my revelation. A dark red crept into his face. "I thought—"

"That you were talking to a dead woman?"

"Well, I was, if you recall," he countered. His dark eyes met mine then, with an impact that rocked me. "Nonetheless, if you need to hear me say it all again, trust me that I meant every word. Never think me false, Meg. I spoke the truth, I do love you to the very edge of madness—and beyond. Nor am I unhappy to see you breathe and speak again. Indeed, I have never known such joy in my life. Only..."

I raised my eyebrows. He had still not touched me.

Alejandro groaned, then came to sit beside me on the bed. His gaze devoured my hair, my face, my throat. "You are so beautiful, Meg. Beautiful and intelligent, with a tongue sharp as a knife at my throat. I do not know how it is possible, but tonight God has spared His most desirable creature from death."

Truth be told, I did not know myself what to think of my unexpected escape from death. I had slipped that dark leash without any stirring on my part, as though someone else had chosen life for me over death. I only knew that I lived. How and why, I had no inkling nor understanding.

He leaned forward and traced a fingertip across the line of my mouth, not quite touching my skin. "Your body is growing warmer," he murmured wonderingly, then watched the rise and fall of my chest. "Dear Lord, I never thought to see you breathe again."

Perhaps the Devil himself had possessed my soul in the otherworld, then sent me back into this body to destroy Alejandro. For I could not conceive that the Almighty would ever have chosen to spare me—a witch, a sinner, and blasphemer, and the possible ruination of his would-be priest.

None of which helped my fervent wish to feel his lips on mine.

"Kiss me," I said huskily, daring him with my eyes.

If Alejandro thought me some kind of unnatural fiend returned from death's wilderness, come perhaps to bait him into sin and despair, he would not touch me.

He hesitated, frowning. "But what if this miracle is undone by my kiss, *mi alma?* Like brushing the dust from a butterfly's wings, I may kill you with a touch."

"So will you never kiss me again?" I demanded, staring up at him. "Never touch me? Never love me again?"

His eyes burnt on my face. "You know that to be impossible."

"Then kiss me."

Alejandro looked at me intently, as though involved in some inward battle, then bent his dark head at last and put his lips to mine.

I did not mean to tempt him further. But I could not help myself. Instinctively, my arms curled up and linked behind his warm neck, pulling him down into the kiss. He groaned my name against my mouth, then pressed me deeper into the pillows.

I was suddenly, almost violently, delighted that I was still alive. If I had died, this would be a distant memory. This love I felt for him.

"Meg," he managed, then disengaged himself, his hands on my shoulders. I had the feeling he was holding me at a distance, as though he did not trust me to stop. Or did not trust himself. "You aren't strong enough for this. I don't want to hurt you."

"You won't hurt me," I whispered, and traced my hand along his cheek.

He turned his head and kissed my hand, his eyes half-closed. "We can both hurt each other. More than you know, *mi querida.*"

I thrilled, hearing the loving words on his breath in Spanish, feeling his breath warm on my skin. Only a few minutes ago I had been cold, an empty shell lying on his bed, nothing but a body without breath or a soul. But now my spirit had returned. I was filled with restless love, this devouring flame that left me unable to turn my gaze away from his face. I did not ever want this moment to end.

Too soon he pulled away, sitting up and then coming to his feet. "It's not right," he murmured, though I could see from his tense expression that he had been sorely tempted to continue. "I should tell the others. The Lady Elizabeth will need to be informed straight away. And your brother is deeply grieved..."

"I know," I told him quietly. "I was there when Richard brought back my body. I saw and heard it all."

Alejandro stared, coming back to the bed. As he looked down at me, I could see the shock and disbelief echoing inside him. "All?"

I nodded. "Every word."

He went to the table, opening a book that lay there. With slow and careful deliberation, he ran a finger along some of the print, turned the page, then shook his head. "It makes no sense," he muttered, speaking almost to himself. "I do not think you were dead, Meg. I do not know what happened to you, nor where your spirit went for the time when your body was cold. But it cannot have been death."

I wrinkled my brow, unsure what he meant. It had felt like death to me, and indeed everyone else had thought so too. I had seen their faces, the horror and pity in their eyes, and Richard had carried me all the way from the circle to the house—he, of all of them, would have known if I was not dead. Yet he had told the Lady Elizabeth that a lightning strike had killed me, and here—I pulled up my bare feet and examined the painful scorch marks critically—was the evidence.

"Why not?"

He had seen me looking at the blackened soles of my feet, and shook his head. "Oh, I do not doubt that you were struck by lightning—or some magickal spell that seemed like a bolt of lightning. But I do not agree that your death was not magickal. I believe it was very magickal indeed. Which is why your soul was not released after death, but lingered, staying close to your body." He turned another page, staring down at the book. "Yes, we were blind, thinking you gone for ever. But your soul knew it had not been meant to leave your body, but had been forced out by some vile magickal trick. When I replaced the crucifix about your neck, your soul was able to return to its rightful place."

I sat up, shivering as I swung my legs out of bed and touched the cold floor for the first time. The soles of my feet stung horribly. But I gritted my teeth and tried to ignore them.

"What is that book?" I demanded. "What have you been reading?"

"Nothing," he said defensively.

"If it's nothing, then you won't mind me seeing the title," I said, and almost smiled, remembering something similar he had said to me on the stairs at Woodstock once. That had been a secret note from William which I had been trying to hide from him. But this book was rather more serious—and not hidden well enough, to my mind. From what he had just said, it sounded to me like one of the books Master Dee had left with Richard.

Alejandro stood back as I swayed towards the table, watching with an anxious expression as though afraid I would fall, his hands poised to catch me. "Careful," he murmured.

I stared in horror at the large, leather-bound book, then turned it over to read the title on the spine.

"*Picatrix*."

It was one of the darkest books on ancient magick ever written. As Master Dee had pointed out when he saw me looking at it before he left, the *Picatrix* was high on the papal list of most forbidden books. This book would earn Alejandro a death at the stake in Spain just by possessing it—and very likely here too, if his priest-masters ever found him studying such a dangerous magickal text.

I was shocked and could not hide it. "What...why is the *Picatrix* here in your room?" I stammered, leaning on the table to support myself. "Do you know what this is?"

He nodded, his calm expression leaving me speechless. His smile was tight. "I had to understand what you were facing, and what the likely outcome of your summoning would be. I asked Richard and he lent me the book. And a few others like it."

"I'll kill him," I swore under my breath.

His eyebrows arched. "You don't think I should be allowed to know what exactly it is that you do out there in the dark, you and Richard?"

My face grew hot. "You know what we do…that it's all perfectly innocent." I saw his dry smile, and stiffened. "Oh, don't tease me, Alejandro. This isn't a jest. Not only is this a dangerous book, a book of the darkest and most deadly secrets known to our craft, but if the priests knew what you were reading…"

"I would be tortured, and then burnt as a witch by my own masters." He nodded, and touched my face fleetingly, a gentle caress that had my blood on fire for him at once. "That is why you should lower your voice, *mi alma*. I trust Alice and your brother not to betray me, but the servants are another matter. I have been hiding the books under the mattress, but then I heard Richard shouting tonight and left them out here on the table when I ran down to…"

He tailed off, no doubt remembering how he had flung open the front door to the house only to see my dead body lying limply in Richard's arms. The pain in his eyes had not yet died.

But that did not excuse *this*. This was a death wish, keeping such dangerous, forbidden books in his bedchamber.

"You're mad."

"Well, I told you that I loved you to the edge of madness. So here I am. Too far gone to return, I fear." He put an arm about my waist as my knees buckled and carried me back to the mattress. "Now back to bed. I insist upon it. You are too weak to be standing for so long. Here, let me make you comfortable."

He shook out his cloak and laid it across me as I shivered on the bed, staring up at the dark ceiling and wondering where I had gone wrong, wilfully leading my beloved astray into such dark territories, into the study of magickal texts that could mean his death.

"I want you to get some rest while I tell your brother you are alive. He may wish to visit you," he added thoughtfully, pausing in the doorway, "but I will ask him to wait a little while until you are stronger. I will wait until first light to inform *la princesa* of your miraculous resurrection. The Lady Elizabeth will be sleeping by now, it's so late." He frowned, then shrugged. "No, there is no better word for it but resurrection—though it feels uncomfortably like blasphemy."

He surveyed me for a moment, clearly concerned by my stillness on the bed. "I hope it will be safe to leave you alone. Is there anything you want before I go? I will be back before you know it, but if you are thirsty or hungry..."

I sighed, and turned my face heavily into the pillow. Now that I was lying down again, I had suddenly realized how exhausted I was. My eyes closed and I let myself stretch out luxuriously under the warmth of his soft woollen cloak.

"No, thank you," I mumbled, already half-asleep before the door had closed on him. "Love you..."

"I love you too, Meg Lytton, and I thank God you are alive," he replied gently, and I fell asleep with those words swimming about in the darkness of my mind.

18

DISMISSED

I had enjoyed so many visitors from first light, Alejandro's chamber felt like a shrine. I had been stared at, and embraced, kissed, and prayed over by almost everyone in the household. Even the Lady Elizabeth had come to the door, and crossed herself at the sight of me alive again, murmuring, "I thank God for this most wonderful miracle."

The princess sent Alice away, who had been salving my burnt feet, then spoke with me alone a few minutes, questioning me about last night and my struggle with the shadowking.

Elizabeth left me with one last, stern look. "I am most grateful for your service in this matter, Meg. My heart is lifted already, knowing the spirit to be gone. I am not pleased, however, that you have become so intimate with Señor de Castillo. He is to be a priest. It is not fitting that you should spend so much time alone with him. I would be failing in my duty if I did not warn you to break off this betrothal. I think it a most dangerous business, and you must know the Queen will never allow such a marriage."

I said nothing, but bowed my head so she would not see the fiery anger in my eyes. It seemed no one here or at court wanted the two of us together—not even me, at times. Yet surely it was nobody's business but our own if we chose to marry?

Now at last everyone had gone to church and left me with Richard for company. Alejandro had been reluctant to relinquish his care of me to Dee's apprentice, hanging over me with dire warnings as he heard of this plan. But I had persuaded him that I needed time alone with Richard to discuss the summoning, and at last he had bowed his head and retreated. But not without shooting Richard the darkest of looks.

My brother too had not wanted to leave me. "But what if you should fall ill again in our absence and need me at your bedside? I was so overjoyed to see you alive again this morning, Meg. I could not stand the shock of coming back to find you dead once more."

Rather than lose my temper with him, I counted silently to ten. "I'm not planning to die while you're out of the house. Does that satisfy you?"

He frowned. "Sweet sister..."

"William, do your duty to God and go to church," I told him flatly, and was glad when Richard ushered him out of the chamber door. I loved William, as any sister loves her older brother. But sometimes he seemed to forget that I could take care of myself these days.

Richard watched from the narrow window as the household walked to church, the Lady Elizabeth riding on a white palfrey beside Alejandro on his black stallion, with the others walking obediently behind.

"They're going," he said with satisfaction. "Now we can talk without fear of interruption."

I rose to look down too, and my heart suffered a little spasm of jealousy when I saw what a lovely pair Alejandro and the princess made riding together to church. The day was warmer too, after weeks of rain and storms, the ground beginning to dry out, the trees bright in the sunshine. I wondered what the Lady Elizabeth would do to separate us, now that she knew Alejandro and I had been secretly betrothed for months. She had seemed to find our intimate head-to-head conversations amusing at first, the witch and the novice. Yet her manner on coming to visit me this morning had been surprisingly cold and distant. Was the princess more annoyed that we had dared to keep our love a secret from her, or that a marriage between us might anger the Queen?

I knew priests of his Order were permitted to marry, under certain strictly imposed rules. But I found it unlikely his Order would condone Alejandro's marriage to an English girl like me, mere gentry rather than nobility, and still under suspicion by the Inquisition of being a witch. It was not as though Señor Miguel de Pero would conceal such a damning piece of information once he heard we were to be married. It was one thing for these Catholic priests to release a suspected witch for lack of evidence—but they would never stomach me marrying one of their own.

Although my legs were stronger now, I still had to lie down again after shuffling back from the sunlit window. Alice—after staring at me boggle-eyed in astonishment, crossing herself at the miracle of my recovery—had gently applied ointment to my blackened feet, then wrapped them thrice in soft rags to protect the skin as it healed. So walking and standing anywhere was difficult: firstly because my feet hurt so much; and secondly because my ankles looked like two newborn babes in swaddling clothes.

Richard helped me to get comfortable on Alejandro's bed, then drew up a stool to sit beside me. "I must ask you to forgive me first," he said quietly, not quite meeting my eyes. I was taken aback, for I had never seen him anything less than confident with me. "I failed you badly out there in the woods. It was my task to watch over you, and instead I nearly led you to your death. If I had kept my wits about me, I would have seen your 'death' was a magickal one. Some magicians have been buried alive on account of such errors."

"You could not have known…"

"Alejandro suspected though, didn't he?" Richard ran a hand through his hair. "I'm a fool. I have read Master Dee's books too, again and again, yet he saw at a glance what I did not. And I have had years of training."

"So has he," I reminded him, "to become a priest. Perhaps the two are closer than you realize, the priest and the magician."

He smiled at that. "Never say so to my master. Nor to any of the priests at court. Not if you value your neck."

I lay a moment in silence, then asked, "I lost my charmstone last night. Did you find it?"

He shook his head. "I will go back later and look for it if you wish."

"Thank you."

Richard rose and went to the table. He poured me a glass of watery ale and passed it to me as though he had sensed my thirst, then settled again on the stool beside me. "Forgive me for watering it down, but you must have nothing strong to drink," he said, when I made a face. "Not until we are sure you are recovered—in spirit as well as body."

"You doubt me?"

"I do not have enough experience in these matters to doubt you, Meg. But my master will wish to hear the whole story of your summoning, from start to finish. So if you tell me everything you remember, I will write to him." He waited patiently until I had finished drinking, then leaned forward with a sombre expression. "Can you start with what happened after you stepped out of the circle? What I saw was a flash of light, then the ground was alight. It sounded like a thunder-clap that followed, so I assumed lightning. But it could have been the last struggles of the spirit as he was banished to the otherworld. Alejandro has heard of violent spirit manifesta-tions where the exorcizing priest suffered burns similar to yours, though more commonly on the hands than the feet."

I looked at him curiously. "Did I fall to the ground after the flash of light?"

"Yes." His face became shuttered, closing off emotion. "I picked you up and ran back to the house with you. You were dead, Meg. I have seen the dead before, and there is no doubt in my mind. You were dead. And it was my fault. For all the good I did, I might as well not have been there."

"No," I insisted. "If you had not been there to carry me back, no one would have found me until today…and I do not think whatever magick brought me back to life could have held out so long. You saved my life by bringing me back to the house."

He still seemed downcast, so I added with emphasis, "Me, *and the crucifix*. I don't know how or why, but Alejandro's crucifix seems to have been the talisman that brought me back to life."

Richard raised his gaze to mine. "But why?"

I shrugged, uncertain myself. "Perhaps Master Dee will know. Though it may be something to do with intention."

"The talisman was intended to protect you, so it did?"

I nodded.

"And because Alejandro's feelings for you are so powerful, the talisman's protection was too." Richard sat back thoughtfully. "Yes, that may be possible. But go on, tell me what happened. Do you remember anything after the flash of light?"

I closed my eyes, thinking back. It was hard to step back into that nightmare world, and I did not wish to do it. But I knew Richard would not be satisfied with my mumbled attempt to avoid questions, as my brother had been, and indeed the Lady Elizabeth too. For Richard, it must be the whole story, and nothing less.

And indeed, I still had questions of my own about what had happened to me after I had apparently died. Perhaps between us we could answer them.

"The spirit was powerful, I remember that." I drew breath, forcing myself to remember. "I have no memory of dying. To me, it was just another vision, like all the others. Except that instead of Marcus Dent being there, this time the shadow creature was with me on the tower." Briefly, I told him what had happened on the tower top, then explained how I had been able to watch him carrying me back to the house, and had heard everything in the Great Hall. "I thought I was dead too. But then Alejandro placed the crucifix about my neck again, and...and kissed me, and suddenly I was back in my body again."

The near-black eyes narrowed on my face. "He kissed you."

"Yes," I said defensively. It was not as though he did not know we were betrothed, for I had heard Alejandro openly announce it in the Great Hall last night. "Is it important?"

"I'm not sure."

"All that matters, surely, is that I survived."

"Barely," he said, bitterness in his voice.

Guilt suffused me. It must have been so hard for him, carrying my dead body back through the darkness, and fearing that it had been his fault. Though of course it had been my own stupidity that nearly got me killed, stepping out of the protective circle like that. I had been lured out of the circle by the seductive power of the shadow-king, but I should have been prepared for his tricks and remained where I was safe. The only thing that had saved me from outright death was that I was still wearing Alejandro's crucifix when the spirit's fury struck like lightning—though my body was caught in a magickal trance of death when the crucifix fell off. That was my best guess, at any rate.

And I would have stayed dead if Richard had not picked up the fallen crucifix and given it back to Alejandro.

"The shadow-king has gone though," I muttered. "We achieved what we set out to do."

"You're sure?"

"The world felt so cold before. Cold and dark and hopeless." I shivered, remembering the black rain that had been falling for weeks, the violent storms, the months of persecution and plague, the terrible flooding up and down the country, drowning people and livestock… Now it seemed as though a weight had been lifted from us all, bright autumn sunshine streaming in through the narrow window, the sound of birds singing again in the trees. "Now everything feels different. Warmer, somehow. As though those dark times will soon be coming to an end. Don't you think so?"

He nodded. "Very well. So although you were beheaded in your vision, you still managed to banish the spirit."

"Hopefully, yes."

"But you said, just before the axe fell, it was no longer the spirit up there with you." He looked at me. "So who was it, or do I not have to ask?"

I did not wish to remember that part of the vision, not least because of the flash of fear that accompanied its memory. But he was waiting for an answer. "It was Marcus Dent," I admitted reluctantly. "But that means nothing. He is always there in my visions. It's a dream. A fear. Nothing more."

"Perhaps."

I was suddenly exhausted by this questioning and closed my eyes for a few moments. When I opened them again, I knew time had passed. Yet Richard had not moved, still watching me with that disturbing gaze that seemed to see deep inside me.

"What?" I demanded groggily, staring back at him.

Richard pressed me, frowning, "What does it mean though? The tower in your vision?"

"I don't know." I was too tired to examine the significance of my strange visions. As far as I was concerned, the fight I had dreaded was over. Could I not simply sleep? "Does it matter?"

He shrugged, but still looked uneasy. "That will be for Master Dee to advise us. I will let you sleep now, and write to him directly. I shall have to write in code though, for all his letters are being intercepted these days. It will take me several hours." He stood, looking down at me with concern in his face. "Would you like me to bring my letter in here, and write while you sleep?"

I smiled faintly, and waved him towards the door. The sunlit room was so unseasonably warm, my eyelids would not stay open, my limbs heavy with the need for sleep. "No, Richard, please go and write your letter. The deed is done, the spirit-king has gone. There's nothing to fear now. I will be perfectly safe."

Some hours later, I heard voices and knew the others had returned from church. Alice popped in to visit me, bringing me a gift of sweetmeats from the kitchen, and then William dropped by to tell me about the new priest, a stern, unsmiling man who had preached long and hard about the need for Protestant heretics to be rooted out of England. Alejandro came in later and drew up the stool, reading to me from the Scriptures in his low, musical tones, until I was ashamed to find I was falling asleep again, lulled to the edge of oblivion by that velvety-dark voice. Finally, Alice came again and shooed Alejandro out of the chamber, removing the damp cloths wrapped about my feet, then helping me dress so that I could descend the stairs and take my place at the table in the Great Hall for dinner.

Dressed in a clean but plain gown, my hair tidily hidden under a white cap, I made my way downstairs with Alice's help. My feet hurt horribly, and my legs were still a little shaky, but otherwise I felt much improved. Certainly I did not wish the Lady Elizabeth to think me a burden on her household—an invalid who would cost her money and not earn her keep.

We were almost at the bottom of the staircase when I heard the sound of cartwheels grating over stones on the track to the house. The dog jumped up from the hearth and barked hoarsely, running to the hall door with sudden excitement.

The Lady Elizabeth had looked up from her book to welcome me, but her face darkened as she too heard the sound of wheels, the words of welcome dying on her lips.

Alice, supporting me down the stairs, frowned and looked askance at William below. "Who can that be?"

"Visitors?" Blanche laid aside her embroidery and stared, first at me—crossing herself, pale-faced at seeing the young dead maid on her feet again—then at the Lady Elizabeth. "On the Sabbath too. It must be important. Do you wish to go up to your chamber and change your gown, my lady? What if it is a message from court?"

Elizabeth stood uncertain. She glanced at Alejandro, who had been reading with her as I descended, and saw that he was looking at me.

"Attend me, sir," she said sharply, and frowned as his head swung back to her. "Pray remember who you serve, Señor de Castillo. Fetch me that shawl, then let us discover who this visitor may be."

He bowed, fetching the lacy white shawl she had indicated and setting it gallantly about her shoulders. Then he escorted the princess to the door where Bessie already stood waiting, shielding her eyes as she stared out into the low evening sunlight.

His dark gaze met mine as he passed, as though asking a question. I shook my head, not wanting him to get into trouble with our mistress. For although the Lady Elizabeth's hostility made me furious, itching to cast a spell which would see her brought to humility, nonetheless I knew she was right. We might love each other, but we were still royal servants. Unless we wished to find ourselves cast adrift in a world where a servant without a master was nothing, we must never forget where our duty lay.

We stepped out onto the track to watch the cart arrive outside Hatfield House. The tall brick chimneys were smoking, for the weather today had been sunny but crisp, and the smoke slipped away through the reddish-gold leaves on the trees that towered about the house. I could not see who it was at first, then saw the driver, an old man in rough clothing, and a cloaked woman in the cart behind him, clutching the side as she was jolted along across uneven ground.

This was no messenger from court, I thought, and saw Alejandro frown, no doubt thinking the same thing.

The Lady Elizabeth took a few steps forward, a hand held to her mouth. "Dear Lord," she whispered.

The cart halted a few feet away, then the driver jumped down and helped the woman descend. She was older than Blanche, but her figure was still neat and her gown, although plain in style, was elegant. A chain was looped about her waist, with a small cross dangling from it, and when she lifted her head, I saw another plain silver cross about her neck. A pious woman then, though she did not have the look of a Catholic. Her face under the black travelling hood was heart-shaped, yet her mouth was stern and her eyes very intense.

The Lady Elizabeth gasped, and ran forward to embrace her. "Kat!" she cried, her voice unsteady. "Oh, my dearest Kat! You have come back to me at last!"

So this was Kat Ashley, the princess's old governess and chief lady-in-waiting, banished from her service by the Queen before I had even been brought to Woodstock Palace.

She looked like a formidable woman indeed. I wondered how this lady would warm to the rest of us, for Blanche had whispered a few times that Mistress Ashley was jealous of her position and liked to keep a tight rein on those allowed near the Lady Elizabeth.

Kat Ashley embraced her in return, bending to touch a kiss to each cheek, then dropped into a deep curtsey before her mistress. "My Lady Elizabeth, I cannot say how overjoyed I am to return to your service. You must forgive my long absence. The Queen forbade me to make myself known to you in any way, by visit or by letter, until I could prove that I was as staunch a Catholic as any at her court. But now Her Majesty relents, seeing me so devout in my prayers, and I am permitted to serve you once more."

"I thank God for it!" the Lady Elizabeth exclaimed fervently.

"As do I, my dear lady." Kat Ashley crossed herself, then rose gracefully from her curtsey. She stared up at Hatfield House, the many narrow windows glittering in the late sunshine. "This place has not changed since I was last here, not a whit. It was like coming home, seeing the chimneys draw ever nearer as the cart came down the track. How I have missed this house…and you, my lady. How have you fared without me?"

Elizabeth was flushed and ecstatic to see her old governess again. "Oh, since my release from Woodstock, I have gathered a small household about myself again. You remember Bessie? She and her sister, Lucy, serve here at the house. Then I have two maids, Alice and Meg. These gentlemen are my men-at-arms, Richard…and William Lytton."

She hesitated, coming to Alejandro, who had been standing silent and frowning throughout this. "And, of course, Señor de Castillo, who came with me from court to be my spiritual guide at the Queen's special request. He reads to me from the Bible every day, and we pray together in the mornings and evenings. He is a nobleman of Spain and came to England in the company of King Philip, no less."

Alejandro bowed to Mistress Ashley. "I am honoured to make your acquaintance, my lady."

Kat Ashley curtseyed, staring at him with undisguised interest but a certain wariness too, as though suspicious that he must be in close contact with Queen Mary.

She looked at each of us in turn, her keen dark eyes missing nothing, then came to me. I curtseyed with a bowed head, as befitted her status as chief lady-in-waiting, then straightened under that searching gaze. I knew at once that I was disliked.

"You are Meg Lytton?" she demanded, looking me up and down.

"Yes, mistress."

"I have heard of you, girl."

Her hostility was like a black beetle crawling down my back under my gown. I could not help myself snapping back, "And I of you, mistress."

Kat Ashley's face stiffened. "Indeed? I hope I do not disappoint in the flesh." She turned at once to the Lady Elizabeth and took her hands, squeezing them warmly. "I am loath to ask this, my lady, but you must send this girl away at once. I have been at court this past week and heard her name linked with that of Master Dee, and such dark deeds…it is even whispered that she was questioned by the Inquisition as a witch!"

The princess looked horrified. "Send Meg away? But she has done me good service, it would be wrong to dismiss her now."

"Hush, my dearest." Kat Ashley drew her close and whispered urgently in her ear, "Have I not done you good service too? Have I not been a loving nurse to you since you were a small child, bereft of your natural mother when you were too young to know what had befallen her? I love you dearly, and would not see you in danger, nor have you sully your good reputation by keeping a suspected witch in your household. Whatever 'good service' this girl has done you, it will only return to haunt you." Her pleas intensified as Elizabeth hesitated. "Send her away, my lady. Send the girl back whence she came, and end this madness once and for all."

There were tears in the Lady Elizabeth's small dark eyes. She stared at me, then at Alejandro—the merest flicker of a glance, her face wary—and then looked at the ground. I could see the warring of guilt and stubbornness in her expression.

"I cannot," she managed in the end, to my relief. "Much as I love you, Kat, you do not know how Meg has served me this past year. To dismiss her so ungratefully would not become the daughter of a King."

"To keep a witch in your service would not become the daughter of a King either, my lady."

"But, Kat—!"

"When have I ever given you poor advice or led you into danger? Remember what happened to your poor mother. Queen Anne once stood accused as a witch…and worse! And your father sent her, his own wife and the mother of his child, to her death on the scaffold. I would not see you make that terrible climb to the executioner's axe, my sweet lady, not for the lack of cold common sense. Send this girl away, or else send me away for ever. For I cannot remain in your service and see you in thrall to a witch."

Elizabeth gave a muffled cry at this ultimatum, and drew back her hands. For a moment she hid her face. Then she turned to me, very stiff and upright, and pronounced the words that sent the blood chilling in my veins.

"Meg, you heard what Mistress Ashley has said. You are to pack up your possessions at once and leave Hatfield. You will be given whatever fee is owed to you for your services."

"My lady!" Alejandro exploded, his face taut with anger.

"Silence!" the Lady Elizabeth countered, equally furious as she glared at him. More furious, perhaps, because she knew that she was in the wrong. "You forget your place, *señor*. I no longer require Meg Lytton's services, and that is an end to the discussion."

When Alejandro started towards me, Kat Ashley stepped between us, not bothering to conceal her triumph. "You too would do well to avoid her company, *señor*. Or would you lose your own good reputation at court for too much intimacy with a suspected witch?"

"I shall take my chances with the English court," he bit out savagely, then added, "Mistress," as her eyebrows arched disdainfully at his tone.

"Since he has no particular duties to fulfil here, your brother, William, may accompany you home," the Lady Elizabeth told me, and I caught a flash of pity in her face. "It is too late for you to leave tonight. You will leave at first light instead."

"Meg Lytton can hardly walk from here to Oxfordshire, my lady," Alejandro pointed out tightly, his eyes seeking Elizabeth's. "She is still too weak."

Elizabeth was flushed now. She seemed to become even more guilty at this reminder of how I had just died in her service, exorcizing the dark spirit that had haunted us all for months. "Very well," she muttered, not looking at me any more, "Meg and William may take the small cart, as long as it is returned within the month. That should be sufficient for her comfort."

Kat Ashley's face held an expression of profound satisfaction. She had won and the whole household knew her power now. She turned her back on me and curtseyed to the Lady Elizabeth. "Shall we go inside, my lady? This autumn air was never good for your chest, and I have much news from court which you will wish to hear."

They filed into the house, Richard frowning darkly as he carried Mistress Ashley's bag inside, Alice trailing in last, her expression one of bewilderment as she looked back at us.

Soon only William and Alejandro remained, looking at me. I stood helpless, my hurt feet throbbing, my arms by my sides, and did not know what to say to them.

The Lady Elizabeth had betrayed me. That was all I knew. I would never have thought it possible, not after what we had been through together. But her loyalty to Kat Ashley had outweighed her loyalty to a witch. Why did that surprise me?

"I had better go up and start packing." I managed a fleeting smile at my brother, but dared not look at Alejandro, for fear I might burst into tears. "Will you help me, William? It should not take long. God knows I have little enough to take with me."

"William, would you give us a moment alone?" Alejandro asked him quietly, his gaze on my face.

My brother hesitated, then nodded. "I will be waiting in your chamber," he told me, and disappeared.

I knew William was unhappy to be leaving Hatfield, but would stand by me whatever happened. I tried not to dwell on how it would feel to go home and face my traitorous father; my impending return to Lytton Park was the least of my problems right now.

"I will speak to her ladyship tonight," Alejandro told me deeply, taking my hands. "She cannot dismiss you. Not after the dangers you have faced on her account. It is too ungrateful."

"When were the Tudors ever grateful towards their servants?" I asked, but shook my head. "No, Alejandro. Mistress Ashley has returned and must have her way, for she is the closest the Lady Elizabeth ever had to a mother. You will only lose your own position here if you try to sway her opinion, and Kat Ashley will hate you for speaking against her."

"You think I care?"

"The Queen herself asked you to guide her sister in spiritual matters," I reminded him gently, "and King Philip asked you most particularly to watch over the Lady Elizabeth and keep her from harm. I do not think you care if you are dismissed. But you will not wish to betray either of them by leaving— in particular your own King."

He closed his eyes in pain, then nodded. "I cannot leave Hatfield, it is true. But I cannot bear for you to leave either."

"I must. It is done."

"Then use your power. You are a witch, and a talented

one. I have seen what you can do. Perform whatever magick you can to—"

I interrupted him, smiling up at him drily. "You would have me strike Kat Ashley down and take her place as the princess's most treasured confidante?"

His eyes darkened, his voice suddenly husky. "I would have you stay by my side and not go out into the world where I cannot protect you."

"The vile shadow is gone," I reminded him. "I am safe enough."

He shook his head. "You have forgotten Marcus Dent."

I had not forgotten him. But to tell the truth, I had hoped he was no longer a threat, except in shadows and visions, his power gone since falling into the void. I knew that was a weak hope. Yet I could not have Alejandro fretting for my safety every day I was away from him, and perhaps putting himself in danger by attempting to persuade the princess to take me back.

"He has not come at me here, though he could have done if he wished. If Marcus Dent is such a threat, why am I still alive?"

"You nearly weren't," he pointed out. "Besides, you said yourself the place is protected by spells that keep him out. What if he pursues you on the road home?"

That was my fear too. But I could not allow him to see that. "Don't," I said softly, and laid a finger on his lips, very aware that we could be seen from the house. "I will be safe enough. And I will write to you, when I have the time."

"I will write every day," he promised me grimly.

"And neglect your duties to the princess?" I shook my head with a sudden weariness. My heart hurt as it had never hurt before, not even when I thought myself dead and separated from him for ever. "Alejandro, it has been a lovely dream for us, being together this year. But it is over now, and I want you to forget me."

"What?"

He was staring now. I could not bear it. It was the worst sacrifice I had ever needed to make, but I knew what had to be done if Alejandro was to survive our dangerous association.

"Finish your duties here with the Lady Elizabeth, then return to Spain and marry a noblewoman chosen by your family. That is your path, and it is an honourable one. I have my own narrower path ahead, a path of magick and solitude, and there can be no space for you on it."

"Meg, no!" Alejandro exclaimed, catching at my arm as I turned towards the house.

"Noli me tangere!" I cried in a voice of power, and suddenly he was on his back on the grassy track, winded, staring up at me in shock. "Let that be a lesson to you, priest. Do not seek me out again before I leave, or I will strike you down again. There can be no love between what I am and what you are— only hatred and fear. I see that now, and am glad we must part before you can betray me to your masters."

As I hobbled painfully into the shadow of the house, I realized that I was crying, and wiped away the tears before anyone could see my weakness.

My heart was breaking. I had thought we would be together for ever. But of course there could be no happiness for us. Our love had been a foolish girl's dream. The Lady Elizabeth had betrayed my trust and loyalty, and perhaps that would prove a good thing in the end. For now I must grow up, harden my heart to love, and become a solitary witch like my aunt.

"Adios," I whispered, bidding Alejandro farewell in his own language, but I did not look back.

19

PRISONER

My father came out to stare when I arrived home at Lytton Park, then hurried to help me down from the cart. He shook hands with William, exchanging a few awkward words with his son. Then he kissed my cheek, not quite meeting my eyes. The last time we had seen each other, he had been drunk and angry in a bedchamber at the Bull Inn in Woodstock, refusing to admit to his betrayal of my aunt. I kissed him back, yet could not find it in my heart to feel love for him, not after he had condemned Aunt Jane to the fire in order to steal the princess's letter of clemency. But he was still my father and I owed him some respect for that, if for no other reason.

"But are you back for good?" my father asked when William tried to explain what had happened, clearly bewildered by our sudden return. "And why was Meg dismissed from the princess's service?"

Warily, he lifted his head to gaze down the dirt track that led out of the park—almost as though expecting to see soldiers galloping after us in angry pursuit.

My father was looking much older, I thought. There was more grey in his hair and beard, and his face was becoming lined. Perhaps he had learned his lesson about meddling with politics, when Aunt Jane died and he nearly lost his children too. But I doubted it.

"Let us talk inside," I murmured, uncomfortable under the servants' curious stares. "It's been a long drive and my throat is dry. Then I would like to rest in my old bedchamber, if the bed can be aired for me."

"Of course." He turned to give orders to the servants and they ran inside. Then he led the way into his study, where a fire was burning cosily and his hound lay sleeping on the hearth. At the sight of me, he jumped up and began to lick at my face. I crouched down to embrace him, and could not help remembering the day I had come down in secret to feed my aunt's magickal books and papers to the fire before the witchfinder could come back and search the house. How it had grieved me to see her precious hoard consumed by fire. Yet I had known it had to be destroyed. Sometimes pain had to be suffered to prevent a greater hurt later. I only hoped Alejandro would soon recover from any pain at our parting.

For my own part, I knew I could never feel love again. Not like this, not with such depth and urgency. But Alejandro was a man, and would soon fall in love with someone else.

Someone better.

I stopped torturing myself, and rose to my feet. I swayed slightly, for they were still tender under the bandages, and saw William's worried glance.

"What is it?" my father asked at once. He had been pouring

us both a cup of wine, but now he stopped, coming to take me by the shoulders. He stared down into my face. "Meg, are you in pain?"

How to answer *that,* I wondered feverishly. But I managed a shake of my head. "It's nothing. I hurt my feet a few days ago, that's all. I just need to get some rest, if my chamber is ready." I glanced without appetite at the platter of meat the maid was carrying in. "I can always eat later. Forgive me, Father. I'm not hungry now. Just dog-tired."

He nodded, but still looked uneasy.

"What is it, Father?" I frowned, searching his face. "Something is troubling you."

His hands tightened on my shoulders and he leaned close to my ear. "Marcus Dent is back. You know that?"

"William told me, yes."

"He came here some months ago, asking after you. I told him you were at court, still in the Lady Elizabeth's service. Did I do wrong?"

I shook my head. "Don't fret yourself, Father. He can do nothing to me now. He has no power left to frighten me."

His mouth twitched. "Are you certain? His face—" He shuddered, remembering. "He is scarred now, and one eye is missing. He speaks so harshly. I did not want him to pursue you to court."

"I told you, Marcus Dent can do nothing to hurt me. I made sure of that before I left for court." I saw his wary look again and regretted saying that. My magick was not something I needed to share with him. It would only lead all of us into danger. "I'm so very tired. Will you be terribly disappointed if I sleep tonight, and we talk more tomorrow?"

My father made no argument against this, but called another servant and had me escorted to my bedchamber. The place was in disarray, the old rushes unswept, the wall hangings stained, and the mattress hurriedly stuffed with fresh straw where it had been sagging. But some recently aired linen had been thrown over it, then enough blankets and covers heaped up to keep out the autumn chill. With the help of a young maid, I was soon out of my gown and snuggling under the covers, trying to get warm. My brother came to see how I was, but went away without speaking, finding me drowsy and already half-asleep.

Since leaving Hatfield, I no longer dreamed of the tower. But I dreamed of Alejandro that first night, and then every night I was there. Always the same dream, the two of us together on a dark stairway, and his arm about my waist, helping me descend. Then his voice in my ear, "I love you, Meg Lytton. And I will never be parted from you again."

Whenever I woke, my eyes were damp with tears. I knew then not to be afraid of my recurring vision of the tower and Marcus Dent with an axe. For I knew Alejandro and I would never see each other again. Or not in this life, at any rate.

So if *that* dream was untrue, all the others were too.

Several weeks passed and we settled back into our old life at Lytton Park with surprising ease. I took charge of the housekeeping now that my aunt was no longer alive, for there appeared to be chaos in some unlived-in parts of the house. My father handed over the keys to the cellar and the store cupboards without demur, clearly happy to have some kind of female presence back under his roof. The kitchen servants took their orders from me after that, and if any of them remembered the day Marcus Dent and his men came to the house, calling my aunt a witch and dragging her away, none of them ever spoke to me with disrespect or mentioned my aunt's fate.

It was hard not to wonder what Alejandro was doing, so

far away at Hatfield House. Sometimes, in an idle moment towards the close of day, I would catch myself thinking of Alejandro with pleasure, and would have to reprimand myself sternly. I did not want to spend the rest of my life dreaming of a man to whom I had once been betrothed. I was not that weak. But it did hurt, recalling how happy I had been in his arms and the plans we had made for our future together.

Happiness is fleeting, I told myself. Better to face the truth now that we will never be together, and focus on what I can do...magick, that is.

Thankfully, such cruel conversations in my head were rare. Mostly, I would remember his lips on mine, then hurry to oversee some unsavoury task—the beating of dusty bolsters and bedcovers outside in the chill autumn air, or the scrubbing of the hall flagstones to discourage beetles and cockroaches from lodging in the gaps between stones.

Eventually, I looked out one morning and saw how the grassy lawns were cracked with frost, spiders' webs turned to icy ropes of white across every bush and fence. The evenings had begun to draw in earlier, fires lit in the downstairs chambers as soon as daylight began to fade, to ward off the dark and cold.

Soon it would be winter, I realized, and we would have been apart more than a month.

He did not write. Nor did I.

It was better that way, I lied to myself, and even stopped looking out towards the gates of Lytton Park every day, hoping to see a servant on a pony bearing a letter for me. After all, what good did it do to constantly pine for someone who would never be mine? Perhaps one day I would cast a spell to banish unwanted love, and that would be an end to it.

Yet whenever I thought of gathering the ingredients for such a spell, somehow I would find an excuse to put it off another week or two. I was half in love with love, that was my problem, and I was wallowing in my loneliness instead of moving on.

One day, as winter began to settle about the house in earnest, I finally heard the sound of an unexpected rider approaching and almost dropped the basket of dried apples I had been carrying down from the attics. They were among the last fruits from the harvest, dried in the sun and wrapped carefully in cloth to preserve them from weevils, and the maid looked at me askance. I handed her the precious basket, wiped my hands on my apron, and hurried outside to see who it was.

I heard shouts of alarm, and looked down the track to see my brother rushing out of the stables to help the rider. "Whoa there!" he cried, bravely trying to grab at the horse's bridle as it careered past.

The rider looked to be a young man, bloodied and bruised, his clothing torn, almost slipping off the horse as the scared animal approached the house at a canter.

Not caring that the servants might be watching, I lifted a hand and spoke a few soothing words under my breath. The horse reared up, then stopped before me, pawing the ground and neighing frantically.

I looked up at the barely conscious rider. Even through the cuts and bruising, I could see who it was.

"Richard?" My brother came running to help him down from the saddle. "Sweet Lord, your face. What happened to you?"

Collapsing onto his knees before me, Richard looked up at me. I could see the apology in his battered face. "Marcus Dent has taken Alejandro," he gasped, then drew a few more shuddering breaths before continuing. "Forgive me, we were both so intent on keeping the princess safe from harm that it did not occur to us that Dent would take one of us instead. He lured Alejandro out of the grounds at Hatfield, sending a note which seemed to be from you. I told Alejandro not to go, that it was a trap, but he would not listen to reason. I decided to go with him, but they took us easily in the end. Fell on us at dusk from behind, like the cowards they are."

My brother swore an oath, still steadying the frightened horse. "Those villains!"

"Go on." I looked at Richard steadily. If he told me Alejandro was dead, I would not long survive my betrothed, but would ride out and kill Marcus Dent with my own bare hands if necessary. "What happened then? Tell me everything."

"Dent took us both prisoner and brought us to a tower he has built at the base of a wooded ravine, some ten miles northwest of here. He is holding Alejandro there, he says, and will kill him if you do not give yourself up to him by sundown tomorrow. That was the message I was to bring you. That, and my face." He spat a mouthful of blood onto the ground at my feet. "I was to say your betrothed would look like this before he dies. Dent will not spare him pain, in other words, if you should fail to arrive."

"How many men does he have?" my father asked.

I was startled, for I had not seen him come out of the house. "Father, please go back into the house, this is not your battle," I said urgently. "Dent will kill you."

"It is you he wishes to kill, Meg," my father pointed out sharply, then helped Richard to his feet. "Come inside, good sir, and let your wounds be tended by my servants. Then we must talk. This message you bear is for me and my son, I believe. My daughter will not be stirring from this place, however many riders come from Dent and his infernal tower."

I stared. "Wait," I insisted. "You…you knew of this tower Dent has built?"

My father shrugged. "The whole county knows. Dent's tower is famous here. He started building it this spring, and paid his labourers well over the odds for it to be finished before winter set in. A monstrosity, by all accounts, built of rough-hewn stone and set in barren countryside, with only one habitable chamber." He frowned, seeing my stunned expression. "Why, is this tower of some importance? I thought it nothing but further evidence of Dent's madness."

Was I the last in Oxfordshire to know that the desolate tower from my vision was real? I looked from him to Richard, whose ironic glance told me he at least understood my despair and astonishment. Then I shook my head. "It does not matter," I managed to reassure him.

Nor did it matter, for all it meant was that this moment was fated, that the malevolent stars had collided to bring me to this day, this hour, when I would have to give up my life in exchange for my beloved's. If I had known of the tower's existence earlier, I might have been tempted to go there and destroy it, or Dent himself.

Instead, I had guessed the danger we stood in, yet had foolishly done nothing to prevent it.

I laughed, and saw them look at me strangely. "Yes, let's get you inside, Richard," I agreed, to hide my sudden exhilaration. "I shall have warm water brought for your cuts, and a bedchamber prepared so you can rest."

"Thank you," he murmured through his cut lip, but I knew Richard was not fooled by my calm demeanour. He knew what I intended to do, and with any luck he would support me in my plan.

I did not want my father and brother to see how excited and nervous I was. For weeks now I had barely been alive, lost in some dreary wilderness of my own making, drifting from one day to the next, overseeing the household, chiding the servants for laziness, labelling bottles, collecting and storing nuts for winter, and mending the ancient tapestries in the hall.

Now at last something had happened. Alejandro needed me. The moment I had been expecting had finally arrived, clear as a trumpet call to battle after a long night of waiting.

After settling Richard in a suitably comfortable chamber, and ensuring that his cuts had been tended with a special tincture of my own making, I hurried to my room and drew out the magickal books from their hiding place beneath my mattress. I had barely looked at them since coming home, preferring to hide my witchcraft from my disapproving father. But now I went hunting for a spell within their pages, turning from one book to the other in despair, knowing I needed a spell that would give me the advantage in a last fight against Marcus Dent.

But Dent was going to cut off my head, I reminded myself, and sat staring down at the untidy black scrawl in my own spell book.

There could be no spell to protect against decapitation, surely?

It was dark now. The moon mocked me through the window, round as a silver coin, shedding light across the icy grounds of Lytton Park. I suddenly wished my aunt was there to advise me, for she had always known the answers to my questions, the right spells to choose, and which to sidestep.

If only I could sidestep Dent's axe.

I closed my eyes, remembering that last vision, how the axe had flashed down and then…nothing.

But that had been a magickal death, a death within my vision which had nearly taken me on this earth too. Would a genuine death by the axe be instantaneous too, or would there be any pain? What if the axe did not quite connect properly and my neck was only half separated from my head? I had heard of such botched decapitations, women staggering about in agony while the executioner tried to catch them, their bloodied necks gushing blood, and men whose gristly necks were so tough they had to be sawn off by the headsman with a short knife, for the axe had only done half its job.

Shuddering, I searched more slowly through the pages of my books, desperate to find something, *anything,* that might allow me to offer myself to Marcus Dent and his axe in Alejandro's place—yet still survive the blow which must inevitably follow.

A tiny sound outside my door brought me upright, suddenly nervous. Someone was moving about on the landing. I could see a shadow passing back and forth under the door.

As quietly as I could, I pushed my magickal books back under my mattress, then crept to the door. With one ear pressed to the wood, I could hear muttering outside, a strange low chanting that reminded me of...

Furious, I threw open the door and stared at Richard. "What do you think you're doing?" I demanded.

He took a wary step backwards into a tiny candlelit circle he had scratched out on the floorboards, but did not stop his chanting. His hand passed to and fro before my door, sealing it with the nine-fold charm I recognized from that night in the wood, one of the unbreakable spells to force me to remain in my room until I was released.

I threw up my hand, and met an impenetrable barrier. Invisible, but as strong as a brick wall.

"How dare you? Release me at once!"

"It's for your own good, Meg," he told me, then finished the charm, I ran through a number of possible spells to dissolve it, but even as I cried out my counterspells, I knew there was little point. Richard had been secretly laying this charm for some minutes while I was reading inside, oblivious to his spell, and it was already too late to break it.

I was well and truly imprisoned in my room.

"William!" I called, throwing as much power into my voice as I could, and heard no sound from below. "Father!"

"They will not come," he said calmly. "I told them the spell I had to perform, and they both agreed it is the only thing to do."

"Why do this?" I asked in disbelief as he knelt to rub out the circle and pinch out the ceremonial candles. My fists clenched, my nails biting into my own palms. Had he no mercy? No pity in his heart? "You want Alejandro to die? Is that it?"

He looked up at me angrily, his cut face still swollen from the beating he had received at the hands of Dent's men. "You don't know much, do you?"

"What does that mean?"

He had started winding the knotted cord around his wrist that he had used to perform the charm. He threw it down, his near-black eyes spat with fury. "It was Alejandro who told me to do this. On the journey to the tower, when he realized what Dent was planning, he told me that if I got the chance, I should seal you in your room until after the time had come for him to die." His voice seethed with bitterness. "I know this will make you hate me even more than before. But I swore I'd do it, and I have. You only have another day to wait, until sundown tomorrow, and then I can release you. Alejandro will be dead by then, and William and I will take you away from here. Somewhere safe where Dent will never find you. Then we will put about the rumour of your death."

"What?"

Richard's face was grim. "Dent believes you to be the witch who is destined to kill him, so he will never stop his pursuit while he thinks you are alive. One day I will find a way to kill him. But until then, this is what we must do to keep you safe."

I stared at him, hating him as he had predicted. "I am not worth all this trouble," I said coldly. "Just let me go to Dent and get it over with. My death will make things easier for everyone."

"Oh, yes, that's true," Richard agreed, his smile twisted. "Hold on while I say the spell to release you. No, wait, perhaps I should not allow a talented witch to go needlessly to her death."

"I am not talented," I threw at him wretchedly, and slammed both fists against his invisible barrier, angrily aware that I was unable to punch so much as the smallest hole in it. "I am a fraud, Richard. I am no witch. I no longer study the magickal texts, I say no spells…I can barely light a fire with my power these days. Let me go, it is Alejandro who must be saved. He is worth ten of me. Do you not see that?"

"No, I do not see that," Richard said violently, and came close to me, though unable to touch me through the barrier his spell had erected. "You're a fool, Meg Lytton."

"A fool?" I repeated, staring into those black, black eyes.

"Do you not know that I love you?"

My lips parted, but for a moment I could not speak. "You… love me?"

"I love you. That is why I was glad to agree to Alejandro's plan. That is why I will keep you here until your betrothed is dead. Because I love you, and even though I know you feel nothing for me, perhaps one day…"

"Never."

He hesitated. "Never?"

"Never." My body was numb with shock as I watched him retreat. He loved me? Richard loved me? I must indeed be a fool, for I had not seen that coming. "You think I could ever love a man who had allowed Alejandro to go alone to his death?"

Richard folded his arms, his face tense, looking away from my expression of contempt. "Hate me, then. But I shall keep my word to Alejandro. I shall not let you go until at least to-morrow evening, once the hour is past when you were to meet Marcus Dent."

"So be it," I said with pretended calm, and stepped back into my room, closing the door on him.

There I stood a moment, my head down, struggling to control my fury. It would do me no good to lose my temper here. What I needed was to find a spell to break Richard's, and that would require a clear mind and an even spirit, not these cloudy batterings of anger.

I knelt, taking out my magickal books again and began to read. Slowly my head cleared. I had one night and a day to find a solution, and this time I knew what I was looking for.

I sat by the window in my sealed chamber the next after-noon, looking above the trees to the flushed clouds in the west and thinking longingly of Alejandro. Was he in pain? Had he steeled himself for death in my place? It must irk him terribly to meet his death in such an ignominious manner, dying at the hands of Marcus Dent and not in battle, not in some glorious charge against the enemies of his people. How brave he was. And how unutterably stupid. Alejandro knew I was the only one with the power to confront Marcus Dent. Yet instead of allowing events to unfold, he had instructed Richard to have me sealed magickally in my chamber until it was too late to save him.

I smiled softly. "Fool," I murmured, and cherished that word on my tongue. "My lovely fool."

I would rescue him from Marcus Dent tonight or die in the attempt. It was as simple as that.

The time had come. I stood and centred myself in the room, my hands spread open to my sides. I lowered my head and called on my aunt's spirit to help me. This would be one of the hardest spells I had ever worked. Indeed, I had never attempted anything even remotely like this before. But then, I had never summoned a dead King before, yet I had managed that. With Richard's help, it was true. But he would hardly help me with this spell—escaping his own—so I would have to find the strength alone. I only hoped it would be enough. For my failure would mean Alejandro's death.

"Diripe!" I called out forcefully in Latin, ordering the very fabric of the house to tear itself apart, and lifted both hands towards the frame of my window.

The thick leaded glass jerked in its frame, the wooden shutters rattled uneasily. But nothing happened.

I leaned against the bricks and timber of my bedchamber wall with the full weight of my mind, calling the word aloud again. *"Diripe!"*

Gently, with infinitesimal slowness, one of the timbers began to move. It shuddered against the dried wattle and daub that held it, then pulled away from the wall with a deep grinding sound. I watched in silent amazement, my hands still spread out towards the window, as another timber loosened itself from its moorings, then jerked free. A brick from the nearby fireplace began to rock, then another, then both were loose, spinning gracefully through the air towards me. I directed them away from my body without difficulty, watching them glide past me to land on the floor with slight creakings and groanings, then turned my attention to the window itself. This was more stubborn. It rattled and shook against its frame, then suddenly cracked. The pieces blew outwards into space with a noise like a bucket of water crashing into a deep well, then at last the whole wall beneath it followed, timbers floating away to the left and right of me, masonry dragging itself free.

At the first grinding sound of the timbers, I had heard hurried steps on the stairs. Then William's voice through the door. "Meg? Is that you?"

Richard joined him a few moments later, and there was a swift exchange. "I can't open the door. It's been sealed magickally until nightfall."

"You must do something. She isn't answering." A pause. "What is that terrible noise?"

"I don't know."

"You don't know? What if Dent grew tired of waiting and has come for her himself?" My brother sounded desperate. "Open the door, Richard! We have to be sure Meg is safe."

The timbers continued to creak and protest as they were released from the wattle and daub. Behind that noise, I heard the sound of Richard beginning to unpick his spell, chanting in a strained voice as he skipped backwards through the nine-fold charm.

Too late, I thought, and stared at the wall. Too late.

At the top of the wall, above the window frame, a single thick wooden beam still kept the ceiling up, sturdy and resilient. But beneath it, where the window had once been, and at the side of my ancient fireplace, was a huge gaping hole in the wall of the house.

Ignoring the shouts from outside my door, I stepped through this hole, my hands held out for power, and leaped into space.

I did not so much fall as glided down on the wintry afternoon air, sinking into a defensive crouch as I landed, then straightening as I realized it was done. I was free. Above me

I could hear Richard undoing the last part of the spell and I picked up my gown, running towards the stables before he could throw open the door and come to the window.

It took me only a few clumsy moments to free all the horses, flinging myself inelegantly onto one horse's back and sending the others scattering into the night. I spoke a single word into its ear and the horse jerked forward beneath me. It clattered out of the cobbled yard and towards the narrow grassy track that led out of Lytton Park. Exhilarated, I felt rather than saw Richard tossing halt-spells after me, but either they missed or some spirit was guiding my flight from home, for soon we were thundering down the track, the wind in my hair, my fingers tangled in the horse's mane as I lay low over the animal's neck.

It was a long way to ride without a saddle, I soon realized. My bottom was sore after only a few miles, my thighs aching horribly. But there was nothing to do but go on. I knew Richard and William would probably be behind me soon enough, once they had managed to catch some of those runaway horses. And they could ride much faster than me.

"Find the tower," I murmured into the horse's ear, and stroked his neck, letting my seeking-spell do its work.

20

THE TOWER

About half an hour before sundown, the sweating horse stumbled and nearly fell down a rocky ravine, tired out by the relentless pace, its head drooping on its chest as I dragged it to a halt. A trickle of water ran beside us between the rocks, and the horse looked at it longingly, its hooves shuffling on the dusty ground. Straight ahead, I saw a vast building rising out of the trees and knew this must be Dent's tower. It pointed towards the sky like an accusing finger, its grim stone walls broken only by a series of tiny arrow slits, no doubt to illuminate some winding stair within. To either side stood tall trees, barren as the ground around them, leafless in winter, their trunks scarred, some leaning to one side as though the tower's foundation had cut into their roots and was slowly killing them. My skin prickled with a sudden awareness of evil. My spell had worked. This was the place.

I swung off the horse and left the exhausted animal by the

side of the icy stream, then picked my way hurriedly across the wasteland and rough boulders to the base of the tower.

A door yawned open in the tower ahead of me. Inside a dark stair beckoned.

"Master Dent!" I shouted, suddenly afraid I was too late, that he had already executed Alejandro. "I have come as you demanded. Come out and show yourself!"

Slowly, a shadow detached itself from the nearby trees. It was Marcus Dent. He stepped into the dying rays of the sun and threw back his hood, revealing his scarred face, one bright blue eye fixed in my direction, the other eye nothing but a dead socket. He looked exactly as he had done in my dreams and visions, which I had not expected. Somehow it had been easier to deal with his intrusions into my mind when I had thought him a work of my imagination. But if he had been able to place himself inside my head...

I pushed the thought away. It would do me no good to fear him now. Fear would only make it easier for him to kill me.

"Where is Señor de Castillo?" I asked coldly.

Dent lifted his hand. I saw other men emerge from the trees, a small band of shuffling men in cloaks and hoods. Amongst them, dishevelled and quite clearly furious, his arms bound behind his back and his mouth gagged, was Alejandro. At his throat was a dagger, clutched in a filthy hand by one of Dent's sharp-eyed men.

The relief when I saw Alejandro was almost more than I could bear. I wanted to kill them with a word and tear him away from his captors. But I knew if anything went wrong and I failed, Alejandro would die.

"Don't waste your breath," Marcus said caustically, coming forward. "Personally, I deplore the spilling of good Catholic blood. But I shall be happy to make an exception in your Spaniard's case if you are so unwise as to attempt to work your magick against us." He gestured to the men to draw back into the shadows of the trees. "You and I will ascend the tower. There is much we need to discuss, and the view from the top is quite breathtaking."

I glanced after Alejandro, but could no longer distinguish him from his captors, a band of shadows moving uneasily amongst the trees.

Marcus had seen my nervous glance. "They await my signal to take your friend and release him a mile away at the edge of the woods. I will not give that signal until we are at the top of my tower." He laid a hand against the rough stone wall of the tower. "Beautiful, is it not?"

I did not trust myself to answer this politely.

"Unfortunately for you, the tower has been designed so that no magick can be worked within its bounds. The walls are worked with wood and stone known by the ancients to repel the dark arts, and even the foundations were blessed and doused in holy water. I would not suggest you pit yourself against such power." He held out his hand to me. "Shall we go up? If my men do not hear my signal by a count of three hundred, the Spaniard will die. So you had better hurry."

"How can I trust you to honour that arrangement?"

Marcus smiled drily. "You can't."

I looked at him, hating the man. There was nothing more to say. "Very well," I murmured, knowing that I had been outmanoeuvred. He wanted me to climb his blasted tower, and to this end his men would hold Alejandro hostage until Marcus Dent had me exactly where he wanted me.

But I still had until we reached the top of the tower to think of how to save Alejandro without using magick. And I was very aware that my brother and Richard might be on the road behind me, perhaps at this very moment riding straight into danger.

"Let me speak to Alejandro first," I insisted. "I did not see his face clearly. How can I be sure that man is even him?"

Marcus hesitated, frowning. Then he nodded towards those hiding among the trees.

A second later, I heard Alejandro's familiar voice cry out, "Get away from here, Meg, for the love of God!" There was a muffled struggle, then a groan, and I knew he had been gagged again.

But I had what I needed. Evidence that it was indeed Alejandro, not a shadowy figure intended to deceive me, and that he was still alive. I had remembered Master Dee's prophecy that Alejandro's life was in danger. This must be what he had foreseen. The realization that it was my fault he had been brought so close to death made my blood run cold, my fingers itching with the desire to work some powerful magick and sweep all those men away.

But I knew how dangerous it would be for Alejandro if I got even the slightest part of such a spell wrong. And the sound of his voice had given me new strength. "Wait for me, Alejandro," I called after him. "I will not be long."

Marcus smiled cruelly at my bravado, gesturing me to enter the tower. "After you, Meg Lytton."

The top of the tower seemed dizzyingly high as I groped my way out of the low arched doorway and into the air. As in my visions and dreams, the wind was stronger here, blowing at my hair and flapping my skirts about me. The sun was still just above the horizon, flushing the sky a wild dusky red, clouds chasing each other above the hills.

At my back was Marcus Dent, close behind me as he had been during the long, arduous climb. I could hear him breathing harshly and knew he was diseased, his body broken from its journey into the void.

Straightening up as he emerged from the dark stairway, Marcus grabbed my hair and dragged me to the edge of the tower. There was no wall built about the top to prevent a fall. The roof of the tower was open to the elements, the grim stones rolling away into nothingness like a cliff top.

"Look down at your fate, witch!" he ordered me, and I looked, my head spinning, my body jerking wildly as he held me out over space for a few horrific seconds. Then he threw me back onto the stone floor, his face twisted with rage. "That is how it was for me when you sent me into the abyss. One moment of divine terror as I was sucked into oblivion, then pain and torment beyond anything I could have imagined. Now I will give you a similar death. Except there will be no coming back for you, no magickal resurrection." He smiled coldly. "Yes, you may well look surprised. I hear everything and I am everywhere at once, Meg. I am in your nightmares and your daydreams. I am the whisper in the walls that you cannot quite get out of your head. I am the shadow in the dark corner that moves whenever you are not looking at it."

He is a madman, I thought dizzily, and scrabbled back along the rough stone floor as he strode towards me.

"I intend to sever your head from your body," he said harshly, bending over me. "Your magick will not save you up here, and there can be no return once the head has been severed. Do you understand? Nod if you understand me, witch."

I nodded, and had to watch my enemy gloat over my impending death.

So my visions had been a prediction of the future, after all. Hope drained from my body. I was going to die here today, on the top of this tower, and as Marcus had rightly said, there would be no coming back this time. But I could not allow him to kill me before I knew that Alejandro was safe.

"Alejandro," I croaked.

"Ah yes, the Spaniard. Well, I shall have him released, for I am a man of my word. But when you are dead, I shall take great pleasure in hunting him down and destroying him. Your other companions too. The Lady Elizabeth is a particularly troublesome female. She cannot be allowed to take the throne. So I shall destroy her too. Once you are dead, the spells of protection you have laid about her household will dissolve." His smile was repellent. "Then I shall simply walk in through the door."

"Make the sign," I told him urgently. "Tell your men to release him. They will have reached a count of three hundred by now."

He looked at me. "Beg for his life if you want me to spare your friend. I would like to hear you beg."

I swallowed my pride. "Please, Marcus," I begged him. "Please keep your word and have Alejandro released. The moon is nearly up."

"Again!"

"Please." I was almost crying. "Please, Marcus. You said you were a man of your word."

"And so I am. But I do enjoy hearing you beg," he said unpleasantly, and nodded. "Thank you."

Marcus put his fingers to his mouth and whistled. A moment later, an answering whistle came from below.

Since Marcus did not seem to have forbidden it, I took the opportunity to crawl to the edge. The tower was dizzyingly high, a vantage point from which Dent must be able to see any approaching enemy long before they got close enough to do him any harm. My belly sickened as I stared down at the boulders below, knowing that even to jump would mean my death. I lay there on my belly and peered down, just about able to make out the men below as they dragged Alejandro through the dark trees and up the ravine.

The helplessness I felt made me want to throw myself down and break my body on the boulders below.

Why wait for Marcus to dispatch me? He would be able to kill me easily enough. I tried to place a shield about myself, and felt my magick push against an invisible wall like the one Richard had set about my door at Lytton Hall. His protection was working. I could achieve nothing on this tower, not the smallest of magickal acts.

Marcus came towards me with an axe in his hand. So that was where he had disappeared to; fetching the instrument of my execution.

It was a familiar weapon to me now, the shaft wound thrice with holly, just as it had been in my visions, the broad blade glinting evilly in the dying rays of the sun.

"On your feet, witch," he said unsteadily.

I obeyed, not seeing any point in arguing, and turned to face him.

"I had this axe specially forged for this moment," Marcus told me, holding up the axe. "Do you admire it? You should. It was made for one purpose only, and that is to take your life. The life of the witch who would take mine."

"The prophecy," I muttered, nodding.

His one blue eye narrowed on my face, examining me fiercely. His scar stood out red and livid in the sunset. "You know about the prophecy? Who told you?"

"You need me to give you a name? I thought you knew everything, Marcus."

"Be silent, witch!"

I made a face. "But I thought you were everywhere at once. Watching us, listening to us. The whisper in the walls, wasn't it?"

He gripped the axe shaft tightly, stepping forward. I could almost smell his anger fulminating on his breath. "Enough foolish talking," he said hoarsely. "I had thought to make you beg for your life, Meg Lytton, but I see your defiance is unchanged. Death is the only way open for such a girl as you. Now it is time for you to kneel and meet your fate."

I backed away until I was nearly at the edge of the tower. "I could just throw myself down. Save you the bother of cutting my head off."

"Your friend will not be free yet," he pointed out coldly, watching me. "And even if he is, a young Spaniard will be easy enough to track down and kill. Give me what I want and he will not be harmed. You have my word of honour on it, Meg."

"And what is it you want?"

He seemed to shudder, staring at me fixedly. "Your head."

I had not wanted to show fear in front of Marcus Dent. He seemed to feed off fear, growing stronger as I grew weaker. Even when I had thought him a mere witchfinder, not a magician in his own right with a hatred for witches, I had never shown him fear. But I put a hand instinctively to my throat, my eyes on the cruel axe in his hand.

Beheading. It was not a death I relished, not least because I had already been through one magickal beheading and knew the fear that accompanied such a death.

"But *why?*"

"If you know what the prophecy said, then you *know* why. That I would die at the hands of a witch who could summon a dead King." His one mocking blue eye glinted in the sunset. "That is you, Meg. Who else could it mean? I watched you for years as a girl, waited as you grew into womanhood, and wanted you for my own. I knew you had power, that you came from a family of witches, even that you might be the woman who would destroy me. But I did not care, you were so different from the others I had met. I wanted to give you my name, to own and control you. I knew if I could marry you when young, I could prevent you from gaining the power which would one day make you dangerous to me."

His voice choked on the words. "Imagine how I felt when you rejected me, when you threw my offers of marriage back in my face. I was so angry, I wanted you to suffer as my pride had suffered. Then you cast me into the pit, into that hellish abyss, and I thought I was dead." He put a hand to his face, touching his scar, the empty socket of his eye. His laughter was hollow. "Sometimes I catch my own reflection and wonder if I did die that day, and this is the creature who took my place."

I swallowed. "Marcus…"

"I lay in the pit for days, perhaps even weeks. Time had no meaning there, nor the needs of my body, just as though it were a dream. But then I found new strength inside myself, a power I had never known before. I used it to claw my way out of that dark place. One night I woke naked on a cold hillside and realized I was back in the world, that you had not managed to destroy me. I knew then that I had to kill you before you could kill me. That it was indeed you in the prophecy. Oh, the irony of it!" His mouth twisted, his scarred face grimacing. "That I should wish to marry the one woman I needed to stamp out."

I did not mean to take another step back, but Marcus was moving steadily forward, the shining axe still in his hand.

I was perilously close to the edge now, the wind pushing at me to lose my balance and fall, to give him the death he required.

What had he said? *But then I found new strength inside myself, a power I had never known before.* Had his newfound "power" been drained from me as he was sucked into the void? My aunt had taught me that all spells had a price; perhaps a transfer of power was the price I had paid for the success of this particular spell. It could explain why I had felt increasingly weakened since that day at Woodstock, as though I was somehow no longer whole. Power I had lost, Marcus Dent had gained...and used to lure me to my death. I wondered if he understood that he might be in danger of becoming the very creature he had spent his life hunting?

"I built this tower as a place of refuge. Somewhere I could climb and know myself safe from your power." He nodded at my astonished expression. "Yes, I fear you and your witch-craft. Does that make you laugh?"

I shook my head.

"But I will never be safe from you. Not while you live." He twisted the axe between his hands. "This axe will finish it. Its sharp blade will ensure your death, leaving no chance of a magickal return to life—such as the one you managed at Hatfield. Yes, I was watching, I was there. How else do you think I was able to step between worlds and take the place of the King you had conjured, just as his shadow left this earth and returned to Hell?"

I remembered seeing his face behind the axe as it swept down onto my neck in my vision. "So it *was* you!"

"Since returning from that...that vile place where you sent me, I have studied hard. I have read texts even a conjuror like John Dee has never seen. Now I am the master, and the rest of you will be my servants." His face flushed, his lips thinning with hatred as he stared at me, Marcus spun the heavy axe in his hands. "Down on your knees and meet the cold kiss of my blade."

"No," I insisted stubbornly.

"Do not make this harder for me than it already is, Meg." Marcus was breathing hard as though he had been running. I saw a flicker of madness in his face and knew he was at war with himself. He pointed with the axe to the stone floor of the tower top. "Kneel."

I turned to him, my hands open, palms up, and felt the wind lift my fair hair. "Marcus, please."

"No," he told me raggedly, but averted his fierce gaze. "Your tricks can have no effect on me here."

"No tricks." I took a step towards him, knowing I could run no further. Nor could I escape, unless I flew from the top of his hateful tower. "You said you wished to marry me once, Marcus. Yet now you are intent on destroying me. Did you never feel anything for me, or was it all pretence?"

Marcus half closed his one eye, shuddering again, then stretched out a hand and spoke one brutal word in Latin. "Kneel."

I gave up and dropped to my knees before him, my head bent. After all the visions I had experienced of this place, perhaps it was inevitable that I should die here?

"You are my enemy, Meg. It is written in the stars that one of us will kill the other. It is a fate that binds our destinies together as the holly is bound to the oak. You tried to kill me, and failed. Now it is my turn." He looked down briefly at my exposed neck, as though fixing on the best place to strike. Then he raised the terrible weapon above his head, his face bleak as the wintry air. "Only I shall succeed."

I would not die at this man's hands. Everything in my soul rebelled at the injustice of such a death.

"Forgive me," he muttered, and brought down the axe with a great shuddering cry.

Pulling on every last iota of magick in my being, I wrenched myself violently sideways as the axe fell.

The last thing I saw was the flint in the stone striking a spark as the axe bounced off it, then the reddened sky spinning over and over. I fell, a wingless bird, tumbling off the edge of Marcus's tower and into space. I knew the end would come swiftly if my magick could not save me. But surely now that I was free of his tower, hemmed about with protection spells, my power would return to me?

I flung my arms wide, as though in prayer or invocation, and my voice soared in Latin above his cry of fury—

"Fly!"

I was most certainly *off* the tower, yet still the spell did not quite work as I had hoped. I did not fly like a bird, but continued to fall. *It was not working! It was not working!*

Breathless with fear, I waited for my body to strike the ground at the speed of a hurtling stone, my arms still outstretched.

"Save me!" I heard myself cry, unsure to whom I was appealing. To my dead aunt, to the spirits all around us, to God—perhaps even to Marcus Dent himself?

Someone must have been listening.

To my intense relief, the cold air suddenly cradled my body like a wave of the sea, sweeping me sideways and into the leafless branches of an oak tree rather than onto the harsh boulders below.

My gratitude did not last long. I thumped violently into the highest icy branch, crashed down from one bare branch to the next, my face slapped and scraped, my gown ripped, but my fall slowed and cushioned so that I hit the ground at a more sedate pace.

I tumbled a short way down the rough slope, lying there too dazed and battered to move. I heard Marcus shouting, and turned onto my aching back to see him high above me, a black figure staring down from the tower.

Behind him the sky was darkening into a stormy night, and for a few crazed seconds I thought Marcus had turned into a wild-eyed hawk and was tearing towards me at a breakneck speed, claws outstretched, screaming his defiance at me.

"Move!" It was Richard's voice.

I just had time to blink in his direction, stunned to see Dee's apprentice there, before Richard was stooping for a large stone. This he weighed in his hand, then hurled it violently through the air.

The rock struck the plunging hawk, knocking it sideways. The hawk uttered a horrible screeching cry, then seemed to shrivel into a tattered shape like an old cloak.

As Richard started towards it with another rock in his hand, no doubt to finish it off, the misshapen hawk flapped away a few feet, blurring into a large black rat. This vile creature dragged itself between the boulders and was soon swallowed into darkness, leaving a trail of blood behind it.

Richard swore under his breath, then dropped the rock and headed back towards me, clambering down the slope. "Meg?"

"That was Marcus," I told him.

"I know. Rest easy, you are hurt."

I was cold, my teeth beginning to chatter. "Is he dead, do you think?"

"He's gone. That's all you need to know for now."

"Where's...Alejandro?"

"On his way." Kneeling beside me, Richard examined me with an expert eye. Grimacing over my bloodied skin and torn gown, he shook his head. "It looks bad, but I think you'll live. I saw you pitch off the tower. Just as well that tree broke your fall or you'd be dead."

"I feel dead."

"Again? Well, you'd know all about that, wouldn't you?" He managed a wry smile at my expression. Then he fished something out of his belt pouch and pressed it into my hand. "Here, before I forget. I went back into the woods after you'd left Hatfield and found this at the circle. Perhaps it will speed the healing of these hurts."

It was my aunt's charm-stone. The leather thong had snapped, the ends charred as though burnt, but the stone itself was unharmed. I clutched it in my tightening fist, once more drawing strength from it.

"Thank you, Richard."

"It's nothing."

His eyes met mine, and I knew that Richard's feelings for me were unchanged. What could I do though? He must know my heart belonged to someone else.

My hurt hand grabbed his shirt. "Alejandro?" I repeated, then let go, wincing at the sudden agonizing pain in my arm.

"Don't fret. I left your brother, William, with your betrothed, just above." He glanced up, his mouth twisting. "Oh, here he is now."

Relief flooded through me as Alejandro dropped to his knees beside me. I stared up at him, memorizing every inch of his body, the broad shoulders, the dark hair swept back, the sheer vitality emanating from him. His face was cut and battered, as though Dent's men had given him the same kind of drubbing they had given Richard, but he did not appear to be seriously hurt.

Alejandro took my hand and kissed my fingertips, making me wince again. *"Querida,"* he muttered. "Forgive me, please forgive me. I was going through hell there. I thought he was going to kill you."

"He made a tidy attempt at it," I agreed, remembering the sparks as his axe bit into the stone where my kneeling body had been.

"Where is Dent?" Alejandro got to his feet, swaying with exhaustion but his face grim, determined. "His men took my sword. But I'll strangle him with my bare hands if I must."

Richard shook his head, frowning as he examined my bloodied right arm. I hissed as he moved it. "You're too late," he told Alejandro. "I threw a rock at him. If he's still alive, he won't be back in a hurry."

"A rock?" Alejandro was bemused.

"This arm is broken," Richard told me sombrely, and began tearing at my underskirt to make a sling for my arm. "No pain in your legs, Meg?"

I shook my head. "I feel sick though."

"Right. Then could you please turn your head away while I put this sling in place? I don't want you vomiting on me if the pain gets any worse."

"So caring," I murmured, fighting back the sickness, and saw Richard's answering grin as he glanced back at me.

Alejandro waited in impatient silence until Richard was finished, then scooped me up in his arms to carry me back to the horses, being looked after by William at the head of the ravine.

His dark gaze met mine, and I could see uncertainty in his eyes. "I failed you," Alejandro admitted heavily. "For the second time I failed you. I allowed myself to be fooled and captured by Dent, to be beaten by his men, and nearly led you to your death because of it. I am not surprised you no longer care for me."

I stroked his face, not sure how to comfort him. I loved him so much, and I knew he loved me back. Yet I did not wish Alejandro to put himself in danger for loving me. And I did not know if that was avoidable if we stayed together.

"You didn't fail me. I told you this wasn't your battle. Besides, Master Dee had already predicted that your life was in danger. Neither of us heeded that warning…and look what happened. It is not enough just to *know* about magick, Ale-

jandro. Sometimes you need to be able to work it too, or you
end up in trouble."

He nodded grimly. "Richard has the skills you need. I
understand."

"No." I shook my head, almost wanting to hit him. "That's
not it. But this fight was between me and Marcus. I could not
involve you in it. That is, it wouldn't have done any good to
ask for your help."

"It is not easy to stand by and watch you suffer. I could
not defend you against Dent, just as I could not defend you
against de Pero."

I shuddered, recalling the cruel gaze of the Spanish Inquisitor on my face as I cried out in pain. "De Pero will get what
he deserves one day."

"That day cannot come soon enough for me," Alejandro
muttered, then looked down at me when I laughed, his dark
eyebrow arched. "My anger amuses you, *mi amor?*"

"No, I just…well, yes, maybe a little," I admitted, and was
rewarded with a brief but intense kiss. My lips tingled pleasantly as he raised his head. I felt myself blush and struggled
to sound coherent, still imprisoned in his arms. "Not every
problem can be solved with a sword. But I still need you by
my side, Alejandro. Never forget that."

I laid my head against his chest, revelling in the warmth
of his flesh, his steady heartbeat. I was so glad Dent's men
had not killed him as I had feared they would. Perhaps Marcus had kept his word over that. Hard to imagine the witchfinder suddenly possessing a sense of honour. But then, there
was still so much I did not know about Marcus Dent—and
ought to find out.

"I think I'm safe enough for now though," I added when
Alejandro did not reply. I worried that I had offended him or
left him more concerned for my safety. "That is, I don't think

Marcus will be coming back for a while. I won this particular battle. But not the war."

His arms tightened about me. "War...yes, now that is something I can understand. So this is a war to the death between you and Marcus Dent?"

"He thinks I am the only witch who can destroy him. So he will keep coming back until either I am dead or he is."

"Then you will need a strategy to defeat him," Alejandro said thoughtfully, and glanced at Richard, whistling a few feet ahead of us as he limped up the steep path up the ravine. "And soldiers to watch your back."

Dusk had fallen while I was on top of the tower, and was darkening to a cold winter's night now. The moon would be rising above the ravine soon, I thought, and found myself grateful to have survived to see another moonlit night, another day tomorrow. I had been determined to sacrifice myself for Alejandro, if that was what it would take to keep him safe. But I was glad that sacrifice had been avoidable. Death, as I had discovered, was not as simple a matter as it looked from life.

"And someone to love me while I am out there, fighting?" I whispered daringly, and saw his brooding look descend to my eyes, then my lips again.

"I thought there could be no love between a witch and a priest? Only 'hatred and fear,'" he said ironically, quoting my parting remarks at Hatfield. "As I recall, you said you wished me to leave England, marry some Spanish noblewoman and have a dozen children with her."

"I don't remember the dozen children," I countered, but smiled at the hurt in his eyes. I had struggled so hard to keep him at arm's length, yet here we were together again. Was it worth fighting such an indomitable bond? "Fool, I said all that to keep you from ruining your chances in the priesthood. You are already reading forbidden texts. Next you will be making magick yourself. I do not want to change you, Alejandro. I just want you to be happy and out of danger."

Alejandro slowed on the path, holding me close in his arms. Over his shoulder I could see the dark rise of Dent's tower, looming ominously out of the shadows, a reminder that we had both just narrowly escaped death.

"I must indeed be a fool then, for being with you seems a dangerous position to uphold, and yet I am only happy when I am with you," Alejandro said deeply, and bent his head to kiss me more lingeringly.

By the time he raised his head, desire had licked along my veins and left me breathless, my eyes staring up at him in longing. I could see by his darkening gaze that his nerves were not quite steady either.

"I should have returned to Spain when I heard that my brother Carlos had died," Alejandro told me. "I could have had my pick of the noble ladies at the Spanish court. Instead I only have eyes for a wild-blooded English witch, half faerie, half temptress. Meg Lytton, are you ready to marry me yet? Because I am more than ready to marry you. Indeed, I fear my life may never be complete until I marry you."

"You gave me a year and a day to make my answer," I reminded him softly, not yet willing to give up my power in exchange for a husband, however much I loved him. Besides, Alejandro was still under obligation from his King to watch over the Lady Elizabeth, and marriage to me would make that oath impossible to fulfill. If he was not so wildly impulsive by nature, he would be able to see that obstacle himself. "By my reckoning, I still have five months left."

"I pray God you do not make me wait that long. I promised myself I would not hurry your decision, Meg, but you would try the patience of the Holy Father himself."

"Then it will be a good test of your own patience," I murmured. "Now hush and kiss me again."

★ ★ ★ ★ ★

Acknowledgments

First of all, my grateful thanks to my agent Luigi Bonomi and his wife, Alison, who are always there when I need them. Then the marvellous team at Random House Children's Publishers, who have been so supportive and enthusiastic about the Tudor Witch series, especially my lovely editor Lauren Buckland (and her cat Stanley), Harriet Venn, Natalie Doherty, Bronwen Bennie, Clare Hall-Craggs and Annie Eaton. Also Natashya, Lisa, Amy, and the whole team at Harlequin Teen who have embraced Meg and Alejandro's story so warmly.

Family-wise, a huge "Thank you!" to my family for being there and for egging me on, which includes my father, Richard Holland—who I suspect is itching to write his own paranormal Young Adult novel—my long-suffering husband, Steve Haynes, and my large parcel of kids: Kate, Becki, Bethany, Dylan, Morris and Indigo, plus grandson Ciaran.

I must also thank all the incredible and fascinating bloggers and tweeps who keep me company every day on Twitter, and who occasionally tell me to go away and do some actual writing. (This is much needed.) With a special shout-out to tweep and blogger Azahara Arenas, who helped me with my Spanish for Alejandro.

And lastly, thanks to Meg and Alejandro, who keep whispering in my ear and asking me to tell their story!

FROM *NEW YORK TIMES* BESTSELLING AUTHOR

GENA SHOWALTER

THE WHITE RABBIT CHRONICLES

Book 1   Book 2

The night her entire family dies in a terrible car accident,
Alice Bell finds out the truth—the "monsters" her father
always warned her about are real. They're zombies. And
they're hungry—for her.

AVAILABLE WHEREVER BOOKS ARE SOLD!

INSPIRED BY CLASSIC FAIRY TALES, WITH A DARK AND SINISTER TWIST, *GRIM* CONTAINS SHORT STORIES FROM SOME OF THE BEST VOICES IN YOUNG ADULT LITERATURE TODAY!

Edited by: **CHRISTINE JOHNSON**

AVAILABLE WHEREVER BOOKS ARE SOLD

Don't miss the thrilling beginning to
The Blackcoat Rebellion

The first move is hers...

PAWN

AIMÉE CARTER

The world is supposed to be equal.
Life is supposed to be fair.
But appearances are deceiving.
And Kitty Doe knows that better than anyone else...

Available wherever books are sold